P9-CBR-635

Wild West Exodus
The Jessie James Archives

An Outlaw's Wrath

C. L. Werner

Zmok Books

Zmok Books is an imprint of Winged Hussar Publishing, LLC
1525 Hulse Road Unit 1
Point Pleasant, NJ 08742

www.WingedHussarPublishing.com
Twitter: WingHusPubLLC

www.Wildwestexodus.com

Cover by Michael Nigro

Copyright © 2013 Wild West Exodus. All rights reserved

Wild West Exodus, the characters, inventions and settings were created
by Romeo Filip and Outlaw Miniatures, who own all rights, registers and
trademarks. This book is published by Winged Hussar Publishing, LLC
under agreement with Wild West Exodus.

ISBN: 978-0-9889532-8-4
EPCN: 2013922910

No part of this publication may be reproduced, stored in a retrieval
system, or transmitted in any form or by any means electronic,
mechanical, photocopying, recording or otherwise, without the prior
permission of the publishiers.

This is a work of fiction. All the characters and events portrayed in this
book, though based in some case on historical figures are fictional and
any resemblance to real people or incidents is purely coincidental.

Something Wicked is Coming

Blood drenches the sands of the Wild West as the promise of a new age dies, screaming its last breathe into an uncaring night. An ancient evil has arisen in the western territories, calling countless people with a siren song of technology and promises of power and glory the likes of which the world has never known. Forces move into the deserts, some answering the call, others desperate to destroy the evil before it can end all life on Earth.

Legions of reanimated dead rise to serve the greatest scientific minds of the age, while the native tribes of the plains, now united in desperate self-defense, conjure the powers of the Great Spirit to twist their very flesh into ferocious combat forms to match the terrible new technologies. The armies of the victorious Union rumble into these territories heedless of the destruction they may cause in pursuit of their own purposes, while the legendary outlaws of the old west, now armed with stolen weapons and equipment of their own, seek to carve their names into the tortured flesh of the age.Amidst all this conflict, the long-suffering Lawmen, outgunned and undermanned, stand alone, fighting to protect the innocent men and women caught in the middle . . . or so it appears.

Within these pages you will find information on wild skirmishes and desperate battles in this alternative Wild West world, now ravaged with futuristic weapons and technology. Choose the methodical Enlightened, the savage Warrior Nation, the brutal Union, the deceitful Outlaws, or the enigmatic Lawmen, and lead them into the Wild West to earn your glory.

As you struggle across the deserts and mountains, through the forests and cities of the wildest frontier in history, a hidden power will whisper in your ear at every move. Will your spirit be strong enough to prevail, or will the insidious forces of the Dark Council eventually bend you to their will? Be prepared, for truly, something wicked is coming!

Learn more about the world of the Jessie James Chronicles at:

www.wildwestexodus.com

Prologue

Heat shimmered from the clay floor of the canyon. Weeds, withered and yellowed by the merciless sun, trembled in the desert wind. Buzzards circled in the cloudless sky, casting their sinister shadows across the rocky ridge rising at the back of the canyon.

Below the rise, nestled against its base, was a ramshackle bunkhouse, planks stripped from its roof by wind and rain, boards torn from the walls by the violence of beasts and men. A stone-lined well, its mouth covered with a piece of lumber, faced toward the building. Across from it was a simple corral with mud-brick walls and a small lean-to cobbled together from branches and thatch. A system of wood fences had once broken up the corral, separating an area for horses and a larger area for cattle. A jumble of iron rods rested against one of the walls, a collection of branding irons with complex and ponderous emblems: the sort of insignia that was condemned across the west as 'robber brands' for their ability to cover and obliterate legitimate marks of ownership.

No cattle milled about in the corral now. It had been several years since the market for steers had been lucrative enough to support large-scale rustling. The advent of RJ-1027 transformed the west, shifting the reins of power from the cattle-men and land barons to those who could provide the wonder-fuel and the mechanical marvels it could power. Where a string of fast horses and a herd of stolen cattle once stood, there were now just the cold steel bulk of machines glimmering in the sun. Iron Horses and Interceptors, vehicles that depended upon only the fabulous crimson ichor that had become the new life blood of the nation to power them.

"Polecats must have stolen them off a patrol somewhere," growled a low, gravelly voice. The speaker was a tall, spindly man. He was sprawled along the top of a shallow draw, lying on his belly as he studied the corral through a set of oversized field glasses. A soft hum and red glow emanated from the RJ cell fitted to the top of the glasses in order to provide the enhanced magnification properties of the lenses. "They haven't even bothered to melt off the Union insignia! Like the peckerwoods were proud of murder and theft!" The disgusted words came from a man whose somber black clothing almost lent him the air of a preacher. The effect was somewhat ruined by the silk cravat around his neck, the gilded electriwork hatband with its RJ-powered automations, and the double-holstered gun belt around his waist.

"Well, Billy's known for being the boastful type." The words came from a man in a grey felt hat; the gaudy carbine in his hands made a jarring contrast to the dull brown that dominated the rest of his attire. Richly engraved barrel, a stock fashioned from pearl, a scope that shone with the red glow of an RJ-powered amplifier, these were the signs of an ostentatious weapon only a renowned gunman would carry. There was scorn in the gunman's eyes as he watched the brown-garbed man. "You are familiar with how he gunned down Sheriff Brady? Just walked up to him in the middle of El Paso, in front of God and everyone, and cut the man in half with his blaster? I mean, you do know who it is you're after?"

The man wearing the cravat rolled over and scowled at the accusation. "Washington is quite aware of William Bonney's history, Garrett. You might not believe it, but we aren't so fool-all as to ride across half a continent without full knowledge of who it is we're looking for."

"And who is that, Charlie?" Garrett wondered. He jabbed a finger at the slope in the direction of the bunkhouse. "Because I'm betting Pinkerton didn't send you all this way just to tangle with a varmint like Billy. Who else do you think he's got in there, Charlie?"

"That's Agent Siringo to you, *Pat*," the detective snarled.

Garrett turned away, pacing past the pair of deputies and UR-30 Enforcers. The grimly silent automatons shifted their cyclopean heads to track the sheriff as he walked toward the group of operatives dispatched by Washington. "Who the hell do you think recommended you for that job, Charlie?" Garrett growled over his shoulder, not bothering to look back at Siringo.

His attention was focused on one of the agents the Pinkerton-man had brought with him.

Garrett adopted his most ingratiating smile and tipped the brim of his hat as he approached the agents. He ignored the two men, concentrating on the woman who was with them. The sheriff had seen his share of femininity in his time, from governors' wives to barhall strumpets, but he didn't think he'd ever seen anyone so splendid as this girl from Washington. Even the mannish style of her outfit, from canvas breeches to waxed cotton overcoat, couldn't smother the appeal of her figure. The cold glint in her eyes and the Navy-pattern blaster holstered at her hip, however, could stifle any man's ardor.

"Miss Loveless, it seems the cat's made off with Charlie's tongue," Garrett stated. "Maybe you might like to tell me what I'm doing out here."

Lucinda Loveless returned Garrett's stare with an unflinching gaze. "Sheriff, you've been told all you need to be told," she said, her tone making it clear there would be no further discussion. "Whoever's down there, just know that your government wants them."

Garrett ripped his hat from his head, slapping it against his leg in disgust. "If that don't beat all!" he cursed. "What the hell do you think I am? Some hired hand?"

"If you don't like it, Sheriff, you could always turn in that badge," Loveless told him. "Or would that mean being taken off the Murphy-Dolan payroll?" A flicker of a smile crossed her face as she saw Garrett wince at the implication of corruption. "Just do your job."

Charlie Siringo crawled down from the top of the draw, brushing dust from his clothes. "The Kid's in there alright. Saw him at the window."

"Did you see *him*?" Loveless asked.

"Nope," Siringo answered, shaking his head. "But we know *he* was riding with the Kid."

Loveless pondered that for a moment, almost laughing at the idea of their quarry taking orders from an impetuous gunslinger like William Bonney. It was far more likely that the Kid had been the one following orders. "We'll have to act accordingly."

"How is that exactly?" Garrett demanded. He waved his hat at the deputies and robots, and then gestured to the corral. "Whoever's in there, they outnumber us almost two to one. And that's if nobody was riding double on them Iron Horses." He pointed at the cliff above the bunkhouse. "Don't forget they've got a lookout up there too. If it's the Kid in there, he'll have posted a good man too. We so much as raise our heads from this draw, they'll know we're coming. You need more men for this hoe-down."

Loveless snapped her fingers at the Pinkerton-men with her. One of the detectives marched over to her, removing the scabbard from a long-barreled energy rifle as he approached. The woman's gloved hand caressed the deadly instrument with an almost loving touch. Raising the gun, she pressed her eye to the telescopic sight. "The lookout won't be a problem."

"Your part, Pat, is to get one of these through that front door," Siringo said. A smooth black bomb was in the hand he held out toward Garrett. "It's an incendiary, something new cooked up by Tesla and his boys. Bonney will have the choice of surrendering or burning alive. Either way, he's out of your hair."

Garrett mulled that prospect for a second, imagining the bonus Murphy would pay him for eliminating the troublesome outlaw. "Bob, I have a job for you," he called over to one of his deputies.

Bob Olinger was a stocky, brutish man; his face looking as though a buffalo had trampled it. For all his roughness, there was a shrewd gleam in his piggish eyes. "Not for what you're paying, Garrett," Olinger replied, punctuating his statement with a hawk of spit.

The sheriff glowered at his defiant deputy, then turned to his other man. "Zeke, how about you? Or are you yellow like Bob here?"

The other deputy, a short, wiry thug with broad features and stringy hair, smiled at his boss. The gleam in his eyes wasn't one of cunning, but of greed. "Fifty dollars," he cackled. "Fifty dollars and I'll do it."

"Of all the low-down, conniving, feckless... It's your bomb, pay the man, Charlie." He grinned at the incredulous expression on the detective's face. "Or maybe get one of your expensive Washington boys to do it."

Grudgingly, Siringo reached into his vest and removed his billfold.

***

Lucinda Loveless crawled into position at the top of the ridge. The long, lethal length of her rifle was wrapped in the dull material of her coat to hide the telltale gleam of metal. Her eyes roved across the top of the cliff, keen for the least suggestion of the Kid's sentinel. She'd only have one shot, but the prospect didn't bother her. There was a reason both Garrett and Siringo left this part of it to her – it was without question that she was the best shot in the posse. The rifle she carried was a specialized weapon designed for sharpshooters in the Union cavalry. It traded the brutal force of the typical blaster for extra range and precision, an exchange that Loveless preferred for this kind of work.

Garrett's deputy made his dash from the bottom of the draw, sprinting across the open ground toward the bunkhouse. As soon as he was clear, Loveless saw motion at the top of the cliff. Quickly, she whipped the rifle to her shoulder and squeezed the trigger. There was a sharp crack as the hot beam of energy leapt from the gun, stabbing upwards. The lookout pitched over as her shot slammed into him, searing through his throat. Soundlessly, the smoking body hurtled to the earth far below.

Zeke reached the wooden porch at a bound. In a final rush, he charged the front door, kicking it open with his boot and flinging the bomb inside. The deputy turned to make his retreat, but it was there that his luck finally ran out. A fusillade of fire erupted from the dark interior behind him, beams of scorching energy that shredded the lawman before he was more than a few yards. Bloody, smoking ribbons of humanity collapsed to the earth in a puddle of steaming entrails and shredded flesh.

An instant later, one of the outlaws appeared in the doorway, the bomb in his hand. Before the bandit could throw it, the incendiary detonated, saturating the porch and the wall with burning jelly. The outlaw himself was transformed into a shrieking torch, stumbling about in a paroxysm of agony.

"Billy!" Garrett shouted from the top of the draw. "This is Pat Garrett! You boys have got about five ticks to come out of that stove with your holsters down and your hands up!" The sheriff ducked as the face of the draw was peppered with shots from the bunkhouse. He looked over at Loveless. "Doesn't seem they're of a mind to surrender, does it?"

Loveless sighted down the scope of her rifle. A second beam of energy dropped the living torch, silencing the outlaw's screams. "Did you really think they would?"

Charlie Siringo and the other Pinkerton agents peeked over the top of the draw, smashing the facade of the bunkhouse with a withering barrage. Wood exploded and rock melted as the blasters delivered their lethal discharge. The agonized shrieks of an outlaw caught in the salvo rang out. The bandit's fate didn't stop the other men inside the hideout from returning fire. Molten flecks of dirt erupted from the rise as the outlaw guns scorched the ground into something closer to glass than sand.

"Sheriff, you'd better send the 'bots to keep them busy," Loveless called out to Garrett. The lawman looked ready to argue, but the icy gleam in her eyes advised him such an approach wouldn't benefit him.

Garrett reached inside his coat, removing the bulky Vocal Reiterator, a control mechanism used to maintain command over the robots from a distance. The UR-30 Enforcers were attuned to the timbre of his voice, and when he spoke into the electrical box, it rotated a different set of waxen command cylinders into activation inside the mechanism that served as the brain of each automaton. Garrett turned the hand-crank fitted to the side of the box, stirring its energy cell into full power. He flipped open the shutter-like grill that protected the bronze speaking tube fitted into the face of the box. A tug of his fingers brought the horn-like tube from the recessed cavity, a string of wires connecting it to the relay buried inside the Vocal Reiterator. Garrett blew into the tube, then tested its transmission by turning his back to the Enforcers and whispering into the control box. "Flank the target. Engage hostiles," the sheriff ordered. He watched as the two machines marched out from the shelter of the draw.

Near the top of the ridge, Loveless saw the outlaws react to the advance of the robots. One ruffian, with the dusky cast of a Mexican and the scruffy gear of a buffalo hunter, appeared in the burning doorway, snapping off shots from the hip with a cut-down carbine. The energy blasts seared the ground but the Mexican's aim was slovenly, missing the robots by a wide margin. With his homebrew customization of his weapon, the outlaw had increased its devastating power but at the expense of accuracy. In close quarters, the carbine could have melted straight through the armored core of each Enforcer, but at a distance he couldn't even hit the mark.

Loveless didn't give the Mexican the chance to close the gap. While he was still pumping shots from the hip, she sent a bolt from her rifle burning through his skull. The twitching carcass toppled backwards into the bunkhouse, eliciting fresh cries of alarm from the men inside.

The Mexican bandit wasn't the only gunman interested in the Enforcers. From a pair of windows on the side of the hideout, other blasters blazed away at the robots. Most of the shots failed to do more than set fire to the woolen uniforms draped about the automatons in a sorry effort to humanize their appearance. One shot, however, blazed through a robot's knee. The crippled Enforcer slammed to the ground, sparks crackling about its damaged leg. Pressing one steel hand against the ground, the 'bot hefted itself upright, shrugging off a blast that slammed into its chest, and a third that crackled across its shoulder and ignited the linen vest draped about the automaton's torso. Before further injury could be dealt to the robot, the concentrated fire from Garrett and his remaining deputy turned the offending window into a burning mass of splinters.

The other Enforcer reached its flanking position. Drawing its own pistols, the robot began raking the side of the hideout with a merciless flow of fire. More agonized wails from inside were testimony to the rapidly diminishing security afforded by the shattered, burning walls.

There was a crash from the side of the bunkhouse nearest the corral, followed by an outlaw leaping through a window, scurrying toward the array of vehicles. Siringo's men opened up on the bandit, but their nimble foe kept a pace ahead of the shots scorching the ground.

Loveless hesitated as she sighted down her rifle's scope. She felt a tremor of doubt tug at her. Only when she saw the man's pinched, pock-marked face, saw that the outlaw wasn't someone else, did she fire. Her shot sheared through the runner's leg, tumbling him into the dust.

"Go to Hell, Garrett!" a venomous voice shouted from within the bunkhouse. The next instant, the burning facade exploded outward as an Iron Horse came roaring through the front of the building. Loveless swung around, but again she felt herself hesitate. Only when she recognized the battered bowler with gold hatband of Billy the Kid did she fire. By then it was too late, the outlaw's mechanized mount was already speeding past the draw and out of the canyon. Her shot blackened the armored plate bolted to the front of the machine, shearing away a fist-sized blob of steel. The outlaw hunkered low in the saddle, juking his mount from side to side before vanishing beyond a bend in the canyon.

Garrett and Siringo were too busy cutting down the pack of robbers streaming toward the corral. Thinking to use the Kid's escape to cover their own bid for freedom, the outlaws were scrambling to reach their own Iron Horses. The fire from sheriff and operatives alike took a withering toll, turning the area between bunkhouse and corral into a bloody abattoir. In less than a minute, nearly a dozen men were splattered over the parched earth.

Loveless was the first to break cover. Discarding her rifle and drawing her pistol, she hurried down to the killing field. In rapid precision, she went from one savaged body to another, turning each onto its back. She knew the face she was looking for. She felt a strange sense of relief each time she failed to find it.

"Don't seem right," Garrett snarled as he came marching over to join her. The sheriff scowled down at a shapeless mass of burned flesh that had lately been a man. "Some of Billy's crowd had posters on them. I figure even without the Kid there was around two thousand dollars holed up inside there."

"I guess doing your civic duty is all the reward you can expect," Loveless said, flipping over another body with the toe of her boot.

"Any sign of our man?" Siringo asked as he came striding down from the ridge. Uneasiness had replaced arrogance in the agent's expression. For the first time since setting up the ambush, it seemed he was worried he'd made a mistake.

Garrett exploded at the question, spinning around and gesturing angrily at the Pinkerton-man. "If you mean Billy, he's already lit out! Just like that sidewinder to keep his Horse inside with him! I've lost a deputy and have a damaged 'bot and all I have to show for it is a bunch of carrion their own mothers wouldn't recognize!"

"Your government will make good your losses," Loveless told the sheriff as she started toward the burning hideout itself. She didn't have any worries about lurking gunmen. If anybody was still alive in there, the UR-30 Enforcer wouldn't have holstered its weapons.

"It sure will," Siringo agreed. A smile worked itself through his worry. "Just as soon as you dispatch all the proper forms to Washington. In triplicate."

Garrett's reply was both vicious and incoherent, involving Siringo's parentage and several feats of physical impossibility.

Loveless sighed at Siringo's attempt at humor. She could almost hear Henry Courtright, the agent she'd usually been paired with, saying something to that effect, only he'd have said it with more panache than Siringo. Overall, next to the brash Siringo, Henry was cultured and refined, positively cosmopolitan. He also had a better knack for getting his job done without upsetting the local law. She didn't know what secretive affair Henry had been detached to investigate, but she hoped it wouldn't be a lengthy diversion. Partnering with Siringo made her miss Henry's stolid presence.

Peering through the flames crackling about the hideout, Loveless tried to see the bodies strewn about the place. She counted eight men in the carnage, bringing the total to just under a score. By rights, it should be a resounding feat for the forces of law, order, and federal government. Instead it represented wasted time and resources. The man they wanted wasn't there, if he ever had been.

She didn't need to see the faces of the men inside the bunkhouse to know it either. In the shadowy gloom of the shack, his presence even in death would have been betrayed by the dull crimson glow of his augmetics, of the mechanical arms grafted to his body; the 'quick-devil' arms developed by the renegade Dr. Carpathian for the notorious Jesse James.

"He's not here," Loveless reported as she stalked away from the burning hideout. Siringo nodded grimly. He'd made some big promises to Washington. It'd been a big gamble, one that he'd lost. If he didn't find himself reassigned to the Alaska Territory he'd count himself lucky.

Garrett glowered at Siringo. "Last time, Charlie, who were you really up here gunning for?"

Loveless waved a warning finger in the sheriff's face. "For the last time, that's information the Sheriff of Presidio County doesn't need to know." The gunmetal chill in her gaze was such that Garrett quickly looked away, hurrying to chastise Bob Olinger as the callous deputy pawed through Zeke's remains in search of Siringo's fifty dollars.

"We'll find him," Siringo swore in a low whisper after Garrett was out of earshot.

The statement sent a quiver through Loveless. The certainty of that fact was beyond doubt. The Union had resources to ferret out a hundred needles in a thousand haystacks. It wasn't a question of *if* they found Jesse James, simply a matter of *when*.

What happened then, that was the real question. One that Loveless no longer felt comfortable trying to answer.

Chapter 1

With chiseled features, broad shoulders, and a smooth smile, Jim Younger was accustomed to the attentions of the fairer sex. Whether he was sitting in a church pew or striding through the batwing doors of a saloon, he was sure to turn a few feminine heads. Even those twenty some odd years ago during the war when he rode with Colonel Quantrill, Jim'd always been able to whistle up a companion to while away a lonely night. Since then, there was hardly a town west of Kentucky that was without a woman he'd been friendly with. More than a few of those liaisons had ended with Jim skedaddling out a back window or dueling some outraged husband. Such complications were simply part of life, the spice of danger that made the encounters all the more thrilling.

Enforced isolation was something that came much harder to Jim. It made his body subject to nervous tics, his attitude to become surly, and his temper to be somewhere between that of a badger and a rabid wolverine. Most men stepped lightly around him when he was in such ill humor, warned off by the malignant curl of his lip and the ugly gleam of light in his eye.

"You're going to wear them cards out if you keep staring at them." The lean man sitting across the table affected an indulgent grin as he baited the discomfited outlaw. It wasn't ignorance of Jim's smoldering temper that made him prod the bushwhacker, but rather contempt for the man's ire born of long familiarity.

Jim Younger pounded his palm against the table.

"Now I know those cards you're holding ain't worth a spit in Hell," his adversary quipped, running a thumb across his moustache. "Guess you didn't find any ladies in the deck either?"

"Leave it be, Cole," the admonition came from a spare young man straddling a bench across the room. He set down the bit of wood he'd been whittling at with a large Bowie knife, favoring the two card players with his full attention. "I don't understand why in tarnation you always have to needle him like that."

Cole Younger leaned back in his chair, careful to keep his cards facing inward as he waved his hands in a helpless gesture. "Brotherly devotion. I can't stand to see any of my little brothers being led into distraction." He leaned forward again, letting his elbows rap against the edge of the table and rattle the gold eagles sitting in the pot. "Shoot, Luke, or give up the gun," he told Jim. The other bushwhacker glared daggers at his eldest brother.

"Women are a distraction, but robbing banks is respectable?" the whittler asked. His eyes darted from Cole to the fourth man in the room, a youth who was little more than a boy. Seated on a stool behind the shack's only window, he was keeping his young, sharp eyes trained on the trail leading up to the building. It was little more than a dirt track, a goat path that even an Indian would think twice about using, but Cole had given him orders to keep a steady watch.

Cole scowled over his cards. "Bob's grousing about us robbing banks, Jim. What do you make of that?"

"We're robbin' Yankee banks," Jim snapped. "Ain't like we were takin' money from decent folk!"

Bob Younger sighed. He slid the knife he'd been whittling with back into its sheath. "I know." Again his eyes strayed to the youth sitting at the window. "Somehow it just don't seem right no more."

Jim slammed down his cards and came to his feet. "Devil hang what's right! Yankees killed Pa and them blue-belly bastards are gonna pay for that, so long's there's a Younger with a lick of life left in him!"

Color rushed into Bob's face. "You think you have more cause to hate them blue-bellies than me? While you were out raising Cain with Quantrill, I was in Kansas City when they gunned down Pa like a sick dog. I was the one who brung him home to be buried only to have Jayhawkers pitch his body into a ditch and burn down our farm!"

Cole rose from his seat, interposing himself between his two brothers. "Hell, wasn't much of a hand anyway," he observed with disgust as he tossed his cards on the table. Sternly, he eased Jim back into his chair, then turned and faced Bob. "He didn't mean that. You know he's on the prod when he's put out to pasture this long. We're all a bit on edge since the split. A nice, juicy mine payroll and things won't look so bleak."

"You have the next job all laid out, Cole?" The exuberance of the question brought an indulgent smile to the man in question's face.

"I told you to keep your eyes on that window," Cole said, taking it for granted that the youngest member of their band had allowed his excitement to entice him away from his post.

Bob pointed to the enthusiastic youth. "That's what I'm talking about. You, me, Jim, we're used to this. It don't seem right to bring John into it."

"He's just as much stake in this as any of us. It was his father they murdered. His farm they burned. His state they stole." There was reproach in Cole's tone as he spoke. "The few years you've got on him don't make it right he should tuck tail and crawl back to Missouri. Feed pigs and mend fences for some carpetbagger on land that should be his."

Bob gripped his eldest brother's arm. "He's the last chance for us, Cole. Last chance for the Youngers to be respectable. He hasn't killed nobody yet. Let him get out before he does." Bob could see his words weren't having any impact, so he tried a different tact. "You know he's started favoring a cross-belly draw? Started calling himself 'Kid' Younger?"

Cole frowned. "He can call himself what he likes, just so long as he minds himself who's 'Boss' Younger."

"Cole!" John cried out suddenly. The youth leapt up from his stool, half-raising his rifle. "Somebody comin' up the trail!"

"Kid makes a good lookout," Cole smiled at Bob before turning toward the excited John. "Don't put a hole in him until you know what he is. It ain't respectable."

John pressed close to the glass, peering intently at the figure he saw approaching. "One man riding an Iron Horse. Looks like somebody knocked the stuffing out of it. Ain't moving so good."

Jim Younger pushed away from the table, fingering the guns he wore. "Sounds like a star-packer. I told you I should have gone with Potts and Danby for the supplies."

Cole shook his head. "I want to eat, not wait around a few days until you dry up your credit with the box herders." He smiled coldly. "If Potts and Danby did get in some trouble, obviously they didn't tell nobody who it was holed up in here."

"How do you figure that?" Jim growled.

Cole stared back, wondering if Jim's wits had become addled by isolation. He rose to his feet and patted the leather of his gun holster. "Who in their right mind sends one man to bring in the Younger Gang?"

At the window, John gave vent to a Rebel yell, whooping as he danced away toward the door. "The *James-Younger* Gang!" he hollered as he flung open the door and dashed outside. Cursing, Bob and Jim hurried after him, blasters clenched in their fists.

Calmly, unhurried, Cole went to the window and looked out. "So much for a good thing," he grumbled as his eyes focused on the lone rider. Scooping up the gold coins from the table, he stepped outside to join his brothers.

The rest of the Youngers were fanned out between the cabin and the trail. Jim's arms were crossed, a pistol gripped in each leathery fist. Bob kept a hand close to his holster, his attitude one of wary attentiveness as his eyes scanned the craggy hills to either side of the trail. John was anything but cautious, his entire body quivering with excitement.

The Iron Horse slowed and stopped a good dozen yards from the men. The machine's hull was battered, its left side disfigured by an enormous dent. Red phosphorescent liquid drooled from its undercarriage, mute evidence that its fuel system was compromised. A smell of ozone crackled from its engine and as it powered down, a sputtering wail rattled through the vehicle.

Cole appeared on the cabin's porch just as the Iron Horse shuddered to a stop. He nodded toward the conveyance. "If that thing had legs, it'd be on the last of 'em."

The rider dismounted from his damaged vehicle. He was a tall, broadly built man, his body draped in the somber folds of a brown linen duster. A wide-brimmed leather hat covered his head, casting his face in shadow. It wasn't necessary to see his face to know who he was, however. The sleek metal arms fixed to his shoulders proclaimed his identity louder than any face. Those arms had become infamous throughout the west, the widow-makers that could snatch a blaster from its holster faster than lightning. A string of corpses from Missouri to California could attest to the lethal precision that guided those mechanical killers, the unerring marksmanship that had been honed on the bloody battlefields of Kansas.

Jesse James, the most wanted man in the Union, the most ruthless robber and bandit in the whole of the west.

"It got me where I need to be," Jesse said as he looked up toward the cabin.

There were a lot of things that ran through Cole's mind as he met Jesse's stare. They'd served together in Quantrill's Raiders throughout the war. They'd ridden with Archie Clement together, robbing Yankee banks in Kansas and Missouri. After that gang broke up, Jesse had been the center of a new gang and Cole was among his very first recruits. From the bayous of the south to the plains of the north, they'd earned themselves the reputation as the most notorious outlaws in the country. They'd been in more gunfights than he could remember, killed more sheriffs than small pox. Pottersonville, Fidelity, Franklin, all those towns had earned their part in the lore of the west when Jesse James and his men descended upon them. The double-bank heist in Dodge was still the subject of dime novels. Two banks at the same time, and with twenty regulators guarding the vault that held the season's proceeds of the Stockton Cattleman's Society and Trust. Not to mention, Cole counted Jesse's brother Frank as his best friend in the world. He knew there wasn't a braver, bolder man to have as a comrade in arms. At the same time, Jesse was headstrong, impulsive, and prideful; qualities that Cole had tried his best to restrain himself after taking on the mantle of leadership and the responsibility of taking care of his brothers. A leader needed to be careful and calculating, not rambunctious and flighty. Since the accident that had removed his real arms, Jesse'd also developed an ugly vein of temper, a propensity toward violence that bordered on sadism at times. All things told,

Cole had more reason to resent than welcome the notorious gunslinger.

Reason, however, wasn't something that applied once a man felt Jesse's eyes on him. There was an innate charisma, a natural magnetism about Jesse James that compelled a man regardless of careful planning and common sense. Jesse was like a force of nature, terrible and irresistible - even when your name was Cole Younger.

"You can stop eyeballin' them hills for hidden marshals," Cole told Bob and Jim. "Any lawdog who got his hands on Jesse James would hardly risk his blood money bringing in the likes of us."

Bob nodded and strode toward Jesse. Still nursing his distemper, Jim merely stood his ground and watched.

John dashed ahead of Bob, wearing a wide smile and uttering another celebratory whoop. "Jesse James!" he crowed. "*The* Jesse James!"

Jesse stared past the boy, removing his crimson-tinted goggles and directing his attention to Bob. "Who's this one?"

"You remember our little brother? Once we set up here, John came out from Missouri to join up." Bob laughed and wagged a finger at his brother. "Calls himself 'Kid Younger' these days. Wants to be the terror of the territories."

Jesse cast an appraising eye over John. "Find a new moniker. I'm not too fond of 'Kids' at the moment." He turned away and started marching toward the cabin.

"Things go sour in Diablo Canyon?" Cole called out.

Jesse glowered up at the bushwhacker. "Might have gone less sour if'n the Youngers had stuck around. Law showed up the day after you lit out."

"I didn't know there was any law around Diablo Canyon," Cole snarled back. "You think I'd have left compadres in trouble like that and just moseyed off on my own? Hell, if'n you think that, we'll slap leather right now. Don't matter none if'n those arms of yourn are fast as quicksilver. I ain't gonna stand fer that kind of insult." Cole's face twisted into a sneer when he saw the fire in Jesse's eyes. "If'n you're so fool-all stupid to believe that of me, then maybe I'd better talk to Frank. He was always the smart one anyway."

Mention of Frank James caused Jesse to stand stock-still. Cole could see the gunman's shoulders sag as though some great weight was pressing down upon them. The fire he'd seen in Jesse's eyes drained away, all the angry strength of a moment before evaporating in the desert sun.

Jesse was close enough that Cole could see the pinched, drawn visage hiding in his hat's shadow. He could see the lines of pain etched into those lean features, the wince of agony that pulled at his mouth every time he had taken a step. More, he could see the hollow emptiness in the outlaw's eyes, the haunted look of a man whose suffering goes far deeper than flesh and bone.

"Things went bad," Jesse said, his voice hollow and empty. "Leave it at that."

"That's a tall order," Cole said. "When you and Frank lit out, you were full of talk about a big payout. You want to waltz back in here and build back the gang, might be some of that loot should be ours."

In a blur, Jesse's arm came whipping up, snatching at Cole. Halfway to the bushwhacker's throat, the metal limb froze, the fingers flexing like the talons of a buzzard. "There weren't no payout," Jesse growled. "Just a pack of lies and liars." He glanced away from Cole, staring instead at his extended arm. A look of cold fury blazed in his eyes as he stared at the mechanical limb. His face contorted in pain as he rolled his shoulder and brought the arm slowly down to his side.

"I need to rest," Jesse said, brushing past Cole. "I'm gonna hole up here for awhile. I'm sure you don't mind." He paused as he opened the door. "Frank's dead," he said, his voice a low, anguished whisper. Without giving Cole a chance to say one word, Jesse started into the gloom of the cabin.

"What do you mean 'Frank's dead'?" Cole demanded. He caught Jesse by the shoulder, cringing at the cold feel of the steel augmetics beneath his hand. "How?"

"Blue-bellies got him after you lit out," Jesse said, his voice as cold and hollow as the steel shoulder under Cole's hand. "A Yankee patrol just outside Diablo Canyon. They got Frank. Didn't even leave me enough chance to fetch back his body." He slipped free from Cole's grip, not by brushing him off, but simply by shrugging clear. His eyes, as they stared at Cole, were absolutely empty. "I had to leave him there, with them damn blue-bellies."

Words caught in Cole's throat. He didn't know what to say. Except for John, they'd all ridden the outlaw trail long enough to know what became of a dead gunfighter like Frank James. The body would be put on display somewhere so that yokels could gawk at it and the law could crow about how mighty powerful it was and how nobody was beyond its reach. Depending on how much hate there was in the sheriff or marshal, they might even let some of the locals take bits of clothing as souvenirs. The more sadistic might even let them cut bits off the body. Archie Clement's trigger finger was said to be in a bottle of preserves in Kansas City and there was still a cantina out California way exhibiting the mangled hand of Three Finger Jack, old Joaquin Murrieta's lieutenant.

The idea of Frank ending up like that was something to make the blood boil. Feeling that rage building up inside him, Cole recognized the magnitude of Jesse's hurt. Losing his brother had drained everything out of Jesse, leaving him as cold and lifeless as Carpathian's arms. He was too empty to hate, too filled with pain to think about revenge. He might be back among friends, but he was still as alone as though he were the last man in the world.

"Anything you need, Jesse?" Cole asked.

The barest flicker of a smile was the only show of emotion Jesse made. "Just a place to hole up for a time, and the time to clear my head." He stared into Cole's eyes, acknowledging the concern he saw there. "Just let me lie for a bit," he said, turning to withdraw into the cabin.

Cole stared after the departed outlaw, digesting everything he'd seen and heard. He wondered if the shot that had killed Frank James hadn't done for Jesse as well.

"In all my born days, I ain't never seen no man so big!" The statement came from John as the boy scrambled up onto the porch. Cole directed a sour look at the youth's enthusiasm.

"Boy, you sure go whole-hog, don't you?" Cole scowled. "You're supposed to be *my* kid brother, not Jesse James'!"

John stepped down from the porch, a sheepish expression of apology on his face. "I didn't mean nothin'. It's just, well, that's Jesse James!"

Sighing in disgust, Cole turned his attention to his other brothers as they returned to the cabin. The germ of an idea was starting to form. The best thing for Jesse right now was to heal up, let the hurt settle a bit. After that, he'd need to be busy, keep his mind from dwelling on Frank and leaving him behind. Cole knew exactly how to keep Jesse busy and at the same time make the Youngers a lot richer. "Have a look at his 'Horse?" he asked Jim. "Does it look like it can be salvaged?"

"Might be we could fix 'er up," Jim said, "but I wouldn't like to bet my stake on it."

Cole frowned. Getting new equipment of that sort would mean tangling with lawmen or Union troops, circumstances that always involved high risk. "Keep a good watch on ours then," he told Jim. "Jesse's welcome to stay a spell, but if he gets the notion to rustle one of our 'Horses, he's gonna find out in a hurry that the Youngers ain't nobody's boot-licker!" He jabbed a finger at John. "That includes you. I didn't shoot no regulator just so's you can give your 'Horse away."

"Jesse won't like that," Bob pointed out.

"Jesse be damned," Cole growled back. "I'm runnin' this outfit." His expression darkened. He was remembering all the good times he'd had with Frank James. Frank had been a man cut from the same cloth as Cole, a careful planner and shrewd thinker. Whatever trouble had put him in a boot orchard, he was certain that it was Jesse's impetuousness that brought it about. Frank'd never been able to shrug off his little brother's charisma, even as a kid he'd allowed Jesse to talk him into the most fool-all ventures.

"We ain't been doing so good, Cole," Jim stated. "Might be Jesse's got some ideas to turn that around."

Cole slapped his hand against one of the beams supporting the awning above the porch. "Sure he's got ideas. One of his ideas put Frank in the ground. Bad enough he got his brother killt, I ain't gonna see one of mine dropped into a grave patch. He wants to stick around; he'll start listenin' to me."

"Jesse'll have something to say about that," John declared, squaring his shoulders in a brazen show of defiance. "He's too big to be takin' orders from a two-bit border ruffian…"

Again Cole's hand slammed against the post, this time with enough force to knock little streams of dust from the awning. "Gettin' a lot of sass, boy. Keep it up and big brother'll be fetching a switch to your hide." The threat brought John a pace nearer, one hand closing about the grip of his pistol. Cole arched an eyebrow when he saw the menacing gesture. "Us Youngers done a lot of bad things, but we ain't yet drawed on kin." The anger drained out of the youth, replaced with a crimson flush of shame. Cole grinned and clapped his little brother on the shoulder. "I said it afore, you got brass, kid."

Bob breathed a sigh of relief as he watched his brothers reconcile. Still, there was a nagging worry in his expression. "John's right, Cole. What'll we do about Jesse?"

"There's a fire gone out of him," Jim said, shaking his head sadly. "Don't even seem like the same man. Like somebody just went and scooped out his innards."

John rounded on his brother. "You callin' Jesse yeller?" he demanded, one hand clenched into a fist.

"He's sayin' the heart's gone out of Jesse," Bob said, trying to keep tempers from flaring up again. "Frank's death is bound to have tore him up inside. Imagine what'd be like for us if Cole was gone."

The three brothers looked to the eldest Younger. Cole had a pensive expression. He was thinking about this reunion with Jesse, pondering it like a preacher might ponder a passage of scripture. He was careful about putting what he thought into words until he was certain there was some veracity behind them.

"There's somethin' wrong with them quick-devil arms of his. I could see it in the way he moved." Cole nodded his chin toward the Iron Horse. "Maybe his 'Horse weren't the only thing got shot up."

"You thinkin' Jesse needs doctorin'?" Bob wondered.

"Nope," Cole stated. There was a cunning gleam in his eye. "I think he's just fine way he is. If them arms of his are givin' him problems, he'll be easier to handle. More apt to listen to reason."

John grabbed Cole's arm. "But if he's hurt, we gotta help him."

"Hardly," Cole answered, pulling away. "When Jesse started focusin' on chasin' tall tales, he cut his string with us. We ain't under no obligation to him now." He nodded pensively. "We do right by the Youngers first."

"What you got in mind, Cole?" Bob asked.

Cole glanced over his shoulder at the darkened cabin behind him. "I've got a few jobs in mind, but we'll need more men. Good men, not buckaroos like Potts and Danby." A foxlike smile spread across his face. "Right people hear we've got Jesse James behind us, we'll get all the guns we could ask for." He jabbed a thumb at the cabin. "See Jesse stays put," he ordered as he stepped down from the porch.

"Where are you goin'?" Jim demanded.

Cole paused in his march to the barn where the gang's Iron Horses were stashed. "Tombstone. I'm gonna look up Ringo. He's been runnin' with the Clantons last I heard. I'll see if him and his pals might be interested in doing some work with the Younger Gang."

"The *James*-Younger Gang," John corrected him.

"Yeah," Cole grumbled as he swung open the barn door. "The James-Younger Gang." It hurt his pride to admit it, but he needed the bandit's fame to work things the way he wanted. For most of the outlaws of the west, the name of Jesse James was like a sacred banner waving up on high. Ringo might balk due to his loathing of Jesse, but he was kin to the Youngers, and Cole knew he'd never be turned away by his cousin. For the rest, he'd use Jesse's notoriety, play it out to the last card to bring them onboard. It might be a gamble, but the rewards were too big to pass up.

His Iron Horse growling beneath him, Cole Younger emerged from the barn and set out on the long ride to Tombstone and his cousin, the notorious Johnny Ringo.

***

John Younger stood in the doorway to the back room Jesse James had taken for his own. It had been Cole's room, but any amusement John might have felt at his eldest brother's expense was stifled by his concern for the man now lying sprawled across the bed.

Despite the assurances of Cole, John wasn't so certain about the severity of Jesse's wounds. The outlaw's flesh had a ghastly pallor and perspiration beaded his brow. Jesse's breathing came in ragged gasps and several times an inarticulate cry rattled past his lips. Jim and Bob both claimed that this was usual for Jesse, that the mechanical arms Dr. Carpathian had fitted him with often provoked bad dreams and fitful sleep. It was the price, they claimed, for his supernatural speed and reflexes. Nothing came without a cost; not even the medical miracles of the so-called Enlightened.

John wasn't convinced. As he watched his idol sleeping, he felt a growing sense of anxiety and frustration. The callousness of his older brothers toward this man they'd rode with and fought beside made him feel guilty. Standing by while this man he admired, this unrepentant rebel who'd become a hero to the Secesh of Missouri, suffered, was a thing that made him ashamed.

Hang what Cole said! His older brothers were a damn sight too cautious. They were too afraid that if they went someplace to fetch a doctor for Jesse that they'd be recognized! Well, the Devil could take their timidity! The faces of Cole, Bob, and Jim Younger might be well known, posted to marshals and sheriffs across the territories, but John hadn't earned the same notoriety. He could slip into a town without drawing any notice; do what his brothers were afraid to do.

The boy nodded his head as he made his decision. He'd heard Potts talk about a sawbones in San Diablo who was a wonder-worker when it came to knife wounds and blaster burns. Well, then Doctor Fletcher would have his chance to show off his skill! John would ride out and fetch him, bring him back to work on Jesse!

John stared at the unconscious Jesse, his eyes drinking in the image of the prostrate outlaw, letting the picture of his infirm hero sink into his mind. Whatever lay ahead of him, the knowledge that Jesse was depending on him would spur him on. He wouldn't let him down.

Quietly, wary lest the slightest sound alert Bob and Jim to his intentions, John crept out of the cabin and made his way to the barn. It took him the better part of an hour to accomplish the arduous task of pushing the dead bulk of his inert Iron Horse far enough down the trail as to be out of sight of the cabin. It was a Herculean task. Before he had gone more than a couple of yards, the boy's shirt was soaked in sweat, his face scarlet with the strain of his exertions, his palms blistered where they pushed against the dead bulk of the machine. Soon, the muscles in his arms began to feel as though they were on fire, shivers of pain pulsing from them to infect every inch of his body. Fatigue dragged at him, the breath that he sucked down into his gasping lungs burned and tormented, perspiration dripped into his eyes and cascaded down his neck. The outlaw's body begged him to relent, to abandon this impossible task he had set himself. He resisted the pleas of his abused body, forced himself onward with imperious resilience. Jesse was depending on him, and the boy wasn't going to let his hero suffer because of his own weakness. Only when he was certain his brothers couldn't see him did John activate the machine. In that moment, the thrill of prevailing at the end of his ordeal washed away his exhaustion, the raw exhilaration of victory energizing him even more fiercely than the RJ fuel in his 'Horse.

Shouting a Rebel yell, the young bandit rode off into the darkening night.

***

Lucinda Loveless presented a far more comely appearance sitting in the Territorial Governor's office than she had crawling in the rocks outside Billy the Kid's hideout. Her long tresses were plaited and piled atop her head, vibrant ribbons of lace holding the complex arrangement of hair in place. A flowing gown of silks and satins clung to her shapely frame, accentuating each curve with the most lascivious detail. Powder hid the dark tan her skin had acquired on the long trail while expensive Parisian perfume blotted out the acrid stink of RJ.

Behind the sprawling mahogany desk, Governor Lew Wallace smiled at his attractive guest, extending a teakwood cigarette case toward her. A graceful twist of her hand retrieved one of them from the velvet-lined box. The governor leaned forward with a pearl-inlaid lighter, its tiny RJ-1027 furnace glowing with an infernal crimson light as it ignited the cylinder of tobacco.

"There was one thing the Secessionists knew how to do: they knew a proper blend of tobacco," the bearded governor proclaimed as he returned the lighter to the brass holder sitting on the desk. "This weed from Hispanola simply doesn't have a civilized flavor. It smells of swamp and malaria and the old tyrannies of the Spanish Dons. " He drew a breath from his own cigarette, frowning at the taste of the smoke. "It is keenly to be desired that the Midlands be restored to the Union and we can see about cultivating a decent tobacco leaf again. If Grant would only consider dispatching a division or two to install a territorial governor in the old Carolinas, the matter would be quickly rectified."

"The Secessionists still pose a problem, governor," Loveless observed. "There are still considerable…"

"Rabble, nothing more," Wallace declared with a wave of his hand. "But for the outrages of the Warrior Nation, General Grant would have cleansed this Union of all rebel elements. Instead we must be content with containing the remnants while we attend to these savages."

"And these marauding outlaws, governor. Do not forget them." The speaker was a middle-aged man with a thin moustache, his trim suit screaming of New York and its expensive clothiers. He didn't wear any weapons openly, but the bulge under his coat betrayed the presence of at least one shoulder holster. "Day by day they grow more bold and ruthless. Frankly, Washington is finding them an embarrassment. Their crimes make the whole country look barbaric and uncivilized. We will never impress the crowned heads of Europe while their newspapers recount gunfights in the streets of El Paso and hold-ups on the Union-Pacific."

Lew Wallace darted a venomous look at the man. The barb about Europe coupled with a reminder about the lawlessness in El Paso had been thrust at the governor with all the cruelty of a Bowie knife. Wallace had risen to his posting as

Governor of Texas Territory especially because it was felt the former general could reign in the outlaw elements and lingering Secesh attitudes until such time as the region could be partitioned off into smaller, more manageable states and territories. His true aspirations, however, were to achieve a position as American ambassador to one of the European courts.

Wallace appreciated exactly how precarious his posting really was. When he'd accepted the position as Governor of Texas Territory, he'd been led to believe the land was firmly in Union hands. Nothing could be farther from the truth. Bands of Warrior Nation marauders were a constant threat, massacring entire communities before vanishing back into the trackless wilds from which they emerged. The forces of the Confederate Rebellion were a persistent menace, slipping across the Mississippi to raid for supplies and assassinate Union soldiers. Close to the frontier between the borders of Texas and the region claimed by Dr. Carpathian and his Enlightened, there had been numerous incidents involving bio-mechanical abominations that had either escaped from or been loosed by the sinister cabal of scientists and inventors. The southern border was always menaced by the Golden Army of Mexico and the potential for further violence with those fierce legions.

To all of these threats, Wallace had to add the depredations of the outlaws. Texas Territory played host to the most infamous criminals in the nation. The Wild Bunch and the Daltons, the Rufus Buck Gang and the Burrow Brothers, all of them had chosen the wide expanses of Texas for their hunting ground. To their numbers had to be added the James-Younger Gang and, more recently, the murderous Billy the Kid. The other malcontents menacing the area were forces of such magnitude that the solution to dispatching them would require federal resources. The outlaw bands, however, were something his superiors in Washington expected Wallace to resolve with the assets already at his disposal. If some progress wasn't forthcoming, some example that would impress upon the still-rebellious population of Texas that the Union was firmly in control of their country, the governor's political career would crash in flames.

"Your agents, Mr. Pinkerton, had their chance to bring down Billy the Kid," the governor declared. He'd long ago decided that of the two, Billy was the target to focus upon. His was a name that would carry weight in Washington, but at the same time he didn't have the experience and resources of the more established outlaws. Wallace tapped his fingers against a stack of papers. "I have Sheriff Garrett's full report right here. He places the blame for the Kid's escape on your man, Charlie Siringo." Wallace bowed his head apologetically to the woman seated across from him. "I fear he also mentions you, Miss Loveless."

Loveless took a long draw from her cigarette. "Billy is only a symptom. Jesse James is the disease. Once he... once he is apprehended this wave of outlawry will come to an end."

"You will forgive me, Miss Loveless, but my constituents are more worried about Billy the Kid. Removing the menace this crazed gunfighter poses the people of Texas will impress upon them far more keenly that the Union is here to help and protect them from these lawless elements."

Pinkerton smiled at the governor. "I was unaware your sense of civic responsibility ran so deeply. Perhaps I should inform Washington that General Longstreet should assume the position of Minister Plenipotentiary to the Ottoman Empire?"

Wallace leaned back, stubbing out his cigarette in a marble ashtray. One glance at Pinkerton told the governor that the agent was fully aware of his fears regarding the precarious state of his political future, should one of the many threats hanging over Texas Territory suddenly explode into full-blown warfare. "What is it that Washington would like me to do?"

"Post a reward for Jesse James," Loveless stated.

"That's been done before. I believe the reward currently stands at $5,000."

"Yes," she agreed, "but this time in addition to the reward, you will offer amnesty. Complete exoneration for all past crimes."

The governor shook his head. "That would be condoning murder. The people would never stand for it."

"The people will stand for what Washington tells them they will stand for," Pinkerton retorted. "The only way we're going to catch this man is by getting the scum he associates with to turn on him. That won't happen if they think there's a necktie party waiting for them if they come in."

Wallace drummed his fingers against the desk, still shaking his head. "It's an affront to law and decency," he declared.

Loveless stared into the governor's eyes. When she spoke, her tone was sympathetic yet firm. "Think of all the havoc these men will do if Jesse isn't brought in. We can't think of past crimes. We have to prevent new ones."

"Yes," Pinkerton agreed. "Don't dwell on the past. Think of the future. Think of Istanbul and the Sultan's court."

It was a visibly shaken governor who made his apologies a few minutes later, claiming a sudden illness prohibited him from attending his guests further. There was certainly a drain of color about the man as he bowed himself out and retired to his quarters.

"He'll do it," Pinkerton predicted as he escorted Loveless from the governor's palace. "Grant knew exactly who they were putting in charge down here. A man bold enough to follow orders but not brave enough to stand on his own. It might take his conscience a few days to come around, but in the end we'll get what we want. When he does, every paper in the country will carry notice of the amnesty offer."

Loveless shuddered under the heavy wrap she'd adopted against the chill night air. The darkening twilight was broken by the sputter of automated lamps. Much of San Antonio remained an isolated backwater, a confusion of narrow dirt streets that hadn't been improved since the days of Mexican rule, but the immediate vicinity of the palace of the governor sported the latest in the way of eastern technology and improvement. As the lamps burst into brilliance, bats swooped down to attack the congregating swarms of moths.

"How long do you think before somebody turns him in?" Loveless's question came in a flat, emotionless tone, giving no hint to the strange flutter that twisted her stomach into a knot.

Pinkerton paused, scratching his chin as he contemplated the answer. "If he's keeping to the company of Missouri border trash, we might be in for a long wait. But if he's playing around with malcontents like Bonney, we could hear something within a few days of the announcement. There's no honor among thieves, you know, and most of these outlaws don't even feign the justification of being Secesh for doing what they do."

"They'll want to get him alive," Loveless stated. "Find out how closely he's working with Lee."

"I don't think so," Pinkerton said. "Alive would be nice, but James has grown too dangerous. At this point, however we get him, so long as we get him." He smiled as he withdrew an envelope from the breast of his coat. "That won't be your problem, though. You've been reassigned."

A quiver of alarm ran through the agent. "Reassigned?" she wondered as she took the envelope from Pinkerton and started to read its contents.

Pinkerton laughed. "Don't worry, you're not joining Siringo in Alaska. Washington thinks you'd be better employed doing the same sort of thing Courtright's working on. Seems there's some Indian holy relic the Army's gotten wind of. They're worried about the Warrior Nation getting ahold of it and using it to whip the savages into an even worse frenzy. They've asked us to slip some of our top people into Carpathian's kingdom to find it." His smile broadened. "Naturally, you are on the list of our top people."

Loveless shook her head and tried to return the document to her superior. "My assignment here isn't done."

Pinkerton's expression hardened and he thrust the envelope back into her hand. "I apologize if I made that sound like a request, Agent Loveless. I assure you it wasn't." He reached into his vest and examined his watch. "There's a stage to Lawry in two hours. From Lawry you can catch a train to El Paso down near the border. Get this hoodoo for the Army and then we'll discuss Jesse James. That is, if he isn't already swinging from a noose by then."

Chapter 2

An old kerosene lamp sputtered on a clapboard table, casting long shadows through the room. The mangy head of a buffalo hanging over the stone fireplace was transformed into a demonic goblin by the flickering shadows. The iron framework of an old bed standing in one corner became a skeletal slashwork of wire. Most of all, the men gathered around the table were twisted into ghoulish apparitions, their eyes glittering wickedly from the darkness.

Cole Younger shrugged. Where the men were concerned, more light would hardly make them more appealing. When he'd ridden up to the dilapidated ranch house, he'd seen some of the ruffians in broad daylight. 'Cowboys' they styled themselves, but Cole doubted any of these desperados had ever punched an honest steer in their lives. They might have rustled their share, but men with faces like these didn't take to hard work and regular hours.

They'd rather steal.

The Missouri bushwhacker kept a ready hand on his pistol. He felt like a wolf that had plunked itself down in a coyote den. It didn't matter that he could whip any five of these contemptible backshooters, not when they had the guns at hand to make up the difference. Of course, if they didn't have the numbers, he'd never have made the trip to Tombstone. The Cowboys hadn't taken part in the train heist that had brought arms and gear to so many of the west's badmen. They'd been raiding in Mexico during the heist and their absence from the train attack had left the gang at a distinct disadvantage, one that no amount of terror and brutality could overcome. They needed blasters and Iron Horses, needed those the way a starving wolf needed meat.

The only real gunman among them was Johnny Ringo, the only one who'd taken part in the great train heist that had enriched the arsenals of most of the badmen in the west. Where the others would plug a man through a window or from behind a door, Ringo had too much brazen conceit. It wasn't any sense of decency or fair play that made him prefer an open fight. It was a sick sort of pride, a sense of accomplishment he simply couldn't get any other way. Ringo'd once told his cousin that he never really felt alive until that second when he looked into the eyes of a man he was about to kill. It was that moment, that instant, when he could feel Death standing at his shoulder that made everything else worthwhile.

He cut a sinister figure, Johnny Ringo. He sported a long duster and a gaudy crimson vest with gold embroidery. The grips on the brace of blasters that hung from his belt were ivory, engraved with writhing dragons by Chinese artisans of Tombstone's Hoptown. The gunfighter wore them butt-forwards, favoring a cross-draw that he always claimed caught his adversaries off-guard. Cole thought it more likely was that it was Ringo's way of giving his opponent an edge, of making the duel more interesting for himself. Among pistoleros, Johnny Ringo was held in a class all his own, feared because when he stepped out in the street to square off, it seemed he really didn't care who it was who ended up on Boot Hill.

The other men in the ranch house had reputations far more unsavory. 'Curly Bill' Brocius was a horse thief, stage robber, and rustler. His trim beard and heavy features, the scruffy and soiled garb he wore, everything about him screamed aloud his savage and untamed disposition. He'd earned a reputation for viciousness after the grisly Skeleton Canyon Massacre when he'd personally tortured six vaqueros to death with the heated induction coil from the engine of a ranger's Interceptor. He was also a vicious drunkard, having shot off a preacher's feet with a blaster when he'd tried to make the man dance during a sermon. He'd narrowly escaped a lynching after blasting Marshal Fred White in half during a drunken escapade outside the Birdcage Theater.

Frank Stilwell was a weasel-faced Texan with mean little eyes and the morality of a rattlesnake. He'd been a deputy sheriff in Tombstone until Wyatt Earp discovered Stilwell's rampant extortion and embezzlement. In his time, he'd been both stage robber and claim-jumper. He was a human rat to whom life was cheap, having once murdered a man for serving him tea instead of coffee.

'Indian' Charlie was a half-breed Mexican, reputed to be a deserter from the feared Golden Army. More than half-deranged, he was given to psychotic fits and bizarre mood swings. During one raid on a fuel station, he'd insisted the stationmaster and his family dance naked until the outlaws were out of sight, blasting the hand off one man who tried to quit early with a buffalo gun. Another incident had involved him wandering into a saloon and smashing every bottle behind the bar over his own head, utterly oblivious to the blood streaming from his slashed scalp.

Pete Spence, Tom and Frank McLaury, Pony Deal, Frank Patterson, 'Rattlesnake' Bill, Jim Hughes, Jack Gauge – all of them robbers and rustlers. However, the guiding force behind this confederation of desperados and renegades were the Clantons. Ike Clanton was a spruced-up scoundrel who styled himself like a gentrified landowner; the sombrero on his head offset by the sleeves of his shirt adorned with gilded elctriwork garters with tiny RJ-powered horses prancing around his arms. His younger brother, Billy, was a hulking brute with a penchant for opium. The oldest brother, Phin, was a reclusive and submissive personality always ready to follow the rest of the gang.

Though Ike and Curly Bill acted in the capacity of captains or foremen of the Cowboys, the leader was Ike's father, the bearded patriarch of the Clanton family, Newman Hayes Clanton, commonly referred to as simply 'Old Man' Clanton. He was a tough, grizzled veteran of the Missouri border wars, a man upon whose face was etched all the cruelty of a hard and unforgiving life. Skin like boiled leather, eyes like chips of lead, he was the despotic chieftain of crime in Arizona's Cochise County and whatever regions of Mexico were unfortunate enough to attract his savage attention. He was a throwback, an atavism from a more brutal time. Like Curly Bill, Clanton was fighting tooth and nail to keep the complexities of this modern age at bay. The avarice in Old Man Clanton's eyes, however,

was unmistakable as he listened to Cole describe the benefits of
joining up with the James-Younger Gang.

"Some of your boys are packing some slapdash
shooters and I saw a mighty sorry bunch of blackhoofs in that
corral outside." Many of the Cowboys carried old-fashioned
blasters that looked like they might have come from a US cavalry
scrapyard. The corral had only a few Iron Horses and
Interceptors in it, the bulk of the gang riding a motley array of
blackhoofs; mechanical horse-like automatons that were
fabricated by blacksmiths and horse-traders throughout the west.
The robot stallions were immensely varied; no two machinists
constructed them in exactly the same pattern. The ones in the
Cowboy corral, despite bearing the magnetized stamp of a
Clantonville workshop, exhibited a range of styles that
encompassed the handiwork of at least a dozen different
manufacturers. Slower and more fidgety than the vehicles built by
the Union, blackhoofs weren't the sort of thing any outlaw wanted
to rely on. The fact that the Cowboys had so many of them told
Cole all he needed to know about how their fortunes had been
faring.

Cole swept his gaze across the Cowboys. "Guess you
boys missed out not bein' around for the big train heist. You
fellas have been bushwhacking prospectors and raiding
sodbusters when you could have been layin' siege to ranches
and bustin' banks. You been hidin' from the law when you could
have been spittin' in its eye. How many men'd you lose that time
Wyatt Earp sicced his Enforcers on you down in Gila Crossing?
Seven, was it? And what about when that range detective Horn
came nosin' around lookin' for Chisum's cattle? Think he
accounted for nine men with that long-distance blaster of his
afore you paid Chisum for the cattle you stole.

"I also hear tell it was only six who got themselves
planted in a bone orchard when you tried tacklin' that refueling
station in Apache Creek. I imagine Ringo's told you all about the
difference modern arms and modern mounts will make until he
was blue in the face. Behind the times, runnin' round Old Mex,
rustlin' when you could have been gettin' yerselves dandied up
with proper shootin' irons. Well, I'm sayin' we can fix all that. Get
you enough blasters and Iron Horses to arm a whole company."

"We ain't doing so bad now," Ike stated, scowling at the seated Cole. "Indian Charlie gutted two marshals just last month, brought us their blasters and their hosses. What do we need you and James for?"

The Old Man turned a withering glare on his son. "Set your backside down and shut yer gob. Can't you see big folks is havin' a palaver?" He turned his snake-like gaze on Cole. "Say yer piece son, but make it good."

Cole smiled indulgently at the assembled Cowboys. "Well, I mean Ike's already said it for me. You can just keep moseying on out and kill all star-packers. 'Course I imagine it won't take 'em long to reckon just who it is planting marshals and rangers in the ground. What do you think'll happen then? My way, we rush in and everybody gets what they need in one go. Then you can meet the lawdogs on their own terms."

"That the way Jesse figures it?" Curly Bill asked.

"That's the way Cole Younger figures it," Cole scowled back. He noticed the flicker of uncertainty that crept into Curly Bill's eyes. "The scheme's good enough for Jesse," he told the Cowboy.

From the corner of the room, Johnny Ringo's cold voice rang out. "I hear tell Billy the Kid split off from Jesse. Musta been a good reason fer him to do that. Maybe Billy figured Jesse ain't such a sharp blade to be around. Maybe him and his boys decided to find themselves friendlier company. Company who ain't so full of themselves like Jesse. Ask me, it sounds like the James-Younger Gang's on the skids. Why should we hitch our wagon to a train that's going downhill?"

Old Man Clanton rounded on the gunfighter. "Because there's damn good money to be had. Enough sugar to keep you coyotes in booze and women for a good long spell." The outlaw patriarch frowned when he saw his words made little impact on the baleful Ringo. He turned his tyrannical oratory on the rest of the Cowboys. "Cole's promisin' us blasters, armor, and Iron Horses. Enough so's we don't need to fret over Neri or the damn Earps!"

"I still don't like it," Ike grumbled. He flinched as the back of his father's hand cracked across his matted beard of a cheek.

"I told you once afore to shut yer gob!" Old Man Clanton snarled. He turned back toward Cole. "You can set yer war bag over in the bunkhouse. Might take us a day or two to get things situated here, but I speak for all the Cowboys when I say we'd be right proud to ride with Jesse James."

Cole hid his annoyance at that last statement as he rose from the table. "Fair enough. But don't keep me waitin' too long. Jesse's the impatient type. He might decide he wants different partners if'n you dilly-dally."

As soon as Cole Younger had withdrawn from the room, the assembled Cowboys erupted into a babble of argument, some excited by the proposal Cole had brought them, others clearly angry that they'd be giving up their autonomy and taking orders from Jesse James. Old Man Clanton silenced the discord by slamming the butt of his blaster against the table. The weapon discharged in a violent blaze of energy, the shot searing through the shoulder of Rattlesnake Bill and throwing the outlaw to the floor. The maimed man writhed in agony, shrieking as blood spurted from his ravaged body. The other Cowboys stared down at their stricken comrade in mute horror, then back at their glowering boss.

Old Man Clanton was careful not to let on that shooting Rattlesnake Bill had been accidental. Assuming an imperious scowl, he glared at his underlings. Stepping around the table, he gave the bleeding rustler a savage kick.
"Quit yer hollerin'!" he snapped. "I said we're gonna ride with Jesse an' that's what we're gonna do!"

Still caressing his cheek, Ike turned toward his father. "It don't make no sense, Pa! We get mixed up with James and it won't be marshals and rangers dogging us, it'll be Pinkertons and the damn Union Army!"

An ugly chuckle bubbled up from behind the Old Man's beard. "Don't think I knowed that? Just 'cause we sign on with 'em don't mean we stay signed on!"

The statement had the outlaws eyeing their boss uneasily. Curly Bill was the first to vocalize why the plan seemed so appalling. "You're fixin' to cross up Jesse James?" With the exception of Johnny Ringo, every Cowboy in the room looked like he'd rather arm-wrestle an Enforcer robot than cross the infamous outlaw.

"Jesse'll have bigger problems than us to occupy himself," Old Man Clanton said. His malignant eyes roved across the faces of his followers. "Biggest nuisance we've got are those damn carpetbagger Earps. Well, we'll kill two buzzards with the same rock! We'll fix it so's the Earps take up Jesse's trail. He'll be so busy tryin' to stay ahead of them, that he ain't gonna have time to think about us. And while the Earps are busy hounding Jesse, we'll have a free hand here."

The Old Man waved his hand, drawing his followers closer. "Now just you listen to how I figure we'll fix it…"

***

The town of San Diablo stretched along the barren, rocky slope of a large hill. In better days, a string of rich gold mines had burrowed down into the hillside above the town. Indiscriminate blasting, spurred by the Union's frenzy for the particular breed of gold the San Diablo mines offered, had led to catastrophe. Trying to sink shafts on the reverse side of the hill, miners had instead collapsed many of the existing workings. Hundreds of men had been buried alive in the blink of an eye and the richest gold veins sealed off by tons of solid rock.

The hunger of the Union, however, wouldn't let the gold slip away so easily. A private firm from Chicago had been contracted to examine the feasibility of reopening the mines. A small army of surveyors and engineers had descended on San Diablo, bringing with them all manner of strange technological inventions from the east. Henry Irons, bulky automatons cast in the vague semblance of men, were lowered into the few shafts remaining. Day and night the robots toiled away, striving to unearth what human sweat and muscle claimed to be impossible. Some of the old miners who had lingered on resented the robots, but most of San Diablo welcomed their advent. Without the men from Chicago and their machines, they knew their town would have dried up and blown away like so many other boom towns before them.

Like the eye of the Devil himself, the hot West Texas sun scorched the winding main street of San Diablo. Many of the structures perched upon the jagged hillside were simple canvas tents with wooden facades. Only a few were proper buildings, chiefly the offices of the various mining companies that had once headquartered in the town. One of these had been repurposed into a replacement for the crumbling adobe hovel that had served as combination courthouse and jail for the community.

John Younger kept a wary eye on San Diablo's new bastion of law and order. There was some commotion there with people dashing to and fro. He could see the menacing metal chassis of an Enforcer standing on the walkway just beside the entrance, its cyclopean optic glowing menacingly each time someone rushed past it. Sometimes, one of the men would pause to yell something at the robot as he ran past, but the machine was indifferent to whatever abuse was being thrown at it. The Enforcers would only listen to those they'd been programmed to obey.

Still keeping one eye on the jail, John looked down the street. He could make out the smoky lean-to of a blacksmith, the lumber-strewn workyard of a cooper, even the tent where the local undertaker must have established himself, judging by the profusion of coffins lying stacked outside. Of anything that might resemble a doctor's office, however, he could see no trace.

The young outlaw let his Iron Horse drift slowly toward the sprawling structure that seemed to be the center of town, a gigantic mass of logs and adobe that bore the title of Blackheart's Hotel and Saloon. Judging by the charred ground outside the building, it seemed to be frequented by men who had access to Iron Horses and Interceptors. The thought gave John a moment's pause – lawmen and soldiers were the sort of folk who had easiest access to the vehicles, most civilians making do with blackhoofs. A careful look at the single machine currently parked outside made him feel a little easier. A big brass plate was bolted to its hull, proclaiming it the property of the Illinois Mining and Assay Company.

Powering down his vehicle, John dismounted and stepped through the bat-wing doors. After the harsh light of the sun, the interior of the saloon seemed black as a cave. The young outlaw stayed in the doorway until his eyes had adjusted to the gloom.

"Don't dawdle there, boy," a sharp voice with a Texan twang called out. "With the sun at yer back, you make a damn fine target."

John's cheeks turned red at the reprimand, but he shifted to one side just the same, putting the saloon wall between himself and the street outside. Now that his eyes had started to adjust to the darkness, he could see the extent of the saloon. A long timber bar stretched across the back of the room, a series of glass mirrors mounted to the wall behind it. A few mechanized lanterns swung from the ceiling, but in the middle of the day none of these had been activated. A motley collection of tables and chairs were scattered about the main floor, and in one corner a small stage had been erected. He could see a narrow set of stairs climbing up to the second floor where he imagined the private rooms for hotel guests were situated. Flattened against the wall, just beside the stairway, was the splayed hide of some strange animal the likes of which John had never even heard tell of before.

"That would be Blackheart," the same Texan drawl announced. "Warrior Nation medicine man. The proprietor of this establishment was with Kit Carson when they brought down his warband. They say Blackheart changed himself into some horrible devil-buff when they caught up with him. Killed seven men before Carson's bullet punched through an eye and into its brain." The speaker laughed. "They have the heart pickled in a bottle behind the bar, but it'll cost you ten cents to see it."

John's gaze strayed back to the bar, for the first time really noticing the man standing behind it. He was a middle-aged, brawny-looking man, his hair just starting to abandon his head. He was wiping glasses with the apron he wore, but there was a nervous intensity to his chore that at once struck John as far from normal. When the bartender happened to look up, he didn't look John's way, but instead toward the right-hand side of the room. There was an unmistakable look of fear in his eyes, the terrified expression of a rabbit who sees a coyote.

John followed the direction of the bartender's gaze. Seated at one of the tables was a lone man dressed all in black, from boots to hat, offset only by the ruby-encrusted electriwork armbands he wore and the crimson vest peeking out from beneath his frock coat. There was a strange-looking blaster in his hand, its cylinder looked to be a single octagonal piece with a long hose snaking away from it to what looked like a ring of metal bottles fastened to the man's gun belt. There was a look of grim determination and almost sardonic amusement on the man's face. When he saw he had John's attention, he waved the barrel of his pistol at the outlaw. "Sit a spell," he ordered, kicking one of the chairs opposite him away from the table. One look into the man's cold eyes told John all he needed to know about his intentions. They were utterly without empathy, the eyes of a practiced killer. So much as a threatening twitch on his part, and John knew this man would gun him down like a dog.

Keeping his arms raised and well away from his own blasters, John marched over to the stranger's table and sank down into the chair. Inwardly, he chided himself for walking into such a predicament. He wondered if any of his brothers would have been so foolish as to let someone get the drop on them so easily. Most of all, he felt guilty. He had come to San Diablo to get help for Jesse, and he knew deep inside that his hero was depending on him. Failing himself, he could accept, but failing Jesse James was too bitter a pill to swallow.

"You a bounty hunter?" John asked as he lowered his arms and set his hands palm-down on the table.

The question seemed to pique the stranger's curiosity. "What an interesting thing to ask," he observed. He leaned back in his chair, his free hand twisting the end of the thin moustache he wore. "Why on earth would you ask such a thing? Is it maybe you're a wanted man?"

John just stared back at the stranger. The man could shoot him, but he wouldn't tell him anything that would lead him back to Jesse and Cole.

"Better answer him, kid," the bartender warned. "That's John Wesley Hardin and he'd as soon shoot you as spit."

Hardin shifted around in his seat, glaring at the interruption. "Mind your bottles and mind your mouth. I was having a discussion with this gentleman." He turned back to the outlaw. "Now you know who I am. Maybe you've heard of me."

John nodded slowly. There were few men who hadn't heard of John Wesley Hardin, a name that blazed large in dime novels and newspapers. He was an unrepentant Rebel who'd started on the outlaw trail in the days immediately after the Union claimed victory over the Confederacy. Hardin had celebrated the end of the war by killing an emancipated slave with an old shovel. He'd been twelve years old then. It was the start of a long and bloody career. Throughout the west, Hardin was infamous for burning down a man with his blaster just because he'd been snoring too loud.

"I'm John," the boy outlaw declared. He hesitated, then added "John Fletcher from Missouri."

Hardin smiled. It was the cheerless smile that might belong to a snake. "A fellow John and a Southerner to boot? Tell me, John, you Secesh or a Yankee bootlicker?"

The mocking scorn in Hardin's tone stirred John's pride. Defiantly, he glared back at the gunman. "I ain't got no cause to love them blue bellies," he snarled. "Drove me and my brothers off our land. Burned our farm and killed my Pa!"

Hardin nodded his head, appreciating the fire in the outlaw's voice. "Too young to fight in the war," he said. "Just like me," he added, tapping his chest. "But we'll learn them tyrants just the same, won't we John?" he shifted around, snapping his fingers at the bartender. "Whiskey for me and my new friend. If you're fast about it, I won't shoot off one of your feet."

John watched as the bartender scrambled to obey Hardin. "I thank you for the drink, but it'll have to be just one pull. I came into town lookin' for the doctor."

The statement brought a gasp from the bartender. The man dropped the bottle of whiskey on the floor, shattering it into a puddle of booze and glass. Hardin rolled his eyes and sighed. "Get another one and try again," he ordered with a wave of his gun. The bartender scurried off to do as he'd been told.

"Fetchin' the doctor might be a sight difficult," Hardin explained. "You see, I shot him last night. The way folks are carryin' on, I suspect he died sometime this morning."

John sat back, his face going pale. "You killed the doctor?"

"Well, what else could I do?" Hardin laughed. "I burned the sheriff and the galoot was tryin' to patch him back together! Don't cotton to folks who meddle in things ain't none of their affair!" The gunfighter looked up as the bartender set the whiskey down on the table. He tapped the bottle with his finger. "You may add that to my account," he declared before waving the man away. When he saw the bartender glance toward the door, Hardin sprang to his feet.

A man was framed in the entranceway, much as John had been. There was a rifle clenched in his hands. Before his eyes could adjust to the dark, Hardin fired. It wasn't a beam of energy that left the gunman's strange blaster but something that looked more like a little ball of red clay. When it struck the rifleman, the ball exploded into flame, bathing the man in molten fire. The man shrieked, swatting desperately at the flames as they quickly spread and engulfed him. He pawed in agony at the wall, leaving little slivers of fire crackling down its length before he crashed to the floor in a blazing heap.

"Be happy I heard your Iron Horse and knew you weren't a local," Hardin told John. The gunman reached down and bolted a last glass of whiskey before dashing toward the front of the saloon. "If you're a stranger to San Diablo, you might want to light out. Don't think they'll be too particular who they lynch!"

From outside, a barrage of energy beams came sizzling through the front of the saloon, scorching holes through the timber facade. Displaying reckless bravado and incredible luck, Hardin dodged the murderous fire. Rolling across the floor, he aimed under the sweep of the batwing doors and opened up on the vigilantes. A shrill scream told that at least one of his shots struck home.

"Never thought they'd have the spine!" Hardin laughed. "Guess they got tired tryin' to coax some action out of the sheriff's 'bot and figured they could do it themselves!" He flattened himself against the floor as another vengeful barrage raked the building. He looked back at John. "I'm gonna make a play for my 'Horse afore some wiseacre gets a mind to start shootin' at it. If'n your of a mind to leave, I suggest you join me."

Shaking his head at the stream of fire pouring into the saloon, John unholstered his pistol. He didn't have a personal grievance against the people of San Diablo, but at the same time he wasn't going to take a chance that Hardin was right. 'Ride with outlaws, hang with outlaws' was a truism many men lived by in the Territories. Shot down by vigilantes was far better than dancing from a rope.

Checking the charge on his blaster, John scrambled to where Hardin was stretched along the floor. Nearby, flames were starting to spread from the body of the first man Hardin had killed. "What's the plan?"

Spinning around like a striking sidewinder, Hardin fired on the bartender, burning the man's head from his shoulders. A sawed-off shotgun tumbled from beneath the slaughtered man's apron. "Was wonderin' when he'd find the sand to use that," Hardin said as he turned his attention back to the vigilantes in the street. He squinted down the barrel of his gun, calmly squeezing off a shot. An agonized shriek answered the blast.

"How do we get out of here?" John demanded as he added his own fire to that of the gunfighter.

"We rush out of here, hop on our 'Horses and ride away, shootin' anything that moves while we're doin' it," Hardin answered. He winked at the young outlaw, and then ducked his head as another fusillade slammed through the saloon.

"It's always worked for me before," Hardin assured him.

***

Jesse James rolled onto his back, twisting the sheets tighter about his body. Every coil impressed itself upon his slumbering mind, conjuring up a hempen noose that drew close around his neck. He could feel his feet mounting the thirteen steps to the gallows, he could smell the blood of executed men that had soaked into the old rope. The crowds were there, mocking and jeering, resplendent in their uniforms of blue and their garish three-piece suits. There was Pinkerton himself, waving at him with the severed arm of Jesse's mother, an arm blasted from her body when the detectives had thrown a bomb into her house thinking Frank and Jesse were there. He could see Captain Laine, his Union uniform caked in the blood of murdered men, his red leggings filthy with the gore of slaughter. Laine smiled up at him and fondled the bullhide whip in his hands, the same whip he had used to stripe Jesse's back when his band of Jayhawkers had come raiding into Missouri before the war. Just behind him was Starkweather, the abolitionist fanatic who'd marched with John Brown at Harper's Ferry and who had later served with murderous glee in the Kansas Red Legs.

The crowd of soldiers and carpetbaggers parted, allowing a troop of painted savages to march toward the scaffold. With every step, the Indians seemed to discard a little more of their humanity, their eyes glowing with an eerie blue luminance, their bodies becoming more and more beastlike until they were nothing but a pack of snarling animals gnashing their fangs at him. He saw one of them, a great bearlike horror, rear up on its hind legs. Its roar echoed the jeers of the Yankees, filled with scorn and mockery. Dangling from the necklace it wore, Jesse could see the gnawed debris of human arms. He knew they were his own.

"We declare that this Union is indivisible, with tyranny and oppression for all." The words growled through Jesse's mind. The executioner was stalking toward him now, but with each step, like the Indians, he was changing. The black hood lengthened into a beaverskin hat, the uniform thickened and darkened into a long frock coat. A pale, leprous face grinned at him, diabolic in its malevolent expression. Eyes like pits of hellfire bore into his own as the fiendish visage leered at him. There was a bright flash, the familiar blaze of a blaster shot. The ogre-like head vanished in a burst of fire, smoke billowing away from a charred stump of neck and exposed spine. Despite the obliteration of the deadman's head, his hateful voice roared in Jesse's ears. "There can be no Secession from this Union."

The rope around Jesse's neck drew tight and he was jerked up into the air. His breath was choked off, his lungs turned to fire. He tried to grab at the rope, to ease its strangling pressure, but his mechanical arms refused to obey. They remained frozen at his sides, unhearing of his desperate demands.

In the crowd, he could see an old man in a white suit smile up at him. Dr. Carpathian shook his head and a strange brace appeared in his hands, a metal funnel sporting a riotous confusion of wires and pipes. "Don't worry. We can fix anything. Even a stretched neck. Just as long as you are willing to pay the price."

Screaming, Jesse tried to lunge at the scientist. He felt the rope saw into his flesh, felt the last wisp of breath ripped from his body. Still he persisted, persisted until he felt the rope snap, felt his body hurtle down from the scaffold. The fire of rage throbbed through his veins, through his nerves. Under the intensity of his fury, his arms rose, his fingers tightened into claws. There was a gratifying look of terror on Dr. Carpathian's face as Jesse brought his hands closing about the old man's throat.

Tighter and tighter Jesse clenched his grip. He felt the scientist's neck crumpling beneath the pressure, groaning with a shriek of tortured metal...

With a start, Jesse emerged from his nightmare. He discovered himself crouched on his knees, his hands wrapped about the bedstead. The brass frame was twisted out of any semblance of shape, the marks of his steel fingers stamped into the metal. He blinked in surprise at the display of raw strength. Since his confrontation with Dr. Carpathian, since the scientist used one of his infernal inventions to shut down Jesse's arms, the outlaw had believed such strength beyond him. It had been pain beyond compare simply to move them.

Yet they had responded before, acted almost of their own accord when he'd reacted to Cole's taunting. There was some secret there, something maybe even Carpathian didn't understand. Some link between the mechanics that had been fused to his body and the mind that controlled that body. Not the rational thought, the deliberate exertion of control. It was something stronger than that, something more primal. Something that didn't fit into Carpathian's books and experiments.

Jesse turned away from the crumpled bedstead. Sitting on the mattress, he stared down at the arms Carpathian had given him after the beasts of the Warrior Nation left him mutilated and crippled. He'd been so proud of these arms, so vain of what they could do. Yet in the end, they had betrayed him.

"Feeling better, Jesse?" The outlaw raised his head to see Bob Younger standing nearby. The way his eyes kept straying to the bedstead, it was easy to guess the reason for his uneasiness.

Without concentration, allowing only the slightest thought, Jesse reached out and grabbed the brass ball at the foot of the bed. His hand tightened, crushing the ball into a tangle of brass.

"Not yet," Jesse told Bob. "But I'm getting there."

Chapter 3

John Younger idled his Iron Horse at the top of the rise overlooking the isolated cabin. He knew at least one of his brothers would be on guard, allowing that Potts and Danby hadn't returned with the supplies yet. Cole might even have returned with Ringo and the desperados from Tombstone. Not knowing who might be keeping an eye out, the young outlaw was especially wary. The hideout had been chosen not only for its isolation but also for the view it commanded. He had no great desire to be gunned down by a friend who didn't recognize him.

"You sure this is the place, Kid?" Hardin asked. He leaned from the saddle of his 'Horse and spit a plug of tobacco into a patch of dry weeds.

John nodded and cupped a hand against his mouth. A shrill noise vibrated through the bowl of his hand, a sound that was part bird-call and part savage war-whoop. He waited a few seconds and then repeated the strange cry.

"Don't seem to be anybody home," Hardin commented. Even as the words left his mouth, a man appeared on the porch. A moment later, John's signal was repeated by the man below.

"That's my brother Jim," John said, a note of pride in his voice. "He's tellin' us we can come on down and we won't get shot doin' it."

Hardin slapped the holster on his hip. "Folk find I don't get shot none too easy," he declared.

John smiled back at the notorious gunman. They'd traveled together a fair distance, Hardin content to follow the young outlaw back to whatever hideout he'd been holed up in. The boy had told him that much, and the gunfighter hadn't pressed for more details. It was one thing every man respected in the Territories, the decency not to pry into another man's past. If someone wanted to talk about who they were or where they had been, that was something they would do in their own way and their own time.

John decided now was the time to let Hardin know exactly who it was he'd been riding with - to knock the gunman's arrogance down a couple of notches. "My brother Bob's probably inside still. Don't think my brother Cole's back from Tombstone yet."

Hardin laughed. "Bob, Cole, and Jim. Who do you fellas think you are, the James-Younger Gang?"

The youth bristled under Hardin's laughter. "That's exactly who we are!" he snapped, gunning his Iron Horse down the rise and toward the cabin. Still laughing, Hardin opened up his own machine and followed John down.

Jim glared at the two riders. Only when John was close enough to recognize did he wave a hand toward the barn. Potts scrambled out from the loft, an energy rifle slung over his shoulder. Danby emerged a moment later from behind the fuel shed, a carbine in his hands.

"Who's the dude?" Jim demanded as the riders parked their 'Horses in front of the cabin. His surly temper had only blackened since John's unannounced departure three days before.

Hardin glared down at Jim. "I been called lots of things. Smart folks call me 'sir', but you don't look so smart, so I'm inclined to let you slide this once."

John dismounted and hurried to put himself between his brother and the gunman. "This here's John Wesley Hardin of Texas," he said, hoping Hardin's name and reputation would get Jim to back down. One look at his older brother told him it wouldn't matter if it was King Fisher sitting there, Jim was spoiling for a fight. "I went to San Diablo looking for a doctor."

"That explains why you left," Jim growled. "Doesn't tell me why you brought this buzzard back with you."

Hardin favored Jim with a thin smile. "That lip's gonna get you in trouble," he said.

Potts and Danby circled around at the edges of the conflict. The two men wore anxious expressions on their faces, clearly unhappy with the prospect of going up against the infamous Hardin. At the same time, they'd been with the Youngers long enough that Jim could depend on them to back any play he made.

"Trouble's one thing we Youngers make plenty of," Jim said. "Be sure you don't pick off more than you can handle."

Hardin leaned back in the saddle. His eyes darted from one side to the other, judging where the other outlaws were. He nodded to John. "Well, kid, you stayin' out of this or do I carve four notches instead of three?"

The sharp crack of a blaster exploded the tension in the air. Hardin watched in shock as his hat went flying into the air. Before it could fall, it was struck again, the energy bolt setting the felt of the brim on fire.

"Before somebody goes puttin' holes in members of the James Gang, they better ask my permission."

Stalking out from the cabin, a blaster gripped in each of his metal hands, was Jesse James. Jim and the other outlaws gazed in open wonder at their leader's approach. All of them had assumed Jesse would be laid up for weeks yet. To see him up and around, much less spry enough to shoot the hat off a man's head, filled them with awe.

Hardin raised his hands, keeping them well away from his holster. Quick-tempered and violent as he was, a fool he was not. He'd heard enough about Jesse's mechanical arms to know a man would have to be an idiot to think he could outdraw the bandit. With pistols already in Jesse's fists, a man would have as much chance as a three-legged mule in a horse race.

"I'll bear that in mind," Hardin said. He went to tip his hat in apology, and then remembered it was lying on the ground burning. "I didn't half believe the boy when he said his compadres were the Younger Brothers."

"You know better now," Jesse told him. "Matter of fact, only reason I don't burn you off that 'Horse right now is because of your reputation." The outlaw paused in his advance. His metal arms slowly lowered, sliding his blasters back into their holsters. Jesse frowned when one of the trigger guards got hung up for a moment. Not too long ago, it would have been the easiest thing in the world to holster the weapons faster than the eye could follow. Damn that traitor, Carpathian!

"I'm obliged for the courtesy," Hardin said, doing his best to watch Jesse and the other outlaws at the same time.

"Don't be," Jesse told him. "Frankly, I can use a man like you. I've got a job in mind for a nice juicy bank. A few extra hands would make it a plumb prospect."

The statement brought an excited whoop from John Younger. Jesse smiled at the boy's enthusiasm, and then fixed Hardin with a steely gaze. "Being new to the gang, you'll understand getting the small end of the split."

Hardin bristled at the remark, then uttered a bitter laugh, staring down at the blasters Jesse'd returned to their holsters. The outlaw was making a point, reminding him that he was the boss, whether his guns were in hand or not. After a moment, Hardin shrugged. "So long's you buy me a new hat outta your share, I'll oblige you." He jabbed a thumb at the smoldering ruin of his old hat.

"What's the job you got picked out for us, Jesse?" John Younger wondered.

Appearing in the doorway behind Jesse, it was Bob who answered the boy's question. Unlike Jesse, the look on Bob's face made it clear he didn't approve of John's excitement. "A bank in a town called Charity. Jesse says it'll be a push-over."

Jim snorted derisively. "Sure it will," he agreed. "That's because there ain't nothin' in it. I used to cowboy out that way. Big horse ranches back then, only nowadays, with the Yankees using Iron Horses and everybody else 'spected to use blackhoofs, there ain't a plugged nickel to be had bustin' broncs. Land up there ain't no good for cattle…"

The icy glower in Jesse's eyes silenced Jim's protest. "Some money is better than none," Jesse told him. He glanced over at John, then fixed his gaze on Hardin. "Besides, I don't cotton to draggin' new blood on a big job when it's their first dance."

***

Cole Younger scowled at the lack of progress they'd made since leaving the Clantonville ranch. He longed for the thrill of opening up his 'Horse and speeding across the desert, the throb of the RJ engine rattling through his bones and the feel of the wind whipping through his hair. Instead, he had his Iron Horse throttled down to its lowest pace, something between the waddle of an overstuffed duck and the lumber of a pregnant bear.

The reason for such delay rode beside him. Old Man Clanton and his gang didn't have Iron Horses; at least those of his men now riding out across the desert. Instead, they were mounted on blackhoofs, mechanical stallions patented by Tesla and assembled by blacksmiths across most of the west from whatever parts they could barter, scavenge or hammer out on their own. Some of the Cowboys sported extravagant steeds, their metal frames adorned with silver conchos and gaudy spangles. Curly Bill had even gone so far as to display the scorched stars he'd plucked from the chests of dead lawmen to the saddle of his blackhoof.

On its best day, a blackhoof would be eating the dust of an Iron Horse or an Interceptor. The machines gave the Union speed and mobility far in excess of what any outlaw gangs who hadn't taken part in the great train robbery could manage. It allowed them greater facility to react to the depredations of the Warrior Nation and the intrusions of Carpathian's Enlightened.

The Old Man and Curly Bill were too locked in the past to readily accept the advantages of the new devices and inventions that streamed out of the east, but even they had to grudgingly allow the necessity of progress. One glance at either of the Cowboy leaders was enough to hammer that point home. The men were throwbacks to the days of highwaymen and road agents – Old Man Clanton even had a black powder pistol stuffed into the waist of his pants to compliment the blaster holstered at his side. Curly Bill, with his grizzled garb, was like some wild beast. He had a gigantic knife strapped to his leg, some Mexican contraption called a machete. Dangling from his gun belt by little leather cords was the handiwork of that brutal-looking blade, a collection of shriveled objects that closer inspection revealed to be trigger fingers hacked from the hands of those unfortunate enough to cross Curly Bill. Cole was reminded of Colonel Quantrill's right-hand man during the War, Captain William T. Anderson, known to friend and foe alike as 'Bloody Bill' Anderson had a penchant for collecting the scalps of the men he killed, festooning the tack and harness of his horse with them until the animal resembled a Mongolian pony. But that had been war. Curly Bill was just unabashed meanness.

"See somebody you know?" Curly Bill laughed when he noticed the direction of Cole's gaze.

Cole smiled coldly at the bandit. "Nope, just marveling that there are so many slow gunmen hereabouts. Must be the heat sucks all the quickness out of a fella."

Curly Bill surprised Cole by laughing at the taunt. "Never did cotton to standin' in the street like some fool-all idiot waitin' for the galoot you come to plug to call the dance. I decide to kill a man, I kill him. Simple as that, and I don't make no particulars about how it's done." He brushed his hand across his gruesome collection, setting the fingers wiggling against his gun belt.

"The Devil takes pride in his work too," Cole said, shaking his head.

Old Man Clanton grinned at the bushwhacker. "Never would have figured you for the sensitive type, Cole. Guess you fellas ridin' with Jesse, gets used to livin' high on the hog. You start to ferget the things what need doin'. Get all squeamish inside."

Cole glared at the old outlaw. "Maybe we just remember there's a difference between killin' and murder."

"Dead's dead," Curly Bill stated coldly. "Every finger here came off'n a lawdog or a Unionist or some damn fool who didn't hear so good." The Cowboy's smile broadened. "Some Mex and Indians too, but it don't seem right to go countin' that sort."

Cole turned away from Curly Bill and his sadistic smile. In that moment, he looked just a little too much like Archie Clement, Bloody Bill's chief scalper and torturer. Cole'd seen Little Arch do things to a man that would make the Devil sick. Somehow, he felt that Curly Bill could have taught even Little Arch a thing or two about viciousness.

A fine band he was bringing back to Jesse, Cole reflected bitterly. Robbers and gunmen he'd expected, but a lot of the men who called themselves "Cowboys" were just murdering marauders; only difference between them and with the

Nations on the warpath was a lick of paint on their faces. He wondered why his cousin Johnny Ringo had taken up with such a brutal outfit. He also wondered if Jesse's name and reputation would be enough to keep the Cowboys in line. Cole knew it was more than he could do, unless he gunned a few of the leaders like Curly Bill.

"Let's talk again about the split," Old Man Clanton said, turning the subject away from the macabre collection of his lieutenant. "I have a mighty big gang to keep comfortable. I think maybe our cut of the take should reflect that."

"All I'll promise is a third," Cole said. "You want more than that; you'll have to talk it over with Jesse. Might be he'll see things your way. Might be he'll figure a third is too generous and whittle it down a bit." He slapped his hand against the Iron Horse he was riding. "What I will say is that any man rides with us is gonna get one of these under him and sooner rather than later. Jesse likes his gang to be fast and mobile. Can't really be trotting around on a four-legged chunk of pig-iron."

"They done good by us this far," Old Man Clanton said.

"If that's so, then why are you still hidin' out from the Earps?" Cole asked.

Old Man Clanton's eyes took on a steely glint. "Who says we're hidin'?" he asked as turned away.

Something about the Cowboy's tone made Cole look back over his shoulder, to stare out across the desert. Johnny Ringo, Ike Clanton, and several of the other Cowboys had lingered behind in Clantonville to 'attend to business' as Old Man Clanton put it. The outlaws each had one of the Iron Horses the Cowboys had acquired from dead lawmen, so there was no question that the men would catch up to the slow moving blackhoofs. What disturbed Cole, what he'd wondered about ever since they rode out from the Clanton ranch, was what sort of business was so important as to delay Ringo and the rest.

***

Dust billowed up from the parched dirt of Fifth Street as three Iron Horses came rumbling through Tombstone. Townsfolk scrambled into shops and saloons after one look at the three riders. At first, with the speeds in which the vehicles moved in, it could be thought that these men were lawmen. Upon closer inspection, there was no mistaking these men for anything associated with the law. The darkbrown linen dusters the three men wore were infamous throughout the west. They were the 'uniform' adopted by the Archie Clement gang after the War, when the vicious bushwhacker led embittered Rebel guerrillas in robberies across Kansas and Missouri. After the death of Little Arch, the same style of duster had become the recognized mark of his even more notorious successor: Jesse James and the James-Younger Gang.

The men sitting on the benches outside the Tombstone Cattlemen and Miners' Trust scattered when the three machines swung toward the brick-faced bank. A leathery-faced guard stepped out onto the plank walkway that ran down past the front of the bank. Even behind the brick wall, there was no mistaking the growl of an Iron Horse's engine, much less three of them. He'd come out to investigate, his hand already closed upon the grip of the blaster holstered at his hip. He visibly paled when he saw the brown dusters and the bandanas pulled up over the riders' faces. Any doubt about their intentions was gone when they dismounted and started toward the bank.

The guard started to back away, but then his eyes fixed on the elegant blaster resting across the belly of one of the men. He'd seen that ivory grip with its Oriental dragons before. There couldn't be another pair of guns like them in the whole Territory. He looked up into the gunman's eyes. The words that left his mouth came in a quivering whisper. "I know you..."

"Well ain't that unfortunate," the gunman hissed back. Before the guard could even start to raise his blaster from its holster, the man in the duster had ripped the ivory-gripped gun from his belt and loosed an energy bolt into his breast. The guard didn't even scream, his burned body simply folded in on itself and crumpled to the street, the bricks behind him scorched black by the heat of the beam that cut him down.

Screams rang down Fifth as those still abroad saw the brutal murder. Alarm accompanied the frenzied cries as they spread along the street.

"That tears it," one of the masked outlaws snarled. He pushed past the gunman, brought a silver-toed boot crashing against the bank's iron-banded door. The portal crashed inwards, bowling over the teller who had dashed forward to bar it against the men in the street. The outlaw stormed onwards, pausing just long enough to kick the fallen teller's face as he started to pick himself off the floor. The blow sent the man sprawling.

"This here's a robbery!" the outlaw declared, brandishing his blaster and sending a bolt searing into the ceiling overhead. With his other hand, he pulled a pair of canvas bags from the pocket of his duster and threw them at the teller who'd remained behind the steel bars of the banker cage. "I'd like to withdraw my money," the bandit laughed, "and everybody else's too. Be quick about it and don't get any fool ideas," he wagged the smoking barrel of his blaster at the man. "This'll cut clean through them bars and I won't be none too happy if I have to waste my time doing it." The warning took, and the teller began to stuff the bags with handfuls of bills and coins.

The other two robbers brought their weapons to bear on the few customers standing in the bank's lobby. One of them shook his head when he saw that one of their captives was a woman. "This don't seem right, Ike," the outlaw said. Immediately he cried out in pain as the gunman with the ivory-gripped blaster clubbed his ear with the butt of his gun.

"Seeing you done mentioned Ike by name, it sort of settles matters, don't it?" Johnny Ringo snarled down at Pete Spence.

The teller inside the cage froze. He stared in terror at the outlaw on the other side of the bars. "Ike Clanton?" he gasped. His shivering grew so bad that he started to drop gold coins onto the floor. "Honest, Mr. Clanton, I won't give you no trouble."

"Glad to hear it," Ike snarled back. "Maybe you get to live awhile longer." He turned his head and glared over at Ringo. "You'd better hope Stilwell and Indian Charlie are where they need to be. We weren't countin' on any shootin' this soon."

"Then we'll just have to improvise," Ringo said. "I told you I'm your huckleberry for that job."

"Old Man wants them ornery, not dead," Ike said. "I can trust Stilwell to do that, which is more'n I can say for you."

Ringo spun around, loosing another blast from his gun. One of the customers in the lobby crashed to the floor, a gory hole drilled through his midsection. "Don't anybody else get the notion of inchin' toward that door," Ringo warned.

Ike reached through the gap in the bars of the cage and snatched the filled sacks from the teller. For an instant, his eyes drifted toward the huge safe at the back of the building. He shook his head sadly. "Too bad we don't have more time," he grumbled. A quick lift of his gun and he turned the teller's head into a smoldering husk.

The brutal murder of the man in the cage was Ringo's signal to let loose. Without hesitation, the gunfighter swept his gun across the customers, burning them down where they stood. One of the terrified victims made it as far as the door before Ringo's blast caught him in the back. The impact of the blaster flung the man's body out into the street where he lay like a bundle of burning rags.

Money bag in hand, Ike motioned for the other Cowboys to quit the bank. They'd accomplished what they needed to do here. The rest would depend on Stilwell and Indian Charlie on the roof of the Bloody Bucket Saloon.

***

Virgil Earp rushed down Allen Street, hurrying toward the sounds of gunfire and screaming. He'd been dining with his wife in the restaurant in the Cosmopolitan Hotel when the shooting started. Dashing from his interrupted breakfast, the marshal had hesitated for an instant, debating if he should race down the street and get the Enforcers. Turning as he heard more gunfire, he decided he didn't have time to race down to the marshal's office and fetch the 'bots.Every moment he wasted might mean someone's life.

The direction of the gunfire told Virgil what was happening. Somebody had taken it into their head to rob the Cattlemen and Miners' Trust. He glanced down Fifth Street, watching people fleeing the area of the bank. Longingly, he looked back down Allen Street toward the building where the marshal's office was situated. Wyatt wouldn't be there this early, but Morgan should be. It wasn't like he had anywhere else to be.

Virgil shook his head. Yeah, Morgan was probably there, but ever since he'd been gunned by outlaws and had most of his body replaced with machinery by Dr. Carpathian, he'd been distant and apathetic. The cyborg was dependable enough in a fight, but he lacked the initiative to investigate trouble on his own. Sometimes, Virgil was tempted to agree with Wyatt. In moments of anger, Wyatt would berate his eldest brother, saying they'd given Carpathian their brother and what they'd gotten back was little more than a 'bot.

More gunfire erupted from within the bank. Virgil watched in disgust as a man's body was flung through the doors to crash in a heap in the middle of the road. His hands tightened about the blasters he gripped in both hands. If these murdering varmints were to be stopped, the job was one he'd have to do all on his own.

Rounding the façade of the Crystal Palace, Virgil ducked down behind a balustrade and drew a bead on the bank's doorway. The moment the bandits made their break for the Iron Horses parked outside the building, he'd cut them down as ruthlessly as the man they'd left burning in the street and the guard slumped on the walkway with his chest turned into a blackened crater.

A masked man wearing a brown duster was just starting to poke his head out the door when a fresh burst of gunfire sizzled through the air. Virgil screamed as he felt searing agony race down his side. The balustrade exploded into splinters, the planks of the walkway were scorched by the withering energy of a blaster fired from above and behind the marshal.

Rolling among the cinders, clutching at the charred flesh of his arm, Virgil blinked through the flames of his pain to see two men in brown dusters drop down from the roof of the saloon on the corner opposite the Crystal Palace. The back-shooting assassins went running off toward Toughnut Street, smoke rising from the red-hot barrels of their carbines. The sound of Iron Horses roaring into life turned the marshal's gaze back toward the bank in time to see three more men in brown dusters leap into the saddles of their 'Horses and tear off toward Fremont Street. As they sped away from the bank, each of the robbers vented a fierce Rebel yell.

Virgil wriggled across the charred walkway, propping himself against the wall of the Crystal Palace. Now that the shooting was over, he could hear people rushing back into the streets, babbling about the attack, bemoaning the carnage that had erupted on Fifth Street. Through his agony, Virgil heard horrified citizens describing the massacre inside the bank. More than one voice gave a name to the perpetrators of this atrocity: the James Gang.

The anguished shriek of Virgil's wife Allie sent a fresh spasm of pain rushing through the lawman. Mustering what strength he had left, Virgil propped himself against the wall of the saloon and pulled himself up onto his feet. He embraced her with his remaining good arm, holding her tight.

"For God's sake!" Allie raged at the gawking people around them. "Someone get the doctor!"

Virgil shook his head. "Somebody get Wyatt," he groaned. "Tell him it was Jesse James. Jesse James shot up his town and bushwhacked his brother."

Fighting to stay conscious, Virgil let Allie lead him into the Crystal Palace to await the doctor. As the barman cleared away one of the poker tables and helped Allie lay him down on it, he kept picturing the night Morgan was shot and what had happened afterwards. In a sudden burst of panic, he reached for the arm the assassins had shot, his fingers sinking into the burned flesh down to the bone within.

With a moan of agony, the crippled lawman fled into the mercy of unconsciousness.

Chapter 4

The dusty main street of Charity was bustling with activity, farmers and ranchers streaming into the town in hopes of securing contracts to provide food for the workers at the new RJ refueling station that was set to be constructed on the trailhead leading back to Abilene. Along with the inhabitants of the outlying homesteads, a number of itinerant tradesmen had descended on Charity, intending to peddle their wares to the citizenry. The overall atmosphere was that of a market day, complete with a snake oil salesman loudly extolling the virtues of his medicinal elixir in a breathless harangue.

Such a climate of distraction suited the seven men who started to drift into town just after the clock tower above the assay office began to toll away high noon. In a less congested and confused time, the people of Charity might have paid closer attention to the Iron Horses the men rode or the brown dusters they removed from their saddlebags when they parked the vehicles and threw across the crook of their left arms. They might have wondered about the blasters the strangers had holstered at their sides or the carbines they carried with them.

Just now, however, Charity was too involved in its own business to be vigilant. The farmers and ranchers were worried about getting their deals with the RJ station, contracts that might mean the difference between survival and ruin for men who'd been hard hit by the collapsed demand for horseflesh. The shops in town were trying to lure customers off the street and exploit the sudden boom in potential profit. Wives and children scurried about the stalls and wagons of the traveling traders, trying to secure anything that seemed exotic or unusual, particularly the mechanical devices brought out from the east. Powered by a little button of RJ, these came in almost every shape and size, from little automated toys, to elegant armbands and hatbands, watches, and even rings.

The people of Charity had no idea that the grim-faced men who slowly made their way through the crowd were anybody special, much less that they were the notorious James-Younger Gang.

Jesse had been careful to pick this day for their raid on Charity. The crowd was effective camouflage for the outlaws as they advanced upon the bank. Later, they'd provide the gang with a smokescreen of confusion when it came time to stage their escape. Nothing was quite as chaotic as a mob of terrified civilians. That was a lesson Jesse had learned well from his years as one of Quantrill's Raiders.

Individually and in pairs, the outlaws moved on the Central Union Bank of Charity. The first men through the doors of the adobe building were Bob and Jim Younger. Once they were inside, the two men made a pretense of gawking at the rich appointments inside the bank, running their hands along the mahogany runners along the walls and extolling the exquisite etching on the glass hood of the RJ lamp hanging from the ceiling.

Hardin came in next, scowling as he strolled toward the tellers' cage. He paused before reaching the bars, fishing in the pocket of his vest and removing a little leather pay book which he made a great show of consulting. Though his eyes seemed to be focused on the pay book, the gunfighter's gaze roved across the faces of the other occupants of the bank. He didn't like the scrutiny with which the armed guard was studying him, much less the scattergun in the man's hands.

Jesse James and John Younger were the next inside, Jesse's metal arms hidden in the sleeves of a bulky cattleman's coat. As they came in, Jesse was explaining how banking worked to the boy, telling him all about deposits and interest in such a simplified fashion that it brought chuckles from the tellers inside the cage and a smile from the elderly rancher who was just making his own deposit.

"First time inside a bank, son?" the rancher asked, turning around to address John.

"Nearabouts," Jesse answered. "I can't seem to convince him his money'll be safe. He's all worried Billy the Kid or somebody's gonna ride right in and steal it."

The rancher laughed. "They got a safe back there that'd take an elephant to break open," he said. "Operates on a time-lock too. Some new gewgaw from back east. Can't be opened 'cept at particular times of the day."

The rancher's eyes went round as saucers when Jesse suddenly pulled both his blasters from their holsters. "Unfortunately we don't have the time to wait," he said, pushing the man aside and leveling his guns at the tellers inside the cage.

Across the lobby, the guard was startled when he suddenly found one of Bob's Bowie knives at his throat. The man was so suspicious of Hardin, he neglected to keep an eye on the older Younger brothers, who he'd dismissed as country bumpkins. Hardin replaced the pay book in his vest and came strolling over toward the frightened guard. The gunfighter's gloved hands drummed ominously against the grips of the smokers he carried.

"Seen something funny?" Hardin challenged the guard. The gunfighter's eyes gleamed like those of a snake as he glared at the man. "Maybe you'd like to cut loose with that hog-shredder of yourn?"

"Settle yourself, Hardin!" Jesse's voice cracked across the gunfight like a whip. "I'll tell you who to shoot and when." He nodded to the windows at the front of the bank. Jim Younger had drawn down the shades and was now peering out from behind one corner to keep an eye on the street. "Help Jim keep watch," Jesse advised the gunman. Sullenly, Hardin turned away from the guard and stalked over to the window.

Jesse turned back toward the tellers. Neither man had dared to twitch a muscle even with the robber's attention focused on Hardin. In drawing his blasters, Jesse's coat had slid back, exposing the metal sheen of his mechanical arms. Those arms told the bank-men exactly who was robbing them. Neither man was suicidal enough to oppose Jesse James.

"I suspect you fellas know what I want, so get to it," Jesse told the tellers. He glanced aside as the men behind the cage began emptying their tills into a canvas mail bag. The outlaw smiled when he saw that John had the barrel of his blaster planted in the belly of the old rancher.

"Step back a pace," Jesse told the boy. "Close like that, if you have to shoot you'll foul up the exhaust when all the fat in his belly turns to grease and goes splashing across the gun. Never stick iron up against a man, hang back a bit and give you both a little space to think. You about why you should shoot, him to think about why you shouldn't. Man don't think clear when he feels a gun prodding into his gut."

As Jesse spoke, John slowly backed away, color rushing into his face. He kept both his blaster and his eyes fixed on the rancher.

"Thank you, Mr. James, sir," the rancher said, drawing a deep breath now that the gun wasn't pressing into him.

"You a Yankee?" Jesse asked him, studying the rancher's expression as the man reacted to the question.

"If'n I were a Yankee, I coulda stayed back in Virginia," the rancher grumbled. "Wouldn't been drove out by them damn carpetbaggers."

Jesse nodded. Turning back to the cage and the tellers he snapped his fingers, relieving one of the men of a bundle of bills. "How much of your money's in here?" he asked.

"Jesse, we ain't got time for this!" Jim complained from his post at the window. Every minute that passed increased the chance that somebody would come into the bank or maybe start to wonder about the seven Iron Horses parked out in the street. Potts and Danby were keeping watch over the vehicles, but even with them providing cover, it would go hard on the outlaws if they had to fight their way back to the Horses.

The rancher was pensive a moment. "I reckon there's two hunert fifty four dollars and two bits of mine in here."

Jesse counted out the bills and then fished a twenty five cent piece from his own pocket. Sternly, he placed the money in the rancher's hands. "We rob banks, we rob trains, but we don't rob good folks," Jesse said. "Next time, bury your money in a coffee can before you go handin' it over to a Yankee bank."

The outlaw turned back to the cage. "You fellas just about done in there?"

"Yes, sir, Mr. James," one of the tellers said, hurriedly relieving his co-workers of the bags they'd filled and pushed them one after the other out the cage. "I'm sorry it's not more, but most of it's in the safe and as Mr. Parker explained, there's a time-lock."

Jesse took the bags, handing them off to John. He glared back at the teller in the cage. "Where's the banker?" he asked.

Bob rolled his eyes. "Jesse, Jim's right, we don't have the time. Forget about the safe!"

Jesse ignored Bob's protest and continued to train his threatening gaze on the teller. "Where's your boss?"

"Mr. Temple isn't here," the teller stammered. "He… he always dines… takes lunch… at the Palace Hotel…"

"Satisfied, Jesse?" Jim asked. "Can we light out now?"

Jesse looked around the office behind the cage. He pointed at a tintype in a gilded frame hanging on the wall, motioning for the teller to give it to him. Snatching the picture from the man's hands, he tossed it across the lobby. It landed on the floor and slid almost to Jim's feet.

"Have a gander and tell me if'n he's not worth the wait," Jesse told Jim.

Confused, Jim reached down and picked up the tintype. He squinted at the picture a moment, but then went livid. Spinning around, he shook the picture at Jesse. "This is why we came here!" he shouted. "It warn't the money! It was him!"

"Him who?" Bob wondered, craning his head to try and get a look at the picture while still keeping his knife against the guard's throat.

"Captain Thomas Archibald Temple," Jesse hissed. "Late of the Kansas Redlegs, now a respectable bank president." A murderous glint crept into Jesse's eyes. "He's gonna be the first notch in payin' the Yankees back for Frank."

Hardin rounded on Jesse. "You drug us out here knowin' there warn't any money?" the gunfighter roared.

"Yeah. Yeah, I did," Jesse said. He punctuated the statement by firing both of his blasters. The shots sizzled past Hardin, striking the windows behind him. Glass exploded across the boardwalk. Townsfolk screeched as blobs of liquefied window spattered across them.

"Now you're all elected," Jesse told his horrified gang. "You can break for the Horses like a pack of coyotes or you can stand with me and make these curs pay for what they done to Frank!"

"Dammit, Jesse!" Hardin raged. The gunfighter darted for the door, but no sooner had he poked his head outside than he was ducking back. Energy bolts sizzled through the front of the building. "Must be fifty rifles out there! How're we supposed to get out of here now!"

"Calm down, Texas," Bob growled. "Can't be more'n six out there."

Jim shook his head. Hardin might be overreacting, but that didn't mean he was entirely wrong. The plan, as Jesse had explained it to them in the hideout, was to hit the bank quietly and then slip out the same way they had come into town, using the crowd as camouflage. Now, Jesse's shots had scattered that crowd and stirred up the town. The only way out now was to shoot their way out.

"You... you have a plan... right, Jesse?" John asked, shocked by the duplicity exhibited by his hero.

Jesse smiled coldly at the boy and nodded. "Hardin, keep them farmers busy with your smokers," he said. "Don't matter if you hit nothin', just so's you make lots of noise. Bob, you start them prisoners out the door when I give the high sign." He spun around to the cage, burning open the door with a shot from his blaster. "Gentlemen," he told the tellers. "You'll oblige me by getting over there by Bob Younger."

"Please, Mr. James," one of the bank-men pleaded. "They'll shoot us if we go out there."

The outlaw's eyes were as sympathetic as two slivers of steel.

"Then you'd best squawk real loud like and make damn sure they know it's you," he advised. Jesse turned to the rancher.

"You can try and light out with them or stick around in here," he told the man. "Either way you're apt to be duckin' a fair parcel of gunfire." The rancher swallowed the knot that had grown in his throat and ambled off to join the bank-men, reasoning his chances would be better with them alone.

"Jim, John," Jesse called to the last men in his gang. He swung around toward the far wall of the lobby. "You're gonna help me blast a door over here. With all them Yankees watchin' the front, we'll see how they favor a flank attack."

John barked out a Rebel yell, aiming his blaster at the wall. Jim was more cautious in his enthusiasm, impressed by Jesse's reasoning but also mindful that once they'd burned their hole in the wall they'd still have a town full of riled up farmers to deal with.

Jesse raised one of his metal arms, then brought it flashing down. At his sign, Bob rushed the prisoners out the front while Jesse, Jim, and John opened up on the wall.

***

The captives from the bank were screaming as they scrambled through the door, shouting and wailing to their friends and neighbors to hold their fire. A few shots sizzled down at them from across the street, but the aim was hasty and the fire uncoordinated. Moreover, the men firing at the prisoners were themselves rattled by the tumultuous explosion that shook the town as the sidewall of the bank burst outward in a cloud of smoke and dust. The gritty fog of pulverized adobe went billowing out into the street, blinding the men arrayed around the bank and forcing them to retreat back behind whatever cover as was near at hand.

Through the murk, the outlaws scrambled out into the street. Bob and Jim dove behind a wagon that Hardin's smokers had set on fire, tipping it onto its side. Hardin himself slithered behind the iron bulk of a blackhoof dropped by the barrage the townsmen had fired at the bank. Jesse and John rushed the carriage of the snake oil salesman, knocking over the table on which he'd set his noxious wares. Crouching down by the steel steps leading up into the charlatan's wagon, Jesse stared into the cloud of dust, his sharp eyes picking out the silhouette of a rifleman creeping out from the boardwalk. A bolt from his blaster ripped across the street and splashed the man against the wall of a tobacconist's shop.

"This here's Jesse James," the outlaw barked out. "Anybody don't want to get shot better clear out now. Anybody sticks around best be warned the James Gang fights under the black flag!"

Silence held the town as men trembled at the threat in Jesse's words. The black flag; the warning that no quarter would be shown to the enemy, no mercy given. It was under such warning that Confederate guerrillas had burned Lawrence, had massacred Union soldiers in Centralia. It took some men a few moments of hesitation for the words to sink in. Even though it had been a very long time ago,the image of such wartime atrocities cast a long shadow and it fell squarely upon the defenders of Charity.

One of the riflemen across the street emerged from behind the sacks of feed where he had taken shelter. Whether to take aim at the outlaws or to flee to safety was a question never to be answered. From where he lay,concealed by the chassis of the mechanical horse, John Wesley Hardin peeled off a shot from one of his smokers. The rifleman shrieked as the blob of jellied fire splashed against him, and his body erupted in flame. A living torch, the stricken man stumbled and screamed, flailing about as the flesh melted off his bones.

The sickening display sent many of the townsmen throwing down their weapons and running off in total retreat. Others, those with more courage or a sharper sense of justice, held their positions and began to direct a vindictive fusillade against the robbers.

The outlaws returned fire, blasting holes in walls and shattering windows and doors as they tried to roust the townsmen from their cover. Jesse, exhibiting the almost preternatural speed of his mechanical arms and the unerring accuracy that had been honed during the War, caught two of the defenders on the run as they tried to dash from the cover afforded by a stack of wooden crates for the more promising shelter of a water wagon. A third man he picked off from the roof of a saloon, sending his mutilated remains dripping from the overhang onto the boardwalk below.

"Jim! Bob! Help Potts and Danby!" Jesse shouted to the two Younger brothers. With the set of their wagon, the two bushwhackers were the closest of the gang to the livery stable where the buckaroos were being hard-pressed by a mob of a dozen men. It didn't need to be impressed on any of the outlaws what would happen should they lose their Iron Horses.

"Give your brothers some cover," Jesse told John. Both of them dashed across the street, blazing away at the cluster of buildings around the hotel where the defenders seemed most firmly entrenched. Their rush to the far side of the street brought a withering stream of fire sizzling after them, but it served to keep those same rifles from menacing Bob and Jim as they rushed toward the livery stable and attacked the rear of the townsmen who had Danby and Potts bottled up inside.

John threw himself behind the stack of long wooden boxes piled up in the work yardon the other side of the street. As he leaned up to fire at the townsmen, the boy shouted in alarm, recoiling from what he now realized was a pile of coffins.

Jesse glanced over at him and shook his head. "You don't believe in that kind of thing," he told the boy. "I ain't never seen no omen could stand up to one of these," he added, spinning back around and tapping off shots from each of his blasters in turn.

More than a little ashamed by his display of superstitious fright in the presence of his hero, John leaned back over the coffins and started to take aim. What he saw had him throwing himself flat into the dirt. An instant later, the coffins exploded into splinters.

Marching down the middle of the street was a UR-30 Enforcer. The robot bore a pair of military pattern blasters; ugly snub-nosed weapons that traded accuracy for destructive power. It was a fair trade where a 'bot was concerned, as its mechanized brain couldn't match the speed and marksmanship of an experienced gunfighter. At the same time, the 'bot was absolutely fearless and hideously tough to bring down. That was proved when Hardin opened up on the thing, striking it with one of his incendiary pellets. Fire splashed across the Enforcer, burning away the vest and pants that had been fitted to it in a crude attempt to make the thing seem more human. The robot itself was utterly unfazed, oblivious to the licking flames as it continued its march down the street.

Hardin rolled away from the fallen blackhoof, squirming underneath the boardwalk like some overgrown lizard, only seconds before a concentrated barrage from the Enforcer slammed into the iron chassis. It broke apart in a burst of flame and shrapnel, twisted limbs scything through the air and embedding themselves in the facades of nearby buildings.

In the undertaker's yard, John Younger writhed in agony, splinters of burning coffin embedded in his flesh. The boy tried to maintain a brave front as he tried to pluck the slivers from his skin, but the pain of each piece of pinewood imbedded in his flesh was excruciating. Lost in the oblivion of his own pain, he was shocked when a metal hand closed about his shoulder and pulled him back against a pile of boxes. Jesse glanced over John's injuries, deciding that even though they might be painful, they weren't serious. Not as serious as a necktie party, anyway.

"John," Jesse called to the boy as they both crouched amongst the coffin splinters. "I need you to keep these farmers anxious. Don't care if you hit nobody, just so they keep their heads down."

'What're you gonna do?" John asked as they both crawled over to a stack of marble slabs.

"I'm going to take all the fight out of them yellow-livered townies," Jesse swore. Before John fully understood the man's meaning, Jesse threw himself out into the street in a long dive. The Enforcer, starting to shoot up the boardwalk Hardin was sheltered under, turned back around to address this new threat.

The bolts from the robot's guns went wide, gouging craters in the street around Jesse but missing the outlaw himself. Dirt from the explosions covered Jesse's duster and hung in clumps from his hat. Tiny rocks thrown up by the blasts had cut his cheeks and dug a little furrow across one side of his neck. He paid the hurt as little notice as the Enforcer would have. Displaying the steely nerve for which he was famous, Jesse took deliberate aim before opening up on the 'bot.

In deploying the UR-30's throughout the west, entrusting them to sheriffs and marshals in hundreds of towns and camps, the Union had thought to make a quick end of the outlawry that threatened the stability of the region. Impressed with the capabilities of their machines, the government had paid little attention to training the men who would be called upon to use them. The sheriff of Charity was one such example. Believing the scuttlebutt that the machines were impervious to gunfire, that they would boldly walk through blasters to get their target, that no man had the stomach to trade shots with the things, he deployed his Enforcer with all the subtlety of a bull in a china shop. Instead of using cover, instead of having the 'bot working in tandem with the armed citizens, he sent the machine lumbering down the middle of the street, thinking to use the mere threat of the Enforcer to force the outlaws to surrender.

Jesse tapped off two blasts from his pistols. With the enhanced speed of his quick-devil arms, the shots struck almost simultaneously. Sparks and flame erupted from the Enforcer's chest as the robot staggered back under the double impact. Pivoting at the waist, the machine returned Jesse's fire, sending him scurrying across the street as the 'bot's fire scarred the earth.

Jesse thought back to the UR-30 Enforcer his gang had faced in Diablo Canyon. Destroying that machine had taken the entire gang and even then there had been moments when the outcome looked to favor the 'bot. He'd made the mistake, then, of thinking the thing would go down like a man. Now, he prayed that Charity's sheriff had made the mistake of expecting the Enforcer to fight like a man.

"Bob! Jim! Try an' get its attention!" Jesse shouted, lunging across the boardwalk just as the Enforcer's guns reduced the façade of a dentist's office into a charred wreck. From their vantage, the Younger brothers opened fire on the robot. Jim's aim was more accurate than that of his brother, but all the shots did when they struck was scorch the machine's hull and cause its ponderous march into a leftward lurch as a lucky hit fused some of the gears together just below its hip.

The Enforcer reacted just as Jesse had hoped. The fresh assault from the Youngers brought a speedy reprisal. The 'bot swung around and started pumping shots into the livery stable, blasting chunks from its loft and sending a spent fuel cell skittering down the street.

In Diablo canyon, the Enforcer the James Gang had fought had been almost loquacious in its mechanized demands for surrender and capitulation. This 'bot was utterly silent, the only sound rising from it was the whizzing of gears and the tromp of its steel feet. Jesse suspected its silence was because, unlike the Enforcer in Diablo Canyon, this 'bot wasn't acting with independence of its own. It was operating under a far less flexible liveliness, enslaved by the commands given to it by the sheriff. It could react to the situation, but it wasn't allowed to interpret the stimuli. It wasn't given the freedom to think and act for itself.

"Hardin!" Jesse yelled. "Try yer smokers again!"
The Texan poked his nose out from under the boardwalk. "Hell with that," he snarled.

Jesse glared at the black-clad gunslinger. "Do it, Johnny, or the 'bot will be the least of your worries."

Hardin blanched at the threat. Screwing up his courage, the gunfighter scrambled out from under the walkway. Shots from some of the townsfolk peppered the street as he dashed across. As he drew parallel to the Enforcer, he peeled off a shot from his smoker. The incendiary pellet splashed across the robot's side, turning it into a walking torch. The machine swung around, tracking Hardin as he ran to the opposite side of the road. The Texan gunned down a townsman who rose up from behind a heap of grain sacks, and then threw himself through the window of an assay office. The next instant, the front of the building was hammered by the Enforcer's shots.

"Jim! Hold off on shootin' the 'bot!" Jesse hollered. For what he had in mind, he needed the UR-30 focused on the assay office, its back to him. Any stray shot from the livery stable might bring the machine turning back around and spoil his plan.

Rising up from the burning dental office, Jesse ran toward the middle of the street. A few farmers fired at him, but his bold dash toward the Enforcer threw off their aim. The last thing anybody expected was that the outlaw would run *toward* the murderous robot. Jesse rushed to within a few yards of the machine before it reacted to him. As it swung around, the left side of its body still wrapped in flame, the outlaw chief brought both of his blasters to bear. The double shot struck the Enforcer in the neck. Jesse thought of the 'bot back in Diablo Canyon and how it had gone wild when its head had been blasted from its shoulders. He intended to use that to his advantage. As the head was ripped from its shoulders, the 'bot's body froze, its automation seizing up. Jesse ran past it, rushing at the head and kicking it down the street like an old tin can.

"What'll you do now, you mutton-punchers!" Jesse shouted at the horrified townsfolk. He rushed to cover as vindictive fire pursued him across the street. The outlaw felt a cold satisfaction at the violence his jeers had provoked. The farmers had acted exactly the way he wanted them to.

The decapitated Enforcer turned around once more. Loss of its head had removed much of its cognitive ability and reduced its sensory input, but the machine was still capable of functioning. The 'bot swung around and began firing at the shooters its reduced senses could detect. Oblivious that it was now firing on the very people it had been dispatched to protect, the Enforcer limped through Charity, both its blasters blazing away. The sheriff appeared on the balcony overlooking a saloon, shrieking orders to the robot, trying to end its mindless rampage. A quick shot from Jesse put an end to the lawman's effort.

The savage destruction wrought by their own Enforcer broke the back of Charity's resistance. Crying out in horror, men threw down their weapons and fled. Jesse spun around at the glint of bronze on the chest of one of the refugees, a blast from his pistol throwing a retreating deputy through the enormous window at the front of the hotel. The Enforcer staggered on, pursuing a group of farmers who kept stopping to take shots at the thing, oblivious to the fact that it was their constant attacks that kept the machine on their tail. Already, the Enforcer had been hit upwards of thirty times, so what the farmers expected to do was a mystery to Jesse. He suspected it was a mystery to them as well. The outlaw almost felt sorry for them as he watched them flee town with the robot still dogging their heels.

Then Jesse saw something of far greater interest. Leaning across the banister on the balcony which fronted the hotel's upper floor was Temple. The banker was dressed in a fine suit of powder-blue, a derby squashed down about his ears, its extravagant metal band shining like gold in the noon sun. Temple had a heavy-bore rifle in his hands, but looked more apt to toss it aside than try to draw a bead on Jesse now that the Enforcer was down.

Jesse didn't give Temple the time to make his choice. Peeling off a shot from each blaster, he blew apart the floor beneath the banker's feet. The blast threw Temple through the air and plummeting to the ground in front of the hotel. The terrified man started up onto his feet, cradling a broken arm against his chest. He made a frantic dash for the open doorway of a mercantile.

He didn't make it.

"Redlegs don't run," Jesse roared at Temple, firing his blasters at the man. The banker's anguished howl thundered across Charity as Jesse's shots tore off both of his legs. "They crawl."

The vengeful outlaw watched Temple flopping about in the street. Jesse didn't see the banker, but instead the murderous Union captain who'd led his barbaric border ruffians in terror raids up and down Missouri. They'd hung any guerrillas or suspected guerrillas they caught, at least once they tired of whittling away at their hides with knives and branding irons. Many times during the War, Jesse had seen the handiwork of Temple and his Redlegs dancing from a tree, birds pecking at what were left of their faces.

The roar of Iron Horses shook the street. The metal steeds of Bob and Jim Younger hurtled down past the ruined hotel toward Jesse. "Potts and Danby are holding the stable," Bob called down to the gang leader. "Better get down there afore these farmers get their second wind."

The advice didn't need to be given a second time for Hardin; squirming out from under the boardwalk, he set off down the street toward the livery stable. John Younger started to follow the black-clad gunfighter, but froze when he noticed that Jesse hadn't moved an inch from where he stood. The long rider was just staring down at Temple screaming in the dirt.

"I'd be obliged for yer rope, Jim," Jesse said, eyes never leaving the mutilated man writhing in the street. "We ain't quite done here yet."

The same vengeful light was in Jim's eyes as he pulled a coil of old hemp from his saddle bag and threw it over to Jesse. In a blur, Jesse holstered one of his pistols and caught the rope. He glanced up at the smoldering balustrade along the balcony, and then returned his hateful gaze to Temple.

"You might'nt have a leg to stand on, Captain Redlegs," Jesse snarled at the man, shaking the rope at him. "But by thunder, yer gonna dance just the same!"

***

They met in the office on Allen Street, the noise of the traffic outside drifting in through the open door. Wyatt Earp, ever a stickler for observing propriety, always a staunch exponent of law and order, couldn't bring himself to use the Over-marshal's office for this meeting. What he had in mind was less about law and more about vengeance.

Pacing across the hardwood floor, Wyatt presented an imposing sight. He was tall, dressed in a long leather lawman's coat with steel plates reinforcing its shoulders to afford some degree of protection against back-shooters. The metal cleats in his boots grating across the boards, his broad-brimmed hat casting most of his face into shadow, Wyatt presented the image of an enraged lion prowling in its den. When his face did emerge into the light, there was stamped upon it such an expression of fury that even close friends and kin hesitated to look on him.

"First Morg, now Virg!" the Over-marshal roared, slamming his fist against the cherrywood top of the desk that dominated one corner of the room. "Them mongrels think they can go gunning the law and then skedaddle back to their hidey

holes and brag about it!" He tapped his finger against the
emblazoned bronze pectoral he wore, setting his finger against
the star engraved at the center of the metal plate, causing it to
jounce on the chain that held it across his chest. "Not anymore!
They're gonna learn *this* means somethin'!"

"And how do you aim to learn them?" The question was
distorted; the voice was rendered into an almost metallic quality
as the words were forced through the silvered grill of an ornate
mask. The speaker leaned against one of the book cases lining
the walls of the office. Neither so tall nor solidly built as Wyatt,
the metal casing that covered the lower half of his face leant the
man a menacing aspect unmatched even by Wyatt's fury. Thin,
almost shriveled in build, the man's eyes seemed the only thing
vibrant about him, glistening with a callous, sardonic intensity that
was at once mocking and threatening. The ruffled front of his
Spanish-style shirt, the rich embroidery on his vest, the golden
filigree of the garters that circled his arms, all of these stood out
in stark contrast to the bulky gun harness he wore and the lethal
blasters hanging from the shoulder holsters underneath each of
his arms.

"You figurin' to ride out with Bob Paul? Take the county
sheriff up on his gracious offer to include you in his posse?" The
last word was almost distorted beyond recognition by the shallow
cough that rattled through the silver grill. The mask was a wonder
of science and medicine, tiny bars of RJ acting as a filter to burn
away the impurities in the air and provided relief from what many
called the White Plague. It could suppress the affliction and its
grisly symptoms, but it was a remedy rather than a cure. His
coughing might not have John Holiday lying on a hotel floor
spitting up blood as it had so often before, but it still made certain
to remind the gambler that whatever relief the mask provided, the
rot was still down there in his lungs.

"I wouldn't bet a Boston dollar on Bob being able to
catch a cold," Wyatt snarled. "No, Doc, we do this, we do this on
our own."

Doc Holiday nodded. "Just one question, Wyatt. Are we
doin' this for the law, or for your brothers?" The gambler's gaze
shifted from the Over-marshal to the spot where Morgan Earp
was standing. Throughout Wyatt's tirade, the hulking cyborg had

been silent, his expression as impassive as the Sphinx. They might have been talking about the weather for all the effect the discussion had on Morgan. It wasn't that Morgan was daft or dull in his mind, he understood what had happened well enough. It had been Morgan who'd carried Virgil to his home, had watched him through that first night as the maimed lawman kept asking why he couldn't move his right arm. No, Morgan understood everything perfectly, it was simply that the cyborg didn't seem to feel anything about his brother's crippling. Doc had often been accused of being a cold-hearted sidewinder, but on his worst day he'd never become as devoid of compassion as Morgan seemed to be.

Wyatt scowled up at Morgan, pain clouding his eyes as he looked upon the cyborg Dr. Carpathian had sent back to Tombstone after Virgil brought their dying brother to the wonder-worker's enclave. Losing Morgan had been the hardest thing he'd gone through in his life, far more painful than even the death of his wife had been. What Virgil had done was worse. There were moments, times like now, when Wyatt wondered if what had been brought back from Carpathian was still their brother. Certainly it was Morgan's face, sometimes even acted like Morgan, but something important appeared missing. It pained him to think like this, but it was like a 'bot playing at being Morgan, a machine with oil where it should have blood and pistons where it should have a heart. Just looking up at Morgan was a reminder of what the family had lost. At his lowest, Wyatt wondered whatif Virgil had only let him die; they'd have been able to bury the memory of their brother and move on. Instead, everyday, they were forced to watch that memory walking around, a steel echo of their brother.

Wyatt could almost hate Virgil for what he'd done. Now, it was Virgil lying in bed, waiting for the doctors to decide if he would live or die. Their older brother, James, was with him now, standing vigil over him. Unlike the younger Earps, James wasn't a fighter; he was instead content to tend bar in the saloon the brothers owned. He didn't have the ability or the drive for what Wyatt was planning. It was just as well. The Earps had too many enemies in Tombstone between the Clantons and the rest of the Cowboys. He'd already deputized 'Texas' Jack Vermillion and seven other men, but he'd feel better knowing there was somebody who was family keeping an eye on Virgil.

"This is all about family, lunger!" the growl came from a gruff, bull-necked man leaning back in a cowhide chair. He wore the same leather lawman's coat as Wyatt, even copied the cut of the Over-marshal's broad-brimmed hat. The same curled handlebar moustache spread across his lip. To a casual observer, he might have been a reflection of Wyatt that had climbed down from its mirror to sit a spell. A closer look would have revealed the absence of the fierce sense of duty and obligation that framed the Over-marshal's features even in a time like this. This man's face was harsher, his eyes gleaming with a streak of viciousness that didn't need the excuse of vengeance to rise to the fore. For all the youth in that face, Warren Earp had already packed a lifetime of brutality behind it.

"Your puppy's barkin' again," Doc complained to Wyatt.

A simple glance from his older brother had Warren sinking down in his chair. Wyatt turned back to Doc. "He's right. This isn't about the law. This is about family." He turned and addressed the other men he'd chosen to form his posse. "'I'll understand if the rest of you boys want to sit this out."

A few of the men glanced anxiously at one another, but it was Doc who broke the tense silence. "That's mighty considerate of you, Wyatt, but I've got nothin' more important on my dance card." He nodded at the other men. "I rather suspect none of us does. And there is that nice fat reward to take into consideration," he added, raising his voice so that he was certain the other men heard every word despite the distortion of his mask. "Split nine ways," Doc added, then glanced over at Morgan. "Or are marshals excluded from taking bounty money? That'd make a seven way divvy, six if you'll pin a star on Warren before we ride out."

"Why you brayin', lowdown..." Warren had barely started to climb out of his chair before another glower from Wyatt made him choke down the rest of his outburst.

Wyatt looked across the men he'd gathered together. He waited for each man to give his nod, feeling pride deep inside him as Sherman McMaster, 'Turkey Creek' Johnson, and the others each gave him their nod. Last of all, he turned toward Doc.

"You know better than to even ask," Doc said. "But before we light out after them, you'd better give me one of them stars."

The Over-marshal reached into his vest and drew out a simple tin badge. "Getting superstitious, Doc?" he asked as he handed it over.

The gambler shook his head. "Nope. I just feel there's things you do for money and things you do for friendship. Wearin' this'll remind me why I'm tradin' shots with Jesse James."

Chapter 5

It was an impressive pack of outlaws that Cole Younger led back to the old hideout. Even after he gave the signal, he was certain that Potts or Danby were going to open up on them, convinced that such a big mob could only mean a posse. It took the familiar cadence of Cole's Rebel yell to get the lookouts to be uncertain enough to dash back to the bunkhouse and fetch one of the senior members of the gang.

Even from a distance, Cole recognized the refined coachman's top hat that was his little brother Jim's prized affectation. It always amazed Cole that Jim spent so much time trying to dandify himself for the ladies, when he'd invariably just take up with the first wag-tail who gave him the squiny. Jim had another of his prized possessions in his hands – the nickel-plated carbine he'd stripped off a Pinkerton-man down near Centralia. Cole gave out a second Rebel yell to make sure Jim didn't snap the weapon up to his shoulder and peel off a shot. His brother wasn't an especially fast gun, but he could pick a coon out of a tree at five hundred yards. Cole figured he wouldn't tempt fate.

Jim waved his carbine overhead when he heard the second yell. Cole waved the men following him forward. The threat of being shot by their new allies having diminished, the Cowboys reverted to the grumbling and complaining that had characterized the long ride from Clantonville.

"Don't look like much," Ike Clanton observed, spitting a plug of tobacco into the dirt. "I'd have figured the James-Younger Gang would be keeping themselves in style. This sorry set-up wouldn't impress a bean-eater."

Cole growled under his breath. He'd crossed half the territory listening to the Cowboys grouse about everything from saddle sores, to fleas in their bedrolls, to the severity of the weather. Most of it was just the sort of venting you'd expect from men on the trail. The big exception was Ike. If it wasn't something that already had a Clanton brand on it, the slicked-up saddle tramp went out of his way to find fault in it. If it wasn't in his pocket, he could make a gold eagle sound rowdy-dow. Cole figured he must have offended the Almighty at some point, since it was Ike who had to be the most loquacious of the Tombstone bunch.

"We like to keep on the move," Cole snapped back at Ike, not appreciating the rustler's high-handed tone. "Old habit we picked up ridin' with Quantrill a long, long time ago. You keep movin' and any folks lookin' fer you have a plum difficult time trackin' you down. Beats havin' the law knockin' on the door every time a steer goes missin'."

Ike scowled back at Cole. "Might's well be livin' like a pack of Indians," he sneered. "You fellas take up with squaws too? Oww!" He clapped a hand to his ear, massaging the enflamed skin where his father had slapped him with a cow-hide cattleman's gauntlet. The metal ribbing lining the fingers had split the skin in a few spots, bringing blood oozing up from the shallow cuts.

"I warned yeh afore!" Old Man Clanton yelled at Ike. "Shut yer gob and mind yer manners!" He looked apologetically at Cole. "Don't mind Ike's bark. He's either half way to makin' hisself a ringster or a half-wit, and the jury's still deliberatin' on which."

"Just see he remembers who's big auger of this outfit," Cole said.

Old Man Clanton leaned across the saddle of his blackhoof. "And just who is tall hog at the trough? That be you or would that be Jesse?"

"Far as you Cowboys are concerned, it's both of us," Cole answered. The rustler had a way of getting under his skin just like his son Ike, only the Old Man was better at it. Ike just made himself obnoxious; but the Old Man would needle a man where he lived, dig around in his skull, and figure out what made him tick before stinging him with his tongue. Cole was constantly fighting to keep either from getting to him, or at least letting them know that they were. Maybe it was just sheer cussedness on the Old Man's part, but Cole couldn't shake the impression that he was scouting out the terrain for reasons of his own.

As the outlaws came riding close to the hideout, Jim ambled toward the newcomers. He waved at his cousin Johnny Ringo, and then turned toward Cole. "You said you was gettin' more guns. Didn't 'spect you to come ridin' back with a whole damn regiment."

Cole smiled, looked over his shoulder at the Cowboys following him. All told, there were twenty five men who'd mustered up with the Clantons. Even though it was a relic of a memory, Cole recalled that during the war, Quantrill and Bloody Bill had put whole towns to the torch with fewer men.

"You know me, Jim. When I do something, I like to do it big." Cole smiled and waved his hand at the men around him. "You already know Cousin Johnny. The mean fellow who looks like a twenty-card speeler is Ike Clanton, the curly wolf sittin' on that tin crowbait there is Bill Brocius, and the head honcho beside me here is Old Man Clanton, Ike's pa."

Jim nodded to each of the outlaws as they were introduced, and then turned back to his older brother. "Cole, Jesse's up and about. Took the whole gang out to tackle the bank at Charity."

Cole felt a cold shiver rush down his spine. "He take John too?" was the first thing that leapt off his tongue. He knew Jesse's penchant for just bulling into a place and trusting to luck and brass to carry him through. Without the restraining influence of Frank James at hand, Cole didn't like to think about how the raid on Charity might have gone.

"John's fine," Jim assured him. "Everybody came out in one piece, though Hardin'll be picking splinters from his prat for a few weeks and John's got a few along his forearm."

Ringo straightened up in his saddle when he heard that name. "Hardin? You mean John Wesley Hardin?" An ugly light crept into Ringo's eyes. "I heard of him. Folks say he's fast."

"Not sure about fast, but he'd win a contest for plum meanness," Jim said. "He favors a brace of ugly-looking irons that don't just shoot a man, but light him up with fire. Watched him laugh when he done it, too."

"What was the take from Charity?" Ike asked.

"Near on two thousand dollars," Jim said.

Ike laughed. "Two thousand? Jesse'd make more turnin' himself in for the bounty!"

"He didn't ride us in there for the money," Jim growled at Ike, resenting the rustler's mockery.

"What did he ride you in there for?" Cole wondered, feeling as though he already knew.

"We rode in there to hang a banker," Jim said. "Man named Temple who'd been a captain in the Redlegs."

"And did Jesse hang him?"

Jim shuddered. "Yeah. We hung him, or what Jesse left for us to hang."

Cole felt an icy cold creep into his veins. That first day when Jesse'd come back, when he'd talked of Frank's getting killed, Cole had seen the look in the outlaw's eyes. The same look he knew had filled his own eyes when his father had been murdered during the war. The look of a hurt, pained animal that only wants to ride out and kill, to kill and kill again until the empty hole inside was all filled up.

***

"You promised us blasters and Iron Horses!" The words exploded from Ike's mouth like a volley from a cannon. He pushed his chair away from the table and glowered down at the outlaw seated across from him. "We didn't ride out all this way just to divvy up some chicken feed cash box or penny-ante payroll!"

"Then maybe you Arizona boys have wasted your time," Jesse James snarled back, metal fingers drumming against the raw wood surface of the table, leaving little dents in the soft pine.

The air within the bunkhouse was tense. The two groups of outlaws eyed each other suspiciously, keeping among themselves while their leaders discussed their next job. The Cowboys were spread out across the left side of the room, the Youngers to the right with Hardin keeping off on his own near the stone fireplace. Danby and Potts, along with two Cowboys, were outside keeping watch.

Old Man Clanton wagged a finger at Cole Younger. "My boy's got the right of it. It was a lot of fine talk about newfangled guns and hosses that brung us all this way. You'll understand our displeasure to hear it ain't so."

Cole turned toward Jesse. "I've had a plan drawn up for a while now. The Union's got a nice cache of gear over at Fort Concho and they've been pullin' troops out for months to send out with Grant and his expedition against the Warrior Nation."

Jesse's expression darkened at mention of the Indians. He folded his metal arms across each other, working his fingers along the shoulders, feeling along the join where flesh gave way to steel.

"I didn't try tacklin' it afore," Cole explained, "since we didn't have enough hands to do the job. But with Ringo and the Clantons along, takin' the fort'll be screamin' simple. We can just waltz right in and take whatever we like."

Jesse shook his head and glowered at the Cowboys. "I don't cotton to ridin' with men I don't know. I like to see how they handle themselves in a scrap. Find out who's a dabster and who's a spooney."

"And how you figurin' on findin' that out, Mr. Bushwhacker?" Ike growled.

"We could throw down," Jesse suggested, "but that wouldn't do none of us any good. Bunch a folks'd be restin' in a grave patch with a sin-buster prayin' over 'em."

"You have somethin' better in mind?" Old Man Clanton asked.

"I figure'd we mosey on out a ways and slap leather where it'd do some good," Jesse said, fingers still feeling along his scarred shoulders.

Beside Jesse, Cole noted the ugly light in the outlaw's eyes. Killing the banker hadn't even started to fill that hole inside the outlaw chief. It hadn't even made much of a start.

***

Old Man Clanton squinted through the telescopic lens, frowning as he felt the heat from the optical intensifier's power cell against his cheek. He didn't like all these modern contraptions, far less when he was reminded of the weird ways in which they worked. He liked them still less when they told him things that weren't to his favor. Just now, he felt like taking the telescopic glass and smashing it on the ground.

"You teched in the head, Jesse?" the rustler asked. "Ain't nothin' down there but a bunch of Indians!"

Ike snatched the glass from his father and peered down the lens. "Don't that beat all!" he cursed. "What're we supposed to do, steal their beads?!"

The outlaws had ridden hard for most of the day to reach this spot. Jesse had insisted they hit an easier target before tackling Fort Concho, a plan that Cole had finally endorsed and which Old Man Clanton had eventually come around to. When Jesse'd led them up into the foothills, they'd thought it was a mining camp or a refueling station that they were striking.

Now, they found themselves lying on their bellies on the top of a ridge, staring down at a cluster of domed shaped huts known as "wickiups" and a dozen or so young warriors. A few elk hung from wooden frames and several of the natives were busy cutting steams from the animals. A couple of the other Indians were tending the fire that was smoldering in the stone-lined pit between the huts.

"Looks like a hunting party," Curly Bill suggested, using his own set of field glasses to study the encampment. "Mostly young bucks. Don't see any women or children. If I were pressed, I'd make 'em out as a hunting party."

"They wearin' paint?" Bob Younger asked the Cowboy.

The rustler shook his head. "Nope. These bucks are just hunting, not a war band." He waved a hand toward the rugged mountains rising above the foothills. "Probably got themselves a village somewhere yonder."

"I don't care what they got or where they got it," Ike grumbled. He turned onto his side and fixed Jesse with a scowl. "I want to know what business we got with a bunch of scruffy Indians."

Jesse returned Ike's scowl with a cold stare. "Better change that look on your face afore I change it for you."

Cole was familiar enough with Jesse's moods to know that Ike was within a hairsbreadth of opening up more trouble than he'd ever want. He also knew that if things came to that pass, the gang would bust up in a blaze of violence. Ideas about hitting Fort Concho would go up in that same blaze. They needed the Clantons if they were going to steal supplies from the Union garrison.

"Think about it, Ike," Cole interjected himself into the standoff before it could boil over. "Jesse wants to see how we operate together, wants to see for himself how good you Cowboys are and show you how good the James-Younger Gang is. We go hittin' a ranch or a town and folks'll notice, start spreadin' the word." He smiled and waved a hand down at the camp below. "Who'll notice or care if we attack a parcel of scruffy Indians?"

Cole could tell his words had little impact on Ike, but they took root with his father. Old Man Clanton scratched the stubble on his chin as he mulled them over.

"Makes a right bit of sense at that," he decided. "I still don't like it, but I kin see the sense of it."

Cole looked back at Jesse, watching with dismay as the outlaw glared down at the camp, as one hand reached to the scarred shoulder beneath his coat. Cole didn't know what it must be like, having your arms torn to shreds. He didn't know what something like that would do to a man's mind, the kind of hate it would kindle in a man's heart.

What was about to happen here wouldn't be over the loss of Frank. It would be for Jesse and the arms he'd lost. The outlaw had purposefully brought the gang here knowing there'd be Indians around. It wasn't for some tactical purpose as Cole'd managed to sell Old Man Clanton. Jesse hadn't had anything so pragmatic in mind. For him, this attack was about nothing except revenge.

This was almost to be expected. Jesse was always the emotional type, living in the moment, acting on his desires and impulses without first scoping out the trail ahead. It was always left to Frank to work out the details. With Frank dead, Cole was the most obvious choice to fill that role. Jesse was not about to change who he was to fill that void; so it fell to Cole, the only other person that knew best how Frank's mind worked.

"We'll spread out from here," Cole told the Cowboy leaders. "We leave five men back with the mounts. You don't have to worry about an Indian stealin' one of 'em, but he'll damn sure try to wreck it if'n he gets half a chance." The bushwhacker paused a moment. "Two men from our outfit, three from yours. We'll leave Potts and my brother, John. Whoever you like from your end." He knew his youngest brother would object to being left behind, but Cole's mind would rest easier knowing he was out of the way. Just now, he needed his wits as sharp as they'd ever been if he was expected to juggle Jesse's thirst for revenge and appease the Cowboys.

"We can circle around from the left," Curly Bill pointed a finger at a dried-out creek bed. Thick clumps of brush lined either bank of the creek, ample cover for the outlaws until they got within a couple hundred yards of the camp.

Cole nodded. "There's a gulley down along the back that'll keep us hid until we get within spittin' distance." He pulled his watch from his vest. "I reckon three quarters of the hour and everybody can be in place."

"Just mind everyone stays downwind of that camp," Jesse said, his steely gaze sweeping from Cole to the Cowboy leaders. "They can smell a man coming long afore they can see or hear him." He slapped a metal hand against a steel forearm to emphasize the point. Even Ike lost some of his bravado as he thought about how Jesse had lost those arms.

"Hit 'em hard and hit 'em fast," Jesse told the outlaws. "Shoot to kill and be sure what you shoot stays dead. Remember that and you might see yourself through with all your parts still attached."

***

From the gulley, Jesse watched as the Indian warriors prowled about their camp, skinning the elk they had taken. It was hard for him to focus on the young natives; his mind kept drifting, conjuring up visions of the Warrior Nation. He could see half-human monsters rearing up from the dark, fangs and claws flashing in the moonlight. He could hear the crunch of bone as it twisted and remolded itself into new shapes, the shredding of skin as it split apart and the flesh beneath shifted and flowed into the foundation of a monstrous form. He could see the shimmer of spectral arrows as they rained down from the sky, granted unholy powers by the medicine men. He could smell the sharp tang as the ghostly arrows came hurtling down. He could feel again the phantom chill as they dropped down toward him in a shower of death.

Jesse's hands dropped to the blasters at his sides. He almost tore them from their holsters; he almost rose up from the gulley and charged into the camp, not so much to gun down the warriors but to vanquish the gruesome images swarming inside his head. Action, the imperative of battle; that would drive down the nightmares, force them back into the shadows where they belonged.

Grimly, Jesse fought to restrain himself. He had to wait, had to hold back until everyone was in place. Attack now and some of the Indians would almost certainly escape. And that was something the hate inside him just wouldn't allow. The savages had taken his arms and the Union had taken his brother. One and all he would pay them back. He would teach them all what it meant to trifle with Jesse James.

Beside him, Cole Younger was keeping one eye on his watch. Jesse could hear the soft buzz of the RJ button inside as the chronometer slowly ticked off the minutes. How many minutes had passed during their crawl along the bottom of the gulley? How many more were left until they would spring their ambush? Jesse held back from asking. It would be an exhibition of weakness to ask Cole, a confession of the anxiety he felt inside, an admission of the bloodlust thundering through his veins. He had to be bigger than that. He was the leader of this gang and he had to have the respect of every man who followed him. He couldn't have that if they thought he was weak, if they stopped thinking for even one minute that he was bigger than they were.

Jesse glanced away from Cole, studying the other men in the gulley. Jim Younger had his carbine already aimed at the camp beside him; Bob had his hands filled with both a blaster and one of his Bowie knives. The buckaroo Danby, much like Jim, had his rifle trained on the camp, but he kept looking away to wipe at the nervous sweat that beaded across his forehead and threatened to drip down into his eyes. Hardin's attitude was more eager, his fingers fondling the grips of his smokers as though impatient to draw them from their holsters and burn down the Indians and their brush-wood shelters.

Time slowly ticked away. Every moment, Jesse expected one of the Indians to turn and stare directly at him, warned of his presence by some preternatural sense unknown to any white man. He expected any one of the warriors to suddenly collapse, for his body to undulate and spasm while his flesh reshaped itself into something obscene and monstrous. He could almost hear the half-human howl of an abomination that was neither man nor beast echoing across the darkening sky.

Then, with an abruptness that startled him, the agony of waiting was over. Cole stuffed his watch back in his pocket, peered down the sight of his carbine, and shouting a fierce Rebel yell sent a blistering bolt of energy slamming into one of the natives butchering the elk. The Indian was lifted off his feet, shot straight into the hanging animal. Corpse, carcass, and frame all came crashing earthward in a smoking mess.

Cole's shot was the signal that caused the entire gang to open up. From the creek bed, the Cowboys sent a withering fusillade pouring down, blasting apart stunned warriors who had just turned away from their chores. The men in the gulley added their fire to the barrage and the Indians were locked in a murderous crossfire.

Jesse peeled off shots at the natives, scowling when his first shot went wide, roaring with dismay when the second fell short. He glared at his metal arms; those fantastic contraptions Carpathian had so graciously endowed him with, the miraculous remedy for his horrific mutilation. They'd betrayed him once, when Carpathian had treacherously shut them down. Now, they were doing so again, refusing to coordinate with the demands made of them by his eyes.

The twilight exploded into light as one of the wickiups caught fire. Soon, a second hut erupted into flame, and then there came a piercing shriek as one of the warriors was turned into a living torch. Jesse spun around to see Hardin laughing like some devil from hell. The gunman had broken cover, risen up from the gulley to slowly walk toward the Indian camp. With each step, he squeezed off a shot from his smokers, immolating either a hut or a man with each shot. Watching the sadist's brazen attack poured fire into more than the camp, it set a fire inside Jesse too. Angrily, Jesse shoved his blasters back into their holsters. He didn't need the guns to do what needed doing.

Lunging up from the gulley, Jesse rushed toward the burning camp. He heard Cole curse loudly behind him, listened with half an ear as the bushwhacker started shouting at his brothers to give Jesse cover. A few of the warriors had managed to reach their wickiups and fetch their rifles, the mystic blue aura of the natives' spirit energy flowing through the air as they were channeled into their weapons. Jesse ignored the fitful shots, too fixed on the hate boiling inside him to worry about insignificant things like keeping his own hide intact.

As he came into the burning camp, what Jesse thought had been a dead native lying on the ground, suddenly leapt to his feet and rushed at him with a tomahawk that was wreathed in blue flame. Jesse met the warrior's charge, catching the downward sweep of the hatchet with his metal forearm. The scrape of steel against steel shrieked out across the camp for a second, but Jesse brought his other hand flashing for the Indian's wrist. His steel fingers tightened, and with a twist he snapped the warrior's arm, sending the tomahawk tumbling from the Indian's grip, at which point the fire went out. Jesse pulled back, dragging the foe with him, shaking him like he was a child's rag doll. The outlaw brought his fist slamming down on his opponent's arm, snapping it like a twig. The crippled Indian collapsed to the ground, shrieking in pain.

In the next instant, Jesse found himself bowled over by a tremendous force. He could hear his coat being shredded by vicious claws, could feel sharp talons raking across his armored vest. A heavy, animal smell was in his nose, a musky stench so overpowering that he could taste it in his mouth. Rolling across the earth, it took every speck of power Carpathian had endowed his mechanized arms with to push the bestial bulk of his attacker off of him. Grunting with the effort, Jesse was just able to thrust his attacker back, pushing it toward one of the burning wickiups.

By the flickering firelight, Jesse could see that the thing was an Indian shapechanger, one of the ghastly and rare monsters that were sacred within the Warrior Nation. This one had the brawny build of a grizzly bear, a kindred beast to the one that had torn Jesse's arms to shreds. The thing's massive body hunched forward, a great hump of fat rising between its broad, almost manlike, shoulders. Manlike too were the powerful hind legs of the beast, taller and straighter than the bandy legs of a natural bear. The muscular forelegs weren't quite like human arms, but the clawed paws at the end of those legs were uncomfortably like human hands. The head and face, however, were utterly devoid of anything human, the low brow and broad snout of a bruin jutting from the merest stump of neck. The beady black eyes that stared out from the bear's face shone with intelligence beyond any animal, yet they glowed in the light like those of any beast.

Jesse stood frozen for a moment, staring in horror at the monstrosity. His body trembled, every nerve afire with the remembered agony of when a beast such as this had torn him apart and left his mangled body helpless on the ground. The bear snuffled, lips peeling back from its fangs in a grisly smile. It could smell the outlaw's fear.

A blaster cracked from either the creek or the gulley, glancing across the bear's back, burning a bloody furrow along its side. The sudden discharge broke the spell of fear that gripped Jesse. Terror became hate in the outlaw's heart, a blazing fury that enflamed every fiber of his being. Throwing up his arms, Jesse shouted at his gang. "This one's mine!" he cried, ordering his men to hold their fire. The bear glared back at him, opening its fanged muzzle in a rumbling roar, as though accepting Jesse's challenge. The next instant, the enormous brute was marching toward Jesse on its hind legs.

"Jesse! Are you loco?!" Cole's cry rang out across the night. Jesse heard similar cries of disbelief from the other outlaws when, instead of drawing down on the bear, he charged straight at it.

The beast swiped at him with one of its claws, a powerful blow that would have split Jesse in two had it connected. The bear was built for strength and power, it couldn't match the infernal speed of Jesse's quick-devil arms. Catching the bear's forepaws as it swatted at him, Jesse wrenched the beast around, using the trapped limb to shield him from the other claw with brutal jerks and tugs that kept forcing the trapped leg into the path of the other paw.

For a moment, the bear roared and raged, trying to break free from Jesse's clutch. Again, Jesse mustered every last ounce of power in his mechanized arms, taxing their superhuman strength to the limit. By degrees, the bear's roars became less furious and more anguished. It flailed desperately in Jesse's grip, trying to pull itself free. Finally, there came a sickening sound of tearing meat and cracking bone. Blood jetted into the twilight as with a howl of triumph, Jesse tore the bear's leg from its shoulder.

Some of the Cowboys, less concerned with Jesse's longevity than the Youngers, had been whooping and hollering from the creek bed, relishing the spectacle of the infamous Jesse James wrestling a bear-changer. The most callous of the Clanton crowd had even wagered on the outcome. Now, even these ruffians fell into a stunned silence, awed by the Herculean feat of the outlaw leader.

Panting from the strain of his fight, Jesse staggered away from the maimed bear. He braced his legs wide and defiantly waited for the monster to come at him again. All the fight had gone out of the bear, however, draining away with the blood spurting from its ripped shoulder. The brute stood there for a moment, glowering at Jesse, then slumped to its knees.

Tossing aside the leg he'd ripped free, Jesse lunged at the dying monster. His metal arms closed about the bear's remaining foreleg. Sweat streamed down Jesse's face, soaked his torn vest, and dripped across his slashed pants as he bent himself to a repeat of the awesome feat that had so stunned his gang. Wrenching the bear's leg backwards, using the beast's own body as a fulcrum, the outlaw pulled until he'd ripped the limb clean from its socket.

Brandishing the gory limb overhead, waving it like a captured flag, Jesse screamed his rage into the night. It had been a beast like this which had cost him his arms, now he would do the same to every skin-changer unlucky enough to cross his path.

"Jesse!" a panicked voice cried out from almost beside the outlaw. He spun around in time to see the young man, whose arm he'd broken, rushing at him. The Indian was holding his tomahawk in his offhand now, the metal glowing with eerie blue energies as he charged. But it wasn't that which gave Jesse pause. It was the anguished look in the native's face, the tears spilling from his eyes as he gazed past Jesse at the dying bear.

Before the warrior could close with Jesse, he was struck down, sent spinning into the dirt by the impact of a Bowie knife slamming into his back. For a moment, the Indian tried to pick himself up, for an instant, the young warrior glared up at Jesse with eyes completely consumed by hate. The outlaw found himself transfixed by that dying gaze, unable to look away until the boy's dead face slumped back down into the dust.

"That would'a been plum tragic," Bob Younger declared as he came stalking over to the dead boy and ripped his knife from the Indian's back. "You go and kill that bear-walker with your bare hands and then this little sidewinder gets you."

Jesse barely heard Bob's words. He was still looking down at the dead warrior, thinking about the ghastly look that had been in his dying eyes, the look that Jesse saw staring back at him whenever he gazed in a mirror. It was the look of love twisted in upon itself until it became a burning knot of hate. What, Jesse wondered, had the bear-changer been to this boy. Uncle? Father?

Brother?

"They'll all be eating out of your hand after this," Bob said, nodding toward the creek where the Cowboys had emerged from cover and were now waving their hats and firing their guns into the air, celebrating Jesse's astounding victory. "Right now, I think those boys will follow you to the gates of Hell."

Jesse turned away from the dead warrior. "Good," he growled as he walked away. "Because that's just where all of us are headed."

Chapter 6

Fort Concho was nestled at the convergence of the North and Middle Concho Rivers, surrounded by miles of treeless prairie. The Union had started construction of the fort immediately after the war, intending to protect the trailheads that passed near to it from the lingering pockets of Secesh in West Texas, while at the same time suppressing Warrior Nation bands. Border violations by Mexico's Golden Army and the criminal activities of Mexican and American Comancheros had, for a time, increased the importance of Fort Concho to a degree where the whole of the 3rd and 10th Cavalry were based there.

The very importance of Fort Concho, the grand ambitions of the generals and politicians who lobbied for its establishment, had played against the post almost from the start. The original site selected for the fort had been abandoned after being flattened and cleared for construction when it was deemed too constrained for the immense compound the generals had envisioned. Part of a perimeter wall had been built from pecan wood before the hard, rough timber was determined to be too difficult to work with. Ugly mounds of earth scattered outside the walls gave evidence to another failed construction material – nearly one hundred yards of wall had been constructed from adobe brick before a demonstration of the penetrating power of an RJ blaster convinced General Grant to order all adobe fortifications dismantled and replaced.

The new construction was sandstone, drawn from local quarries. Thick enough to obstruct light arms and even small cannon, the sandstone brought with it a different problem – the expense of importing stone masons from the east to work it. The added expenditure, in the face of the rising threat posed by the Warrior Nation in the north, finally forced a budget conscious War Department to suspend construction of Fort Concho.

The end result was a fully garrisoned and operational outpost with large gaps in its stockade, guarded by nothing more substantial than wooden posts and steel wire. The size of the garrison and the commanding position of Fort Concho were felt, in a show of insincere optimism by those in Washington, to be sufficient to discourage any attack by hostile elements.

One of those hostile elements now gazed on Fort Concho through an optical intensifier, a broad smile on his face. When he'd first seen the fort, Cole Younger saw it as a ripe plum just waiting to be plucked. That opinion hadn't changed in the months since. If anything, Fort Concho had only become more attractive to the outlaw. The 3rd Cavalry had been withdrawn to the north to address the Warrior Nation's depredations, and whole troops of the 10th Cavalry had been sent to other posts in the area like Fort Clark and Fort Richardson. This left only a hodge-podge of units from other Infantry divisions and Cavalry companies manning the fort, each with their own array of commanders and officers over them.

Cole had seen enough during the war to recognize, whether Union or Confederate, the more brass there was hovering over any group of soldiers, the less effective and slower to react they became. The situation was bound to be made still worse by the commander that Grant had put in charge of Fort Concho; Colonel Ranald S. Mackenzie, a bold cavalry officer but a strict and exacting disciplinarian who tolerated no initiative in the officers under his command. His men were there to follow orders, not discuss them. Since 'Perpetual Punisher' had taken command of Fort Concho, many soldiers had deserted the post, several of them just bitter enough to air the fort's dirty laundry in the cantinas and saloons they drifted through on their way west.

"It looks good, Cole," Jesse observed, peering through his own scope at the fort. "The big stone building at the end of the parade ground is the storehouse?"

"Just to the left of the headquarters' building. There's two of 'em. First one's the commissary, second one is the quartermaster," Cole explained, drawing a rough map of the fort in the dirt. "I figure we set fire to the commissary and at the same time we hit the quartermaster. Them blue-bellies will have to waste time roundin' up vittles in San Angelo if'n we burn up all their hardtack before we skedaddle."

Jesse stared in surprise for a moment at Cole. He was impressed, these were the sorts of military tactics he'd expect to hear from Frank, not a gunman like Cole. "Seems a might of Frank musta rubbed off on you."

"Might be," Cole replied. Despite himself, he relished the fact that he'd managed to impress Jesse. "You're the boss, Jesse. Who'd you like where?"

"Hardin, Stilwell, and Spence can take care of the commissary storehouse," Jesse said. "I want you, Jim, and any decent shots in Clanton's crowd pinning down them blue-bellies in their barracks buildings."

"Ringo and Indian Charlie," Cole said. "Maybe Curly Bill too," he added after a moment's consideration.

"The Old Man and the rest of his crowd can hit the stock yard," Jesse said, pointing at the long stone building where the Union troops kept their Iron Horses. He smiled at Cole. "They want to ride 'em, then they can fetch 'em themselves." He gestured to the stockade wall and in particular the watch towers at each corner of the forty acre base. "We can forget about the towers out to the east, but we'll need to take care of the ones up close." He laughed grimly. "Bob's still damn handy with a knife. He can take out the guard in the tower close to where we slip in. Once hell breaks loose, somebody'll have to settle the guard in the other tower."

"I'll give that job to Ringo. He'll enjoy the challenge and it'll keep him away from you. You ain't exactly his favorite person, you know." Cole pulled at his moustache, hesitating before broaching the subject that had been nagging at him. "What job do you reckon for John?"

"He'll come in with me," Jesse said. "John and those two buckaroos of yourn. We'll bust into the quartermaster storehouse and swipe anything not nailed down."

Cole's expression remained worried. "John ain't exactly used to all this."

"He did just fine in Charity," Jesse said, a hard edge in his voice. "Don't worry about John, he'll make out." The outlaw chief fixed Cole with a steely gaze, almost daring him to flout his decision.

Cole clenched his teeth, biting down on the angry retort that was on the tip of his tongue. Challenging Jesse now wouldn't do him or his brothers any good. He couldn't explain that it wasn't John who had him worried, but Jesse himself. The man who'd used the attack on Charity as a pretext, an excuse to kill a Yankee officer, wasn't about to listen to reason now. There was a whole headquarters full of Union officers right next to the storehouse. He knew Jesse's penchant for taking risks, his impulsiveness once the shooting started. This was the same man who only three days before had waltzed out and wrestled an Indian bear-changer. Cole still wasn't sure if the word for that was brave or crazy.

What he was certain of was he didn't like the idea of his youngest brother taking the kind of chances Jesse James accepted as just part of the job. That sort of recklessness might be fine for Cole Younger, but not for John.

***

The dull crunch of vertebrae being crushed told Jesse he could release his grip on the sentry's neck. The man in the dark blue shell jacket collapsed to the ground, a look of surprise frozen on his face. The first the soldier was aware of Jesse James lurking in the shadows near the brick guardhouse was when the outlaw's metal fingers closed around his throat. Except for a strangled gasp, the trooper hadn't even made a sound.

Danby crept forward, snatching up the dead trooper's rifle and dragging the corpse back into the shadowy alley between the guardhouse and the nearest of the stone buildings where the enlisted men were bunked. Potts and John Younger eased their way forward to join Jesse against the guardhouse wall. When Jesse tapped Potts on the shoulder and pointed to the guard patrolling in front of the two storehouses, the buckaroo drew his knife from his boot and nodded. Unless Hardin or one of the Cowboys caught the soldier when he came to the corner of the commissary storehouse, it would be left to Potts to eliminate the man when he passed them to make his circuit around the quartermaster storehouse.

"How's your shootin' iron?" Jesse whispered to John, gesturing toward the massive headquarters building beside the storehouse. There were two more sentries patrolling the front of the building, a soldier on the ground and a second making a circuit of the roofed belvedere rising above the headquarters. He was especially worried about that man. There were outlaws creeping all over the fort at this point. The men in the watchtowers had their view of the base obstructed by the buildings; the guards on the ground were a bit too comfortable with the routine of their patrol to be vigilant enough to spot anyone unless they walked up and shook their hand. The trooper up in the belvedere though, with its commanding view of the parade ground, wouldn't have to be particularly on the ball to notice furtive activity below. That one soldier could sound an alarm that would turn out the whole fort against them before they were ready.

"Bob reckons I'm a damn good shot," John said with pride.

"Is that brag or fact?" Jesse demanded, fixing the boy with a commanding gaze. "It'll be all our hides if you can't do what I need you to do." He pointed at the headquarters. "I've got to knock out the blue-belly up top there. I can't risk gettin' tripped up settlin' the fella down below and maybe warning his pal. So I need you to watch him. If it looks like he's got wise that I'm around, there won't be any more need to play sneaky, so you just let him have it."

John's face spread in an exuberant smile, thrilled that his hero trusted him, *him,* to guard his back. "You can count on me, Jesse."

Jesse nodded once, then slipped away from the guardhouse. He had three different men to keep tabs on as he dashed across the front of the parade ground: the two men outside the headquarters and the sentry patrolling around the storehouses. His thoughts strayed back to similar times many, many moons ago when he'd ridden with Quantrill during the war, hiding out from Redlegs and Jayhawkers.

He'd been fighting for his country then, trying to push back the Unionist tyranny. Now, Jesse had far less lofty ambitions. All he was fighting for was himself.

Darting across the parade ground, Jesse pressed close against the side of the storehouse, feeling a bit safer with the building's shadow wrapped around him. He watched the guards in front of the headquarters building and tried to listen for the man making the circuit of the storehouses, unable to see the soldier now that he was around the corner. He gritted his teeth as he saw both of the sentries outside the headquarters turn their backs to him, stalking off in the other direction as they paced back and forth. Unable to hear the sound of footfalls at the front of the storehouses, Jesse decided that Potts or one of Hardin's men had settled the man. He had to, because with every passing second the chances of the man in the belvedere spotting one of the raiders grew.

In a bold dash, Jesse raced toward the headquarters and leapt at the wall. His metal fingers dug into the sandstone and he pulled himself partway up onto the belvedere. Wrapping his legs around the base of one of the columns supporting the Spanish-style roof, he drew himself up against the side of the building. He felt like a raccoon slinking around in someone's attic as he shifted his position, squirming along the outside of the belvedere toward the footsteps of the sentry.

When he drew parallel with the marching steps of the guard, Jesse lunged up and over the side of the belvedere. He hurled himself full on the man, crushing him down beneath the impetus of his lunge. The outlaw's steel hand closed across the soldier's windpipe, crushing it beneath his vice-like grip before the man could even think to shout.

It was then that things started to go wrong. The boom of a blaster sounded from the area of the guardhouse, and Jesse felt the air turn hot at his back as an energy beam went sizzling past. A Yankee officer, just climbing out onto the belvedere, crumpled against the wall, his head reduced to a steaming ruin. Almost immediately, Jesse heard another shot sizzle away from the guardhouse. Shooting the intruding officer had forced John to shift his attention away from the sentry on the ground. Now, the soldier was scrambling for cover, avoiding John's shots as the boy tried to burn him down.

The nimble soldier ducked behind the steps leading up to the headquarters, using it for cover as he tried to draw a bead on John. The protection offered by the steps, however, wasn't any obstacle for Jesse up in the belvedere. The Union trooper had made the mistake of not realizing there was an enemy already above him. Taking careful aim, Jesse sent a bolt searing straight down into the top of the soldier's head. The trooper pitched across the steps, his carcass flung back when one of John's shots slammed into the twitching corpse.

From his vantage in the belvedere, Jesse watched as chaos erupted throughout Fort Concho. Hardin and the men with him blasted open the door to the commissary storehouse while Danby and Potts did the same to the quartermaster storehouse. Cole and his shooters, however, weren't in position yet, nor were the Clantons and their rustlers. Both groups of outlaws were still crossing the parade ground when soldiers began swarming out from the barracks. The troopers might have been half-dressed, but not a man-jack of them had failed to snatch up his rifle. Caught in the open, the outlaws would swiftly be massacred.

Jesse's vision went red. He thought of Frank, he thought of their home in Missouri, their old mother with her arm blown off by a Union bomb. Between the beats of his heart, his quick-devil arms snapped down to his holsters and ripped his blasters free. Before he even realized what he was doing, Jesse began pumping shot after shot down into the soldiers scrambling from the barracks, mowing them down with the remorseless intensity of a gatling gun. Shocked by the intensity of this one-man fusillade, most of the soldiers scrambled back into the safety of the buildings. The few still exposed out on the parade ground were quickly settled by the vengeful fire from Cole and his sharpshooters.

Jesse could see that Cole and Ringo were slowly falling back toward the stockyard, snapping off shots at the barracks to keep the soldiers penned inside. The original plan had been for Cole's outfit to provide cover from the roof of the fort's chapel, but the early alarm now forced them to support the rustlers more directly, Jim and Curly Bill helping the Cowboys force their way into the stockyard.

Flames crackled from the commissary storehouse as Hardin's men set fire to the Union supplies. As the outlaws dashed away from the burning building, a group of black cavalrymen came rushing out from behind one of the barracks to intercept them. From the top of the belvedere, Jesse could hear Hardin's sadistic laugh as he opened up on the soldiers with his smokers, splashing the entire group with liquid fire.

The roar of engines rumbled from the stockyard. Ike Clanton came barreling out of the building on a shiny new Iron Horse with 'US Cavalry' embossed on its hull. He was followed an instant later by Indian Charlie. The two outlaws made a half circuit of the parade ground, peppering the front of the barracks with shots from the blasters of their Iron Horses before racing away toward the unfinished stockade wall. In short order, other Iron Horses came whipping out from the stockyard. Curly Bill slowed his steed just long enough for Johnny Ringo to clamber aboard. Jim Younger began to brake in order to pick up his elder brother. Cole waved him on toward the guardhouse, ordering Jim to pick up John instead. As Jim sped off, Cole turned about and dashed into the stockyard to secure a mount for himself, almost getting plowed over by Old Man Clanton as the grizzled rustler bolted out from the building on his Iron Horse.

Jesse did his best to keep the soldiers pinned down inside the buildings. The more care he seemed to take with his shots, the more accuracy he seemed to lose; Carpathian's cursed arms refused to adjust to the demands of his mind. Perversely, when he didn't really think about what he was shooting at, when he just snapped off a shot more or less from sheer instinct, the bolts struck true. For an accomplished gunman, it was an infuriating vexation, another reason – if he needed one – to squeeze the life out of the treacherous doctor.

Accuracy, however, wasn't a tall order to keep the soldiers penned up. With almost a dozen of their comrades scattered about the parade ground, it didn't need much to make them keep their heads down. The buildings themselves were large enough that even with his mechanical arms defying him,

Jesse couldn't help but hit something each time he squeezed off a shot.

"Jesse!" John's voice shouted up to the outlaw. "We gotta git!" Jesse looked down to see John slung up behind Jim. Fire from the porch in front of the headquarters sent Jim speeding off around the side of the fort. Jesse smiled when he heard John shouting in protest, insisting Jim wait until Jesse could join them.

The outlaw shook his head. The boy would have to learn that, in a fight, worrying about anybody but yourself was the best way to get yourself killed. That was a wisdom that had seen him through many decades of outlawry. You just didn't stick your neck out for anybody.

Not unless they were family.

The hairs on the back of Jesse's neck suddenly prickled, causing him to spin around. He snapped off a shot at the Union major who was creeping up over the body of the officer John had dropped. The major shrieked as Jesse's blast caught him in the chest, but even as he started to fall, a second officer was rushing up after him, thrusting the body before him like a shield.

Jesse threw himself flat as the second officer started shooting at him. He'd wondered how long it was going to take before the men in the headquarters realized there was somebody up on the belvedere and decided to do something about it. From the floor, the outlaw sent a shot shearing through the officer's forearm. The soldier screamed and clutched at the spurting stump. Jesse silenced his shrieks with a second, mortal shot to his gut.

The distraction presented by the officers gave the soldiers in the barracks the opportunity to come rushing from the buildings. Cole, the last man to come riding out from the stockyard, had to dodge a gauntlet of fire as he tore across the parade ground and hurtled into the night. Before he vanished into the darkness, the bushwhacker shouted a defiant Rebel yell at the enraged Yankees he left behind.

With all the other members of his gang fled, Jesse considered it was time he made himself scarce too. As he rose from the floor, however, he was nearly cut down by a blaster.

Hastily he snapped off a shot at yet another officer climbing up onto the belvedere. There was a dull, metallic clang followed by the sound of splintering wood and a body crashing to the ground.

Leaping to his feet, Jesse dashed across the belvedere; throwing himself out over the balustrade before any other officers could come climbing up from below. He flung himself into the open air, hurtling across the span between the headquarters and the quartermaster storehouse. He slammed into the tile roof, feeling it crack and crumble beneath his impact. Before he could consider if the roof would bear his weight, shots came sizzling up at him from both the parade ground and the headquarters. Flakes of terracotta slashed across his face as the soldiers did their best to pick him off the roof.

Jesse didn't give them the chance, sliding off the back of the building to the earth below. Almost the instant his feet touched the ground he heard a shout of alarm, and the wall beside his ear exploded as a shot barely missed taking his head off his shoulders. The outlaw swung around, blasting the black cavalry trooper trying to burn him down with a rifle. He could hear more soldiers rushing around the side of the storehouse, their officers bellowing at them to cut Jesse off before he could reach the perimeter wall.

The prospect of being surrounded seemed a certainty until Jesse heard the roar of an Iron Horse. Speeding out from the smoke boiling up from the blazing commissary storehouse, was Cole. The bushwhacker fired at the advancing blue-bellies, driving them back as he sped toward Jesse. The outlaw leaped up into the saddle behind Cole as he brought his machine roaring around the building.

"You know better than this," Jesse growled at Cole as he brought the Iron Horse whipping around. Shots from Union rifles pursued them as they raced off into the night.

"Somebody has to watch out fer yer neck," Cole said. "Frank's not here, so I figured that means I'm elected."

Jesse was quiet as Cole's steed punched through a gap in the stockade wall and went racing across the dusty prairie. It had been a long time since anything had made Jesse James feel humble, but Cole's gesture and the sentiment behind it came close.

***

Colonel Mackenzie was sprawled across the divan in his drawing room, his shirt torn away so that Fort Concho's surgeon could pull slivers of wood from the commander's flesh. One side of the colonel's face was an angry welt, the skin blistered by the heat of a near-miss from Jesse's pistol. The eye that stared from that side of Mackenzie's face was like a pool of blood, the white turned red by all the little blood vessels that had boiled and burst.

Mackenzie glared up at his subordinates while the doctor worked on him. "That makes eight," he snarled, rapping his hand against the metal plates bolted into the left side of his body. "Six times I was wounded by Secessionists during the war. A damned spirit arrow nearly took my leg off last time I rode against the Warrior Nation." His hand clenched into a fist, a grotesque gesture with half his fingers replaced by steel talons and a steel plate bolted to his forearm. The Indians called Mackenzie 'Bad Hand' because of that mechanical claw, a memento from injury number three during the siege of Petersburg. Tonight, Mackenzie's metal hand had saved his life, deflecting the shot Jesse James had fired at him, earning him his eighth injury in the line of duty.

"Death reached out for me this night, gentlemen," Mackenzie snapped. "I want to know how such a thing was possible. I want to know how a bunch of outlaw vermin snuck onto my post, fired my buildings, killed my men, and stole my supplies."

"Colonel, sir, the stockade wall..." A glower from the wounded Mackenzie caused the infantry captain to choke down the rest of his speech.

"Put yourself on report, Hawkins," Mackenzie growled. He swept his gaze across the other officers. "The stockade wall's condition is one you've all known about. I expect it to have been taken into account when posting sentries and assigning duties. Men secure perimeters, not fences!"

"It's them colored troops, sir," a cavalry officer declared. "You can't expect them to obey like regular soldiers."

"You're on report too, Lutherlyn," Mackenzie said. "Discipline and training don't recognize the color of a man's skin. If you can't get an African to fight like any other soldier then you need new officers, not new men!"

"Sir, we weren't attacked by just any border trash," a young lieutenant said. "It was the James-Younger Gang that raided us."

Mackenzie waved aside the surgeon and leaned up from the divan. "Jesse James," he mused. "He rode with Quantrill and Bloody Bill. He used guerrilla tactics on us."

"Yes, sir," agreed Captain Hawkins. "No disgrace being tricked by Rebel raiders. Some of the best generals have been..."

Mackenzie fixed the captain with an angry stare. "Failure is always a disgrace. Whatever James might have been before, he's an outlaw now. Nothing more. He isn't owed the dignity of military consideration." His sullen gaze swept across his officers. "Governor Wallace already has a $5,000 reward on Jesse James. We're going to double that, even if it has to come out of the pay of every man in this command. I want every bounty killer and scalp hunter in the territory after that man's hide!"

***

The smell of smoke was what drew the warband down into the foothills. Even in his human shape, Broken Fang could smell smoke from seven miles away. The scent of a fire had guided the medicine man and his warriors across the prairie in the dead of night to strike a lonely homestead or a settler's camp many times.

This time, the smell guided them to a very different scene. The warriors prowled among the ruin of the hunting camp, poking about among the ashes of the wickiups. Only a generation ago, Broken Fang's warriors would have looked on the slaughtered young men as so many dead enemies. That was before the great chief Sitting Bull had started his big talk about all red men being brothers, about how they must all come together if they would keep the white man from ravaging the land and poisoning the earth. That was before the Warrior Nation and the spread of the great secret.

Broken Fang stared down at the butchered carcass of the slain elder. In death, the bear-like shape had started to slip away from his corpse, reverting back into a semblance of human form as decay began to rot the skin-changing magic. By the time the body was reduced to bones, there'd be no sign that he'd been anything other than just another man.

If not for the smell of metal and the taint of devil's blood lingering around the corpse, Broken Fang might have thought another skin-changer had killed the bear. The spirits of beast and man weren't always in harmony, and a skin-changer had to be very wary of how much of the beast he let into his mind.

Broken Fang shook his head. The lowest beast was a clean thing beside these crazed white men and their unclean inventions. They could never be content, never be satisfied, until there was nothing left for them to destroy. The dead warriors had been mere boys. Their faces didn't have war paint; they'd been on a spirit walk with their elder, seeking the isolation of the wild in order to commune with the Great Spirit.

Broken Fang's lips pulled back in a vicious grin, exposing the long sharp canine tooth, the wolf-tooth that never turned back when he changed from man into animal. The massacre wasn't old, the scent of the men who had done this would be easy to follow.

As the white men had shown no mercy, as they had spared no one, Broken Tooth and his warriors would do the same.

No mercy. No pity. Only the fury of tooth and claw.

Chapter 7

The James-Younger Gang doubled back upon their own trail several times as they sped across the prairie, putting ground between themselves and whatever pursuit Fort Concho would send after them. Cole didn't think there'd be much to worry about from the Union soldiers. He'd shot up a fair number of the Iron Horses the gang hadn't been able to steal. The danger, as he saw it, was more likely to come from Concho's sister forts, Clark and Richardson. Those garrisons would have full compliments of equipment and regiments that hadn't already been shot up by outlaw raiders.

Jesse's thoughts echoed those of Cole. As they crisscrossed the area, they were careful to give the two forts a wide berth, avoiding them as keenly as they did the cache where they'd stashed the Clantons' blackhoofs and the extra Iron Horses they'd stolen from Fort Concho. After going to all the trouble of stealing the vehicles, there was no sense in leading the Union right to where they were stashed.

They'd have to pick their next target carefully. Jesse's mind wavered between picking something quick and easy like a mine payroll or intercepting a stage and going after something that would set the Yankees quaking in their boots. Rob one of the Texas-Pacific trains or maybe head down to San Antonio and burn down the governor's mansion. Something that would send a clear message to the rattlesnakes in Washington that they didn't have everything their way; that there were still people who weren't just going to lie down and let themselves be walked over by carpet-baggers and ringsters.

Making his escape from Fort Concho on the back of Cole's 'Horse, rather than speeding away on a mount he'd stolen on his own, stuck in Jesse's craw. It irritated his pride to know that ruffians like Ike and Curly Bill were riding fresh mounts while he had been forced to take up his old steed at the cache. The continuing vexation made him irritable and short-tempered to a degree where even the Youngers were giving him a wide berth. All except the imperturbable John. The boy's worshipful regard for the outlaw chief blinded him to Jesse's black mood.

"We're gonna be the terror of the territory now!" John crowed, a grin on his face as his 'Horse raced across the prairie. The outlaws had entered the vastness of West Texas, travelling through a seemingly endless swathe of rolling grass. The inland sea of blue grama stretched to the distant horizon, swaying like ocean waves in the crisp breeze. Cole had chosen this route deliberately; reckoning that with such an unlimited view there could be no chance of any pursuit from the Union forts catching them by surprise.

It took a moment for Jesse to react to John's enthusiasm. He'd been watching Johnny Ringo off to his right, casting more than a little envy on the gilded molding around the engine casing of his 'Horse and the electriwork ornaments fitted to its saddle, their internal RJ-cells making the ornaments whirl in intricate spirals. The steed Ringo had taken must have been that of an officer – probably the commandant himself – to heighten his grandeur when on parade. Whatever its purpose, Jesse coveted the machine. It was too fine by a damn sight for a scoundrel like Ringo. By hook or crook, he intended to get the gunfighter into a hand of poker and take the gilded vehicle from him.

With a bit of reluctance, Jesse glanced away from Ringo's machine. "We're already the terror of the territory."

"Them Yankees ain't gonna forget it, either!" John declared, his hand slapping against the blaster holstered on his hip.

Jesse started to echo the boy's sentiment, but in that instant his sharp eyes spotted a disturbance in the long grass. Years spent as a guerrilla fighter under Quantrill and Bloody Bill, many decades plying the outlaw trail first under Little Arch and then as the leader of the James-Younger Gang, had honed his senses to an almost preternatural keenness. Even from the saddle of his speeding 'Horse, he noticed the disturbance in the swaying grass. For an instant, a brief blink of time, part of that rolling vista had been upset. A clump of grass had shuddered more violently than the greenery around it, the tall stalks moving *against* the breeze.

The outlaw's hand flew to one of his holsters. Every nerve in his body bristled with instinctive alarm. A sense beyond the ordinary thundered in his ears, warning him that danger was near.

The senses of those lying in wait for the outlaws were even sharper than Jesse's. Knowing that their presence had been betrayed to the metal-armed gunman, the lurkers sprang up from the tall grass. Before Jesse could shout a warning to his comrades, dozens of savage warriors materialized before them. Savage, primal cries of wrath and fury howled across the prairie as the Warrior Nation attacked the mounted badmen.

Arrows whistled through the air, their heads ablaze with the ghostly blue fire that so often empowered the weapons of the Warrior Nation. One of the Cowboys was pierced by a glowing arrow, the shaft catching him in the breastbone and rocketing him from the saddle of his 'Horse. The stricken outlaw's body tumbled through the grass, forcing the others following behind to juke and brake to avoid the cadaverous obstruction that had been thrown into their path.

The Indians whooped and howled as they continued to launch flights of glowing arrows into the speeding outlaws. Grotesque in their grisly warpaint, savage in their dress of buffalo hides and bone talismans, the fighters of the Warrior Nation seemed more like inhuman devils than anything born of woman. As each archer loosed his arrow, the warrior would drop down into the grass, hiding beneath the greenery only to pop up again some distance away and loose another deadly shaft of spectral malignance.

For Jesse and the other outlaws, the tactics of the savage warriors were infuriating. The steady volleys of arrows forced them to constantly shift and weave, never presenting the Warrior Nation with a steady target. At the same time, the frustrating habit their foes had of ducking back down into the grass every time they fired an arrow made it all but impossible to draw a bead on them and try to strike back.

Except for their first casualty, the outlaws had good fortune in eluding the attack of their enemy. It was Cole who sickeningly realized why. He shouted in alarm to Jesse and the others. "They ain't fightin' us! They're herdin' us!"

Jesse appreciated the dire import of Cole's warning. The volleys of arrows were driving the outlaws toward the left and it didn't take long to figure out why. Ike Clanton was ahead of the other Cowboys when the grass suddenly disgorged a howling, shrieking savage. The Indian warrior was stripped to the waist, his chest daubed in primitive designs that echoed the warpaint spread across his face. In his hands he gripped a tomahawk, its head blazing with the same phantom luminance as the arrows. The half-naked warrior lunged at Ike, and the speed of the outlaw's 'Horse thwarted the blow directed at his head. Instead of smashing into Ike's skull, the tomahawk scraped across the side of his machine, gouging the metal and sending sparks dancing.

Before the Indian could turn and leap at Ike's back, he was ripped in half by the murderous fire of Curly Bill's blaster. The gory fragments of the warrior were thrown asunder by the brutal discharge, further mutilated an instant later as the trim rustler drove his 'Horse over the mangled carrion.

The slaughtered warrior wasn't the only savage lying in wait for the desperados, however. As they drove their 'Horses further away from the archers, every clump of grass seemed to disclose a hidden Indian. Whooping their primitive war cries, the warriors threw themselves at the mounted badmen with glowing knives and tomahawks, with brutal clubs and vicious spears. A scene of pandemonium ensued as outlaws tried to dodge the screaming Indians who threw themselves at the speeding 'Horses. Jesse saw three of the Cowboys pulled from their saddles by the attacking warriors, the men shrieking as glowing knives and blazing axes bit into their scalps.

Jesse snapped off a shot from one of his blasters, scoring a hit against the flank of an Indian with a tomahawk as he leapt at John's 'Horse. The savage was sent rolling through the grass, one leg nearly torn from his body. The startled John recovered his wits enough to gun his 'Horse forwards and smash down a second warrior as he came charging out from hiding.

There was no chance for Jesse to render aid to any of his other men. Squeezing off that shot at the Indian threatening John had caused him to neglect his own defense. Screeching a long, low howl, a warrior festooned in a long headdress of eagle feathers leapt up onto the crumpled hood of Jesse's steed. Before he could even think to fire at the man, the Indian's glowing club cracked into the outlaw's gun hand, forcing his arm sideways. Jesse braked his 'Horse hard and without a lick of warning.

It was as though the Iron Horse had struck a stone wall. With the weight of the warrior on its hood, the abrupt arrest of the machine's motion set it spinning end over end. Jesse was thrown from his saddle, but the Indian, in a panic, tightened his hold on the hood of the machine. He was still holding fast as the 'Horse spun forward to crash down upon its back.

Jesse ripped his other pistol from its holster as he slammed against the ground. Even as sparks flashed through his vision and his teeth rattled in his jaw, the outlaw brought his blasters sweeping toward his crumpled steed. A blaze of energy, the smell of vaporized flesh, and Jesse's attacker was reduced to a smoking tangle of meat.

"You wrecked my ride," Jesse snarled down at the smoldering corpse. "You shouldn't mess with a man's ride."

A low snarl to his left brought Jesse spinning around just in time to see a grisly figure turn away from the wreck of another Iron Horse. It was an Indian warrior, his body spattered with blood. In his gory hands he brandished a dripping human scalp. At the warrior's feet, Jesse recognized the tortured ruin of the buckaroo Potts.

Jesse took aim at Potts's killer just as the savage came charging toward him, murder shining in the warrior's eyes, eerie blue flame pulsating about the blade of the Indian's knife.

Again, Jesse's arms betrayed him. Aiming directly at the man, his shot instead went wide, scorching the grass just to its left. The Indian didn't give him time for a second shot, leaping on him in a long, low tackle that bounced the back of his head against the sun-baked earth. The knife slashed at Jesse's face, only a last second roll keeping the blade from raking across his flesh.

The Indian's savagery intensified. There was vengeance in the warrior's eyes as he reared back and brought his glowing blade stabbing down at the outlaw's throat.

***

Old Man Clanton peeled off a shot from his blaster, sending another warrior hurtling back as though fired from a cannon. The rustler sent another shot chasing after the savage. "Dry-gulchin' cur!" Clanton roared at the Indian, spitting in contempt in the direction of the corpse.

"They don't seem in any mind to call it quits!" Curly Bill declared. The marauder's shirt was torn and bloodied, his trim beard matted with blood from a wound across his cheek.

"Be that as it may," Old Man Clanton said, a greedy light creeping into his eyes. "These ornery galoots 're gonna help us."

Curly Bill frowned, dabbing a handkerchief at his torn cheek. "How's that?"

The Old Man chuckled darkly. "We got the rides and the shooters Cole promised. I don't see where's we exactly need Jesse James no more." There was an agonized screech from nearby as Johnny Ringo blasted the arm off a spear-wielding warrior, then finished the cripple with a shot that splashed his skull across the grass.

"You fixin' to turn on Jesse?" Ike asked, a trace of horror in his tone.

"I'm sayin' we light out of here and let nature take its course," the Old Man laughed, waving his hand at the ongoing fray. Most of the Cowboys had won their way clear of the fighting. It was Jesse and the Youngers who were still surrounded.

"Don't seem right, leavin' men to die like that," Ike said.

The Old Man glared at his son. "That's a strange sentiment for a man that done what he's already done to that outfit," the rustler snarled. "Or maybe yer forgetin' that little job you done in Tombstone to set the Earps on Jesse's tail? This ain't cowardice, it's just good business." The Old Man laughed again when he saw Ike's embarrassed expression. "You just keep playin' at respectability and leave the strategizin' to me." He made a quick count of the Cowboys around him, scowling at the result. "We've got six men lying around here someplace. That's all we're givin' Jesse James. It was his damn fool idea to attack that huntin' party," he added, ignoring his own endorsement of Jesse's plan. "He called the tune, now he can pay the fiddler." Waving his arm, the rustler pointed westwards and threw his Iron Horse into full gear. The other Cowboys followed after their boss, speeding out over the prairie without a backwards glance at the men they were abandoning.

* * *

Pinned beneath the warrior, Jesse brought one cyborg arm up to catch the descending knife. For an instant, the spectral blade bit into the cold steel of his hand. Then the glowing blade was snapped by the mechanized might of the outlaw's hand as he twisted it to one side. Taking hold of his attacker's neck, Jesse quickly ended the man's life, squeezing until he felt the Indian's bones pulverized by his steel fingers. Grimly, the outlaw tossed aside the warrior's twitching corpse.

Jesse was back on his feet in a flash. Nearby, he could see Bob Younger trying to hold off an Indian armed with a glowing spear with his Bowie knives. The longer reach of the spear was keeping Bob on the defensive, denying him any chance to slip in and strike his foe. Off to Bob's right, Jim was struggling with a hulking warrior gripping tomahawks in each hand. It seemed the two brothers had crashed their Iron Horses together in the confusion of the initial ambush. Cole and John were still mounted, making a wide circuit of the shortgrass as they tried to drive more lurking warriors from hiding. John Wesley Hardin's strategy was both more direct and more brutal, using his smokers to set the grass alight and burn the men right where they lurked. As the fires caught the Indians, the eerie blue glow of their weapons flared brighter, expanded into a purplish aura before fizzling into a wispy gray smoke. The fires caused by the Texan seemed to be poison to the enchantments of the Warrior Nation's spiritual powers.

Those same fires, however, would settle for white men as well as red. Jesse watched the spreading flames with alarm. A shift in the wind, and Hardin's fire would be blown straight back at the outlaws. Indeed, the way the flames were spreading, it might eat up thousands of acres before it spent itself out.

More troubling than Hardin's psychotic pyromania, however, was the desertion of the Cowboys. Jesse could see the Clantons and their followers speeding off across the prairie, turning their backs on the rest of the outfit. Such base treachery made the blood rush hot in Jesse's veins. This was the second time Ringo had deserted him. He was reminded of how Billy the Kid had run out on him and Frank when the Union had come down on them outside of Diablo Canyon, leaving them for dead while he skedaddled off to safety." Ugly visions of what he'd like to do to such traitors blazed before the outlaw's eyes.

Viciously, Jesse snapped off shots from his blasters. Seemingly awed by the rage boiling inside him, his metal arms didn't stray from the demands imposed upon them by his brain. His aim was precision itself when he blasted the leg off Jim's foe and tore the head off Bob's enemy. The same withering stream of shots cut down a squat axeman and pulped the chest of a lanky bowman.

Then, Jesse himself was knocked flat, bowled over by the hurtling bulk of his ruined vehicle. Something inhumanly strong and powerful had tossed it through the air, deliberately throwing it at him. Another inch and Jesse would have been pulverized by the wreckage; as it was, the glancing blow left him sprawled across the ground, his blasters flying from his hands.

A fierce howl rolled across the prairie, and Jesse could see his attacker loping toward him at a run. This creature was more lupine than human in shape, covered in short gray hairs. Its body was lean and powerful, great cords of muscle rippling as it moved. The head was stretched into the elongated muzzle of a wolf, long and sharp teeth gleaming in its fanged smile. One of those fangs, longer and thicker than the others, protruded over the beast's lower lip like the blade of a dagger.

Before the monster could charge him, the deafening roar of an Iron Horse powering forward at full throttle rumbled over the shortgrass. John's steed was just a steely blur as it hurtled toward the huge skin-changer. The boy was trying to ride down the beast. However, he'd underestimated his enemy.

Broken Fang sprang upward just as John's 'Horse came streaking toward him. The great wolf threw its body forward, over and across the speeding machine. Its immense claw raked out at the boy, catching in his brown duster and tearing him from the saddle. John was flung across the ground in a violent tumble, pitching and rolling across the grass. Broken Fang growled at the stunned youth, the animalistic impulse to rend this helpless prey driving the wolf-beast into a fierce leap.

As Broken Fang started to lunge, the metal hood from Jesse's Iron Horse swatted across the monster's face, breaking its dagger-like tooth and ripping the ear from the side of its head. The wolf-beast's leap became a slide, its paws digging at the ground as it spun to face its original enemy. Jesse flung the crumpled hood he'd torn from his steed at the creature; forcing it to duck as the crude missile went sailing over the skin-changer's head.

Then it was Jesse who was charging Broken Fang. He hadn't wasted any time looking for his blasters when he saw John's peril. Much as he had against the bear-beast, the outlaw had only his bare hands to fight the monster.

But they were hands fixed to the mechanical devilry of Dr. Carpathian's perverted science, the wondrous miracle that merged man and machine. Broken Fang's speed was inhuman, but the speed of Jesse's arms, the power behind them, was superhuman.

A bloody cough erupted from Broken Fang's jaws as it reeled back from Jesse's assault. For only an instant, the huge wolf-beast stood there, towering over its enemy. Then the cold glaze of death settled across Broken Fang's eyes and the skin-changer fell to the ground, blood jetting from the hole Jesse's fist had punched into its chest and the ruptured heart behind the wolf's shattered ribs.

Jesse turned away from the dead wolf-man. He could hear the yips and yelps of alarm as the surviving savages fled across the prairie, their appetite for battle lost with the death of their leader. Behind them, the Warrior Nation's warriors left a landscape of mangled bodies and ruined machines. He could see Bob and Cole crouching beside a prostrate Jim, trying to peel away their brother's vest and coat to tend the wounds the enemy had inflicted on him. Danby tried to help by tearing off bandages from an old shirt he removed from his saddlebag. Hardin's contribution was the sadistic execution of every wounded Indian he could find.

Jesse hurried over to where John Younger had been thrown. Reaching down with a bloodied hand, he helped the boy back onto his feet.

"Thanks," John panted, the terror of his ordeal still pounding in his veins. "I...I... thought I was a... goner."

"Just returning the favor, kid," Jesse said, clapping John on the shoulder. He spun the boy around, pushing him in the direction of his brothers. John gave a cry of alarm and ran off to see if he could help the injured Jim. Jesse didn't follow after him. Instead he turned away and stared out across the prairie, not at the fleeing Warrior Nation, but at the distant cloud of dust thrown up by the Cowboys and their stolen vehicles.

"They're some other favors I'll be returning afore long," Jesse snarled under his breath, his steel hands tightening into fists at his sides. He knew it wouldn't be straight away; Cole would want to see that their wounded were tended to first, that they had time to strategize and make careful plans. He knew it might be weeks, even months before everything fell into place. But he knew somehow, somewhere, he'd be paying Old Man Clanton a visit, and only one of them would be walking away from that reckoning.

***

The atmosphere in Colonel Mackenzie's office was heavy enough to cut with a knife. Fort Concho's commanding officer still had half his face swathed in bandages and was forced to employ a cane to amble about the base. Despite the assurances of Governor Lew Wallace and the War Office, little had been done by way of sending fresh troops and supplies to the fort, the attitude of both politicians and military appearing to be along the lines of seeing no point in pouring resources into a place that had already been hit by the outlaws. Lightning had already struck, what sense was there in worrying about its striking twice?

Seated in a leather-backed chair, Over-marshal Wyatt Earp had listened with mounting annoyance to Mackenzie's tirade against his superiors tying his hands and making it impossible for him to do his job. The colonel seemed to take great pains to blame his subordinates for what had happened, but didn't seem to find any fault in his own leadership.

"Colonel," Wyatt addressed the officer. "What you're telling me is that these outlaws absconded with fifteen Iron Horses and enough military-grade weaponry to start a range war. If that don't amount to dereliction of duty, I don't know what does."

Mackenzie lurched up from his chair, shaking the metal talons of his maimed hand at the lawman. "I was fighting to defend this Union when you were still swindling chuckleheads at a faro table! I been shot eight times protecting this nation..."

The metallic rasp of Doc Holiday's laugh scratched across the office. "Sounds to me like maybe you should practice gettin' out of the way sometime."

Mackenzie's eyes narrowed. "You can tell the sort of man you got by the company he keeps," he snarled. "What're *you* palling around with, Earp? Card-artists, lead-bellied 'bots, and cow-town copperheads!"

Wyatt returned the colonel's hostile glare. "You call me what you like," he warned, "but watch how you talk about my friends and my kin."

Standing behind Wyatt's chair, Warren Earp pointed an accusing finger at the officer. "And I ain't no damn copperhead!" he growled. "Just 'cause I said Jesse James must know a thing or three to pull off a raid like this don't mean I hold no Secesh sympathies!"

"Gentlemen, this arguing gets us nowhere." Stepping away from where she'd been standing against the wall, Lucinda Loveless had shucked fine gowns and fancy dresses for riding breeches and a corduroy shirt. She moved stiffly, her body still sore from the injuries she had taken during her recent trip into Carpathian's Kingdom and the ancient Anasazi cliff ruins nestled within the territory's canyons. She had been promised a vacation after successfully bringing to Washington the eldritch Indian relic she'd been sent to find. Any notion of rest had evaporated when news of Jesse's raid on Fort Concho came across the wire. Pinkerton knew, of all his agents, Loveless had developed some sort of connection with the outlaw. She would be the most likely to have some insight into how his mind worked, and what he might be expected to do next.

The problem right now was getting Wyatt Earp to understand that. "We're all on the same side," she reminded the lawmen. "We want the same thing. We want to bring Jesse James to justice."

The smile Wyatt turned toward Loveless was thin and cold. He knew she was a special operative connected with Mackenzie and ultimately his superiors. That didn't impress him any. Not when it was a question of avenging his brother. "*I* want Jessie," he said. "Washington can have what's left when I'm done with him."

Loveless arched her eyebrow. "That sounds like revenge talking, Over-marshal," she said. "What we want is justice. You swore an oath to uphold the law, remember?"

"Ride out to Tombstone and take a gander at my brother Virg, allowing he's not already planted in a bone orchard," Wyatt advised her. "Or better yet, just look over yonder at Morg," he added, jabbing a thumb at the hulking cyborg. "There's some things the law'll just have to settle for second helpings."

"Hell, leave the tin-badge be," Mackenzie told Loveless. "Maybe him and James'll shoot each other and do the nation a big favor." The unmarred side of the colonel's face pulled back in a snide grin. He stabbed a finger against the electric bell set into the side of his desk. The door at the back of his office swung open and a young adjutant poked his head in. "Send the bounty hunter up," Mackenzie ordered. As the adjutant withdrew, the colonel returned his attention to Wyatt. "I'm going to get you some help."

Wyatt shook his head. "I don't need any bounty killers."

"My mistake," Mackenzie said. "I thought you wanted Jesse James." He turned and waved his clawed hand as the door swung open again.

Framed in the doorway was a tall, lean man, a wide slouch hat shading a thin, sharp-featured face. It was the face of a ferret or a weasel, the face of a hunting creature that relies on cunning to wear down its prey. The eyes in that face were like flattened bullets, leaden and lifeless. A long leather slicker, its collar padded with wolf fur, framed the man's body. An armored breastplate, still retaining the glimmer of brass beneath its patina of dust and grime, protected the man's chest, serpentine shapes in the stylized patterns of Meso-America etched across its surface. The heavy gun belt that circled his waist was reinforced with steel ribbing, chains securing the holster against his right leg. At the left side, the grisly spectacle of three shriveled human heads, shrunk and mummified by some obscene process, grinned at the marshal.

"Thomas Tate Tobin," Mackenzie introduced the bounty killer. "Finest tracker and man-hunter in the Territory. Man who single-handedly brought in the Sanchez brothers."

"And where would they be now?" Doc asked.

"Shakin' hands with Old Scratch down in the infernal fires, I reckon," Tobin answered in a voice that sounded like a snake shedding its skin. His hand brushed across the scalps of the shrunken heads on his belt. "Leastwise, those bits that wasn't worth a payday."

"We don't need no damn headhunter!" Warren growled, echoing Wyatt's earlier position.

Tobin sneered at Warren. "You two shop at the same chandler, or are you just wearin' your older brother's hand-me-downs?"

Warren bristled at the bounty hunter's mockery. He started to reach for the long-barreled buntline holstered at his hip, but Wyatt slapped his hand away before his fingers could even start to ease around the grip.

"I want Jesse bad," Wyatt said. "But not bad enough to partner up with a bounty-sniffin' buzzard."

"Then you don't want Jesse at all," Tobin hissed back. "Because I'm the man who can show you right where he is." The bounty hunter jerked the chain he held in one hand, dragging into the office the man shackled at the other end. Wyatt leapt up from his chair in surprise, shocked to find that he recognized Tobin's captive.

The bounty hunter's catch was Ike Clanton.

Chapter 8

Jim Younger's jaws clamped tight against the wooden block in his mouth, his teeth digging into it as pain lanced through his body. A muffled scream dribbled from his throat as raw, searing agony pulsed down every nerve. The stink of his own burning flesh was heavy in his nose, causing him to clench his eyes tight and try to crush the tears of agony streaming down his face.

Bob's face was almost as agonized as Jim's. Standing over the table where his brother lay, the knife fighter pulled his smoking blade away from Jim's exposed chest. He squinted down at the scorched flesh, studying it to see if the heated blade had sealed the outlaw's cut. Grimly, he nodded to the men holding Jim down. Cole and Hardin maintained their unyielding grip on the wounded man's arms and legs while Bob stepped away from the table and approached the iron stove.

"Has to be done," Cole reminded Jim, more too soothe his own conscience than to succor his brother. In his current state, Jim was beyond reasoning, beyond being placated. All that mattered to him right now was pain and making it stop. The necessity of his suffering wasn't even a thought. "That Injun cut you good," Cole said, frowning at the hideous string of slashes running across Jim's chest. "We don't stop the bleeding, you'll end up in a bone orchard."

"Hold him tight," Bob warned as he came toward the table. He'd removed the Bowie knife that had been nestled in the belly of the stove; its tip glowing like it had an RJ fuel-cell fixed to it. He waited a moment for Cole and Hardin to secure their grip, and then he leaned over Jim again. "I'm sure sorry about this," he said as he brought the red-hot blade against Jim's chest. The outlaw's body thrashed wildly as pain shot through him, his back arching as he struggled to free himself.

Cole cursed lividly as Jim slipped one of his arms free. Before he could try to grab him, Jim's hand was clawing at Bob's arm, trying to pull him away and stop the burning pain of the knife he was using to cauterize the wound.

"John, get over here!" Cole shouted, his eyes still fixed on Jim.

John Younger came limping across the cabin. After being pulled from his 'Horse by an Indian warrior, the boy's whole body seemed to be one big bruise. Nothing had been broken though, and such cuts as he'd taken weren't serious enough to warrant the agony Jim was going through. John reached out and pried Jim's hand away from Bob's arm. Slowly, he forced the clawing hand back against the table, holding it flat against it while Bob continued his torturous work.

"Take over for me," Cole told John. "I can't do it by a long chalk." As John grabbed hold of Jim's other arm, Cole stepped away from the table. Immediately after he was relieved of holding Jim down, Cole was clutching at his side, poking his hand under his shirt. He smiled when he failed to see any blood on his fingers. He'd worried that the strain of pinning Jim down had opened his own wound, but it seemed the bandage was holding tight.

Cole turned away from the table and the agony on Jim's face. More than the physical strain, the ordeal of watching his brother suffer was taking an onerous toll on him. He hadn't seen Jim so bad off since the war when they'd ridden into a Yankee ambush. That time, they'd at least been able to fetch a surgeon for him from a Confederate encampment. Now, they'd have to tend him on their own until they could figure out where and how to smuggle him into a doctor.

Cole walked back across the cabin, taking up John's position at the window. Jesse was already standing there, his steely gaze roving the landscape. He didn't look up when Cole approached, just kept his eyes staring out over the rocks.

"How's Jim?" Jesse asked.

"Above snakes," Cole answered. "He's not ready for a boot yard yet, but we need to get him to a doctor to make sure he stays that way. All Bob's doing is makin' sure he don't bleed out before hand."

Jesse nodded, a grimace coming across his features. "That'll be a damn sight dangerous," he said. "Lawdogs will be sniffin' around for us. Blue-coats too, more than like."

"We'll lose too much time sendin' someone out to fetch a sawbones back," Cole said. "Jim don't have any to spare. The Indian that cut him didn't do him no favors. We have to take him out soon's Bob gets the drippin' stopped."

"Hardin burned the doc in San Diablo," Jesse said. "That means our best bet is Tucumcari. Sheriff there's a copperhead. Long's we don't cause him a ruckus, he's liable to play dumb about who we might be."

"Damn those Clantons anyway!" Cole snarled, smacking his fist against the wall. "Yellow-backed polecats! Never expected them to cut dirt like that, leave us danglin' in the wind!"

The wood frame of the window splintered under Jesse's metal fingers as they tightened. It was the only physical sign of the anger boiling inside him. "

"They cut and run, but I don't think it's because they got funkified by them Indians. The Old Man and that barber's clerk son of his probably reckoned they'd got all they needed from stringin' along with us. Lightin' out while them Indians were tryin' to cut us down must have been mighty appealin' to a low-down four-flusher like Clanton."

"You lie down with snakes, yer apt to get bit."Cole looked back at the table, at Jim's agonized form;he looked at John's bruised face, and thought of his own hurts. It was bad enough to think that all of this had come down to the Younger Brothers because of cowardice, but to think it stemmed from treachery, from callous opportunism, it was almost too much to bear. "Well, I figure once we get Jim settled, we go and pay Clanton's brood a visit. It was a long ride from Tombstone and Johnny Ringo told me a fair deal about how the Cowboys operate." The outlaw spat a cold laugh. "And whatever he didn't tell me that brayin' ass Ike did with his brag and boast show."

Jesse turned away from the window, fixed his hard stare on Cole. "We'll have to talk a spell, Cole. Because I'm tired of wearin' other people's dirt. Clanton thinks he can play Jesse James like a fiddle, then he's gonna find out he has to pay the band."

***

"That's the place," Ike Clanton said, waving his hand at the lonely hideout. "Jesse James and the Younger Brothers are all holed up in there. Just like I said."

Lying against the side of a boulder, Wyatt Earp kept his eye pressed against the lens of the optical-magnifier, studying the bleak terrain, checking for any sign of ambush. "You also said we'd find the whole gang lying butchered by Indians on the prairie."

The Cowboy cringed at the snarl in Wyatt's tone. "Listen, I don't know how he got hisself out of there," Ike protested. "He should have been strewed across half an acre by them braves."

"I believe you, Ike," the Over-marshal said. "Not because I trust you, but because I figure you're just the sort of coyote who would leave a fella in a heap of trouble like that." He looked away from the scope, fixing the shackled outlaw with a contemptuous gaze. "What happen, Ike, you get to worryin' that the Warrior Nation didn't finish the job? It start botherin' your insides that Jesse might still be alive and maybe lookin' for the varmint that left him to die?"

Ike yelped as he was struck in the side by the long barrel of Warren Earp's pistol. The thuggish lawman glowered at Ike as he pulled back and swatted him against the ribs a second time with his Buntline Special. The pistol had a barrel over twelve inches long with a large bore and at close range would do maximum damage. "Answer my brother, crow bait."

"You ain't got no cause to treat me poor!" Ike whined, clutching at his side. "Alls I was doin' was sellin' some beef to this here outfit and soon's I realized who they was, I lit out and tried to do my duty as a respectable citizen."

The outlaw's statement brought a raspy, metallic chuckle from further back among the rocks. "If'n a buzzard could sing, it'd call itself a canary," Doc Holiday proclaimed. The gambler's eyes were like chips of ice as they stared from above his breathing mask. "Whatever the song, it's still a buzzard. Mighty fair trail to ride to sell beeves, don't you think? Unless maybe you don't have a good brand artist down there in Clantonville and were afraid somebody'd recognize their stock if you sold them closer to home?"

Ike scowled back at the gambler. "Nobody asked you nothin' lunger," he hissed. "I come in of my own accord. Least I would've if that rattlesnake Tobin hadn't bushwhacked me!" He looked back over at Wyatt, more than a tinge of fear on his face. "You can't let that headhunter keep me," he said, making the statement half demand and half plea. "The governor's promised full pardon to anybody brings in Jesse!"

Warren brought the barrel of his gun slamming into Ike's ribs again. The finely etched design in the metalwork glinted off the light. The length of the barrel put a great deal of space between the two men, so Ike could see it better than he would have liked "You figure you earned that?"

Wyatt waved his brother off. Warren was a good, dependable man in a fight, but he had a mean streak in him as wide as the Missouri. Let him off the leash too long and he'd push his authority to the limit and then some. The last town he'd been sheriff in had voted him out of office because of his brutality; even Bat Masterson over in Dodge had been obligated to ask him to hit the trail after only a few weeks serving as his deputy. Of course, Wyatt had an edge over Warren that his friend Bat would never have. His little brother looked up to him like he was Hercules, King Arthur, and George Washington all rolled into one. The bully had never grown out of his childhood hero worship of Wyatt.

The Over-marshal looked out across the rocks to where the rest of his posse was arrayed, their numbers augmented by a dozen cavalry troopers from Fort Concho. The black cavalry troopers and their lieutenant had proven a mixed blessing; they gave Wyatt the firepower he felt he needed to ensure a fight with the James-Younger gang wouldn't go sour. At the same time, the troopers had been forced to ride blackhoofs commandeered from the inhabitants of San Angelo. The plodding metal horses had slowed the posse's progress to a crawl compared to what they could have managed on Interceptors.

At least the lethargic advance had produced one satisfactory result. Thomas Tate Tobin had parted company with the posse a day out from the gang's hideout, turning Ike over to Wyatt and declaring that he could fare better on his own. Wyatt wasn't deceived. The bounty hunter didn't want to share the reward with anybody. Like a blood-sniffing weasel, he'd gone to try to get Jesse all on his own.

Studying the hideout, Wyatt couldn't help but smile. Whatever had become of Tobin, it was clear that the bounty killer had failed to get Jesse James. Through his RJ-powered glass, Wyatt could see Jesse appear at the window of the cabin. There was no mistaking those metal arms of his. Other men who had appeared at the same window could have been some of the Youngers. There was a man prowling around outside who matched Ike's description of one of the buckaroos who rode with the Youngers. There was no sign of the other brothers or John Wesley Hardin, but Wyatt reasoned they might just be lying low inside either the cabin or the barn-like stables.

Wyatt tried to control the eagerness that burned inside him; the same eagerness that he knew was making Warren even more ornery than usual. Jesse James and his gang, the scum who'd bushwhacked Virgil, were so near he could just about smell them! It took all of his will power to keep from rushing in there with guns blazing. That'd be too easy and a damn sight better than Jesse warranted. Wyatt wanted the outlaw alive, wanted to drag him back through the streets of Tombstone on the end of a lasso. He wanted to lead Jesse up the courthouse steps and then up the steps of the gallows. Virg deserved that. He only prayed that his older brother was still alive to see justice brought crashing down about Jesse's ears.

"Better settle for the pardon and the colonel's handshake," Wyatt advised Ike in a low snarl. "I'll gun you here if you so much as ask about the reward money. That's for men who rode out to help the law, not exploit it."

"You listenin' to him, cur?" Warren snapped, cracking Ike's ribs with the barrel of his Buntline.

"Yes, you damn tin-badge pimps!" Ike growled back. "You just go ahead and keep all the money!"

Wyatt scowled, but didn't bother to correct the rustler's allegation of corruption. It would be wasted breath on his sort. Ike'd never believe the Over-marshal if he said the money would go to Turkey Creek Johnson, Sherman McMaster, and the other men in the posse.

"Doc, I'll be leavin' you up here with Ike," Wyatt said. He turned his cold gaze on the would-be ringster. "We get down there and it looks like they're waitin' for us, you'll know what to do. Unless, of course, there's something Mr. Clanton would like to say first."

Ike turned his head, blanching when he saw Doc Holiday checking the charges on his blasters. Of all the men in his posse, Wyatt could not have picked a more threatening presence. Wyatt, Morgan, even the bullying Warren might have shown some restraint, might have hesitated to sink so low as to shoot down an unarmed prisoner, even if saidcaptive had led them into an ambush. With Doc there wasn't any such question. The gambler had few scruples and even less charity. If he thought Ike'd led the posse into an ambush, he'd shoot the rustler down like a sick dog and not blink an eye while doing it.

"If you hear a loud noise from these parts, that'll be Mr. Clanton shaking hands with the Devil." Doc stuffed one of his pistols back into its holster.

"It's all on the line!" Ike swore, panic in his voice. "Jesse don't know yer comin', I swear it on…"

Ike's oath ended in another yelp of pain. "Don't blaspheme," Warren growled at him.

Wyatt picked up a stone from the ground and tossed it over to where the cavalry lieutenant had concealed himself. The officer turned toward him, nodding when he saw Wyatt give him the high sign. Following the marshal's example, the lieutenant passed word along to the rest of his men. Wyatt turned and repeated the procedure, getting the notice of Turkey Creek and the other men of his posse. The best long-distance shot among them, Turkey Creek raised his rifle and drew a bead on the man patrolling outside. It would be his job to drop the outlaw the moment the ruckus started. All the other men had to do was keep the gang pinned down inside the cabin.

The heavy work was going to fall to Wyatt and his brothers. He wouldn't have it any other way. As he scrambled back down from the rocks, he tapped Warren on the shoulder. "Let's to it," he told his brother. With a last vindictive swat of his

Buntline against Ike's back, Warren followed the marshal down the slope.

The posse and their cavalry allies had parked their steeds below, but it wasn't toward these that the two lawmen made their way. Beyond the Interceptors and Blackhoofs was a gigantic steel behemoth, an armored carriage supported on three enormous wheel sets that looked as though they might have been stripped from a locomotive. Similar to a train engine in overall appearance, the machine boasted a huge blade-like cattle-catcher at the front of its chassis and an elevated turret of armor plate from which projected the menacing barrel of an energy cannon. A mobile fortress, the vehicle was designated as a 'Judgement' by its manufacturers in the East, but for the inhabitants of the west and the still-contested hinterlands of Texas Territory; it was more commonly referred to as a 'lynch-wagon'.

The sight of a posse riding out with the support of one of these armored RJ-engines had killed the fight in many an outlaw band. Only the most reckless or determined would try to hold out against such an imposing machine. A part of Wyatt hoped Jesse would be one or the other. He hoped the outlaw would try to make a fight of it. It would make the bushwhacker's defeat all the more satisfying.

As he approached the rear of the Judgement, Wyatt climbed up into the bed of the carriage. A trio of UR-30 Enforcers sat against the walls, still as statues, blasters holstered at their sides. Standing between the unmoving 'bots, displaying the same stony silence, was Morgan Earp. The cyborg nodded his head when he saw Wyatt.

"Everything is ready," Morgan told the Over-marshal.

Wyatt winced at the steely lack of emotion in his brother's voice or on the cyborg's face. The fact that they were about to attack the lair of the most notorious outlaw in the west didn't seem to concern Morgan whatsoever. Wyatt shook his head.

"When we get up to the cabin, I want you to deploy the 'bots," Wyatt told Morgan. Perhaps because the cyborg was more machine than man, he had an incredible facility with the Enforcers, able to coax them to an efficiency nobody else seemed able to match. Morgan accepted his assignment with the same emotionless nod. Wyatt turned toward Warren, who was just climbing up into the carriage. "I want you in the cab, driving. Get us as close to the hideout as you can and turn the Judgement to its side to give Morg and the 'bots some cover." The Over-marshal glanced over at the steel ladder suspended below the turret. "I'll be up there manning the cannon."

"We'll do for those skunks," Warren vowed.

Wyatt nodded. "Jesse's gonna learn right fast that he's played out his string this time." An ugly light shone in the Over-marshal's eyes. "Nobody bushwhacks an Earp and lives to brag about it."

***

Jesse James had been uneasy for most of the day. Years as a guerrilla fighting for the Confederacy and the years of crime afterward had honed his instincts almost to an animal keenness. There were times when he didn't need any trace of danger to be visible for him to know it was there. He could *feel* when someone was hunting him; when somebody was lying in wait just around the next bend or stalking his trail just over the horizon.

The uneasiness Jesse felt now was no different than the impulses that had kept him one step ahead of the Pinkertons in Missouri after the war. Throughout the morning, he'd kept close to the window, watching and waiting for whatever was coming. He was waiting for the threat hanging over him to show itself, thenhe would know how to react. Maybe it was the betrayal of his mechanical arms, maybe it was Cole's new facility for strategy rubbing off on him, or maybe it was the death of Frank. Whatever the cause, he was trying to be less impulsive and more cautious. Work out a plan rather than leaping headfirst into trouble.

Beside him, Cole was going into detail about how the Clantons and the Cowboys operated. He was fixated on the idea of getting revenge on the gang from Tombstone; maybe that was why Cole didn't have any premonition of danger until the desert solitude was broken by the sharp crack of a rifle shot.

Reflexively, without conscious thought, Jesse's quick-devil arms had his hyper-velocity blasters drawn from their holsters. Through the window, he could see Danby lying in the dirt near the stables, smoke rising from the ugly hole in his chest. The way the dead buckaroo was strewn on the ground drew Jesse's gaze toward the rocks along the eastward rise. He cursed when he saw about a dozen men up there, more than half of them dusky Africans wearing blue shell jackets.

"Down!" Jesse snapped at Cole as the other outlaw turned toward the window. Both men dropped low an instant before energy beams came crashing against the cabin's exterior. At such range, the rifles the men on the ridge were using didn't have the strength to penetrate timber, but as Danby gave mute testament, they still had more than enough punch to put a man in a grave patch.

"Posse?" Cole snarled, drawing his own blasters.

Jesse nodded, peaking up from below the base of the window frame to fire a pair of shots up at the ridge. "Buffalo soldiers from Fort Concho and some civilians," he said.

"Might be a posse from San Angelo paired up with them," Cole suggested. As Jesse dropped down, Cole popped up at the other corner of the window and sent a bolt sizzling up toward the rocks. "Could be vigilantes or bounty hunters. Maybe even them damn Pinkertons!" He glanced over at the table where Bob and John were carefully lifting their brother down to the floor. Hardin was dashing over to the door, one of his smokers in his gloved hand. Cole yelled in warning at the gunfighter before he could pull open the door. "They're up on the ridge!"

Hardin glared at the smoker and thrust it back into its holster. The incendiary bullets that the gun fired weren't made for anything resembling accuracy at more than a hundred yards. Scowling, the gunfighter rushed to where Jim's gear had been stowed, rummaging about until he could find the man's blaster.

"Whoever they are," Jesse said as he snapped off two more shots, driving two of the black cavalry troopers into cover, "they've got us cold. They can sit up there and wait us out until the Jubilee."

As Jesse dropped back down, Cole popped up to fire again. He spat a curse and ducked down again as soon as his head peaked above the sill. "They ain't of a mind to sit anything out! They've got a lynch-wagon rolling up on us!"

Cole's shout froze Hardin just as he was about to pull open the door and add his fire to the barrage against the men on the ridge. "That about tears it," he hissed. "Ain't no way we can fight one of them steel armadillos. Can't even put up a decent fight without a damn sight more iron than we've got."

Jesse kept his head low as another fusillade from the rocks crackled against the frame of the cabin, a few beams even flashing through the open window to scorch the back wall. When he judged the worst of the barrage was spent, he peaked over the sill. What he saw confirmed Cole's grim report. A Judgement rumbled at full steam toward the cabin, dust billowing about it as it charged toward them. He could see the cannon mounted in its turret. It didn't take any stretch of imagination to know that weapon would tear through the cabin destroying anything in its path.

"What'll we do, Jesse?" John Younger asked as he came rushing over to the window with his hands wrapped around an energy rifle.

Jesse frowned as he slid back down to the floor. "Ain't too much choice left. The deck's stacked and them fellas out there are doing the dealing."

***

Wyatt peered through the narrow viewport in the Judgement's turret, watching as the outlaw's hideout rapidly drew closer. He was coming within range now. If he was so inclined, he could use the cannon to blast the cabin into splinters along with everyone in it.

That wasn't appealing to the Over-marshal. He was determined to see Jesse hang for bushwhacking Virgil. That meant dialing down the power of the cannon and using it with far more discretion. It would make a powerful threat, might even persuade the James-Younger Gang to throw down their guns and surrender. If it came to ferreting the outlaw from his lair, then the heavy lifting would fall to Morgan and the Enforcer 'bots.

As the Judgement rumbled closer to the cabin, Wyatt opened fire. Crimson streams of crackling light exploded from the barrel, scything into the roof of the structure, blasting planks and timbers into the sky. Whatever wasn't obliterated outright by the cannon began to burn, crackling and popping as flames licked across them. Ugly black smoke billowed into the air. The Over-marshal turned and barked down to Morgan in the Judgement's cargo bed below. "Get the Enforcers movin', Morg!" he shouted. There was little of Wyatt left to worry about family at this point. He was focused on his objective. Blasting the roof off the hideout would give the outlaws an incentive to keep their heads down while the Enforcers deployed.

The Judgement slowed to a stop a dozen yards from the cabin as Warren cut the impetus of the wheels and brought the armored machine into a leftward slide. Even before the wagon came to a complete stop, Morgan had the back door open and was jumping down to the ground. The cyborg hefted his blaster and sent a shot burning through the cabin wall. Instantly, he was in motion again, his mechanical legs propelling him at superhuman speed to the cover afforded by the corner of the cabin itself.

After Morgan came the robots. Lacking a human brain to guide them, the Enforcers moved with less speed and precision than the cyborg. They clomped down from the bed of the Judgement with the steely resolve only an unliving automaton could exhibit, indifferent to the threat of gunfire from the enemies holed up inside the building.

"Ten-Nine, cover the rest of the troop," Morgan ordered one of the 'bots. At his shout, one of the machines dropped to one knee and began to pump shots from its carbine into the door of the cabin, a steady fusillade to hold back any rush from inside the building. The other Enforcers fanned out, using the armored hull of the Judgement to block their deployment from the attention of the outlaws.

Wyatt glowered through the viewport. He pressed his mouth to the speaking tube set into the side of the turret. When he spoke, his words were transmitted and amplified by the metal horn fixed to the top of the Judgement's hull. "Jesse James! This is US Over-marshal, Wyatt Earp! You are under arrest for the crimes of murder, bank robbery, horse stealing, treason, firing upon a law officer in the performance of his duties, and a dozen other outrages against decency! I have you surrounded! Lay down your guns and come out grabbing sky!"

The Over-marshal waited a few seconds for any sort of response. He expected at least some jeers and catcalls from the outlaws; maybe even a futile sally against the armored Judgement. He wasn't so naïve to think Jesse James would surrender without a fight, but what he didn't expect was to be greeted with stark, stony silence. Wyatt fingered the energy cannon's actuation lever, dialing it to the next intensity. Maybe taking the roof off hadn't impressed upon the outlaws the severity of their situation. Vaporizing one side of their hideout might be the next step to hammering home the hopelessness of their position.

Before Wyatt could fire, the wooden doors of the stables exploded outward. As he brought the turret swinging around, he saw a number of Iron Horses leap out from the building. A half dozen of the machines charged out at full throttle, speeding away across the broken ground. Three of the machines sped northward, two headed south. The last came hurtling straight at the Judgement.

Wyatt tried to train the energy cannon on the 'Horse as it came streaking toward him, but the angle was too steep and he couldn't bring the gun to bear against a target so near to the wagon. The marshal cursed and called down a warning to Warren. "Grab somethin' and hold tight!"

In his effort to shoot down the 'Horse, Wyatt had seen that it didn't have a rider. Its throttle had been tied back with a loop of barbed wire. Aimed by the outlaws while they were inside the stables, the Iron Horse had been launched at the Judgement like a steel thunderbolt.

The Judgement rocked on its chassis as the unmanned machine smashed into it. For an instant, Wyatt thought the wagon would roll over onto its side, but the tremendous impact failed to provide the collision with that much force. Even so, he was thrown about in the turret, his head cracking against the metal hatch, a stream of blood gushing from his torn scalp. His right arm, looped about the top rung of the ladder, felt like it had been all but wrenched from his shoulder. There was a salty taste in his mouth from where his clamping teeth had bit down on his lip.

Dust and smoke drifted before the turret, obstructing Wyatt's view. Angrily, the Over-marshal threw back the armored hatch and peaked up, spitting a mouthful of blood into the dirt. He could see the smoking wreck of the Iron Horsethrown twenty yards away by the collision, its frame reduced to a tangle of tortured metal. Further off, he could see the outlaws making their retreat. There were three Iron Horses speeding to the north, one of them lagging with the double-weight of two riders. To the south there were only two riders. While he watched, he saw them divert slightly, angling toward the ridge and trading shots with the posse up in the rocks.

"Warren, get this buzzard-box moving!" Wyatt roared down at his brother. Warren grunted back an inarticulate reply, but the Judgement's engine soon rumbled into life. The armored wagon started to lurch into motion, but then shuddered to a stop. The grisly shriek of metal grinding against metal assailed Wyatt's ears. Looking down, he saw the crumpled side of the Judgement where the Iron Horse had crashed into it. One of the wheels was pushed up against the hull; Warren's efforts to get it moving only serving to dig the wheel still deeper into the armor.

Cursing, Wyatt dropped down from the roof of the Judgement. He watched in impotent fury as the two bands of outlaws made good their escape. He didn't have to go inside the cabin to know that he'd find some sort of tunnel connecting it to the stables. While he'd been closing the noose around the cabin, Jesse and his men had simply slipped out to their rides.

"Morg, get the 'bots together and see if you can't get the wagon fixed," Wyatt called out to the cyborg. "Warren, hop over to the stables and see if these coyotes left any transportation behind."

The posse up on the rocks broke from cover, the soldiers galloping off on their blackhoofs, the rest of the men speeding down to the hideout on their Interceptors. Wyatt waited until the men drew close, his fury mounting with each passing breath. By rights, they should be splitting off and taking up the outlaws' trail, not stopping for anything. Even for him.

When the riders pulled up beside the crippled Judgement, Wyatt glowered at his men. "I suppose you've got a good reason for dilly-dallying when you should be riding down Jesse James?"

Doc Holiday met his friend's anger with a rasping chuckle. "The cavalry boys have called it quits and are riding back to Fort Concho. McMaster was wounded, so they're taking him along to get patched up." The gambler shook his head. "Long odds if we split up, Wyatt. Unless that lynch-wagon gets rollin' again, we'll have to leave Morg and the 'bots. We just don't have enough mounts for everybody and if we leave the Enforcers behind there won't be enough of us to light out after both packs and still have the advantage."

Wyatt glared up at Doc. "What're you sayin'? We just up and let Jesse slip through our fingers? After what he did to Virg, you have the gall to ask me to do that?"

Doc's voice was an angry hiss when he answered. "What I'm sayin' is we can only chase one pack of them critters. I felt it was your call to make, your choice which one we mosey after."

The Over-marshal nodded in apology to Doc. Being old friends, the gesture was enough to smooth over any ill feeling his harsh words had engendered. He realized Doc was right, chasing after both bands of outlaws would only split their strength, especially with Morg and the Enforcers out of the picture and with McMaster wounded. They had to try for one or the other. Wyatt mulled that over, considering what he knew about Jesse and balancing it against the way the two groups had made their escape. The bravado displayed by the two riders who'd traded shots with the men in the rocks seemed like just the sort of thing Jesse would do.

"We run down those varmints who headed south," Wyatt said. He turned his head as Warren came running back from the stables. "Any luck?"

Warren shook his head and cursed lividly. "They left one 'Horse, but the polecats trashed it afore lightin' out! Won't be doin' anybody any good for quite a spell!"

The report brought a gruff laugh from Ike Clanton. "Gonna be a long walk, marshal," he cackled. "You bein' without a ride now and all. Gotta say you lawdogs really made a mess of things! I hand you Jesse James on a silver plate and you let him get away!"

"Over-marshal to you, Ike!" Wyatt rounded on the smirking rustler. Seizing him by his vest, he dragged Ike from the saddle of his 'Horse and threw him into the dirt. "I ain't the one who's walkin'."

Ike rolled onto his back, his face black with dust and dirt. "You damn star-packer! You can't treat me like this! I got a pardon! I'm a reg'lar citizen now!"

Wyatt scowled at the rustler. "I should burn you down right here, Ike," the lawman hissed. "Do the territory a favor and save some respectable folk a spell of trouble down the road. But, like you say, you got a pardon." He reached into the pocket of his vest and drew out the keys to Ike's shackles. The rustler reached up to take them, but before the keys were in his hands, Wyatt pulled back and threw them into the rocks.

"Work for it," Wyatt told the rustler, leaving the cursing Ike to scramble in the brush. He mounted the outlaw's Iron Horse and turned back to Doc and the rest of his diminished posse. "Turkey Creek, you figure you can pick up their trail?"

Turkey Creek Johnson nodded. "Lessn' they sprout wings or turn Indian," he answered.

Wyatt turned back to his brothers. "Warren, Morg, stick here and see if you can get the lynch-wagon up and rollin'. One way or the other, we'll swing back around for you in a few days."

The lawman stared out across the desolate horizon, picturing in his mind the two outlaws who had sped off toward the south. Jesse James would answer for his crimes. That was a promise Wyatt intended to keep. Come hell or high water, he'd see the bushwhacker swinging from a rope.

Chapter 9

Jesse's Iron Horse sped across the rocky wastes, letting the miles stretch between him and the abandoned hideout. He'd done his best to antagonize Earp and his posse, hoping to goad the lawmen into pursuing him instead of Cole and the others. With Jim wounded, Jesse wanted to give the others as much advantage as he could. If Cole's trick with the spare Iron Horse had played out right, then Earp's lynch-wagon would be immobilized. Unless the lawmancould find enough vehicles for the 'bots,Earp would be forced to abandon a good chunk of his posse with the armored wagon.

Riding beside Jesse, John Younger let loose with a Rebel yell. "Damnation! That was Wyatt Earp and you done made him look ten kinds a fool!"

Jesse couldn't help but smile at the boy's fawning admiration. Still, it was a smile that quickly turned sour. The Earps were the most renowned lawmen in the west. An outlaw with any sense would rather have the whole Pinkerton agency on his tail than the Earps. What had set Wyatt riding out from Tombstone into Texas, Jesse didn't know, but he had an idea it must have had something to do with the Cowboys. Yet another debt he had to take up with Old Man Clanton.

"Don't reckon Wyatt down," Jesse cautioned John. "Man like that'll eat dust a long time if'n he thinks he's got a trail he can follow."

John laughed, his eyes beaming as he met Jesse's gaze. "He catches up to us, then he'll have real trouble! I'd like to see him lock horns with Jesse James!"

Jesse matched John's laugh. It was hard not to feel prideful with John's boisterous faith in his prowess riding right at his elbow. When they'd separated, John had volunteered to ride out with Jesse, leaving his brothers to follow after his hero. It was a testimony to the regard in which John held his hero.

"We'll riddle that star-packer so full of holes, that he'll look like he fell in a briar patch," Jesse agreed. "But let's give him a good chase first," he added with a wink.

John started to say something in reply when his 'Horse juked violently to the side. Smoke belched from the machine's engine. As the boy tried to wrestle with his machine, he cried out in pain, smoke rising from his hands and little slivers of electricity crackling from his teeth. The Iron Horse skewed downwards, plowing nose-first into the earth and launching John into the air.

Jesse didn't have time to swing back around and come to the boy's aid before his own steed was struck. The outlaw saw the flash from a stony butte, even fancied he could see the crackling finger of lightning that came streaking down to sizzle across the Iron Horse. Unlike John, he didn't try to wrestle for control of the machine. Twisting the control neck one direction, he threw himself in the other. The 'Horse veered off, mimicking a half-circle before it dipped its nose and slammed into the ground.

The outlaw landed hard, feeling all the wind kicked out of him as he rolled in the dirt. Before he could rise, he was smashed flat by the explosion of his crippled machine. Shrapnel from the machine scythed overhead, gouging the earth around him. He bit down on a cry of pain as a red-hot sliver of steel sliced across his leg. Pain was something he didn't have the luxury to feel. Not with a sniper lurking somewhere up on the butte.

Picking himself up as best he could, Jesse drew his blasters and fired. He didn't have a target that he could see up on the butte, so instead he fired at the ground between himself and the ambusher. The shots kicked up a screen of dirt and rock, a veil to hide Jesse from the sniper.

The trick worked. When the sniper's electric blasts came crackling down at Jesse, they lacked the precision of the shots that had disabled both of the Iron Horses. The outlaw dashed along, favoring his injured leg as he made for a cluster of boulders. The blind fire of the sniper crackled all around him, sizzling against the ground and leaving ugly craters with each blast. Unable to draw a bead on Jesse, the ambusher was trying instead to lead his prey, following the outlaw's shots and trying to predict his position.

Jesse nearly reached the boulders before one of the ambusher's shots caught him a glancing blow. The entire side of his body tightened like a tense muscle, his metal arm falling limp at his side, fingers clamped so tight that the grip of his hyper-velocity blaster was crushed out of any semblance of shape. He crashed to the ground, shivering as though seized by an epileptic fit. Through the screen of dust, he could see a figure in a long coat and sporting a strange shirt of gold step out from a crevice in the side of the butte, a massive rifle clenched in his hands.

Jesse could guess the sort of trash that had sprung the ambush. Not one of Earp's men, but a scavenging bounty hunter. He'd probably watched the whole fracas at the hideout from a distance and then hurried off to intercept whoever slipped through Wyatt's trap. Jesse only hoped there weren't more of the vultures lying in wait for Cole's group.

Any moment, Jesse expected another blast from the bounty killer's rifle to finish him off. When the shot never came, he realized the scum either thought he was dead or wanted to take him alive. Either way, it gave him a slight edge over his adversary. It was an edge he'd have to exploit to the fullest if he was going to win out over the hunter.

Straining his ears, Jesse listened for the sound that would tell him it was time for action. With his left side still quivering, he didn't know if he'd be able to make it to the rocks. He also knew that if he didn't try, he was as good as a dead man. John would be as well, if the boy had survived the wreck of his vehicle. With the big reward on Jesse, a bounty killer wouldn't look twice at John Younger; he'd be more apt to simply gun him down and save himself any trouble.

The noise Jesse's ears strained so desperately to hear finally reached him. It was the clatter of loose rocks rolling down the slope. The bounty hunter was starting his descent. On such treacherous ground, the ambusher would be paying more attention to his footing than he would the men he'd shot down. That would give Jesse a small lead, perhaps just the briefest instant when the bounty killer would be distracted. It'd take brass and a fair bit of luck to make it to the rocks, but the outlaw had been in tougher spots with nothing more than high hopes and recklessness to see him clear. He just had to trust that his string hadn't run out yet.

Mustering all the strength in his body, clenching his teeth tight against the pain in his side, Jesse lunged up from the ground. Half falling, half jumping, he propelled himself toward the rocks. Up on the slope, there was an instant of confused violence as the bounty hunter rushed downward, seeking a spot of even ground from which to take another shot at the outlaw. Jesse didn't give him the chance. With another bone-wracking effort he threw himself forwards again, slamming down hard into the packed earth at the base of the nearest boulder. The rock just above his head exploded in a burst of crackling energy, splinters of stone peppering his face. He felt his brain pounding against the inside of his skull from the concussion of the blast. It took more strength than he thought he had to reach out with his right arm and claw his way back behind the boulder. If not for the enhanced power of his mechanical arm, he doubted he could have managed to drag himself to safety before another shot from the bounty man's rifle cracked against the boulder.

"Give yerself up!" the bounty hunter shouted. "You ain't got food and you ain't got water! I can sit you out, so you might as well save us both the inconvenience!"

Breathing hard, Jesse pried the crumpled pistol from his frozen left hand and transferred it to his right. His other blaster was lying out there on the ground where he'd fallen. In fact, it had been a bit of a blessing that his left hand had locked itself so tight about the other gun. The grip might be ruined, but the gun was still functional. Accuracy might be a problem, but there was no way the bounty hunter could know that.

Groaning with the effort, Jesse leaned around the boulder and peeled off a shot in the direction of his ambusher. The shot went wide, but it did send the ambusher scrambling down the slope, rushing to get himself some sort of cover. More importantly, it impressed on the man that he was still up and able.

The bounty hunter started to dash toward a stand of cactus, but changed direction abruptly, diving toward John's Iron Horse. Jesse snapped off another shot at the ambusher, but again the blast went wide of the mark. Before he could fire again,

Jesse saw the man pick John off the ground, holding the boy before him like a shield.

"I've got your partner here, James!" the bounty man shouted. "If'n you don't want to see me excavate his head, throw down yer iron and come out!"

"Don't do it, Jesse!" John shouted back. "Don't mind me, just plug this buzzard!" The boy's outburst ended in a moan of pain as the bounty killer smashed the butt of his rifle into the outlaw's back.

"Come out or the kid dies."

Jesse could tell it was no bluff. The scavenger would gun John down the instant he didn't have any use for him, whatever Jesse did. There were a few cards left in the outlaw's hand, however. The bounty hunter was after reward money and it was pretty obvious he didn't favor the notion of sharing it with anyone.

"Better settle for the reward on him," Jesse shouted from the rocks. "That's one of the Youngers you got there!"

The hunter's voice was a thin snarl. "Yeah, and its Jesse James I got pinned down in them rocks."

"Settle for what ya got, buzzard," John hissed in his captor's ear. He'd caught the turn of Jesse's taunting. "Wyatt Earp and his whole posse are gonna be comin' this way any minute."

The bounty killer cast an anxious gaze over his shoulder. He cursed when he saw a distant cloud of dust. Swinging back around, he sent a stream of invective at Jesse.

"Real simple, buzzard," Jesse called out. "Stay here and wait me out, you can share out the whole reward with Wyatt's posse. Or you can take my partner in by yerself and keep the whole poke. Better make up yer mind quick."

The scavenger glared at John, studying him with an avaricious eye. "Which one are you? Bob?" he asked, almost visibly appraising the value of his catch.

"Guess," John spat at his captor.

The bounty man took a step back, and then brought John low by smacking his rifle against the boy's head. Before the outlaw could fall, the killer sprang forward and caught him. "I'll be takin' the boy!" he yelled up at Jesse's refuge. "You can give the Over-marshal my apologies that I didn't wait around fer him."

Jesse watched as the hunter carried John to the crippled Iron Horse and slung him across the saddle. If he'd been able to trust his aim, Jesse might have picked the man off in that moment of vulnerability, but with his arm acting up and the grip of his blaster twisted, he didn't risk shooting. He could only play the part of an observer as the bounty man sat behind John's sprawled body and spurred the 'Horse into action. The damaged machine started off. It was obvious to Jesse that the machine couldn't get far, but it was equally obvious that the bounty hunter didn't need it to. He had his own steed somewhere up behind the butte.

As the assassin started off, he made a final strike against Jesse's refuge, snapping off a string of shots, not from his rifle, but from the pistol holstered at his side. The outlaw was forced to crouch down as splinters of rock exploded from the face of the boulder. He made one halfhearted attempt to return fire, his shot again being thrown wide. It was just as well. With John slung across the saddle ahead of him, any shot that took the bounty hunter was just as likely to claim the boy too.

Snarling in frustration, the scavenger sped away with his prisoner, resigned to leave Jesse behind in the rocks. The last the outlaw saw of him, the ambusher was swinging around the far end of the butte.

The bounty man's retreat seemed to drain Jesse's body of the desperate vitality that had forced him to the Herculean efforts needed to get him into the rocks. The outlaw all but collapsed as the strain of his recent exertions came flooding through his body. Every hurt, every speck of fatigue, seemed magnified by those long minutes of denying them. Like a weary moth, Jesse wilted against the rocks. His last conscious thought was the image of a rabbit hole, then darkness swallowed his senses and he knew nothing more.

***

The sound of angry voices roused Jesse from the clutch of black oblivion. Except for a thin sliver of light, everything around the outlaw was darkness. Dimly, he remembered collapsing to the ground and sliding into a declivity beneath one of the boulders – the rabbit hole that figured so prominently in the confused muddle of his recent thoughts. Without moving his head, without twitching a muscle, he rolled his eyes toward the little sliver of light, the narrow gap that yawned beneath the edge of the boulder. It was through that gap that the voices drifted down to him.

"Has to have been Tobin and that Fancy Dan rifle of his," one of the voices cursed. "He must have laid up somewhere in the rocks and waited for 'em to ride by. Probably hit 'em before they knew he was there."

The exclamation was answered by a voice Jesse recognized as belonging to Wyatt Earp. The Over-marshal's tone was as murderous as a ten-button sidewinder. "I should have shot that bounty-sniffing coyote when he decided to light out and try a lone hand! Well, if he was here, then we know where he's taking Jesse. He'll be riding back to Fort Concho for the reward. He'll have taken him alive; too, otherwise he'd just have hacked off the head and left the rest for the vultures."

A raspy, metallic voice urged Wyatt to caution. "If Tobin's taken him to Concho, then that's an end of it."

"The hell it is, Doc!" Wyatt snarled back. "We'll ride back there and demand Mackenzie turn Jesse over to us!"

"You can't buck the Union," Doc warned. "I know you're upset about what he done to Virg…"

Jesse's brow knotted in confusion. It had bothered him that Wyatt Earp had taken up his trail, but now the discussion between the lawmen put things in a clearer light. For some reason, Wyatt thought the James-Younger Gang was responsible for holding up a bank in Tombstone and shooting his brother Virgil. It didn't take any imagination at all to see the treacherous hand of Old Man Clanton behind such a play. It seemed blasters and Iron Horses weren't the only things the Cowboys had hoped to get from their alliance with Jesse James. They'd also planned things so that they'd have a free hand back home while the Earps were busy pursuing a vendetta against Jesse James.

Well, the Clantons would have a few things coming back to them as soon as Jesse got himself clear of Wyatt and his posse. Nobody made a fool of Jesse James! He'd taken dirt from too many people; from the filthy Union and from the savage Indians and from that lying Carpathian. The Cowboys weren't going to pass this one over on him. He'd settle this treachery and pay the varmints back in their own coin.

"We're going back to Concho," Wyatt declared. "That's the end of it. If Mackenzie has Jesse, he'll have to cough him over. The Union can have him after he stands trial in Tombstone."

Doc's laugh was like the hiss of escaping steam. "After you try him or after you hang him?" the gambler asked.

Wyatt's answer was uttered in a hiss every bit as grisly as Doc's laugh. "That depends on how Virg is when we get back to Tombstone. If I have to plant him in Boot Hill, he won't be going there alone. I'll see the man responsible dead, if it means bucking the army, the Pinkertons, and the whole damn government!"

Down in the hole, Jesse carefully squirmed his arm out from beneath his body, pointing his blaster up at the opening. So far, the lawmen hadn't found him; but if they did, he was going to make sure a few of them rode along with him on the trail to Hell.

"Here I was thinkin' you had some respect for that bit of tin you wear," Doc said. "Imagined you were after more'n just revenge. I thought you were seekin' justice. Ain't that what you say Virg deserves?"

Jesse tensed as he heard footsteps starting to circle around the boulder. Whoever was prowling around the rocks was near enough that he could hear the creak of their leather holsters as they moved and smell the grease in their hair. Shutting one eye, he squinted down the barrel of his blaster and waited for a face to peak down at him. He felt like a rattler, all coiled up and waiting to strike. And just like a rattler, he knew he wasn't apt to get the chance for a second attack, so he'd have to make it count. The little sliver of light shining down into the hole flickered as a shadow passed across it.

"I won't be talked out of seein' Mackenzie," Wyatt said in firm, unyielding voice. "You can ride back to Tombstone if it makes you uncomfortable, but I'm goin' to Concho and I'm tellin' that eagle-button I want custody of Jesse."

Doc sighed, a sound that bubbled like boiling coffee in the filter of his mask. "They say never stand betwixt a fool and his folly," he rasped. "But that don't hold when the fool's your friend. If your dead set on this, I'm plumb dumb enough to stick to you."

A few pebbles trickled down into the hole as one of Wyatt's posse walked past the boulder. Jesse could almost picture the man staring down at the ground, studying the marks he'd left behind. Slowly, his finger tightened around the trigger of his blaster.

"Doc's ridin' with me to Fort Concho," Wyatt's voice was raised to a shout, carrying to the scattered members of his posse. "The rest of you light back and see if you can help Warren and Morg get the Judgement runnin' again. We'll head back for Tombstone after I palaver with Mackenzie."

The man near the boulder called out to the Over-marshal. "We'll string along with you Wyatt. We come this far."

"Thanks, Turkey Creek, but two's enough for this job. If Mackenzie won't hand over Jesse, it won't do any good gettin' the rest of you involved."

"What he's tryin' to say is there's no use in everybody goin' against the law," Doc elaborated. "My reputation's already blighted enough that another black spot won't make no nevermind, but the rest of you have your respectability to take into consideration."

"I ain't of a mind to jaw over this all day," Wyatt said. "Me and Doc are goin' and the rest of you ain't. That's an end to the discussion."

Jesse relaxed as he heard Turkey Creek walking away from the boulder. He listened as the lawmen returned to their Interceptors and spurred them into action. The racket of their firing engines soon faded off in the distance, four of the machines heading northward, two of them rocketing eastward in pursuit of Tobin and the outlaw they were certain he'd captured.

It never occurred to Wyatt Earp that the man he wanted so badly had been practically under his very feet.

Sometimes the turn of Jesse's luck astonished even him.

Jesse waited the better part of an hour before he finally crawled out from under the rock. His left arm still felt like a lump of dead iron dragging on his shoulder, but at least most of the numbness had left his leg. He was able to move with at least a semblance of normality, though he still felt a shot of pain rush through him whenever he planted the sole of his foot against the ground. The same pain struck at him whenever he bent his knee at too sharp an angle.

The outlaw scowled as he contemplated the bleak, inhospitable terrain around him. His infirmity would have been just an inconvenience in more settled surroundings, but out here in the wild, where the odds were already weighted against him, his debility could prove fatal.

One glance at the wreck of his Iron Horse was enough to tell him there'd be no salvaging the machine. A quick examination of the ground showed him that the blaster he'd dropped was gone. Purloined by one of Wyatt's lawdogs, Jesse was certain. He shook his head as he stared down at the crumpled, twisted weapon in his hand. That abused gun was the only tool he had, the only weapon available to see him safely across the hostile west Texan desert.

Squinting up at the sun, Jesse tried to figure out where he was and where he should be going. The frantic ride away from the hideout hadn't left him much opportunity to consider his bearings, and he wasn't as familiar with the area as Cole and the Youngers were. Bitterly, he once again wished Frank was with him. His brother would have made it his first priority to study the lay of the land and pick out the spots where they could secure supplies and remounts. Frank was always the strategist; he was always the one who figured out how something could be done. All Jesse did was tell the gang what it was they were going to do. The details had always been left to Frank.

The Yankees had taken so much from Jesse; it still seemed unreal to him that they'd taken Frank too. His older brother had seemed indestructible to him, able to wade through a shootout without batting an eye, able to brain his way into any bank or supply depot. It chafed his pride to admit it, even to himself, but Frank had been a better man than he was. Left on his own, Frank would have settled down after Little Arch got himself gunned by the law. It had been Jesse's vindictive streak, his refusal to accept the carpet-baggers and the glad-handing Yankees, that had Frank follow him when he formed the James-Younger Gang. Devotion to his brother, more than anything, had kept Frank riding the outlaw trail.

Jesse choked down on the regret and guilt that welled up inside him, and he tried to turn it into something else. Shame wouldn't give him the sand to see his way back to civilization. Thinking about Frank, he turned his mind to the men who had taken him away. He thought about John Younger, the boy who idolized the great Jesse James, and how he'd been bushwhacked and abducted by that bounty killer.

Feeling the fire of determination coursing through his veins, Jesse turned eastward. Wyatt claimed Tobin would be taking John back to Fort Concho. Following the Over-marshal's trail would be Jesse's first step in helping the boy. Grimly, the outlaw started out across the desert.

All through the day and long into the night, Jesse continued to plod along. The pain in his left leg had eased somewhat, or else become so persistent that he became so accustomed to it, that it stopped vexing him. His left arm still hung limp at his side, but in those brief moments when he allowed himself to stop and rest, Jesse found he could force the fingers of his hand to twitch, allowing he concentrated hard enough. Like his body, the shock from Tobin's glancing shot seemed to be wearing off from the mechanisms in his metal arm. However treacherous he had proved, Jesse had to confess that Carpathian knew his business when it came to designing machinery.

As darkness settled over the wastes and night cast its cloak over the sky, Jesse pressed on. The chill of the desert darkness cut at him like a thousand icy knives, yet still he continued his long march through the desolation. Eyes focused on the trail left by the Interceptors of Wyatt and Doc, Jesse didn't appreciate the crumbling edge of the arroyo until it gave out beneath his feet.

The outlaw slid down into the declivity, crashing into a tangle of mesquite. Lying on his back in the dirt, the fatigue he had resisted for so long closed about him. The tyrannical call of sleep drowned all other thoughts, smothered all other intentions. One effort to raise himself off the ground, and then Jesse's head slumped back in the dirt. For a minute, he blinked up at the stars. Then all was darkness.

It was the feel of steel against his throat that awakened Jesse. The outlaw didn't move, didn't twitch a muscle. The only sign of life was when he opened his eyes. When he did, he found himself staring up into the lean, hawk-like face of an Indian. The man's coppery skin was daubed with paint, the white slashes and whorls of the Warrior Nation.

More than the man, however, Jesse noticed the long cavalry saber clenched in his fist, its point pressed against Jesse's throat. A single thrust and the Indian would skewer him like a pig.

"Iron Knife," a sharp voice called from the darkness. "Do not kill. This man must not die."

The Indian with the saber scowled, his face contorting into an inhuman expression of viciousness. "The stink of abomination is on him, Two Wolves!" He pressed the sword just a little closer, drawing a bead of blood as the tip cut Jesse's skin. "He is part devil already."

"He is Metal Hands," Two Wolves declared. Jesse could see the other Indian emerge from the darkness. Like Iron Knife, he had the squat build of the desert and his face was painted for war. "He is the one from the medicine vision. You must not kill."

"I do not believe the medicine," Iron Knife snapped at the other warrior. "I do not believe anything that says I must not kill the white man."

The expression on Two Wolves' face became grim. "Then you do not trust the Great Spirit. You do not trust those to whom He speaks."

The accusation took some of the fire out of Iron Knife. With an inarticulate snarl, the Indian drew the sword away from Jesse's throat. "I will kill you," he glared down at the outlaw. "But first I will take you to see Geronimo."

Chapter 10

Thomas Tate Tobin stalked across Colonel Mackenzie's office, the bounty hunter's fist clenched around the handful of greenbacks he'd been issued by Fort Concho's purser. "Fifty dollars?" he growled. "You're tellin' me I traded shots with Jesse James and crossed up Wyatt Earp for fifty dollars?"

Mackenzie leaned back in his chair, his metal fingers drumming against the top of his desk. "That's the standard reward for any member of the James-Younger Gang. Now if you'd managed to bring in Cole or Jim, you'd have the individual rewards being offered for them. Hell, you didn't even bring in Bob Younger."

Tobin spun around, slamming his hands against the desk and leaning over the colonel. "You suggestin' maybe I should fetch that boy out of your guardhouse and let him run about a spell so's he gets as notorious as his brothers?"

"Maybe you should have tried harder to get Jesse James if you wanted a big pay day." The stern words came from Lucinda Loveless. The Pinkerton operative strolled across the office, her lovely face curled in contempt, her eyes flashing angrily at Tobin. As far as she was concerned, the bounty hunter was no different than an assassin or a range detective; a hired killer devoid of decency and honor. The idea of paying out any blood money to this human vulture was repugnant to her. "If you decide to play it safe and settle for an easy catch, don't go bawling to your government when you don't strike the mother lode."

Tobin leaned away from the desk, glaring at Loveless. "I was head-huntin' Mex for Colonel Tappan when you weren't even a gleam in your daddy's eye. I was one of two men to escape the Battle of Turley's Mill during the Taos Revolt. I was the man who brought back the heads of the Espinosas when every posse and cavalry troop in the territory couldn't."

Loveless turned a cold smile on the bounty hunter. "It sounds to me like you've been at your job too long. Like an old wolf whose fangs are getting too weak to hang onto prey."

"You ten-penny painted cat," Tobin growled back. "Waddle back to yer hog ranch!"

The bounty hunter's crass insult brought Mackenzie up from his chair. The colonel's steel fingers clenched tight as he shook his fist at Tobin. "You ain't got no call to speak to a lady like that, you flea-ridden dog."

Tobin sneered at the outraged officer. "You blacksmithin' for this horse-poker?" he snarled. Before he could say anything more, Tobin felt the cold press of a gun barrel against his side. He turned his eyes toward Loveless, surprised to see a snub-nosed derringer in her slender hand. "Never figured you for a pocket advantage," he said, raising his arms from his sides.

"Take your blood money and get," Loveless told him. "You can be grateful I'm a forgiving sort and didn't take any offense to what you said... this time."

The bounty hunter slowly backed away, bowing his head ever so slightly toward Loveless. "My apologies, ma'm," he said, waving the bills in his hand. "I forgot myself in my excitement. I promise I'll be more mindful of my company when I bring in Jesse James." He looked back to Mackenzie. "You'll have the reward ready, I trust."

"Ten thousand, but I want him alive," Mackenzie reminded the killer. "I've got a hemp party all planned for that bushwhacker."

Tobin smiled as he turned toward the door. "Start makin' out yer invite list, Bad Hand, because Jesse's on borrowed time."

Loveless waited until the bounty hunter was gone before she returned her derringer to the sleeve of her blouse. She was sorely tempted to have Mackenzie arrest Tobin, throw the bounty killer in the guard house along with John Younger. She, however, resisted that temptation. She knew it wasn't Tobin's lack of respect for her or the law that fired her resentment, but rather the thought of the back-shooting killer being at liberty to track down Jesse. She understood that Jesse was the enemy of everything she'd sworn to protect and uphold; he was an unreconstructed rebel, a man still living like a Secesh guerrilla. This strange fascination she held for him, this attachment she had formed; it was a toxic, poisonous thing. By rights, she should be happy an accomplished assassin like Tobin was out on Jesse's trail. Anything that would bring an end to the outlaw's campaign of robbery and murder was something she should support.

Maybe it was naïve of her, but Loveless couldn't bring herself to accept the mantra of the ends justifying the means that Pinkerton and the officials in Washington seemed so ready to adopt. She knew Jesse had to be brought in, but when it happened, she wanted it to be clean and above board. When the outlaw was apprehended, it should be lawmen who brought him in, not some bounty hunter sniping him from half a mile away.

"You ever hear how a Chinaman gets rid of a snake?" Mackenzie asked. "He sends a bigger snake down into the hole. That's what I feel like I'm doin' right now."

"The only way that prairie tenor will get Jesse is by pluggin' him in the back," Loveless said.

Mackenzie shook his head and laughed. "I'm sure he'd favor that approach, but he's too greedy to give up on the bonus fer bringin' Jesse back alive."

"Maybe, but I don't relish the idea of relying on a bounty hunter." Loveless fixed the colonel with a questioning look. "Have you considered my idea?"

Mackenzie frowned. He reached into his desk and produced a sheaf of papers. "I decided against it, ma'am. I'm not keen on the risk involved."

"It's my risk to take," Loveless reminded him.

"Not entirely," Mackenzie smiled. "If anything went wrong, you can bet the War Office would make me the goat. John Younger might not be a big noise, but he is one of the Youngers. This idea to turn him loose so's you can trail him back to Jesse… I'm sorry, but I'm not gonna stake my career on it. Been shot too many times defending this country to give it up on a cracked scheme like that."

Loveless came around the corner of the desk and brushed her hand across the colonel's cheek. "He's the best chance I have of finding Jesse. You know that."

Mackenzie pulled away from the woman's caress. "I've already arranged for his transfer. It's out of my hands." He laughed and flexed the metal talons of his maimed hand. "Or what's left of 'em anyway."

"Then I'll take it up with the warden at the territorial prison," Loveless said, stepping away from the colonel's chair.

"I'm not sending him to the territorial prison," Mackenzie's voice fell cold. "I'm sending that ringy to Andersonville."

Loveless stared in disbelief at the seated colonel. Andersonville housed the most notorious Confederate prison camp of the conflict; it had been renamed as Camp Lincoln and employed for the reeducation and rehabilitation of 'recidivist Secesh.' Most of those sent to the prison to be reconstructed never left. Loveless had never been there herself, but she'd heard it described by other Pinkerton agents as the worst hell-hole in America.

"You can't do that," Loveless protested. "John's too young to have fought in the war. He's not a Secessionist."

"He's a Younger, and that's good enough," Mackenzie countered. "That little mongrel helped shoot up my fort. Now, he can rot in Camp Lincoln." The colonel perked up when he saw Loveless head toward the door of his office. "Leaving so soon, Agent Loveless?"

"I have a job to do," Loveless reminded him. "I came to Fort Concho trying to get a lead on Jesse James. Now you're shipping my only resource to Camp Lincoln."

"So what are you going to do?" Mackenzie asked.

"That isn't your problem," Loveless told him. "If I were you, I'd be more worried about what Jesse James and Cole Younger are going to do if they find out you've shipped John off to Camp Lincoln. Somehow I think they might prove a sight more debilitating to your career than Washington or the War Office."

***

Sweat dripped from every pore in the medicine man's body, streaming into a puddle on the dirt floor of the lodge. Hot vapor filled the tiny room, a stifling mist that transformed the whole lodge into an indistinct gray cloud.

Within that cloud, the medicine man could see two great serpents writhing. They were as pale as snow, their rattles flecked with gold like slivers torn from the sun. A shrill, whistling sound rose from the rattles as they shivered at the end of each serpent's tail. It was the voice of the great iron snake that crawled across the land,leaving a metal trail behind in its wake. As the sound of the whistling rattles grew louder and rose to a frenzied wail, the serpents balled themselves into tight coils. Their flattened heads arched toward each other, their forked tongues flickering as they tasted the air.

When it seemed the whistle of their rattles could grow no louder, the two snakes struck at each other. Their fanged jaws clamped tight about the other's scaly neck. An ugly purple stain spread through each reptile, discoloring the snowy scales. The fangs of each snake pumped poison into its enemy, unrelenting and merciless. Only when both serpents were turned completely purple, only when their rattles lost strength and fell silent, did the reptiles relent. Bloated with poison, their fangs still sunk into each other's neck, the two vipers fell dead.

The gray clouds swept in, blotting out the spirit vision. The medicine man rose from his crouch and flicked the sweat off his fingers before he drew back the buffalo-hide flap that closed off the sweat lodge. He stood for a moment at the entrance, letting his body adjust from the sweltering miasma within, to the comparative cold without. Then, with a firm step, he descended the sandy slope to the camp below.

Young warriors and veteran raiders alike bowed their heads respectfully as he strode past them, many of them touching the iron of their knives or guns as a sign of devotion to him. For he was more than just a medicine man and spiritual leader to these men, he was also their war-chief. Short, stocky of build, his face so weathered the skin seemed more leather than flesh, the Indian was the most notorious marauder in the whole of the American southwest. His name was the terror of a thousand communities from Texas to Arizona and from Utah to Mexico.

He was Geronimo.

As he walked among his followers, Geronimo pondered the vision he had seen. It was a vision that the spirits had shown him many times; always two pale snakes, striking at one another, and killing each other with their poison. After the first time he had seen the vision, he had known its meaning. Each time the vision reappeared, it only reinforced his belief that the way of Sitting Bull was not the way to victory. The war-chief was the great voice of the Warrior Nation; he had forged an alliance between all of the great tribes, overcoming the entrenched animosity of generations. But Geronimo was more than just another chieftain. He had the sight; he had the gifts and knowledge of the medicine man. He had seen that there was another way to stop the white man.

Sitting Bull urged all the tribes to unite and drive the white man's poison from their lands. Geronimo saw another way. The two snakes. Not so long ago, two great white tribes had fought. If their war had persisted, they would have destroyed one another. The vision he had seen seemed to urge him to help the whites make war again.

Geronimo marched through the camp, past the clusters of wooden wickiups. At the very center of the camp, he found what he was seeking. Lashed to a wooden frame by rawhide thongs was the outlaw the Warrior Nation called 'Metal Hands,' and who the white man knew as Jesse James. Many times the medicine man had seen this face in his spirit visions and heard the outlaw's name whispered on the wind. He had an important part to play in bringing the white tribes to war again. It was for that reason he had warned his warriors that they must never harm Metal Hands if they should see him, but must instead bring him to stand before their war-chief.

A large band of warriors stood guard around the prisoner, knives and hatchets at the ready. It was more the threat of the warriors than the restraint imposed upon him by the rawhide bindings that kept the outlaw confined. The Warrior Nation knew the strength in Jesse's mechanical arms and the infernal power of the devil's blood that gave them that strength. It was the great poison which had polluted the spirits of the white men and driven them to ravage the land in search of the red gold. Only evil could come from such poison, an evil that had to be exterminated before it destroyed the balance set in place by the Great Spirit.

Many of Geronimo's warriors held with the teaching of Sitting Bull that, anything touched by the red gold had to be destroyed immediately. This was mostly because they couldn't understand their own leader's talk of turning the white men against each other, letting them destroy themselves. Sometimes, even Geronimo questioned his visions, wondering if they were true wisdom or lies sent by demons to deceive him.

As he stared at his captive, as he felt the outlaw's hateful gaze stare back at him, Geronimo wondered if it wouldn't be better to kill Metal Hands now. There would be none in his war band who would question such an act, none who would doubt the rightness of such a thing. Only he would have doubt, only he would wonder if what he had done was for the good of his people. If his visions were true, then he couldn't kill this man.

"We have brought Metal Hands to stand before the great Geronimo," the hulking warrior Iron Knife announced, waving his captured cavalry saber at the prisoner. "Now we wait for Geronimo's word to kill."

Geronimo was silent for a moment, studying the mood of his warriors. Iron Knife spoke the truth; many of them were expecting, even eager for the war-chiefto give them the signal so that they might butcher Metal Hands. He could understand their attitude. With his mechanical arms, Jesse was a living manifestation of the perversion the white men were practicing, their defilement of nature and the land. He could appreciate their hate, even share in it, but he also knew that they had to strive for things more important than hate if they were to help their people.

Patiently, Geronimo explained his visions to his warriors. He told them of the two serpents and how they killed one another with their poison. He spoke to them of the war he had seen, the war between the white tribes that would destroy them both.

Most of the warriors attended Geronimo's words, listening to his talk about spirit visions with gravity. A few, however, remained unmoved. Even those warriors kept silent, their respect for Geronimo as medicine man and war-chief too great for them to question him openly. Only Iron Knife remained defiant, only he raised his voice in protest.

"The poison of Geronimo's vision already pulses through this man's heart," Iron Knife said, pointing his sword at the outlaw. "He is already a dying thing. Let him die then and bring great power to the Warrior Nation!"

Iron Knife was a vicious fighter, a man who reveled in killing. He had ripped the sword that had given him his name from the belly of its former owner. Around his neck he wore a string of bullets and animal claws on a band of wire, each talisman a memento of some foe he'd killed in combat.

"It is not the Warrior Nation you think of," Geronimo accused. "It is the glory of Iron Knife that fills your heart. What power can our people have if the land cries out with pain? What greatness can we keep in our hearts if the red poison pollutes our hogans? We do not have the strength to stop the white man. Only by turning the white tribes against each other can we find victory."

Iron Knife folded his brawny arms across his chest and glowered down at the stocky medicine man. "Geronimo speaks with the tongue of a sick woman, afraid to fight the white man." He wagged the tip of the cavalry saber in the air. "I am not afraid. Metal Hands is my captive, he is mine to do what I want with! The word of Geronimo said he would see Metal Hands, so I have brought him. Now Geronimo has seen! Now let all the Warrior Nation see the power of Iron Knife!"

The Indian's arrogant taunting was an open challenge to Geronimo, but it was not the war-chief who answered it. Since his guards were distracted by the confrontation among their leaders, Jesse James seized the slim opportunity he'd been given. Rawhide thongs snapped like string as he pulled his mechanical limbs free, the infirmity left by Tobin's glancing shot having dissipated over the long journey to Geronimo's camp. The outlaw roared a fierce Rebel yell as he reached a hand to his neck and ripped away the thong binding his head to the framework.

As Jesse bent down to tear the thongs binding his legs, the startled Indians started to rush in with their spears and knives. It was a sharp cry from Geronimo that stopped them from descending on the only partially freed outlaw in a flurry of stabbing blades. At their war-chief's bellowed command, the warriors backed away. Geronimo nodded to Jesse as the outlaw used the reprieve to break the bonds around his legs.

"Now let all see the power of Iron Knife," Geronimo tossed Iron Knife's words back in his face.

Letting loose a brutal war-whoop, Iron Knife charged at Jesse, his saber held before him like a buffalo spear. It was more than hate of the white outlaw that drove Iron Knife; it was the mockery of Geronimo that sent fire rushing through his veins. The brave's always volatile temper now held complete sway over him, making him forget all strategy and caution in his lust to kill and destroy. Goading Iron Knife into mindless fury was the last gift Geronimo could give Jesse -.the rest would be up to him; it would be up to the outlaw to prove whether the vision of the two snakes was truth or lie. The other question was whether the future of the Warrior Nation lay with Geronimo or Iron Knife.

As the Indian came rushing in, trying to spit Jesse on the end of his sword, now sheathed in a flash of blue flame, the outlaw swung sideways, letting the enraged warrior charge past him. In passing, the outlaw's metal fist smashed into Iron Knife's shoulder with a brutal, meaty impact that bespoke of torn muscle and shattered bone.

Iron Knife reeled away, twisting about and lunging back to the attack. He tossed the glowing cavalry saber from his injured right arm to his left, and then waved it through the air in a savage flourish. The warrior's face twisted into a ghoulish mask of hate; the war-paint staining his features, enhancing their natural harshness. In his eyes were gleaming with azure fire and filled with the malevolence of the hunter who delights in the kill and the suffering of his prey.

Jesse's metal hand closed about one of the poles which formed the frame he had been tied to. When Iron Knife came charging at him again, the outlaw pulled on that pole, ripping it away from the rest of the frame. He cracked the heavy shaft of wood like a whip, swatting the charging Indian as though he were a stampeding steer. Teeth flew from Iron Knife's jaw as the pole crashed against his face, the impact sending him sprawling in the dust. Jesse brought the tip of the pole slamming down, narrowly missing his foe as he scrambled through the dirt on all fours.

Warriors scattered as Iron Knife's retreat brought the fight close to them.

His face rendered demonic by the intensity of the rage boiling inside him, Iron Knife leapt up from the ground. He lashed out with the flame-wreathed saber, knocking aside the pole and rushing at Jesse before the outlaw could recover.

The burning cold steel of the sword came hurtling toward Jesse's head, but before the blade could cleave into his skull, the outlaw caught it in a metal hand. Iron Knife strained to free the blade, but the mechanical strength of Jesse's grip held it like a vise as fat blue sparks dripped from between his metal fingers. Scowling at the enraged warrior, Jesse dropped the pole and brought his other hand slapping against the imprisoned blade. The tang of the sword snapped like a twig and the cerulean energy fled, leaving an overbalanced Iron Knife to stumble into his enemy. Jesse's fist crashed into the Indian, throwing him into the air as though he'd been kicked by a mule.

Wiping blood from his mouth, Iron Knife rose to his feet. The blue feral gleam of his eyes sent the circle of watching warriors back a pace, a few nervous murmurs spreading among the braves. The Indian grabbed his dislocated jaw and pushed it back into place. A grisly popping sound then rose from his shattered shoulder, a sharp cracking sound shuddered from his legs, his spine groaning as it began to bulge outward. Before the shocked eyes of his enemy, Iron Knife's body began to change.

"You have lost. Accept this with dignity," Geronimo ordered the warrior.

Iron Knife's reply was barely intelligible, forced from a throat that was already thickening and swelling into bestial shape. "I accept nothing from the white man except his death," the shape-changer growled. His head began to elongate, flesh cracking and sloughing away as mottled fur pushed itself upwards. Hands lengthened into feline claws, each finger tipped by a wicked crescent razor-like tip. Sharp fangs jutted from cat-like jaws.

Once, the animal whose shape Iron Knife wore had ranged throughout the west, but the encroachment of the white man had steadily depleted its numbers, pushing them steadily southward until the cry of the jaguar was barely even a memory in the lodges of the Warrior Nation. Perhaps it was a manifestation of the hate inside Iron Knife's heart that the animal whose form he should adopt was one that had been exterminated by the white men. Perhaps it was simply that no beast except the jaguar could emulate the warrior's vicious brutality and the thrilling feeling of slaughter.

Uttering a low, rumbling snarl, the transformed Iron Knife lunged at Jesse. The jaguar's claws raked the outlaw's side, sheering through his leather coat and slashing across the ribs beneath. The outlaw was sent sprawling into the dust. Roaring with delight, Iron Knife paused to lick the blood from his claws before turning to pounce upon his fallen prey.

As Iron Knife tensed his powerful muscles and made ready to leap on the outlaw, Jesse's hand clawed across the ground, his fingers gouged into the dirt, and he flung a cloud of dust into the jaguar's eyes. The blinded shape-changer cringed back, rubbing at the grit in his eyes with his paw-like hands. While his foe was blinded, Jesse came charging up, flinging himself upon the monster.

Iron Knife flailed and raged as Jesse's metal arm coiled around the jaguar's chest, holding the brute fast. The outlaw's other hand grabbed the necklace hanging around the shape-changer's neck. The chain hung loosely about the Indian's neck when he'd been in human form, but it was as tight as a choker now that he had transformed. Working his finger beneath the chain, Jesse twisted it tighter.

The jaguar thrashed and struggled, throwing himself to the ground and rolling through the dirt in his effort to dislodge the outlaw. Jesse clung fast, his metal finger steadily tightening the necklace. The chain began to dig into Iron Knife's throat, bright blood streaming as the necklace bit into his skin. The fierce roars of the jaguar were reduced to ragged, choking coughs.

A last twitch of the improvised garrote, and Jesse's bestial enemy went limp. A grisly rattle wheezed from the jaguar's body as its head lolled to one side. Carefully, Jesse loosened his grip and rose from the carcass of Iron Knife. Defiantly, he glared at the surrounding Indians.

Geronimo made a slashing motion of his arms, dismissing his warriors, sending them off to break down the camp. The war-chief stared at the bloodied, panting outlaw. Slowly, he paced over to the body of Iron Knife. Reaching down, he ripped free one of the totems from the dead shape-changer's neck. "You fight," he told Jesse in broken English. "You fight, you kill." Carefully, he handed the totem, the gray feather of an owl adorned in gold and turquoise, to the outlaw.

Jesse replied with a simple nod as he cautiously accepted the grim totem, Iron Knife's blood staining the edges of the feather. "The day I stop fighting is the day they plant me in the ground."

The war-chief smiled. "We go our way," he said, pointing to the north. "Metal Hands goes his way," he added, pointing west. "Keep the feather of Iron Knife. All the Warrior Nation will know what you have done. They will know that it is Geronimo who has allowed you to live. If they believe the vision of Geronimo, they will not seek the life of Metal Hands."

Geronimo reached under the calico sash circling his waist and removed the crumpled blaster that had been taken when Jesse was captured by Iron Knife and Two Wolves. To the Nations, such a weapon was repugnant, a tool of the white man's poison. He tossed the blaster into the dirt at Jesse's feet.

Geronimo watched as Jesse recovered his gun. He saw the brief temptation flicker across the outlaw's face. The idea was there, the thought that with one shot he could eliminate the most feared Indian in the southwest. The idea quickly died, as quickly as Jesse knew he would die if anything happened to Geronimo. It was only the medicine man's protection that kept the rest of the war band from killing him.

"Much obliged," Jesse said as he stuffed the weapon back into its holster.

"Kill much Blue Shirts, Metal Hands," Geronimo told him. Again, he pointed to the west. He stood and watched as Jesse cautiously descended the slope and stole away into the brush. In his mind, however, he didn't see a man striking out across the badlands. What he saw was a great snake, a snake that would soon sink his fangs into the other great serpent and kill it with its own poison. In giving the outlaw the token of the owl, Geronimo had marked him as a man already belonging to the realm of the dead.

* * *

It was well after midnight when the commotion rising from the corral outside drew the old miner from his bed. Catching up the shotgun from where it hung on a hook beside the door, he stepped out into the darkness. The chill of the desert night bit through the threadbare long johns he wore, lending a shiver to his voice as he called out into the dark.

"Who's there? What're you doin'?"

The miner's questions were answered by in a stern snarl. "I'm Jesse James and I'm stealin' your horse." The miner's eyes went as wide as saucers as he spotted the red glow of the outlaw's RJ-powered arms in the darkness. By that crimson glow, he could see the blaster pointed at him.

"Yes sir, Mr. James," the miner said, letting the shotgun fall to the ground and hurriedly reaching his hands into the air. "I'm sorry I ain't got anything better to offer you, but my claim ain't panned out so good. Can't even afford a blackhoof."

Jesse kept his gun trained on the miner as he moved along the corral and began to gather up tack and harness for the grizzled old nag standing behind the fence. "What's the nearest town and how much law's it got?"

"Tombstone, Mr. James, sir," the miner said. "Wyatt Earp's the law there."

Jesse froze as he was reaching to pull down bit and bridle from the fencepost. "I understood Earp was away east somewhere."

"He was," the miner agreed. "Came back a few days ago. Went lookin' for you, matter of fact. Understandable, allowin' how you robbed the bank and shot up his brother and all."

Jesse waved the miner over to the fence. Reluctantly, keeping his eyes on the blaster, the man complied. "Listen, old timer, I done a lot of bad in my time. Some of it I take pride in, some of it I don't, but whatever I done I own up to. So when I tell you I didn't shoot no Earp or rob no bank in Tombstone, you can believe me."

The miner smiled nervously, still looking at Jesse's blaster rather than the man who held it. Deciding the old man wasn't a threat, Jesse holstered the weapon with a quick twirl and flourish.

"I ain't the one you gotta convince, Mr. James. It's the Over-marshal you need to talk to." The old man laughed, a chuckle as dry and cheerless as the Arizona desert. "Only I don't think he'll oblige you. More'n like he'll hang you first and talk about it later."

Jesse nodded his head, as though giving the miner's joke serious consideration. "It's all about how you talk to somebody. Now I'd be beholden if'n you'd help me saddle that nag of yourn."

The miner frowned. "Mr. James, please don't steal my horse. She ain't much, but she's all I got."

The outlaw reached into his pocket and set a gold eagle on the fence post. "I rob banks, not honest folk. Consider I'm just hirin' your horse. You mosey into town and she'll be there wait'n."

"Town?" the miner asked. "Which town?"

Jesse smiled back at him. "Tombstone. I have to have a bit of a palaver with the *marshal*."

Chapter 11

Wyatt Earp left Allen Street's Alhambra Saloon with a belly full of whiskey and a pocket full of money. That night's round of faro had been particularly lucky, but he took little pleasure in 'bucking the tiger.' His thoughts were with his brother Virgil. The doctors had managed to save the lawman's life, but his right arm was crippled and useless. It was a hard blow for someone like Virgil to accept. Wyatt had tried to talk sense to his older brother and get him to at least come to terms with what had happened to him. Every time he looked at Morgan, however, Wyatt felt a shiver of fear run down his spine. If Virgil had gone to such lengths to try to save their brother, what might he do now?

The idea that Virgil would go seeking more of Dr. Carpathian's infernal 'curatives' was something Wyatt didn't want to face. He'd lost one brother that way; he didn't want to think about losing another in the same manner.

Marching alongside the Over-marshal as he made his way down the boardwalk, Doc Holiday muttered something under his breath, the words turned even more indistinct by his breathing apparatus. Wyatt stopped and stared at his companion. "How is that?"

"I said, a man running ace high like you are should playing at the Crystal Palace," Doc replied. "That's where all the real money's going to be on a Friday night."

Wyatt stared down the street. The damage inflicted on the side of the saloon by the men who'd ambushed Virgil was still evident, only the blood had been cleaned away. There was a bit of disagreement between the county and the city about who should pay for the damages. In all likelihood, it would keep getting pushed back and forth until the proprietor of the Crystal Palace took things into his own hands and replaced the scorched woodwork and broken column himself.

"The Crystal Palace ain't been so lucky for my people of late," Wyatt shook his head dejectedly.

Doc shrugged his shoulders. "You won't mind if I take a turn, then?" The gambler held his hand toward Wyatt. "That is if you'll oblige me. I seem to be a bit embarrassed."

Wyatt frowned. "I always thought you kept the advantage." He reached into his vest and brought out a stack of bills. He didn't count it, but just handed it over to his friend. "If anything's left in the morning, you can bring it by. I'm headed over to the hotel to get some shut eye."

Doc tapped the brim of his hat. "You are a credit to your profession, Wyatt. Don't let anyone tell you otherwise." The gambler peeled off as the two men passed the intersection of Fifth and Allen, striding over to the Crystal Palace while Wyatt continued on to the Cosmopolitan Hotel further down the street.

The gambler's parting words recalled to Wyatt the ugly scene when they'd gone to confront Colonel Mackenzie at Fort Concho. He'd been less than cooperative with the lawmen, complaining rather loudly about the troopers who'd been shot up at the James-Younger Gang hideout, and he was exceedingly abusive in his opinion of the Over-marshal's failure to bring in Jesse James. The fact that Wyatt thought he could find Jesse in Fort Concho's guardhouse had made an already hostile encounter even worse. If not for the restraining influence of Doc Holiday on the one side and Lucinda Loveless on the other, it was entirely probable that Fort Concho would be looking for a new commander and Tombstone a new Over-marshal.

Wyatt cursed under his breath as he thought about what Mackenzie had told him, which Loveless confirmed as truth. Thomas Tate Tobin had indeed been lying in wait for Jesse James after Wyatt's posse flushed him from his hideout. But the bounty hunter had been unsuccessful, returning to Fort Concho, not with Jesse, but only John Younger. The killer had gone out to try again, but it was Loveless's opinion that the outlaw was long gone.

Loud, boisterous laughter from the porch in front of the Grand Hotel drew Wyatt's attention. He scowled when he saw Ike Clanton and several of the Cowboys sitting in front of the hotel, drinking and swapping ribald jokes. Curly Bill Brocius was feting

Clanton's return, presenting him in grand style to his comrades. The bearded rustler was bedecked in extravagant new duds, electriwork filigree sewn to the front of his vest and around the brim of the beaverskin hat he wore. With the promise of new wealth that their recent acquisition of arms and machines promised the Cowboys, Curly Bill had cast aside the rough savagery of his old stylings for the gaudy ostentation of a would-be ringster like Ike.

Ike might not have received any part of the reward posted for Jesse, but the varmint had exploited Governor Wallace's pardon to the full. It galled Wyatt to think that if Ike played things careful and kept himself from taking a direct hand in the criminal enterprises of the Cowboys, that he'd be outside the Over-marshal's reach. He didn't believe Ike would go honest for a second, any more than he thought a leopard could change its spots. The outlaw brand was imprinted on Ike's very soul, put there by the Old Man. Where the Clantons were concerned, the apple hadn't fallen far from the tree.

By some irony, the Cosmopolitan Hotel where the Earps had their headquarters was directly across the street from the Grand Hotel, which served as rallying point for the Cowboys when they were in town. As Wyatt marched down the boardwalk, a few of the more intoxicated Cowboys whistled and tossed catcalls his way.

"Next time, lawdog, maybe you should treat me respectable!" Ike Clanton shouted, swaggering out into the street.

"Next time I'll let you walk, instead of letting you ride on a 'bot's lap," Wyatt said, regretting now the twinge of sympathy that had moved him to let Ike ride in the back of the repaired Judgement when the posse made its return to Tombstone. A few weeks without Ike around had not made him miss the Cowboy any more than he had before.

Ike puffed out his chest, poking his thumbs into the pockets of his vest. "You got some nerve jawin' at me like that, star-packer!" He turned and smirked back at the other Cowboys on the porch. "I'm the big bug around here. You'll be workin' for me one of these days."

"The way I see it, Old Man Clanton calls the shots in your outfit. He just lets you off the leash when he gets tired of your yappin'."

Wyatt didn't bother to listen to the tirade of abuse Ike hurled at his back. If it was Indian Charlie or Johnny Ringo or especially Curly Bill, Wyatt would have taken the insults with far more severity. Those men were killers just looking for an excuse. Ike wasn't; he was the sort who got others to do his killing for him. When he barked, it wasn't a challenge, it was just hot air.

The Over-marshal tipped his hat to the clerk at the desk in the Cosmopolitan's lobby, and then made his way upstairs to his room. The instant he turned the key and stepped into the room, he knew something was wrong. When he'd left that morning, the shade over the window had been up. Now, it was down. The maids at the Cosmopolitan had standing orders to leave his room alone unless he was there to watch them. There'd been an incident where somebody had put a Gila monster in his pillow case while he was out. Ever since, he'd been careful about any repeat of that experience.

He just started to ease his blaster from its holster when a cold voice from the darkened room warned him against such action. Wyatt turned slowly. In the blackness, the crimson glow of two cybernetic arms shone with hellish brilliance. The marshal didn't need two guesses to know who those arms belonged to.

"At this range, I can hardly miss," Jesse said. "Take your left hand and unbuckle that belt, then kick it over this way. We're gonna have a little palaver, you and I."

"This is very obliging of you," Wyatt said as he unbuckled his gun belt. "I thought I was going to have to ride all the way back to Texas to track you down."

"You must need that feather in your cap awful bad." Jesse reached down and plucked Wyatt's gun belt from the floor. He holstered the damaged Hyper-velocity blaster he had crushed in Tobin's ambush and armed himself with the Over-marshal's guns. "Never did believe the stories that Wyatt Earp was a glory hound. Lowdown, Free-Soil, copperhead, maybe, but not a braggart chasin' laurels."

Wyatt turned away from the door, taking a step into the room. The glow from Jesse's arms was just enough for him to make out the outlaw's features. He glared at Jesse's disapproving expression. "You want to shoot, then you shoot, you Secesh trash," Wyatt sneered. "But know I ain't interested in money or glory or even the law! I want to see your neck stretch on account of you bushwhacking my brother!"

Jesse shook his head at Wyatt's outrage. "Fair enough, *marshal*, but how would it strike you if I told you tonight's the first time I've been anywhere near this town? What if I told you it wasn't me or any of my people had anything to do with gunnin' your brother?"

"I'd likely call you a liar. Everybody saw the men who robbed the bank and shot Virg from ambush. They were wearin' your brown dusters, the sort of thing nobody outside the James-Younger Gang has the guts to wear."

"Unless maybe they wanted somebody to think they was the James Gang," Jesse mused with a glint in his eye. "We can't be the only people in the county with brown dusters? I understand you've caused Old Man Clanton and the Cowboys a fair heap of trouble. Enough trouble that they'd be mighty keen to see you out of their hair for a spell. Chasin' after me would be one way of removin' you from the vicinity. Wyatt Earp huntin' high and low for the James Gang, while the Cowboys are free to rob and steal to their hearts' content."

"Don't you mean the James-*Younger* Gang?" Wyatt taunted.

Jesse waved the blasters at Wyatt, motioning him to seat himself on the bed and away from the door. Walking across the room, the outlaw put himself between his prisoner and his only avenue of escape. "Just now it ain't my concern whether you believe me or not. I was in the rocks listenin' when your posse rode up. I know you followed after the bounty man who ambushed me. What I want to know is where that polecat took John Younger."

"You're going to shoot me either way," Wyatt spat. "Why should I give you the satisfaction?"

"Shoot you?" Jesse scoffed. "That ain't my notion at all. Did it occur to you, Wyatt, that if my gang went to all the trouble to rob your bank and shoot your brother that we'd just light out for Texas Territory? A man in your position must know somethin' about what we've done and how we operate. When we pick an area, we pick it clean, stick around until there's Pinkertons behind every tree and in every stage. We don't just hit willy-nilly and move on."

Wyatt sat forward on the bed and made a slashing motion with his hand. "Then you really are saying somebody else gunned Virg and tried to frame you?" If anything, the lawman's expression became even grimmer. "Tell me, Jesse, if it was one of the Cowboys, which of Clanton's scum did it?"

Jesse smiled coldly. "We bargain for that answer. First, I want to know what happened to John and if he's alive or not."

"Answer the Over-marshal's question, Jesse," the rasping voice of Doc Holiday sounded from the doorway behind the outlaw. The gambler had eased it open just the slightest crack. The lethal barrels of a chopped-down shotgun protruded from the opening, aimed squarely at Jesse's back.

"Come on in, Doc," Wyatt called to his friend. "The conversation was just turning interesting." He smiled at Jesse. "Drop the irons. There's no way you could know this, but anytime Doc asks me for money it means he thinks I'm being followed. I think he'd rather stake his breather than ask a friend for a loan."

"Only this time I figured it wrong," Doc admitted as he slipped into the room. "I thought somebody was following you on the street. It didn't occur to me he'd already be up here waitin' for you." The gambler's voice trailed off into a mechanical cough.

Despite Wyatt's command and the menace of Doc's shotgun, Jesse kept his blaster aimed at the Over-marshal. "Seems what we have here is a Mexican standoff," the outlaw declared. "The lunger can drill me sure as hell, but not before I burn myself a star-packer."

"So how do we fix things so we both don't end up on Boot Hill?" Wyatt asked.

"We deal," Jesse said. "I take you to the coyotes who gunned your brother, you tell me where John is."

Wyatt shook his head. "Why should I trust you?"

Jesse smiled. "Because you should be askin' yourself a question right now. And that question is, where are the rest of the Younger Brothers? You see, I didn't come here alone. Cole and the rest are keepin' tabs on your kin right now. We didn't come in here gunnin' for any Earps before, but the Youngers feel just as concerned about their brother as you do about yourn." The outlaw's smile broadened when he saw the flicker of concern that crept into Wyatt's eyes. He knew his bluff had been taken as gospel by the lawman.

"Damn you, Jesse," Wyatt growled. "Anything happens to my brothers, I'll stretch your neck from hell to Kansas!"

"Nothin' will happen if you deal square," Jesse said. "Do I have your word of honor that we have ourselves a deal?"

The Over-marshal nodded. "Fine, but you ante-up first. Who do you claim shot Virg?"

"I don't rightly know, but I have my suspicions," Jesse admitted. "What I can tell you is who ordered it done. I also happen to know where he'd be just about now."

Wyatt glared coldly at the outlaw. "Then you take me to him. I get this sidewinder, I'll tell you what you want to know and maybe a little more besides. I'll raise up a posse and we can head out…"

"No posse," Jesse nodded his head toward Doc Holiday. "Just you, me, and the lunger. Call me scared, but I have a notion that if'n you brought more men, you might just take it to mind to have your cake and eat it too. The Youngers wouldn't like it much if you took me into custody. Might give them some funny ideas."

Wyatt rose from the bed. "Alright, we play it your way. Just you, me, and Doc."

A cough wheezed from Doc's breathing mask. "Play a straight hand, Jesse," the gambler warned. "Because whatever else happens, I can promise you'll be cut in half if anything untoward befalls Wyatt." His eyes glittered menacingly as he stared at the outlaw. "You can bet your bottom dollar on that."

***

Mounted on Interceptors drawn from the stockyard, the strange trio sped across the dark, bleak desert. The Interceptors were the top of the line – fully capable of running down blackhoofs, but not as fast as the Iron Horses used by the Union and many outlaw bands. Their major handicap was range, depleting their RJ cells at a far quicker rate than either of the other machines.

As the broken terrain of gulches and wind-etched plateaus receded into the distance, the three riders found themselves on a flat plain. By the moonlight, they could clearly see the mass of cattle being herded along the plain. The guide-lights on the Iron Horses that zipped about the periphery of the herd were dulled, appearing only as the faintest pinpricks against the shadowy terrain. Far more distinct were the whine of their engines and the rumble of their exhausts.

Wyatt activated the brakes on his Interceptor, slowing the machine as he glared down at the herd. It was blatantly obvious that this was no legitimate drive. The closest market for beef would be out toward Yuma, yet these animals were being moved north in the direction of Tombstone... and Clantonville. The Over-marshal didn't need to see the red sashes around their waists to know that the rustlers below were Cowboys.

"Old Man Clanton," Wyatt spat the name like it was the vilest obscenity.

"Give a coyote the best tools in the world and he still thinks like a coyote," Jesse said. He focused on the Cowboys through the crimson lenses of his goggles, analyzing their layout. "Big money these days is in hitting trains and stages or knocking down a refueling station, but Clanton still clings to rustlin' like it's his religion."

"A man behind the times," Doc coughed. "Heard he gunned down one of them two-bit stealin' chance machines over in Campbell and Hatch's Billiard Parlor on account of the noise it made." He chuckled into his mask. "Not that I blame him none, them one-armed road agents is an affront to respectable gamblin'."

Wyatt continued to glare down at the rustlers. "The Cowboys," he said, rolling the word over on his tongue. It made sense, of course. With the Earps out of the way and no effective lawmen in the area, the Cowboys would have the run of the county, free to pillage and maraud without any real threat of reprisal. The closest law would be the soldiers in Fort Yuma and the Mexicans across the river. "I always figured they were behind Morg's ambush, I should have reckoned they'd be behind hitting

Virg too." His eyes narrowed as he reflected on his earlier brush with Ike Clanton outside the Grand Hotel. He was trying to remember all the faces he had seen hanging around on the porch. Curly Bill and Pete Spence for certain; Indian Charlie and Frank Stilwell, possibly the McLaureys as well. A lot of the Cowboys' big guns were in town. That put things into a different perspective. Reaching to his holster, Wyatt checked the cylinder of his blaster.

"How do you reckon we handle this?" Doc asked in his metallic rasp.

Looking up from his inspection of his guns, Wyatt frowned. "What I'd like to do is charge down there and burn those curs out of the saddle, but that scum needs to be brought to trial."

Jesse shook his head. "I'm more particular to the first idea," he said, opening the throttle on his Interceptor and launching the machine full bore down toward the rustled herd. He could hear Wyatt and Doc cursing behind him. An instant later they had their own Interceptors charging across the plain in tow.

It wasn't bravado that spurred Jesse into immediate action. Seeing the rustlers in action, knowing the treacherous Old Man Clanton was so near, these things had set the outlaw's belly boiling with the lust for revenge. Just like Clanton had set the law after Jesse and his gang, so the bushwhacker was going to return the favor. Even the deal he'd made with Wyatt and his concern about John Younger were secondary to that almost primal need to exact retribution.

Speeding toward the rustled herd, Jesse's ears rang with the alarmed shouts of Clanton's outriders. One of the men stood up in the saddle of his vehicle, snapping a rifle to his shoulder since the blasters in the Interceptor had been disabled by Wyatt. Before the Cowboy could fire, the blaster in Jesse's good hand barked. The impact of the energy bolt ripped the rustler out of the saddle and sent him flying back to crash among the herd. The loud noise, the bright flash, and the stench of burnt meat were all too much for the cattle. Bellowing in panic, the herd rushed away from the scorched carcass of the Cowboy.

More shots sounded around Jesse. Some were the hastily loosed gunfire of the rustlers; others were the coldly precise and lethal marksmanship of Doc Holiday and Wyatt Earp, opening up with the high-powered blasters in their mounts. The screams of Cowboys as they were struck down rang out above the roar of engines and the trumpeting cries of the frightened cattle.

"Stop that shootin'! You'll stampede the herd!" the shout came from somewhere at the back of the herd, but Jesse couldn't mistake that gravelly voice. It was Old Man Clanton himself trying to restrain his men and save his plundered livestock. Vindictively, Jesse spun about in the saddle and stabbed a blast right into the middle of the herd. The agonized cry of the steer he hit was all it took to send the cattle into absolute chaos.

An Iron Horse came speeding out of the darkness, swatting aside a steer with the cattle-catcher bolted to the front of its frame. Energy bolts crashed all around Jesse as the rider fired the Gatling blasters built into the 'Horse's faring. The momentary glimpse Jesse had of the outlaw showed him the hateful glower of Johnny Ringo. Jesse snapped off a shot at the gunfighter, the bolt passing so near to him that it scorched a line across the gunman's coat and set the material smoking. Ringo ducked low over the side of his ride, drawing his blaster and firing blind as he rocketed past Jesse.

Jesse sent a few more shots chasing after Ringo as he went speeding off into the darkness, but he didn't pursue the fleeing outlaw. As badly as he'd like to deal with Johnny Ringo, he wanted Old Man Clanton more. Weaving his Interceptor around the edges of the stampeding herd, he tried to work his way past the panicked cattle to reach the outlaw chief.

The ground was a scarred mush of earth that was gouged by hundreds of pounding hooves. Here and there, the carcass of a dead steer lay heaped, crushed beneath the hooves of the herd. Twice, Jesse sped past the grim remains of an Iron Horse and its rider, flattened by the stampede they had tried in vain to turn. He slowed briefly when he passed these macabre markers, lingering long enough to ensure that none of the dead men were Clanton.

When he sped past the back of the herd, Jesse could hear renewed blaster fire ahead. The roar of Doc's shotgun and the shriek of a crippled 'Horse told him that the shots were more than just Cowboys trying to turn the cattle. Driving onwards,

Jesse came upon a violent tableau. Old Man Clanton's 'Horse had been shot down. In crashing, the grizzled outlaw had been unable to clear the stricken steed, and he was now pinned underneath it.

Nearby, Phin Clanton, the Old Man's eldest son, had braked his 'Horse and was using it for cover as he tried to fend off Wyatt and Doc. The speed of the modified Interceptors made a mockery of Phin's efforts to bring them down.

In a sudden burst of speed, Wyatt drove his Interceptor full into Phin's parked 'Horse. The rustler was driven from cover as the Iron Horse was knocked back by the impact. As he scurried away, Wyatt sent an energy bolt slamming into his side. Phin screamed, and then crashed into the dirt, ribs standing stark against the ghastly burn inflicted upon his body. He made one last, sorry effort to aim his pistol at the Over-marshal, then sprawled limp in the dust.

There were no other Cowboys in evidence. The rest of the gang had either fled like Ringo or were still trying to stem the tide of the stampeding cattle. It didn't matter to the two lawmen who now dismounted from their Interceptors and approached the Old Man trapped under his own crippled vehicle.

"Damn you Wyatt!" Old Man Clanton raged. "You killed my boy!"

"And you tried to kill my brother," Wyatt said, fingers tightening about the grip of his blaster.

The Old Man struggled to reach his own guns, but the Iron Horse pressing down on his chest made such an effort impossible. "It was Jesse James, you damn fool! Everybody knows that!"

"Everybody except Jesse James," Jesse snapped as he brought his Interceptor prowling out from the darkness. He brought the machine to a slow crawl, advancing until its nose just touched the edge of Clanton's overturned 'Horse. "Why don't you tell the *marshal* the truth?" Jesse punctuated the suggestion by nudging the 'Horse. The Old Man screamed as more of the machine's weight pressed down on his chest.

"Alright! It was me! I had it done!" the Old Man shrieked, flecks of blood flying from his mouth, his arms pushing frantically against the ponderous weight of his metal steed.

Wyatt Earp crouched down close to the pinned rustler. "Who did it? Who'd you send?" When the Old Man didn't answer quick enough, Jesse gave his wreck another nudge.

"Johnny Ringo!" the Old Man screamed. "Him and Stilwell and Indian Charlie!" The rustler's face contorted with pain as the 'Horse continued to press on him. "Pete Spence too. He was there with Ike…" The outlaw's face contorted with pain of a different sort when he realized that he'd just indicted one of his other sons. He knew enough about Wyatt Earp's ways to know that nothing would stop the Over-marshal from exacting justice from Ike's hide, either from the barrel of a gun or the end of a rope.

"Ike Clanton," Wyatt said as he stood up. "Looks like somebody's pardon ain't gonna be worth a hill of beans."

"It weren't Ike!" the Old Man shouted. "Curly Bill, it was Curly Bill who was there!"

"A man shouldn't lie when he's so close to meetin' the Almighty," Doc said, slamming fresh RJ charges into his shotgun.

Jesse eased his Interceptor back from Clanton. "Well?" he asked Wyatt. "You find out everything you wanted?"

The Over-marshal stared down at the Old Man. Slowly, he nodded his head. "The Old Man tried to do a frame up. Doesn't make you any less a polecat, but at least you're not the polecat I'm lookin' for."

"Glad to hear it," Jesse said with a sardonic smirk. He opened up the Interceptor and slammed into the underside of the Old Man's Iron Horse. The trapped rustler shrieked once as the machine rolled over and crushed him.

"What the hell, Jesse?!" Wyatt roared, looking down in horror at the Old Man's splattered remains. He froze when he looked up and found himself staring into the barrel of Jesse's blaster.

"Lose the hardware," Jesse told the Over-marshal. He waved a pistol at Doc Holiday. "You too, Doc. I don't have time for another Mexican standoff." He smiled as he watched the gambler discard the shotgun and the pistol at his waist. "Better lose your pocket advantage too," Jesse told him, waiting patiently as Doc removed the derringer from his sleeve. "Old Man Clanton owed me for betrayin' me and leavin' my gang to die," Jesse said, spitting at the bloody ooze streaming from under the Iron Horse. He fixed his gaze on Wyatt. "That just leaves the balance between you and me to be settled. What happened to John?"

Wyatt matched Jesse's icy gaze. Still bristling from the outlaw's sudden murder of the Old Man, he took a cruel pleasure in telling Jesse what he wanted to know. He knew the impact it would have on him. "John Younger was handed over to Colonel Mackenzie by Thomas Tate Tobin, same bounty hunter that ambushed you. He was alive when I saw him, shackled in the guardhouse and looking a bit peeked, but alive. Mackenzie didn't keep John in Fort Concho long though. He had him shipped out first chance he had."

"Where'd that blue-belly ship him off to?" Jesse snarled through clinched teeth.

Wyatt's answer was like a sneer of defiance. "Andersonville. They sent him to Camp Lincoln."

A cold chill swept through Jesse's body. Andersonville was home to one of the most infamous Union prison camps in the country; Camp Lincoln! It was a place where recidivist secessionists were sent to be 'reconstructed' and turned into 'loyal' members of society. At least such was the official explanation for its existence. In truth, any man who went there never came out again. Alive or dead, once a man entered Camp Lincoln he never left. It was a fate supposedly reserved for men who'd fought in the war and had never embraced the Union afterwards. For John, a boy who'd been too young to fight for the South, to be sent there was an act of such injustice it made Jesse feel sick inside. A surge of guilt welled up inside him. He should have taken the risk and gotten the answers he wanted from the commander at Fort Concho when he'd first heard it mentioned. His lust for revenge on the Clantons had sent him off in the wrong direction.

"I guess I'll have to let you lawdogs live. You'll oblige me, *marshal*, by dealing with Ike and the rest," Jesse growled. "Much as I'd like to do it myself, it appears I've got bigger things to worry about."

Wyatt scowled up at the mounted outlaw. "You know I'll have to come after you."

Jesse spun around, firing a bolt from each of his pistols. The shots slammed into the engines of the Interceptors, blasting them into shrapnel. Turning his right-hand blaster to keep Wyatt and Doc covered, he sent another shot into Phin Clanton's Iron Horse, disabling it as effectively as he had the two Interceptors. "Walkin' back to Tombstone should slow you down."

"What about the Youngers?" Doc coughed. "You swore to call them off if Wyatt helped you."

Jesse laughed. "Call them off? I'm not even sure I know where they are! I do know they ain't nowhere near Tombstone!"

Uttering a sharp Rebel yell, Jesse sent his Interceptor speeding away into the darkness, leaving behind him two fuming lawmen.

Chapter 12

Jesse James rode into the winding canyon, feeling the jagged cliffs pressing in around him. The chill within the shadowy ravine was remarkable in its contrast to the heat of the west Texas desert he'd been traveling across for days. Except at noon, when the sun was directly overhead, the canyon was always in shadow, allowing it to retain much of the night's cold throughout the day.

The narrow pass channeled Jesse down a familiar path and made him appreciate what a formidable defense the canyon presented. It was a natural choke-point, one well-armed man could hold off an army in this winding ravine. That consideration and the remoteness of the location had been the key reasons the James Gang had employed this place as one of their hideouts. Riding into the canyon now, however, Jesse fully appreciated the uneasiness a posse or cavalry troop would experience trying to root outlaws from this lair. He had no way of knowing if the Youngers had returned to this refuge or if some other party had taken it over – no way at all of knowing who might be watching him from behind the rocks. With his stolen Interceptor loaded down with canisters of extra fuel to feed its powerful but rapacious engine, he felt like he was sitting on a stick of dynamite as he made his way deeper into the ravine.

He was about halfway through the chasm before he was challenged. A sharp voice barked at him from behind a boulder that had fallen into the canyon and partially blocked the fissure. It was as Jesse slowed to maneuver around the rock that he caught the gleam of a rifle barrel and heard the order to power down his steed. Despite the threat of both rifle and voice, Jesse smiled.

"Hell, Bob, you mean to tell me I come all this way just to get shot?" Jesse called out as he pulled the handkerchief down from his face.

An excited yell and the clatter of stones being kicked loose answered the outlaw. Only a moment later, Bob Younger came running out from behind the boulder, his brown duster looking just a bit more worn for all the dirt and sand covering it. Somehow, he'd contrived to keep his bowler clean and even managed to pick up a striking leatherwork hatband for it that depicted a bear hunter stalking a grizzly. Or perhaps it was the other way around, given that the two little silver figures rotated in an endless circle around the hat.

"Jesse!" Bob shouted. "We'd just about given you up! You've been gone near-on a month! Cole's been sendin' Hardin out once a week to snatch a gander at the news sheets over in Wolf Bend, hopin' and dreadin' to read that you and John were caught!" The knife-fighter hesitated, turning away from Jesse and staring down the canyon. It was easy to figure out who he was looking for.

"They got John," Jesse confessed, his heart going sick with guilt. "When we lit out, there was a bounty hunter lying in wait for us. Just luck of the draw he got John instead of me."

The excitement of a moment before vanished from Bob's face, turning into a dour expression. "Them's the breaks," Bob tried to choke back the emotion threatening to overwhelm him.

"He took John alive," Jesse did his best to assure Bob. After what he'd gone through when Frank had been shot, he knew only too well the anguish Bob was feeling. He also knew how dearly he had prayed someone would say those words to him and change all that grief and despair into hope.

When Bob looked at Jesse again, he could see the hope glistening in the man's eyes. "Alive? You know where they took him?"

"Yeah, but it's somethin' I'd rather not tell twice. Take me up to Cole and I'll tell you all about it."

Returning to the Youngers without John was hard enough for Jesse. He felt like a coward and a traitor, the guilt of escaping when John was captured was like a knife twisting around in his gut. Telling them that their little brother was rotting away inside Camp Lincoln was going to be much worse.

Midway along the ravine, the canyon widened out for a mile or so. It was here that some enterprising wag had tried to make a go of a mining operation. Silver, gold, whatever they'd tried to make their fortune on hadn't paid out. Given the remoteness of the area and the difficulty of navigating the ravine, it was likely that the labor of extracting and transporting the ore simply hadn't been worth the effort. Then again, it could have been the attentions of Indians and Comancheros that had driven off the miners. This part of Texas allowed for only the most Spartan law enforcement and the last significant military presence had been during the Mexican War.

Whatever the cause, the abandonment of the mine came as a boon to outlaws like Jesse James. The tunnels and mine shafts presented a hidden warren of bolt holes and hiding places, while the old sheds and storehouses made convenient shelters for their Iron Horses and other equipment, such as an extra pair of Jesse's Hyper-velocity blasters.

For the sake of sparing Jim the long climb up into the cliff and the numbing cold of the mine shafts themselves, Cole had established the gang in the old foreman's office. A few blankets thrown over the broken windows kept out the worst of the wind and dust, while a little RJ-powered heater fended off the chill of the canyon. As hideouts went, they'd all been in far more primitive conditions.

Jim Younger was pale and in pain, lying on a pallet when the group entered the shack. His whole chest was wrapped about in plaster and he was obviously uncomfortable. Little buttons of RJ were embedded in the plaster strips the doctor had banded about his body, each button connected to a wire that was woven into the strips. The end of the wire was fitted to a little iron box with a crank attached to it. Turning the crank sent a little charge running through the wire and heated the RJ buttons. The doctor who'd attended Jim claimed the heat would speed his body's natural healing, selling the whole apparatus as the latest medical marvel from back east. Jesse wasn't sure about that, but he had to admit that for a man who'd been at Death's door the last time he'd seen him, Jim was acting mighty spry.

At that moment, spry meant slowly trying to stuff himself into a shirt too small to accommodate the plaster bands bulking out his body, while at the same time trying to squeeze his feet back into his boots. It was obvious that he should have been staying put, but Jim Younger was not one to sit still when there was work to be done. There was a furious cast to Jim's features, an almost frantic need to leap into action.

"Settle yourself," Cole leaned across the table and pointed a finger at his headstrong brother. "We rush into this, we don't do any good for anybody except them blue-bellies. We have to take our time, think things through."

Bob whittled away at a stick with one of his Bowie knives, angrily slashing strips from the wood. "Thinkin' won't do no good, Cole. They took John to Camp Lincoln! Worst hellhole in the Union!"

"That's why we plan this careful," Cole snapped at Bob. "We think it through, leave nothing to chance." He turned his eyes to Jesse seated across from him. "That's how you figure it, right Jesse?"

Slowly, Jesse nodded. "We can't leave John in there, that's for damn sure. At the same time, this isn't going to be like knocking over some adobe-walled jail in a one-dog town. We have to think this out, plan every move. We don't make a move until Cole's satisfied we've got a chance of gettin' John out of there."

"Then you'll back our play?" Cole asked with a note of eagerness in his voice.

"I can't help but feel that I got John into this," Jesse's voice grew heavy, somber. "I know what it's like to lose a brother. I don't want you to go through that."

Cole rose and set his hand on Jesse's shoulder. There were no words he could use to express his appreciation for Jesse's friendship in that moment. There wasn't any need to. Cole turned away, looking toward the window of the shack and the black-garbed man standing there. "How about you, Hardin? Are you in?"

The gunfighter laughed. "Deal me out, Cole. If you have any sense you'll deal yourselves out too. The Yankees have that place guarded better'n the Washington Mint. Ain't but one man ever escaped from that place."

Hardin's statement brought Jesse spinning around. "I never heard of anybody breakin' out of Camp Lincoln."

The gunfighter bristled at the challenge in Jesse's tone. For a second, it seemed his hand was going to dip toward the smokers hanging from his belt. "You callin' me a liar?"

"I'm sayin' maybe you heard things wrong," Jesse said, shifting around in his chair so that if it came to it he'd be able to draw his own guns without the obstruction of the table. "Or maybe you were a little quick to credit somebody's tall tale."

Hardin scowled back at the outlaw. "I met the man himself. Saw with my own eyes what Camp Lincoln done to him. Man named Kelso Warfield used to ride with Mosby. Said he spent nigh on six years in Andersonville's hellhole after the war."

Jesse turned and looked over at Cole. "What do you think?"

Cole tugged at his moustache as he mulled the question over in his mind. "I think, allowin' for a moment that this Kelso Warfield isn't the biggest liar since Lincoln, that before we make any plans we should look this fella up."

"That's exactly what I was thinkin'," Jesse said as he turned back toward Hardin. "Where'd you meet up with this Kelso Warfield?"

***

Robbers Roost was a hideaway so notorious that even the Texas Rangers gave the place a wide berth. Situated at the extreme edge of the territory, nestled in the contested region on the periphery of what the Union derisively called 'Carpathian's Kingdom' and the almost completely depopulated wilderness left behind by Sitting Bull's Warrior Nation, the old mining town had become a veritable outlaw community. Smugglers, gun runners, Indian traders, Comancheros, criminals of every stripe and brand, all made their way to the security of Robbers Roost when they felt no place else could afford them shelter. A lawless outpost on the very frontier of civilization, there was only one rule in the town: might makes right. It was the kind of place Diablo

Canyon had been before Wyatt Earp had assigned an Enforcer to maintain the law there. It was perhaps only a matter of time before the same happened to Robbers Roost, before a lawman like Pat Garrett or Bass Reeves came along and forced the town to become civilized. Until then, it existed as a way station on the road to hell. The strong could prosper in Robbers Roost, the weak would be chewed up and spit out.

Brazenly, the James-Younger Gang marched down the dirt street, openly displaying their weapons in a show of force that would impress any onlookers too ignorant to recognize the quick-devil arms of Jesse James. Power was the only thing that was respected among these outlaws. By such a bold show, Jesse hoped to keep these renegades and rustlers in their place. It was something of an irony that he could thank Dr. Carpathian for enhancing Jesse's reputation as a gunfighter to a degree where even the most arrogant hot-head wouldn't challenge him now. To face another man was one thing, but these would-be gunslingers balked at the idea of going up against the sinister technology of the Enlightened. Even for men out to steal a reputation off a living legend, there was a reluctance to play against a stacked deck.

"Looks like we have some friends here," Cole said as they made their way into the town. He pointed to several rebel flags fluttering from the facades of the buildings.

Hardin laughed. "Yeah, they'll whistle Dixie while they cut your throat and clean your pockets. Don't make any mistake, the only friends you have here are the ones you bring in with you."

"Comin' from a guy who'd place second to Yellow Fever in a popularity contest, you'll forgive me if I take that with a grain of salt," Jim told the gunfighter, wincing as his own laughter sent shivers of pain coursing through him. He'd improved enough over the last week to sit on a 'Horse, but beneath his shirt his body was still swaddled in bandages and RJ heating pads. He was cagey about letting the others know how much pain he was actually in, fearing they'd leave him behind when they made their play to rescue John.

"Suit yourself," Hardin smiled at Jim with all the friendliness of a rattler. "It's your neck."

Studying the men they passed lounging in front of the saloons and brothels that lined the street, Jesse was more inclined to back Hardin's opinion. The inhabitants of Robbers Roost were the scruffiest, meanest bunch he'd ever seen; a polyglot mix of whites, blacks, Mexicans, and half-breeds. Whatever their background, there was the scurvy cast of a hungry coyote in every face, a predatory gleam that made Jesse grateful for the blasters hanging on his hips.

"How do we even start lookin' for Warfield?" Bob asked.

"Hell, if he's been here any length of time he's probably already been knifed and buried," Cole said, keeping a wary eye on a pack of Comancheros as they prowled past them.

"Sometimes you've got to play the long hand," Jesse said. "Press your luck and hope for the best."

Cole shook his head. "Sometimes I think I used up all my luck in the war. That's why I stick around with you, Jesse. Your run never seems to dry out."

A sharp whistle from Hardin brought the rest of the gang turning around. The Texan pointed across the street at a man leaning against the hitching post in front of a gambling hall. "Would you look at that," he hissed through clenched teeth.

The man Hardin indicated was wearing the grey shell jacket of a Confederate soldier over a buckskin shirt and a cowhide vest. The pants he wore were tucked into a set of cavalry boots with the flared tops favored by rebel horsemen. Among the arsenal of weapons draped about the man's body, the grips of several rebel-pattern blasters were evident. The big brass buckle on his gun belt bore the initials 'CSA.'

What galled Hardin was the fact that the man wearing all this Confederate regalia was black.

"That darkie has some nerve," Hardin growled.

"Yeah," Cole agreed, following the Texan's pointing finger. "I don't see how a man can move around wearing that much iron." The veteran guerrilla made a quick study of his arsenal. "Looks to be two in shoulder holsters, two on the hips, one across the belly and another in his left boot."

"The one on his right hip is a chopped down carbine," Jesse chimed in. "Way his jacket bulges I think he's got another pistol behind him too."

"Shouldn't be surprised if he doesn't have a pocket advantage too," Jim said.

Bob chuckled. "That's a damn big knife he's carryin'. One of them Mexican things they call a machete. Chop a man's boots right off with one of them."

Hardin rounded on the rest of the gang. "You don't see what that darkie's wearin'?" he snapped. "That don't rile you none? It's like he's laughin' at the South just by standin' there!"

"Leave it be," Jesse told Hardin. "We ain't lookin' for trouble."

Hardin sneered at Jesse. "Well that darkie is," he spat as he turned away from Jesse and the Youngers, proceeding to prowl across the street.

"Hey boy!" Hardin shouted at the black man. "Your master know you're wearin' his duds?"

The outlaw flashed a cheerless smile at Hardin. "Givin' he's rottin' in the ground somewhere nears Appomattox, I doubt he knows nothin' just about now."

The gunfighter sneered at the black man's retort. "I'm tellin' you to get out of them clothes, boy."

"Mister, I don't know what your problem is, but if you'd like to settle it, I'm your huckleberry." The outlaw stepped away from the hitching post and ambled out into the street. He nodded his chin at Hardin. "Let's keep this between the two of us. Your friends can wait their turn."

Hardin didn't look around. He could hear the footsteps behind him. Thinking one of the others was coming over to back his play, he simply growled a warning. "I killed one of these baboons when I was barely off my momma's tit. I don't need no help now…"

The Texan's growl ended in a gasp as a metal fist smacked into the back of his head. For Jesse, it was barely a tap, but to Hardin it was like being hit by a sledgehammer. The gunfighter dropped into the street and his eyes rolled back as all sensation abandoned him.

"Bob, Jim!" Jesse called to his gang. "Find someplace where Hardin can sleep things off for a spell. Maybe when he wakes up he'll feel a might less ornery."

"Yeah, and pigs'll fly," Jim said as he helped Bob lift Hardin from the street and carry him off toward a hotel a few blocks away.

The black man watched as his unconscious antagonist was carried away. "I could have handled that myself, Mr. James."

Jesse wasn't surprised that the outlaw recognized him. There were only so many men prowling the west with a set of mechanical arms bolted to their shoulders. "My apologies, friend, but there's a chance I'm going to need that curly wolf later. I couldn't take the gamble." He waved his hand at the departed gunfighter. "Besides, that's John Wesley Hardin. He ain't exactly a slouch when it comes to a fast draw."

The outlaw smiled and slowly eased back the front of his shell jacket, exposing a brace of derringers sewn into the lining. "I ain't so quick, but when you cheat you don't have to be. Just as happy not to have to tangle with you, Mr. James."

"Jesse," the bushwhacker said. "This old guerrilla behind me is Cole Younger and the fellas carting off your would-be playmate are his brothers Jim and Bob."

"Will Shaft," the black man introduced himself. "Virginia by way of Kansas, in case you was wonderin'."

"An Exoduster?" Cole asked. A great many freed slaves had struck out to make new lives for themselves in the plains of Kansas, terming themselves 'Exodusters' after the Exodus of Moses and the Israelites from Egypt and the dusty climate of the Kansas prairie. Finding themselves isolated by their white neighbors in their new land, the blacks had maintained their identity as Exodusters, feeling they'd yet to reach their 'promised land.'

"Yes, sir," Will said. "They told me I was a free man and I should try to make my own way in the world. Only thing those Free Soilers and abolitionists didn't bother to say was that they didn't want me bein' free anywhere they was. Man gets kicked around from town to town he gets a might riled."

"Riled enough to wear rebel gray?" Jesse asked.

"Blue was never my color," Will grinned. "Besides, that ain't such a good thing to wear hereabouts. Anybody spots a speck of Union uniform on a fella, he starts thinkin' maybe he's found himself a deserter. Army pays fifty dollars for a deserter."

His eyes narrowed as he asked his own question. "What is it brings the great Jesse James to a hole like Robbers Roost?"

"I'm lookin' for someone. Though it seems like now I'll have to wait for Hardin to finish his nap before I can try to find him."

Will shook his head. "Most folks drift in and out of here all the time, but maybe I've seen this man you're lookin' for."

"This varmint supposedly escaped from Camp Lincoln," Cole said. He would have said more, but he saw that he'd already said enough. There was an uneasy, almost haunted expression on Will's face.

"You're lookin' for Kelso Warfield," he said. Will closed his hand tight about the rabbit-skin gris-gris bag hanging about his neck. "I don't suppose I can talk sense to you and get you to leave him be. Warfield's... Well, he ain't right. Even in a place like this, he... Well, you feel dirty just bein' around him. Almost like you brushed up against somethin' unclean." His hand closed tighter about the Voodoo bag.

"He's been inside Camp Lincoln," Jesse said. "We need to talk to him about how the prison is laid out."

"I wouldn't trust anythin' Warfield told me," Will said.

Cole scowled and clenched his fist. "I knew the coyote had to be a liar."

"I didn't say he was a liar," Will corrected Cole. "I just said I wouldn't trust nothin' Warfield told me. Still, if you all are determined to see him, I'll take you to where he's holed up."

***

Will Shaft led the outlaws to the edge of Robbers Roost. The crumbling remains of a Spanish mission squatted on the periphery of a disused stockyard. The entire area had a forsaken atmosphere, an uncanny air of desolation that seemed to stifle the very breath the outlaws drew as they walked toward the collapsed chapel. Stepping inside the rubble, they approached the old bell tower, the only part of the structure that was still mostly intact. The man they were looking for, Will had told them, lived on the middle floor of the tower.

A simple wooden ladder led up from the base of the tower. Before starting their ascent, Jesse called out in a loud voice, "Warfield! Kelso Warfield! We're coming in and we don't mean no harm." There was silence. Only the wind whistling through the crumbling walls answered him. After a few moments, Jesse started his climb. Cole covered him from the ground, keeping his blaster trained on the hole leading up into the tower. Only when Jesse reached the platform above did Cole start his climb.

The room was small, furnished only with a rickety table and chair. A crude pallet of straw was just visible in the gloom. Jesse prowled about in the dimness of the room, but he couldn't see any trace of an occupant.

"Where is he?" Cole asked as he joined Jesse.

Jesse shrugged, knowing that the gesture would be visible even in the weird shadows thanks to the glow of his cybernetics. "Not here, anyway. Not unless…" He remembered what Will had said about this being the middle tier of the tower. That meant there was a room above it. He raised his eyes toward the ceiling.

Instantly, he froze. Just visible by the faint daylight drifting through the broken roof of the tower was the silhouette of a man, poised in the gap leading up to the next level. Although it was just a vague, dark shape, Jesse could feel hostile eyes glaring down at him. Not knowing if there was a gun in the shadowy figure's hand, he was careful to keep his own away from his blasters.

"Kelso Warfield?" Jesse called up to the figure. Cole spun around, following the direction of Jesse's gaze even as he darted behind the ramshackle table.

"Some folks call me that," a dry, somehow desiccated voice drifted down from the ceiling. "Other folks call me other things."

"We only came here to talk," Jesse said. "We wanted to ask you about Camp Lincoln."

A grisly chuckle rose from the shadowy phantom. "Then have Cole light the lantern on that table he's crouching behind. I can see you fine as things are, but you'll no doubt feel more at ease if you can see me too."

"He's got us dead to rights already, Cole," Jesse told his friend. "Might as well light the lamp."

As the lantern slowly sputtered into life, Jesse saw a wooden ladder being lowered from the ceiling. A tall, gaunt figure started climbing down, a heavy black cloak draped about his shoulders. Black boots, black pants, black gloves; the only spot of brightness in Warfield's raiment was the hat he wore. Like the scraps of uniform Will affected, it was rebel gray, the floppy hat of a Confederate cavalry officer, one side of the brim curled back. A black plume was pinned to its side by a silver button.

It wasn't until Warfield reached the bottom of the ladder and turned around that Jesse and Cole had a good look at the man's face; and when they did, both gasped in shock. They knew that face, even if it was much more lean and more pallid than they remembered it, even with tinted glasses covering the eyes.

"Some folks call me Kelso Warfield," the recluse said again, bowing with exaggerated military courtesy as if they were children playing adults. "Some folks know me as Allen Henderson." He said the name slowly, lading on the last syllable for emphasis.

"Henderson," Cole echoed in a whisper. Here was the adjutant of their old commander, Colonel Quantrill. Both of them were supposedly killed decades ago in the last years of the war.

"I ain't no ghost," Henderson assured his former compatriots. "The Yankees shot down others and claimed it was us. A band of Red Legs caught us down in Louisiana, but they didn't have no clue who we were. I gave 'em the name Kelso Warfield and that's who I was while the blue-bellies had me. They kept the boss in Camp Davis, but he escaped shortly afterward. Killed a guard, put on his uniform, and walked out. They had already shipped me off to Andersonville when they reopened the camp, renaming it Lincoln." The leather of Henderson's glove creaked as he clenched his hand into a fist. "Wouldn't grovel afore them none, no matter what name I carried. They tried everything they could to break me, make me submit. They beat me and they starved me, and when that didn't work they threw me in the hole."

Henderson raised a hand to the glasses he wore, tapping the side of one darkened frame. "They kept me down in that pit for months on end. Kept me down there without a speck of light so long my eyes got so I can see as clearly in the blackest night as you can in broad daylight." He laughed bitterly. "Of course there was a trade-off. I can't handle the light very well anymore."

"But you escaped, Henderson," Cole shook his head, still in disbelief. "Nobody else has ever done that."

Henderson nodded. "I escaped. After fifteen years in that hellhole. Made my way out west, nearly dead when Captain Quantrill somehow found me. He kept me hid until I could heal up good enough to strike out. The Captain was heading back into Rebellion territory, but I'd had a bellyful. Weren't so many places a man as wanted as me could go, and I ended up in this little Algerine's paradise.

"While I was in Camp Lincoln, the Union didn't particularly care about Kelso Warfield, but now that I've escaped their impenetrable prison, they're as keen to get Kelso Warfield as they would be Allen Henderson or William Quantrill."

"Well, that escape was the whole reason we came to see you," Jesse said with a nod toward Cole. "John Younger's been sent there and we're going to get him out."

"John Younger?" Henderson asked.

"You wouldn't know him, sir. He was too young to fight in the war," Cole said.

"Too young to go through Camp Lincoln then," Henderson said, and then paused to look at each of the outlaws in turn, his expression and tone both etched with stern sympathy. "Believe me when I say it, but if they've sent John to Camp Lincoln, then he'd be better off dead."

***

The timber stockade stood almost thirty feet high, running in an unbroken ring about the acres set aside for Camp Lincoln. At each corner, a guard tower rose above the wall, the sinister frames of Gatling guns projecting over the parapets, soldiers manning the weapons day and night. Spotlights, humming with crimson RJ power, yawned from the face of each tower, able to bath large swathes of the prison in a brilliance to match that of the noonday sun. Decking stretched across the inner face of the stockade, set twenty-five feet above the ground. Along this walkway, marching in ceaseless cadence, were robot sentries, Army models designated as UR-25 Warders. They were slightly bigger and bulkier than the UR-30 Enforcers; less agile and versatile than the 'bots issued to lawmen in the west. One arm of each Warder was replaced by the bulky barrel of an energy rifle, the weapon built into the 'bot's very frame, making it impossible for a prisoner to disarm it and use its weapon against his captors.

The prison itself was a squalid morass of mud, across which a miserable expanse of canvas tents had been pitched. Here and there, small fields were tended by the inmates; patches of rice, beans, and potatoes that the prisoners desperately tried to cultivate in a hopeless effort to supplement the trifling rations their captors issued to them. Along the eastern wall of the camp, a vast graveyard stretched; simple wooden crosses marking the final resting place of men who weren't allowed to escape captivity even in death.

At the center of the camp, surrounded by a stone wall, were the administration buildings and medical facilities. With most of the guards taking the form of robotic Warders, a large machine shop dominated one of the structures, acting to repair and refit the 'bots as they wore down. A contingent of Rolling Thunder assault wagons were parked against the high wall to one side, insurance against the unlikely event of an attempted prisoner riot. The 'bots were the key to the economy of the prison camp. Although there were better than ten thousand prisoners interned in the prison of Andersonville, only a little more than fifty human soldiers watched over them; the rest of the guard duties fell to the untiring, pitiless Warders.

When John Younger was processed by the prison administrator, the official didn't even raise an eyebrow at the youthfulness of his latest captive. The boy was pushed through channels like any other Secesh. His photo was taken, his name and vital statistics recorded. He was dumped into a vat of chemical powders to remove any lice from his body, and then given a hasty shower where a blue-belly sergeant scrubbed him with a hog-hair broom. Finally, he was brought before the prison doctor, a ridiculous-looking man wearing a gaudy, somehow European-looking military uniform and sporting an enormous walrus-like moustache. The doctor gave him a cursory examination, made a few notes in a leather-bound ledger, and then curtly ordered him removed.

It was when John was led away from the medical building and shoved out the gates and into the camp itself that he understood the full level of misery he had been condemned to. The prisoners gathered about the stone walls were a wretched, ragged sight. Many of them had blotchy, diseased complexions; others were missing hands and feet, arms or legs. Men already reduced to a near skeletal appearance were further tortured by wracking coughs and the sweating shivers of malaria. These were the desperate and the forsaken, those whose dignity and composure had ebbed to such a degree that they gathered around the walls of the inner compound to beg their captors for even the slightest consideration or expression of mercy.

In their despair, these wretches turned their ire against John. As he was pushed out the gate, the prisoners jeered at him, mocking him for his youth. They wondered how a boy so young could have fought the Yankees in the war. Several made lewd suggestions about John's mother and her activities during the war. When John reacted to the catcalls and jeers, a crude wooden crutch cracked against his back, spilling him into the mud. Kicks and punches soon followed as the prisoners vented their frustration and dejection against the outsider who had been thrust into their midst.

The strength behind those kicks and punches was too feeble to deal John any real physical harm; the pain was emotional. It was the humiliation, the sense of utter isolation and loneliness, that truly beat him down. Such was his inner turmoil that he didn't realize his tormentors had withdrawn until he felt a hand reach down and lift him out of the mud.

As he regained his feet, John gazed in shock at his rescuer. He would have collapsed back into the mud if the man hadn't helped him to stay standing. He couldn't believe who was in front of him.

His rescuer was Frank James.

Chapter 13

There was an unseasonable chill in the darkened ruin of the mission's old sanctuary. The outline of a cross, long ago stolen and melted down by impious bandits, was etched high upon the inner wall, the adobe brick behind it discolored by the long years when this had been a place of worship. Now, it was just a dilapidated hall; one wall completely caved outward in a jumble of broken bricks, many of the wooden support beams stabbing down from the roof into the floor below. The pews had been broken down long ago to use as firewood, the top of the altar looted so that its granite surface might serve for a hearthstone in some plunderer's home. Except for the dust and tumbleweeds, skittering horny toads and scurrying armadillos, the old chapel was empty.

The outlaws of Robbers Roost gave the crumbling mission a wide berth, uncomfortable with any reminder that they might be answerable to a Higher Power for their sins. For someone wanting to conduct a clandestine meeting, no place in the town could offer better seclusion.

Such, at least, had been Henderson's advice. With strange shadows trickling down through the shattered tile roof, the men of the James-Younger Gang gathered in the forsaken sanctuary, perching on piles of broken brick, sitting on the splintered remains of fallen beams, leaning against the stone columns that reached up toward the decayed roof. John Wesley Hardin, the Younger Brothers, even the Exoduster renegade Will Shaft all watched as Henderson climbed up into the iron-railed pulpit. He adjusted the cloudy glasses he wore, pushing them closer to his eyes when a stray beam of sunlight shot across the pulpit and illuminated the defiled altar.

When he spoke, Henderson addressed his words to the metal-armed bushwhacker sitting on the toppled mass of some defaced plaster saint. Jesse James listened with such an enthralled ear that he didn't even notice when a lizard scrambled over his pant leg on its way across the fallen statue.

"You all know the bold plan Jesse proposes. You all know he's come here to ask me how you can break into Camp Lincoln and liberate John Younger from the vengeful grasp of the Yankees." Henderson shook his head, his hardened voice taking on a note of regret. "I admire your pluck and the nobility of your purpose, but I have to tell you here and now that gettin' somebody out of that pit is above one's bend. The blue-bellies have got walls thirty feet high all around the place, with 'bots prowlin' about 'em day and night. They got seven towers, each with an automatic repeating gun that can splatter two score rebs in the wink of an eye. That ain't to mention the vocal reiterator. Make a move on them and they'll have every Yankee soldier from Virginia to Christmas prowling the roads looking for you."

"You got out," Jesse said. "If'n a man can get out, it means other men can too." He looked around at the rest of his gang. "We figure out how it was done afore, and we see how it can be done again."

Henderson leaned heavily on the pulpit railing. "I don't think you'd much favor the way I got out of there." The shadowy man shook his head and there was a sick curl of his lip as he recounted to the outlaws how he'd escaped from the prison. "There'd been another outbreak of cholera. I'd been there when it happened before and I knew upwards of a quarter of us wouldn't make it through the winter. And sure enough, I took sick. The blue-bellies let me out of the hole when they saw that. They didn't see no sense keeping a man who was more'n half dead down there. Once I was back circulating among the rest of the rebs, I watched and I waited.

"The chief medical officer at Camp Lincoln is a human devil who took full advantage of the outbreak to experiment on the prisoners. He had the camp commandant wrapped about his finger and could pretty well do as he liked. Anyway, he'd send his orderlies out to gather up the sickest men, drag them off to the hospital shed and, well, ain't but a few fellas ever came back from there. Sometimes wagons would leave, always loaded down with big wooden casks."

Henderson's smile projected a wickedness that lingered below the surface and he again pressed his glasses close to his eyes, as though trying to blot out the image he saw in his mind. "A few of us managed to sneak around and crack open one of them casks late at night while the wagon was being loaded. What we found inside was all that was left of a captain from the Texas Cavalry. I can't even describe half what the doctor did to 'im, but what was left he'd stuffed into the cask, leaving it to float in something like a brine mixed with grain alcohol.

"The other prisoners weren't so ornery then. Once they saw that corpse floating about in there, they was done. I was too sick to be squeamish, though I knew if I didn't get out of Camp Lincoln, I'd be a dead man. So I hunkered down in that there cask, down in that briny alcohol, with the bits of that captain floating around me, and I waited. Weren't long before the wagon got moving and the Yankees drove me straight out of the camp. Never did learn where they was taking the pickled bodies they was hauling. A few miles out of Andersonville, I crawled up out of that cask and I kilt both them ghouls driving up front. Afore I left, I set the whole corpse-coach on fire. Burning, I figured, was a damn sight better'n whatever the Yankees were gonna do to them bodies, wherever they was going."

Cole rose slowly to his feet. "Murderin', thievin' coyotes!" he shouted. "Won't even let a man be buried decent and Christian!" He ripped his hat off his head and shook it at the pulpit. "Hang what you say Allen, but I ain't leavin' my little brother in the hands of such low-down grunters. By hook or by crook, we're gettin' him out of there!"

"Ease off, Cole," Hardin said. "You heard what Henderson done told us. That dog won't hunt. Ain't no way nobody is gonna bust somebody out of that pit."

Jim and Bob glared at the black-clad Texan. Cole looked irate enough to go for his guns. Jesse distracted the outlaws before their tempers could get worked into a worse state. He'd seen both Cole and Hardin in action, knew that if it came to a standoff then Hardin would handily outdraw Cole. Then Jesse would be obliged to avenge his friend. That'd diminish his gang considerably right when he needed every gun he could get.

"It ain't open for discussion," he told the outlaws. Jesse held each man's gaze with a steely stare. "We're gettin' John out of there, whatever it takes. Any man feels otherwise can light out now. I won't call him a coward." The way Jesse said the last bit made it clear that while he might not *say* it, he would most certainly *think* it.

Up on the pulpit, Henderson smiled down at Jesse. "You were always a bold one, saw that when we rode in and burned Lawrence. But I wonder if you really are bold enough to tackle Camp Lincoln."

"Ride with us and see for yourself, Henderson," Jesse said.

"I might do that," Henderson nodded. "If I thought you were doing it for something right. For something bigger than just rescuing your own." The shadowy figure pointed his finger accusingly at Jesse. "You used to fight for more'n just one man. You used to fight for a cause."

"We lost the war, Allen," Jesse said. "Only a fool can't see that. The cause is over."

"Is Yankee tyranny over?" Henderson asked. "The Union still imposing its word and its will on folks who don't want any part of it? President Johnson sittin' there nigh-on twenty years without any election? This freedom they're so quick to impose, how many people are they really willing to let share in it? They let our folks down in Missouri live their lives, try to prosper, or are they busy sending copperheads and carpet-baggers down there to steal every speck of land and every yellow hammer they can pick out of man's pocket? Are the courts upholding laws or just rubber-stamping whoever pays them the most? We have representation now, or just whatever skunk Washington thinks will do and say what they expect him to do?"

Jesse brought one of his metal hands crashing down against the fallen saint, sending a jagged crack running the length of the statue. "It don't change facts. The cause is lost."

"It's only lost if you let it be," Henderson told him. "You want to break into Camp Lincoln, I say you go big figure. Don't just do it for yourself, do it so you strike a blow against the whole damn Union! Send a message loud and clear to all those who still keep the Confederacy in their hearts, that the time of tyrants isn't gonna last!"

Henderson lifted his arms, his coat spreading about him like the wings of some black angel. "Be more than just Jesse James the bandit and robber. Set that aside! Be Jesse James the rebel! Jesse James the revolutionary! Jesse James the hero!" The man, who seemed like a prophet at this point, shook his head. "You want to rescue only John from that camp? I say that's selfish and petty! I say what you should really be thinking about is how to liberate Andersonville and rescue every man-jack in Camp Lincoln!"

Henderson's shout reverberated through the ruined sanctuary, but nowhere did it echo louder than in Jesse's heart. The prophetic speech was like lightning searing through him, forcing him to confront the pettiness of his ambitions since the end of the war, making him face the hedonistic materialism that had become his only purpose in life. Even rescuing John – even that had selfishness about it, a personal drive to ease the guilt he felt over the boy's capture. Henderson was right; he didn't think about others, he didn't appreciate anything bigger than himself. He'd allowed everything he'd ever believed in to die inside him; he had accepted that the victorious Union had taken hope from him. What Henderson was saying was that it stayed dead only as long as he allowed it.

Slowly, Jesse walked over to the pulpit. He reached out, laying one of his hands against the base of the platform near Henderson's boot, and looked up at him. "You really think it's possible? You really think everyone can be rescued?"

"If anybody else asked me, the answer would be no. But with the legendary Jesse James leading the charge, I think the chances are good. A lot better than those men have if they stay there under the doubtful mercies of the blue-bellies."

Jesse nodded. "Then we'd better make our plans. Because if it's possible, I'm gonna empty that prison right down to the bury patch."

***

John Younger sat at the opening of the miserable canvas tent, staring at the man sprawled on the thin layer of straw that was the closest thing to a bed most of the prisoners of Andersonville would ever know again. The cotton blanket was pulled tight about the man's body, but it was too thin to effectively fend off the cold; especially for a man wracked by fever.

"I want his boots, boy." The words came in a low hiss from just outside the tent. From the corner of his eye, John could see the speaker; a snaggletoothed villain who still had the remnants of a Georgian insignia on his decayed shell jacket. The human vulture had been perched outside for most of the previous night and all through the morning. "He ain't got no use for 'em, nohow. Give 'em to me."

John looked over at his sick tent-mate, at the bare stockings sticking out from the edge of the blanket, and at the boots standing neatly beside the man's head. Leaning forward, he retrieved the footwear, trying his best not to disturb his companion.

"That's it!" the vulture cackled, but his laughter ended in a pained yelp as John spun around and smacked the heel of the boot across his jaw. The scavenger was knocked onto his rear, sputtering and cursing at the young outlaw.

"You made a mistake boy!" the vulture snarled. "Your pal ain't never gonna get off'n his sick bed! We'll be plantin' him in the bone orchard afore long. Then where'll you be?"

John glared back at the Georgian, a vicious smile on his face. "Where'll you be if his brother ever hears about this?"

The question made the color drain out of the scavenger's face. His curses faded off in a frightened sputter. John's suggestion was more than an empty threat. Every day, the Union was investing more resources in the hunt for Jesse James. When they caught him, there was only one place they'd send him to. The same place they'd sent his brother Frank. The vulture knew this and lost interest in a new pair of boots, instead scurrying off to lose himself in the maze of tents all around them.

The man disgusted John, but at the same time it was hard not to pity him. The inmates of Camp Lincoln had suffered so much for so long that they'd lost most of their humanity. They couldn't afford anything more than whatever would keep them alive, no matter how callous their actions. Before he'd taken sick, Frank James had told John about how he'd seen food stolen from sick men on a regular basis, their fellow prisoners reasoning that it was wasted on men who were going to die anyway.

Maybe it was naïve of John, but he refused to view Frank in that light – he was, after all, Jesse's brother. He was made of sterner stuff. He kept thinking of the wonderment and jubilation Jesse would have when he found out his brother had survived the battle outside of Diablo Canyon. He kept thinking of all the raids Frank had ridden alongside his brothers Cole and Jim. Frank was still the man who had pulled him out from under that sad mob when he first arrived in Camp Lincoln, a thought that kept running through John's mind. He owed Frank for that, if nothing more, that alone would make John beholden to him.

Disease was an omnipresent threat in the squalid, unsanitary confines of Camp Lincoln. Still weak from the wounds he had received when he was captured, Frank had succumbed to the latest round of illness sweeping through the camp. From what Frank had told him, John knew how slim the chances of recovery were. Without the assistance of the camp doctors, few who took sick in Andersonville's prison ever recovered.

Though it rested heavy on his conscience, John realized the only way for him to help Frank was to leave him alone and try to beg help from the camp doctors. The notion of joining that same desperate throng that had nearly mobbed him on his arrival to the prison was revolting to him, but what else could he do?

"I'll be back," John promised the man shivering on the ground. Before he left the tent, he tucked Frank's boots under his arm. The desperate inmates all around them might not stoop to murder, but theft was almost a certainty. The boots would be just too much of a temptation, as the Georgian vulture had so vividly displayed.

Quitting the tent, John looked across the morass of muddy earth and filthy canvas shelters. Many of the prisoners still wore the gray tatters of their uniforms, the garments tied crudely about their starved bodies by bootlaces and strips torn from tents and blankets. Everywhere there was the haunted, empty look of broken men; faces so oppressed by the misery of existence that not only hope, but even fear, had been beaten out of their eyes.

What was left was only a terrible blankness, the unfocused stare of men trying to lose themselves in a landscape of memory.

Very few things could spark an ember of interest or excitement in such men, but one of those things was the appearance among them of what the prisoners called 'rebel angels.' These were volunteer nurses, southern ladies who offered to administer aid to the inmates of Camp Lincoln. There were never many of them, but their presence was the only bright spot in the dreary ordeal these men endured day upon day. It was the strictest rule that these female Samaritans never be harassed or offended; the prisoners were quick about policing any of their own who broke this rule. More than the meager medical aid that the nurses provided, it was the lifting up of their spirits that the mere presence of a woman provoked, that the prisoners held sacrosanct.

As he looked across the camp, John noted some of the inmates displaying the excitement that characterized the proximity of a nurse. Jogging down the muddy path between the tents, John soon saw a figure dressed in white, kneeling down in the mud and changing the bandages wrapped about the foot of a scarecrow-like Virginian. There was no small crowd around the nurse, but John was only recently arrived in Camp Lincoln and he was still hale and hearty, while the men around him were half-starved and sickly. It was moral repugnance rather than physical impediment that delayed John's thrust to the front of the crowd.

"Nurse!" John cried. "My friend, he's taken sorely sick! I wish you'd come and look at him."

The nurse looked up and John couldn't help but marvel at the loveliness of her face, the admixture of natural beauty colored by sympathy and utmost concern. She finished binding the man's foot and then turned toward John. "You're new to this camp, aren't you?" she asked. It was a question he thought fairly obvious by the condition of his clothes, much less the fact that he was at least a decade younger than any other man in the camp. His youth made him stand out like the spots on a playing card.

"Yes, ma'm," John said. "My friend's been here a sight longer. Long enough to catch the fever. Please, you've got to come help him." He injected the last of his words with that desperate, boyish smile that Jim always resented because of its effect on women. The nurse wasn't any exception. Finishing with the man she was ministering to, she made her apologies to the other sickly men begging her for help. John felt pangs of guilt as he led her away from them, but there was nothing else to be done if he was going to help Frank. That was the blunt, brutal truth, as unsavory as it might be to swallow.

Outlaw and nurse hurried through the labyrinth of tents, both of them forcing themselves to be deaf to the weak voices that called out to her as her white uniform was noticed by men too sick to leave their shelters. The guilt John felt turned into a smoldering anger. Rage built toward the Union fiends who would inflict such misery on these men; to abandon them to such slow, lingering torture. It was with a relief more profound than anything he'd felt before that they reached Frank's tent and he pulled aside the flap to admit the nurse.

"Frank," he called to the man lying on the ground. "I've brought you help. This here's Miss… ah… Miss…"

"Lucy," the nurse finished for him, crouching down beside Frank. Frank looked at her through his fever. She looked familiar, but his eyes kept going in and out of focus. She laid her hand across his forehead, feeling the sweat beading his brow and the fever burning inside his head. She frowned and looked up at John. "Has he been like this long?"

John nodded. "It might have been settin' in even afore I was brought here two months ago, but it really struck him down last night. Is there anythin' you can do?"

"It looks like malaria." She reached into the pocket of her coat, drawing out a small leather pouch. Carefully, she counted out a handful of tiny pills. John handed her the battered canteen that the two men were forced to share. "Hold up his head," Lucy ordered. As John complied, she tugged open Frank's mouth with her thumb and forced one of the pills onto his tongue. A swallow of water sent the medicine down his throat.

"Quinine," Lucy explained. "It will help to break the fever, though it should have been more effective if he'd been given it before the disease was ever allowed to settle into him. Now, I'm afraid, he'll have the potential for relapse the rest of his life."

"But, he'll live?" John asked eagerly.

"If the fever breaks," Lucy said, worry straining at her voice and turning her expression grim. She turned her head, wincing when she found Frank's eyes fixed upon her. She could almost feel the outlaw's mind struggling to pierce the confusion of fever to understand why she looked familiar to him. To remember the woman who had been introduced to him as Lucinda Loveless. How he would react when his mind made that connection was a problem that troubled her almost as much as the fever itself.

Despite the hundreds of other men needing her attentions, the nurse remained to watch over Frank for several hours. Only when the fever lessened, and Frank was able to not only open his eyes, but actually focus on those around him, and frame a coherent request for more water, did she accept that her vigil had ended. Handing John a half dozen pills, she gave him instructions for Frank's continued treatment.

"Bless you, Miss Lucy," John said, bowing with that same gentlemanly mannerism with which his brother Cole always favored a lady.

"Yes... thank you," Frank said, lifting his head from the pallet. For a moment, his eyes held the woman's. There was no mistaking the recognition in that look. "Thank you... *nurse*," the outlaw said before sliding back against the pillow.

Loveless rose and made her way to the tent's opening, relieved that the outlaw hadn't revealed her secret. "See that you give him the pills," she cautioned. "If you want him to recover, you need to promise that you'll remember that." She nodded toward Frank. "It would be awful for the brother of Jesse James to die such a useless death."

John gave a start, his eyes narrowing as he looked at the nurse. "You... you know who he is?"

"There's no mistaking Frank James," she said. "They've plastered his picture on wanted posters across the entire Union. It'd take someone far less observant than a nurse to forget a face they've seen every time they wanted to post a letter."

The young outlaw looked back at Frank. "Don't let anybody know he's sick," his voice was pleading. "Frank's big fear was that the commandant would take him back to the doctors. I don't know what they done to him when he first came here, but he'd rather die than go through it again."

Smiling sympathetically, the nurse nodded. "I'll check back on you tomorrow. And I won't tell the doctors." Slipping through the flap, the nurse returned to the maze of tents and the hundreds of sick prisoners clamoring for her help.

"That's... that's a fine... woman," Frank muttered, his voice a harsh croak.

John hurried over to his friend's side. "She gave me medicine. She broke your fever."

Frank managed a weak nod and sank back onto the bed of straw. "Then I'm obliged. I always feel uncomfortable being obliged to women."

"She's tryin' to help," John said. In his fever, it seemed Frank was becoming paranoid, imagining that Lucy was some spy or agent of the camp commandant. When the old bushwhacker spoke, however, he revealed that his fears weren't about spies.

"She can help us," Frank said, "but how can we help... her?"

"I don't understand," John said. "She's got reg'lar meals and a real roof over her head. She's better off'n we are."

Frank's eyes focused on John, becoming fierce in their intensity. "She ain't," he said. "Not by a long shot. Them rebel angels don't tend to last too long." He pointed at the flap of the tent. "You watch for her. If'n you ever see her sent at night to that big wooden ward building on the north side of the compound, you won't never see her again."

John kneeled beside Frank, grasping his shoulder, a sudden surge of panic sweeping through him. "Why? What're the Yankees doin' there? What kinda danger would they pose to a woman?"

John could feel the shudder that passed through Frank's body. Even in the misery of Camp Lincoln, there were some horrors too terrible for the prisoners to speak of. The building in question was one of them. "She goes there, she's goin' into Dr. Tumblety's surgery," Frank said. "Ain't no woman goes in there and comes back again."

The surgery had the stinging pungency of antiseptics in the air, a chemical stink that was restrained and magnified by the closed confines of the building. The many windows were kept bolted and shuttered day and night, many of them nailed closed permanently. The doors were similarly kept locked, a UR-25 Warder standing before each one in perpetual vigil. A regular rotation of the 'bots patrolled the flattened roof of the building, the steady tromp of their steel feet creating a dull throb that pervaded every corner of the ward.

The building was one of the few survivors of the original Confederate prison that had stood there. Defying the flames of the vengeful conflagration that had consumed the rest of the camp, the old hospital had assumed a haunted reputation among the staff of Camp Lincoln. The outrages and atrocities inflicted upon the Union prisoners who had once been confined there seemed to resonate through the grim halls of the hospital. There were few in Andersonville who would willingly venture near the shunned and blighted place.

It was that pungent atmosphere of offense and wrongness that had drawn Dr. Francis Tumblety to select the old hospital for his surgery and recovery ward. He wanted seclusion and isolation, two commodities that were in short supply within the cramped confines of a prison camp. Selecting the one spot which prisoners, guards, and townspeople alike regarded with natural aversion was simply the logical decision.

Tumblety prided himself on his logical, keenly analytical mind. He was a man of pure reason, guided by the principles of rational science rather than emotional urges and the stubbornness of tradition. As he'd taken great pains to illustrate in his self-published volume, *Dr. Francis Tumblety – Sketch of the Life of the Gifted, Eccentric, and World Famed Physician*, he was a man of humble mien and selfless devotion to science and medical advancement. Let self-aggrandizing cretins like Tesla and Carpathian court the press and seek the laurels of an overly credulous public; he would lay before the people of the world a new science that would shake the very pillars of convention! His name would stand above the scions of reason, greater than Galileo, Newton, and Copernicus!

Tumblety leaned back in his chair and smoothed the luxuriant mass of his walrus-like moustache. His eyes roved about the immaculate tile floors, the unblemished plaster walls of his surgery. He frowned slightly at the huge electric lamps arrayed about the various vivisection stations; a concession to Tesla's inventions and the practicality of avoiding the soot from oil lamps. The galvanic batteries that were arrayed around each station were a far more clever creation, derived from Tumblety's own experiments with electrical stimulation of living tissues. It was a magnificent derivation of applied reason, extrapolating such stimulation from the semi-occult researches of Johann Konrad Dippel, the notorious 18th century German alchemist. Only a man of Tumblety's vision could have stripped away the arcane nomenclature of Dippel's writings to recover the anatomical and physiological theories that lay hidden beneath the trappings of soul-transference and the Elixir of Life.

He had, of course, gone far beyond Dippel. The German simply never had the resources available to him that Tumblety had acquired. He had known Lincoln when he was in office and enjoyed the favor of the War Secretary Stimson. He was so renowned that at the snap of his fingers, he could get any consideration his experiments required from the government – the obfuscations of that foreign ass Tesla notwithstanding. It grated on Tumblety's sensibilities that a barely civilized Serbian should be afforded an American citizenship of the same caliber as an Irishman like himself. He was minded to take the matter up with Secretary of War Upton the next time he was in Washington, to impress again on him the erratic temperament of people like Tesla.

Tumblety gave his moustache an anxious twist, his eyes roving over to the rack of bottled surgical specimens that formed his own personal collection. Perhaps it would be better not to broach the subject to the Secretary. He might – irrational though it was – draw a comparison between Tesla's eccentricities and the recent unpleasantness that had accumulated around Tumblety's last visit to London. There was nothing to it of course, nothing but lies and innuendo, but he couldn't quite forget the unseemly haste with which Pinkerton agents had collected him in New York and spirited him away. It was, naturally, preposterous that Scotland Yard had actually sent detectives looking for him, but that was the story they'd used to ensure his cooperation.

The door into Tumblety's surgery slowly creaked open. He swung around in his chair, his eyes focusing on the white-uniformed figure that came creeping into the ward. The nurse was timidity itself, so demure and shy in her manner that he was reminded of a scared rabbit stealing across a meadow. Her face was comely, her hair descending in a dark cascade about her shoulders. He could see the swell of her body beneath her uniform as she moved; the inviting sway of her hips as she walked toward him. Yet, there was a slatternly wantonness in the curve of her lips. Her scent was intoxicating, overpowering the clean antiseptic smell of the surgery. He could feel it seeping down into his body, threatening to overwhelm his senses, to drown his intellect beneath a patina of primitive emotion.

"You… you sent for me?" the nurse asked.

Tumbletey was not deceived by the faltering words and the tremulous voice. He knew every inflection was calculated to entice and entrap. His eyes strayed again to the collection of surgical specimens lining the shelves. He'd built that collection himself, piece by piece and bit by bit. Every organ floating in its solution of alcohol had a memory associated with it, a moment in time when he'd struck back at the irrational tyranny of instinct and nature.

"You sent for me… Doctor?" the woman asked again.

Tumblety's face spread in a cold, reptilian smile. He rose slowly from his chair. Without saying a word, without even looking at the nurse, he stalked across the surgery toward one of the vivisection theatres. He could feel the nurse's eyes watching him, could sense the uneasiness throbbing through her veins. She was perplexed, discomfited that her feminine wiles were ineffective on him. The first flickers of fear were running through her veins, the fear of a man she couldn't control and bend to her will. Fear of a man she couldn't seduce and betray.

Picking up a bone-handled surgical knife, Tumblety turned back toward the nurse, his eyes glittering with undisguised malignance. There was no need for pretense, not here. Let her know what was coming, let her appreciate the magnitude of her defeat. There was no escape. Not from this place.

"My colleagues call me 'doctor,'" Tumblety said as he advanced toward the nurse, the knife gleaming in his hand.

"Whores call me Jack."

Chapter 14

Jesse James sat in the old mission's bell tower, leaning over the table in Henderson's reclusive quarters and studying the map arrayed before him. The former raider had drawn the map from memory and Jesse was impressed by the sharpness of his recollections. Every tent and grave seemed to be picked out, much less the buildings and fortifications that the outlaws would need to overcome if a raid against Andersonville's prison was to be any kind of success.

In many ways, Jesse still found the prospect of such a raid staggering in its audacity. This wasn't going to be a simple attack on a train or bank. This was going to be altogether different than anything he had been involved in since RJ technology had been invented. This was going to be a direct attack against the hated Union itself; he would be spitting in the face of Grant and all of the other reprobates in Washington. It would be no different than the battles they'd fought during the war.

That wasn't quite right either, Jesse reflected. In the war, even for a loose outfit like Quantrill's Raiders, there had been rules and obligations, a chain of command to answer to, a country to support and defend. None of that applied now. This was just Jesse James, answerable only to his own conscience. The decisions were his to make. The risks were his to decide.

"It'll take at least a hundred men to hit that camp," Jesse said, one of his metal fingers sliding along the demarcation of the perimeter wall. "I'll need five for each of the towers, enough to keep the guards pinned down if they can't kill 'em outright. No less than thirty to hit the main gate. We'll need a good cadre of sharpshooters with heavy-hittin' blasters to pick off them Warders as well. Stuff with enough kick to put a bot down for good." The outlaw sighed as he ran his finger into the sprawl of the camp itself and the confusion of tents strewn about the grounds. "Breakin' in will be a damn sight easier than gettin' the men back out."

Henderson sat in the corner of the room, little more than a shadow in the darkness. "You'll do it, Jesse," he assured the outlaw. "You'll do it because it's what needs doing. Those men are depending on you, not just John but all them thousands of rebs in there with him. You won't let them down."

Jesse shook his head. "When we hit that camp, sure as shootin', somebody's gonna call out the troops against us across the whole state. Every garrison between there and Texas will be mobilized. Our only chance is to have enough firepower that there won't be a fort or cavalry troop that'd dare tangle with us. Make the Yankees turn out a whole army to put us down. And while they're gatherin' up such a force, we skedaddle into parts they won't be too keen to follow."

"That'll take resources," Henderson observed. "More men and equipment than you're going to find in Robbers Roost or a dozen places like it."

"We can pick up gear off'n the blue-bellies. Just like we always done." Jesse paused for a moment, picturing the other possibility. Dr. Carpathian would sell guns and mounts for such an adventure, but given his recent encounter with the scientist, Jesse knew that such a price would be paid in more than gold alone.

Henderson seemed to be considering the same option. "We go hitting all these forts and trains like you want, even the Yankees will get wise to what we're up to. They'll start pouring more troops into Andersonville, then turn the prison into a stronghold that we'll never be able to break." The shade's voice dropped to a grisly hiss. "I wouldn't put it past them to start shooting the prisoners just to make sure we couldn't free them."

Jesse's eyes blazed as he mulled over that possibility. Anyone who'd seen what was left after Sherman's March knew there were no limits to what the Union was capable of. Still, if they turned to Carpathian to outfit them, they'd just be trading one Devil for another. "What do you suggest, Allen? We go with hat in hand to beg supplies off'n Carpathian and his Enlightened?"

"I wasn't thinking of Carpathian," Henderson said. "I was thinking that a venture such as this would be of interest down south to President Lee."

Jesse almost laughed at that. The continuing Confederate Rebellion had been isolated and cordoned off in the extreme southeast of the country. Some disparagingly referred to it as the 'Remnant,' and even for the Confederacy's staunchest supporters, there was no denying the diminished, impoverished state of the territory Robert E. Lee and his troops continued to hold. If not for the more immediate threat posed by the Warrior Nation and Carpathian's Enlightened, the Union Army would have smashed Lee's forces years ago. As it stood, the blue-bellies were content to simply contain the secessionist forces and leave them to wither on the vine.

"I don't see how Lee's in any position to help himself, much less anybody else," Jesse said.

Henderson stepped out of the darkness, his face drawn and grave. "Lee doesn't have the resources to fight a prolonged campaign. He can't capture territory or go toe-to-toe with the Yankees. Mustering the troops and providing provisions for a raid on Andersonville – that would be within his capability. The key will be to impress on him the feasibility of such an assault. You'll have to sell him on the idea, Jesse."

"I'm a fighter, not a diplomat," Jesse said with a scowl.

"A leader has to be whatever the situation calls for," Henderson told him. "He has to stop thinking only about himself and start considering the bigger picture. He has to think about all those things that are bigger than himself."

"Is that how Quantrill led us in the war?"

Henderson pushed his tinted spectacles closer to his eyes. "That was war. Things were different. What you're planning isn't war, it's liberation. You aren't leading men to death; you're leading them to life and freedom. That calls for an entirely different sort of man; the kind of man who not only destroys but who can rebuild."

Jesse tapped his metal fingers against the table. What his old commander's adjutant told him was simply the echo of what he already felt inside. He could free these men, of that he was certain. It was what happened after they were liberated, that was the problem which both tantalized and troubled him. On the one hand, it was an onerous burden to be responsible for so many lives. At the same time, the possibilities having an army behind him would open up were all too enticing. He could carve out a new land away from Yankee oppression, a land where those who rejected the tyranny of Washington could be free.

It was a captivating vision. Freeing the men trapped in Camp Lincoln would be the first step toward making that dream a reality.

                              ***

It wasn't long before word of Jesse's presence in Robbers Roost made the rounds, spread along that phantom network that lawmen sometimes termed the 'outlaw telegraph.' It caused a steady stream of road agents, rustlers, and bandits to come trooping into the lawless town. They were all drawn by the same thing: the fame and reputation of the notorious bank robber. The same nebulous network that told them Jesse was in Robbers Roost also claimed he was looking to expand the James-Younger Gang. A position in the infamous outlaw band was something to be coveted by hardened gunslingers and criminals. Around the Laughing Wolf Saloon, where the gang had established its temporary headquarters, a mob of desperados gathered each morning, keen to extol their virtues to Jesse James and Cole Younger. Each man spared no effort as he tried to inveigle himself into the gang's ranks.

The three riders who slowly made their way into town this particular morning had a very different objective in mind. Two of the men, scruffy-looking ruffians, were dressed in sorely weathered oilcloth slickers and sporting the battered remnants of broad-brimmed cowboy sombreros, the felt stained and weathered by the dust of the trail. They had broad, boyish faces with close-set eyes and only the slightest trace of chin. It was clear from a glance that the two were branches from the same tree, brothers or cousins of some close affinity.

The third rider, draped in a black duster to conceal the brass armor beneath that had been bought with blood money, had the predatory cast of a wild beast about him. While his companions rode blackhoofs, he was mounted on a sleek Iron Horse, its hood adorned with the ossified remains of a cattle skull. The eyes of the balding man with a thick beard roved from side to side, watching the outlaw denizens they passed on their slow ride down the street with keen wariness. The brain behind those eyes was putting names to some of those faces, and affixing prices to many of those names.

"I still don't like it," the older of the two brothers hissed at the man in black. "Our part in your plan is the riskier one. We should be gettin' a bigger share of the reward."

Thomas Tate Tobin fixed a withering glare on the boyish rider. "A quarter of the reward is already generous," he said in a low growl. "Don't forget the pardon waitin' for both of you when we turn him in. Or maybe I should have just turned you two over for the bounty on your heads and tried a lone hand?"

The younger brother eased across his saddle, his eyes glittering like those of a snake. "If you'd thought you could pull this on your own, you'd never have offered us a deal."

"A deal you accepted," the bounty hunter reminded him. "You were quite happy to agree to my proposal when I made it."

The older outlaw scowled. "You don't exactly negotiate with a man who has the drop on you and says if you don't do as he tells you he's a goin' to shoot you like a dog and turn your head in for two hundred dollars."

"One hundred dollars," Tobin corrected him. His smile was as cold as ice. "Two hundred is for the set."

"However that might be, Mr. Bounty Man," the younger of the outlaws said. "We still figure we're runnin' most of the risk. We should get more of the reward."

Tobin nodded, seeming to take the question under consideration. He patted the rifle scabbard bolted to the side of his steed. "Well, I reckon if'n we trim my share it might interfere with my marksmanship. Don't forget, I only need one of you to get Jesse's head."

The expressions on the faces of the two outlaws grew vicious. "You do that and you'd better watch your back," the older one warned.

Tobin chuckled at the threat. "I've never seen a rat yet that went out huntin' a wolf. More like whichever of you makes it will forget about the other and start thinkin' about how his own share just got bigger." Tobin laughed again when he saw the brothers cast suspicious glares at each other. Scavenging vermin, they knew each other well enough to appreciate the truth in his assessment of them.

They also knew what the opportunist expected of them. As Tobin's eyes roved the dusty main street of Robbers Roost, his gaze focused upon the old mission and the bell tower rising above the ruins. He pointed a gloved finger at the structure. "That's where I'll be. You'll bring Jesse out into the street, lead him off toward the stables. He gets to about this point, and I'll gun him."

"And what if you miss?" the younger outlaw asked.

"In that unlikely particular, you two will be right beside Jesse," Tobin said. "He'll be payin' attention to me up in the tower. He won't be keepin' his eyes on you. I don't reckon shootin' somebody in the back'll bother you none."

The outlaw brothers glowered at Tobin, but they didn't say anything about his contemptuous remark. There was too much truth behind it to challenge.

***

The bounty hunter climbed up toward the old mission, using the block of crude cabins ranged behind the town's main street to conceal his approach for most of the distance. His hand tightened around the neck of the rifle he carried at his side. Not for the first time, he thought of the reward being offered for Jesse. After leaving Fort Concho, he'd reached the decision that trying to collect the bonus for bringing the outlaw back alive wasn't practical. It was better to settle for a sure thing than play the long odds. Besides, his pride still stung from the way Jesse had slipped through his fingers before. He wasn't going to take any chances of that happening again.

The two desperados he'd recruited would do their job. They'd lead Jesse out into the ambush Tobin was preparing. The story they were to give was that their partner had a number of Iron Horses to sell. The way Jesse was recruiting men into his gang, the outlaw was certain to be in need of mounts. Tobin was relying on that. Necessity was the quickest way to penetrate someone's caution.

They'd lead Jesse off to the stables to examine the 'Horse that Tobin had rode in on, a 'sample' of the steeds they had to sell. As he crossed from the saloon to the stables, Jesse would come in range of Tobin's rifle. The bounty hunter's first shot would settle the outlaw; after that, he would maintain a steady fusillade to drive the inhabitants of the town from the streets. In the confusion, his two desperados would snatch up Jesse's body and make their escape.

Tobin could count on the scum to do that much. The reward was big enough that their greed would pour some iron into their yellow spines. He wasn't fool enough to think they'd stick to the rest of their agreement. They'd try to cut him out of the bounty and claim it for themselves. Well and good. Let them try. It was a long trail back to Fort Concho.

Stealing toward the ruinous mission, Tobin glanced back at the town below. He'd always resisted making a catch in Robbers Roost before, judging the risks to be unequal to the rewards. The outlaw town had been more useful to him as a place to pick up the trail of a bandit or gunslinger, to track his quarry and run them down miles away. After this, those days would be through. There'd be too much chance somebody would recognize him and remember him as the 'man who shot Jesse James.'

The bounty hunter crept into the dim chamber at the base of the tower. He lingered in the darkened setting, letting his eyes adjust to the change in light, listening for any sound from the rooms above. When he was satisfied that he was alone and his eyes were as accustomed to the shadows as they were going to get, Tobin started his climb up the wooden ladder.

He emerged through the trap door into the center level of the tower. At once, Tobin took stock of the sparse furnishings and the clear evidence that someone had been holed up here. Reaching down, he eased the knife out from his boot.

While the bounty hunter's body was bending down to retrieve the knife, a figure sprang at him from the gloom. Tobin was knocked back as arms coiled around him, obviously having had practice at fighting in the shadows as Tobin was locked in a bear hug. Driven against the wall by his attacker, he wrenched the knife from his boot and drove upwards. The tight grip around his abdomen faltered as the knife stabbed into his adversary's body. In the next instant, Tobin was free and his foe was staggering back in the shadows. He could hear his assailant's body crash to the floor.

Tobin leaned against the wall a moment, drawing breath into his gasping lungs. Though they had been around him for only a moment, the awful strength in those arms had come close to throttling him. Warily, he watched the dim shape of the body sprawled on the floor. When he'd recovered his breath, Tobin approached it. Keeping his knife poised to deliver a stabbing thrust, he reached out and seized a wrist. A moment passed and then another. A cold smile formed on Tobin's face. He could feel no pulse under his fingers. The enemy he'd knifed was dead.

Tobin didn't trouble himself about who his late adversary had been. Comanchero, rustler, or madman, it mattered nothing to the bounty hunter. The attacker had been an obstacle, an inconvenience standing between himself and Jesse James. No, he was nothing but carrion, unable to obstruct Tobin further.

Moving away from the body, Tobin started toward the ladder leading up to the bell itself and the parapet overlooking the main street of Robbers Roost. It was from here he would watch his 'partners' bring Jesse out into the open. The first the outlaw would be aware of Tobin's ambush was when a bolt of electricity came crackling down from the bounty hunter's rifle. So much cleaner than the destructive charge of a regular blaster, the electrical ammunition would kill the target, but leave him intact enough to be identified when it came time to collect the reward.

As he climbed up into the tower, Tobin didn't notice the body on the floor stir, watch it raise its head, or see the pallid face gazing up at him with its red, glowing eyes.

***

Jesse followed the two horse-traders out from the saloon. Their arrival had been opportune. Many of the recruits the gang had taken on had ridden into Robbers Roost on blackhoofs; a few were even in such dire straits that they'd made the trip on live horseflesh and mules. Without proper mounts for his men, Jesse knew it would be a long trek to the Confederate Rebellion and any meeting with President Lee. After coming around to Henderson's way of thinking, he was once again reconsidering that position. A solid raid against a Union outpost or two would get his men mobile, and it would drastically cut down the time they'd waste making contact with Lee.

Every day they spent in preparation was like a knife twisting in Jesse's gut. The image of John Younger rotting in Camp Lincoln was sickeningly omnipresent. After hearing firsthand from Henderson the horrors of the prison camp, Jesse couldn't abide the thought of leaving John there any longer than he had to. His sentiments were vociferously echoed by Bob and Jim Younger. It was rather ironic that Cole was the voice of caution. Even with his little brother languishing in captivity, Cole considered himself the shrewd strategist and tactician. He wanted to free John just as badly as any of the others, but thoughts of the loss of his best friend, Frank James, also urged him to make sure that when they made their raid they would be successful.

It was for that reason Jesse brought Cole along with him as he followed the two rustlers out to the big stable yard. As eager as he was for action, Jesse was apt to take anything that was offered. Cole would appraise the quality of the stock with a far more critical eye. The outlaw knew that such discrimination was exactly what they needed right now. Anxious men made mistakes. It was a lesson Jesse had been slow to understand.

Iron Horses. Jesse cast a wary glance at the two horse thieves. He didn't care for them at all. There was a rat-like meanness about them that set him on edge. Their story didn't sit easy on Jesse's mind; they didn't strike him as the kind of men with the grit to go stealing anything from the Union. Unless this third partner of theirs had a good deal more sand than these two displayed, he had misgivings about where exactly they might have come by their stock. That was why he was thankful to have Cole along. Cole would be able to pick apart the quality of their 'Horses. If they hadn't been stolen then they'd likely been scavenged, picked off some battlefield up north. The Warrior Nation had settled for more than a few troops of cavalry in their war against the white man, and the Indians had a religious repugnance for anything powered by RJ. Blasters, Iron Horses, even fob-watches and electriwork garters would be left to rot if the victorious Indians didn't have a medicine man around to destroy them more thoroughly in a ceremonial fire. Some human buzzards would follow troops of cavalry, hoping to pick up any technology that might be left lying around if the 'Horse soldiers were massacred. Sometimes these jackals would even go so far as to give the Indians warning so that they could prepare an ambush.

Jesse had no love for the Union, but such murderous treachery was beyond the pale. It was the lowest thing a man could sink to. Looking over the two horse thieves, he considered that they'd be perfectly capable of that kind of villainy. Cole swore that the older of the men had ridden with the James-Younger Gang many years before, down in Missouri just after the war. The man had been with them on a few train robberies Cole thought, but it had been so long ago that even he could not be certain. Usually Jesse's memory for names was excellent, but he just couldn't place Charley Ford and he was certain he'd never seen that baby-faced weasel Robert Ford before.

"You sure this ain't wampum you're tryin' to sell?" Jesse asked as they walked down the street. It was a question he'd asked the brothers before, but he still wasn't satisfied with their answers.

The Ford brothers scowled at the question. "Wampum" was tantamount to the vilest slur a man could invoke, indicating something that was either bartered or otherwise acquired from Indians. Before the vicious rise of the Warrior Nation, Indian traders had been held in the lowest repute, the bottom rung on the hierarchy of criminal society, lower than horse thieves and slavers. Now, they were considered traitors; even worse than Comancheros. A Comanchero might sell Indians guns and liquor, he might take whatever loot the braves had in trade, but he'd draw the line at scavenging massacred soldiers for plunder.

"As I said, Mr. James," Charley whined. "Me and my brother are just agents, facilitators if you would. Our partner, Mr. Howard, is the one who actually takes in the stock. I can't say for sure where he gets it."

Robert shook his head. "It ain't wampum," he declared, the fire in his tone reminding Jesse of a rat backed into a corner. "Howard's been a good deal evasive on where he gets his rides, but they look too good to be wampum." He waved his hand toward the stables. "You'll see for yerself when you look over the one he brung as a sample."

Jesse frowned at Robert, the intensity of his gaze wiping the smirk off the 'Horse thief's face. "Yeah, I'll see. And I'd better like what I see. Because, if I don't, it's going to go hard on you fellas and your friend Howard."

"Where is this Howard?" Cole asked. Because Charley had ridden with the gang in the past, he was less dubious about the Ford brothers, but their unknown partner was what kept his guard up.

"He's in the stable yard," Charley said quickly.

"A place with a reputation like Robbers Roost, Howard felt he'd stay close to his stock," Robert explained. "He didn't want some coyote ridin' off with the sample before he had a chance to show it to you."

Jesse nodded. It was a reasonable precaution to take. There was a certain rough code of honor among the outlaws of Robbers Roost. They didn't steal from one another; that was one of the things that could see a man lynched by his fellow bandits. However, that rule didn't apply to any outsiders who came into town, such as the mysterious Howard. "Well, let's mosey over and meet your partner and take a gander at what he's got to sell," Jesse said as he stepped down from the boardwalk and out into the street.

The four men had only started to walk across the dusty road when a voice shouted in warning to Jesse. The outlaw spun around, startled to see Allen Henderson rushing toward him. From Will Shaft's description of the habits of his old colonel's aide, the old guerrilla was pretty much a hermit and kept to the ruined mission. Even in his meetings with Jesse, Henderson insisted they have their talks in the ruins. To see the recluse running down the street, his black clothes and pallid face jarringly incongruous with the bright noonday sun overhead, made even more of an impact on the outlaw than the words he was shouting.

"The tower!" Henderson yelled. "There's a rifle in the tower!"

Jesse didn't need to ask which tower. If Henderson had been rousted from the ruins, he could only mean the bell tower. He also didn't need to ask what a rifle would be doing there. The instant he heard the man's warning, Jesse was throwing himself to the ground. Almost in the same instant, a bolt of electricity went crackling past his ear to scorch the dirt beside him.

There was a terrible familiarity about that crackling blast and the acrid smell its discharge left behind. It wasn't the usual explosive burst of a blaster or even the incendiary flare of Hardin's smokers. It was the sizzling electrical shock that had struck at Jesse when he'd escaped Wyatt Earp's posse. Without so much as a glance at the sharpshooter in the bell tower, Jesse knew in his bones that he was once again in the sights of Thomas Tate Tobin.

Jesse rolled along the ground, a second blast searing into the earth as he shifted position. There was no question that the shot came from the bell tower, and the outlaw didn't give the bounty hunter any opportunity for a third chance. The quick-devil arms Dr. Carpathian had grafted to his body leapt to his holsters, his guns clearing leather in less than a heartbeat. Two bursts of energized annihilation leapt from the pistols.

Unable to sight Tobin up in the darkened bell tower, Jesse instead fired his Hyper-velocity blasters at the base of the structure, shattering it in a staccato series of savage blows. The crumbling brick shattered as though struck by a mechanized hammer. With a groaning roar, the base of the tower exploded outward, the upper floors telescoping downwards in a catastrophic collapse. Dust and debris billowed from the jumble of cracked beams and smashed adobe, the tarnished bronze bell tolling dolefully as it crashed atop the rubble.

Somewhere under the mound of destruction, the body of Thomas Tate Tobin was buried. There'd be no more electrified blasts fired at Jesse James from ambush. Not from him. The entire incident, from the first attack to Jesse's dramatic demolition of the tower, took less than half a minute. As he picked himself off the ground, Jesse found that both Cole and Charley were still standing in shocked silence. Only Robert Ford had made any action, his own pistol half-clear of its holster. Jesse smiled and waved one of his smoking blasters at the young 'Horse thief. "You can leave that where it is. I've settled with the polecat."

Robert hesitated, and then slowly slid his gun back into the holster. "Thought you might need help, Mr. James."

Jesse nodded. "Damn quick reflexes," he said. "It might be I didn't remember your brother Charley, but it's damn certain I won't go forgetin' you, Bobbie." He looked over at the crowd that had come rushing out from the saloon and several of the other buildings. A wave of his metal hands reassured Bob, Jim, and the other members of his gang that their leader was alright.

"Any idea who that back-shooter was?" Cole's voice was full of fury, not least at his own lack of action in those critical seconds when the first shot had been fired. He glowered over at Henderson. "How is it you knew this fella was up there?"

Henderson chose to ignore the suspicion in Cole's tone. "He snuck up on me when he was climbing up. Threw me down the ladder and left me for dead." He continued with a description of the ambusher. With every word, the faces of the Ford brothers grew paler and sweat began to bead across Charley's forehead.

It was Robert who spoke first. "Damnation!" he cursed. "That's Tom Howard!" he glanced over at his shaken brother, then back at Jesse. "That's the man who wanted us to help him sell 'Horses to you!"

"His name was Thomas," Jesse said, turning his head and staring at the dust still rising from the pile of rubble. "But it weren't Howard, it was Tobin."

"The bounty man?" Robert gasped.

"He's the one who caught John," Cole spat. "He must have picked up your trail again, Jesse."

"I reckon," Jesse turned his gaze on the Ford brothers. "He must have figured to use you two for camouflage. Nobody'd pay too particular attention if'n he rode in here with known outlaws."

Robert nodded his head. "We didn't think he was anythin' more'n he told us he was," he declared, eliciting a quivering affirmation from the still shaken Charley. "Hell, if'n we'd know'd he was a bounty killer, I don't know how we'd have made it this far. There's posters out on the two of us, you know."

"That's right," Charley said. "Two hundred dollars."

"We'll have to see if we can't make you more valuable," Jesse said before he started toward the stable yard. "For now, let's see about puttin' Tobin's 'Horse to good use."

Henderson stepped into Jesse's path. "There isn't the time to dawdle anymore," the guerrilla cautioned. "If Tobin could track you here, other bounty hunters can do the same. We'll have to fit out what men we can and leave the rest." He raised his hand to deflect the protest he saw forming on Cole's tongue. "When Jesse explains his plan to President Lee, he'll get all the men and gear he needs to raid Andersonville."

Henderson's words evoked Jesse's own irritation at further delay. "Allen's right, Cole. We stay here and who can say how many more of these buzzards will come swoopin' in." He turned toward the Ford brothers. "I'm sorry boys. The furtherin' of your reward posters will have to wait. Rest assured, I'll remember you if'n you want to sign on once my business in Andersonville is done."

Robert nodded. "Well, Mr. James, if it's guns you need, my brother and I will be glad to sign up!"

"W-We will?" Charlie stammered, but a glare from his brother shot the nerve back into his spine. "I mean, w-we will! Of course we will!"

"We got no more business here, so if'n you'll let us, we'd be glad to ride with the famous Jesse James!"

Jesse stared at the brothers for a few moments, as if contemplating their offer. He eventually nodded and gave them a grim smirk. "Normally, I wouldn't be so sure, but since we're needin' more hands, it's you boys' lucky day." With that, Jesse turned back toward the stable yard. "Come on, Cole! Least we can do is check out Tobin's 'Horse. Will Shaft ain't got one and I reckon it'd be a mighty fittin' present for him."

"That'll really make Hardin hot," Cole warned.

A boyish grin formed on Jesse's face. "All the more reason," he said.

The two outlaws headed across the street. The Ford brothers watched them for a moment and then gradually drifted back to the saloon and the crowd that had gathered in front of it. Nobody paid any particular attention to Henderson as he studied the ruins of the mission before following Jesse and Cole into the stock yard.

Nobody noticed the tear in Henderson's shirt just above his belly or the pale, unblemished flesh beneath. His gaze lingered on the dust-shrouded ruins, a crimson glint sparkling behind the thick glasses.

***

Colonel George Armstrong Custer stalked into the laboratory-surgery of Dr. Francis Tumblety with a face that could have sent a lion cringing into the back corner of its cage. A bold, reckless general during the war, Custer had been effectually put out to pasture by the War Department. Demoted after the official cessation of hostilities, he'd been bounced from one desk job to another until he'd finally ended up here, as commandant of Camp Lincoln. A dirtier job in the whole Union Army was something Custer didn't believe existed. His posting was all the more onerous for the very vivid memory of the fate that had befallen Captain Wirz, the Confederate commandant of Camp Sumter during the war. For the mistreatment and torture of the Union prisoners under his charge, Wirz had been executed, hung by the neck in Washington.

Custer was a tall, strongly built man. Partially out of pride, partly out of protest for his unglamorous posting, he wore his blonde hair long, well past the military custom of being cropped above the collar. His moustache was broad and thick, curling across his cheeks. Over his regulation uniform, he wore a buckskin jacket with a long leather fringe across the shoulders. He was a commanding presence, his every motion overlaid with a quality of energy that quickly affected the men he led. It was more his personal vitality and drive, his ability to inspire and lead, rather than any tactical acumen that had won him his victories in the war.

As he stepped into the sanitized sprawl of Tumblety's surgery, Custer reflected bitterly on how little those victories had won him. He was a man who longed for the glory and acclaim afforded to a hero. Instead, he found himself a mere jailor and custodian of a degenerate monster.

The costume Tumblety had adopted for this meeting with the commandant was still more infuriating to Custer. So far as he was aware, exempting some especially dubious claims that he'd done some espionage work for the Union during the height of the war, Tumblety had never served in the United States military, or the military of any other country for that matter. Yet here he was, bustling about his laboratory in a starched uniform of such ostentation that it would have shamed the extravagances of a Napoleon. Royal blue tunic over purple trousers adorned with a single stripe of crimson down the leg. Gilded shoulder boards struggled beneath coils of jade-colored brocade. Across his breast was a menagerie of medals and honors simulating everything from the Congressional Medal of Honor to the German Iron Cross and the French Pour le Merit. Custer noticed with extreme revulsion what looked to be Tumblety's own profile etched into an ivory cameo that served as the centerpiece for an enormous sunburst of bronze and silver – a decoration that its Latin inscription indicated was an award for 'excellence in the fields of science and humanity.'

Tumblety was fussing over one of the contraptions that had caused him to award himself such an honor. Resting on a steel table, the device looked like nothing Custer had ever seen. It was a bulky armature of steel and wire, pipes and hoses running away from it to a small RJ engine that had straps fastened to it so that it might be worn across the back like a mountaineer's rucksack. Protruding from the side of the armature was a hopper of some sort, a platter-like feeder that dropped serrated metal disks into a slot fitted to the top of the armature.

"My dear Commandant," Tumblety beamed as he looked up and saw Custer walking toward him. "It is so good of you to accept my invitation."

Custer frowned at the experimenter. "I've told you before, my rank is colonel. You will address me as such."

Tumblety stroked a finger across his walrus-like moustache. "Of course, yes. Forgive my lack of propriety. I sometimes forget myself. The weight of my indignation for the War Department's lack of foresight sometimes is too onerous to bear! They squander so much time and resources on that foreign charlatan, Tesla! Do you know what that crackpot has them believing he can do now? He actually has them convinced that he can translocate physical material! Imagine! The audacity! To suggest it is possible to transmit an object or a person from one place to another in the same way a sound is transmitted by the vocal reiterators! Have you ever heard anything so absurd?!"

The colonel barely heard Tumblety's tirade. He was more interested in the scrawny prisoner pinned to the wall of the surgery by a set of steel staples. For a moment, he wondered if the wretch was a more reasonably formulated specimen of Tumblety's research, the creations he sardonically termed his 'Reconstructed.' A brief study, however, didn't reveal any of the surgical scars that would have indicated the man had been subjected to one of the ward's vivisection theatres. This prisoner, it seemed, was there to indulge one of the experimenter's side projects.

"The Secretary of War expects results from you," Custer warned the scientist. "Don't worry about Tesla, worry about your own work. The War Department has invested a lot of money on you. They've put all the resources you need at your disposal, turned a blind eye to a lot of things just so you can further your work."

Tumblety started to strap himself into the device he'd constructed. "My work proceeds apace," he assured Custer. "There's no fear on that count. The process just needs a little more refinement and then you will have a weapon that will make those painted savages in the Nation only too eager to sign every treaty and smoke every peace pipe Washington sees fit to send their way!" He stroked the steel armature, closing his eyes and giggling as he savored the feeling of his fingers running down the framework of his creation. "Genius doesn't limit itself. If I were a boastful man I might describe myself as a prodigy. A scientific virtuoso." He nodded his head, endorsing his own statement. "You have seen my facility with surgery, but now let me exhibit my expertise with mechanical engineering."

Custer stepped aside as Tumblety walked toward the exposed section of wall, the metal armature supported by the straps across his back and a broad belt around his waist. The experimenter wound the tiny crank set into the contraption's side, generating the spark that set the entire armature aglow with crimson lines of energy. One of the saw-edged disks came sliding down from the hopper and into the slotted top of the armature.

"This will revolutionize warfare," Tumblety promised. Swinging around, he aimed the device at the man shackled to the wall. The prisoner flailed under the steel staples, opening his mouth in a grisly croak of terror. Custer could see the jagged stump where the captive's tongue had been.

With a ghastly screech, the saw-blade was launched from Tumblety's weapon. It whirled across the lab to slice into the wall… easily missing the prisoner by a dozen feet. The scientist glared at the shivering metal embedded in the wall. "I fear my aim isn't what could be expected of a trained soldier," he apologized. Taking a few steps closer, he fired a second disk at his prisoner. This time, the blade went sweeping high above the man, slamming into the wall a good two feet over his head. The mute screams of the wretch increased in their frantic violence.

"A few bugs still," Tumblety said, coughing loudly to clear the knot in his throat. Again, he took a few steps closer to the prisoner. When he launched a third disk at the captive, it glanced off the floor and went spinning into the wall. Deflecting off a support beam, the deadly missile careened across the lab to shatter several of the biological specimen jars before it sliced into the opposite wall.

"Leave the technology to Tesla," Custer growled. Casting a withering gaze at the experimenter, he started to storm from the lab. "Just concentrate on the research covered in the War Department's orders."

Tumblety shrugged out of the armature and hurried after the withdrawing officer. "Give me time!" he pleaded. "I will work out all the problems! It is this tension, this foolishness with Tesla! I am not in a proper mood to perform at my best."

Custer spun around at that last statement. His expression was one of complete disgust. "No."

"I need another one! My nervous disposition requires recalibrating."

"No!" Custer snarled. "I'll not be a party to your outrages. What you do to these Rebs is despicable enough!"

An unctuous smile formed on the experimenter's face. "Shall I wire the Secretary and tell him you won't give me what I need?" he challenged.

Custer shook his head. He knew that the murderous scientist had him at a disadvantage. When he'd protested to the War Department before about Tumblety's activities, he'd been told in no uncertain terms that they were both aware of and indifferent to the bloodthirsty peccadilloes of the experimenter. "It'll take a few days. Try to control yourself until then."

Tumblety clapped his hands, rubbing his palms together like a little boy anticipating Christmas. "Pick a nice one. Soft and pretty with nice white skin. The sort of skin just made for a knife."

Custer didn't answer the madman's request, instead hurrying from the surgery and back into the comparative wholesomeness of the squalid prison camp. Tumblety laughed at the officer's agitation and then turned back to his malfunctioning device. Lifting it back onto the table, he started to attack its workings with screwdriver and wrench.

"Don't worry," Tumblety told the captive bolted to the wall. "I'll have everything set to rights soon. Then we can try again."

Tumblety reached under the table and retrieved a new supply of saw-edged disks. He smiled as he started to stack them on the platter inside the weapon's hopper. "We have all night to get things right, after all."

Chapter 15

Jesse was able to outfit eighteen men by the time his gang left Robbers Roost. Grudgingly, he'd been forced to leave the Interceptor behind. It was simply too fuel hungry for the long trek across the Texas Territory, and at any event, it would draw too much notice from lawmen. They might be able to buffalo sheriffs and rangers into thinking they were an outfit from one of the big eastern companies, but if a lawman spotted an Interceptor among the Iron Horses, he'd need to be a half-wit not to appreciate that something untoward was going on.

Keeping to old Indian trails and back roads known only to Hardin and other Texan desperados, the gang was able to avoid any contact with the law until they were well past the panhandle region. It was there, in the desolated region south of the old Indian Territory, that the James-Younger Gang found themselves confronted by a Union patrol.

The outlaws were just clearing a stand of scruffy pine trees, heading into the grassy plain beyond, when the sound of whirring motors brought them whipping around in their saddles. From both sides, blue-uniformed soldiers came streaking toward them, blasters firing from their vehicles as they charged. For an instant, Jesse considered trying to outrun the Yankees, but a warning hiss from Henderson brought his attention to a rocky hill at their left. Jesse could see the gleam of metal reflecting among the rocks. The soldiers hadn't left much to chance, positioning sharpshooters up in the rocks. Any move to try to speed away would simply draw the outlaws into the killing ground the Yankees had prepared.

"Ease off, boys," Jesse warned his men, powering down his 'Horse and bringing it to a stop.

A yowl of pain sounded from Jesse's left. He glanced aside to see Hardin rubbing at his hand and glaring daggers at

Cole Younger. "The man said leave your smokers alone," Cole growled at the gunfighter.

"We're just out surveyin' for the Texas-Union Railroad," Jesse reminded his men. They'd been fortunate enough to buy some stolen surveying equipment off a claim-jumper in Robbers Roost, and Will Shaft had provided the gang with two fellow Exoduster outlaws who'd previously worked as laborers for a surveying crew out in the Dakotas. "We ain't got no cause to be afeared of the law."

"And if they don't buy that?" Bob Younger asked.

Jesse nodded his head toward the hill and the glint of gun metal shining among the rocks. "We try to give as good as we get. Might be a few of us can win our way clear."

"Won't come to that, Mr. James," Will Shaft assured the outlaw. He gestured with his thumb to the other Exodusters. "Freddy and Moses know what to say if'n the blue-bellies get inquisitive."

"See that they do," Hardin snarled. "Or it won't need any Yankee gun to settle things where you darkies are concerned."

Jesse rounded on the gunfighter, but before he could reprimand Hardin, he saw the Union patrol closing in. "Everybody play nice," he reminded his men, adopting a broad smile as he removed his hat and waved it in greeting to the uniformed cavalry troopers. "Mornin' gents!" he called out.

The Union captain commanding the patrol didn't respond to Jesse's greeting. Keeping one hand on his blaster, the officer studied the well-armed gang of riders, his gaze lingering on the faces of John Wesley Hardin and Cole Younger. Then he turned his attention directly at Jesse. "You folks are mighty well-heeled and a damn fair sight off the beaten path," he said.

"We're surveyors for the Union-Texas," Jesse told the officer, then laughed. "That is, some of us are. The rest of us're engaged as guards to see their hair stays in place. Word is this region's crawlin' with dog-soldiers."

"Did you say, 'dog-soldiers?'" There was the slightest crack of a smile from the otherwise gravel-faced sergeant at the naivety of the phrase. "The Nation's on the war-path alright, but that's away over in the northern part of the territory. These parts it's the Hole-in-the-Wall Gang causin' all the ruckus."

The captain shot his subordinate a warning glance, immediately producing a sullen silence. The officer turned back around, staring suspiciously at Jesse. "Surveyors?" he asked, craning his head to one side as he looked over the equipment strapped to the Iron Horses.

"Yes, sir," Will Shaft said. "We's been sent out to figure a new route up into Tulsa." He lowered his voice to a confidential whisper. "I don't think the company has any intent of layin' track, they just want to secure the rights to the land so's nobody else can do it. Have to make sure they keep their monopolies."

The captain scowled at all the Confederate regalia adorning Will's body. "Where'd you pick up all that Secesh trash?" he asked, pointing at the hat and belt buckle.

"War trophies," Will said, adding a wide grin. The comment brought some laughs from the surrounding troopers. The captain allowed himself a faint semblance of a smile before turning toward Jesse.

"How about you?" the officer asked. "You have any trophies off'n the rebs? Seems to me I've seen you somewheres."

"I don't see how that's possible," Jesse said. His metal arms were hidden beneath the long sleeves of his duster and a set of cow-hide gauntlets, but even so, it would only take a fraction of a second to rip his blasters from their holsters and hurl the inquisitive officer into eternity.

Will Shaft hurried to explain to the officer. "We weren't in the reg'lar army during the war, sir. We was in a raider outfit. Chased Bloody Bill all across Missouri and Kansas we did."

The captain turned back around. "You two rode together in the War?" he asked.

"Come on, Cap'n," the sergeant grumbled. "These fellas don't look like the Wild Bunch and if'n they're ridin' with the Emancipated, it's damn sure they ain't any o' Lee's scum."

The captain whipped his head back around at the sergeant. "You tellin' me my job?"

"No, sir," the sergeant said, straightening up in his saddle.

The captain held his subordinate's gaze for a moment, and then addressed Jesse. "The Butch Cassidy bunch has been on the prod lately. With them 'Horses, your outfit would make a temptin' target for them. I suggest you forget all about scoutin' the terrain hereabouts."

Jesse shook his head. "Railroad wouldn't like that much. Some of us got wives and children to feed. Can't go offendin' the big bugs back east. 'Sides, like you said, we're well-heeled. I don't think any outlaw'd be fool-all enough to tangle with us."

The captain nodded. "You might be right about that," he conceded. Reaching into the breast of his coat, the captain pulled out a crumpled wanted poster. "Been puttin' these out at every stage stop and fuel depot. Cassidy's gang was brazen enough to have their picture took." He handed the poster over to Jesse. The officer gave him a moment to glance at the faces in the picture. "You boys keep that one. If'n you see one of them, get yerself to the nearest telegraph and signal the closest fort. Worth a two thousand dollar reward if'n your information lands us the whole gang."

Jesse smiled and slowly folded the poster, tucking it into a pocket of his duster. "We'll be sure to keep our eyes open, Cap'n."

The captain gave a last lingering look at Jesse, some familiarity about him nagging at the officer's memory. Finally, he gave up the elusive connection he was trying to make. Raising his arm, he waved Jesse's outfit onward. The outlaw wasn't fooled; the gesture wasn't for his benefit, but a signal to the men in the rocks to let the 'surveyors' pass.

Opening up their Iron Horses, the outlaws sped off across the plain. In a few minutes, they'd put the Union patrol and their lurking sharpshooters far behind.

"Damn lucky back there," Jim Younger winced from the lingering pain of his wounds as he spoke. Soon, the Yankees were a distant memory over the horizon.

"I thought for certain that eagle-button officer recognized me," Cole said. "Would have had a bad fracas with them shooters up ahead and Yankee 'Horses to either side."

Jesse slowed his steed, dropping back until he was riding beside Will Shaft. "You're the one got us out of that spot,

Will," he told the Exoduster. "If not for you, I don't think them Yankees would have believed a word we told them."

"Darkie camouflage," Hardin sneered. "Now that we can't have 'em pickin' cotton, it's nice to know they're good for somethin'."

Will glared at the Texan, a cold glint in his eyes. "Any time you'd like to dance, buckra, you jus' say the word." He noticed Hardin start to reach for his smoker. Before the gunfighter could finish the move, Will whipped one of his own blasters from a shoulder holster.

Before either man could bring a weapon to bear, he found himself looking into the barrel of one of Jesse's guns. While gently guiding the Iron Horse with his knees, the quick-devil arms Carpathian had given the bushwhacker made a mockery of both Hardin's speed and Shaft's cunning.

"I happen to need both of you right now," Jesse warned the outlaws. "So if I'm goaded into shootin', I'll just have to oblige both of you." The warning didn't need to be repeated. Hardin scowled and shoved his smoker back into its holster. Will nodded and put away his blaster. "Hardin, seein' you know this country, why don't you light out ahead and play scout for a time. Give you a chance to act civilized when you get back." Hardin glared at the guerrilla and then cast a murderous look at Will. Without saying a word, he opened the throttle on his 'Horse and sped off down the trail.

"He's gonna be trouble, Mr. James," Will said.

Jesse holstered his weapons. "He'll bide his time a spell yet. He's ornery as a curly wolf, but he's still a damn good hand in a fight. I'm hopin' he doesn't push things too far until after we get John and the others out of Camp Lincoln."

Will looked dubious. "As you say, Mr. James, but I wouldn't turn my back on that sidewinder for nothin'."

"Call me Jesse," the outlaw said. "Damn if you didn't earn that much and more back there." A distant look crept into his eyes. He might not have been as belligerent as Hardin, but he'd been brought up in the same culture. He'd been taught that black men were only partly human, that they couldn't think or act for themselves. He'd been raised to think of them as property, like a horse or a dog, not as people. Certainly not as equals.

He repented that attitude. Listening to Will speaking up for them, trying to ease off the Yankee officer's suspicions, had made him confront his old prejudices and beliefs. It was a hard thing to set aside everything you'd been taught, even more to grow past everything you'd believed. It was worse to think that maybe the Confederacy's defeat had been necessary, that the Union tyranny which followed had in some ways done some good. At least for Jesse, the Union oppression made him understand what it was to not have freedom. It made him experience what it was like to have men standing over you telling you what you could do and where you could go. It gave him a taste, however slight, of what it must have meant to be a slave.

The blacks, they were people too. It was a realization that came hard to Jesse. He could feel all the things he'd been reared on resisting that idea, but something far deeper and more profound within him knew it was the truth. He knew it was the right and decent thing. He'd taken up arms because the Union thought it could glad-hand the South; to rob and steal without conscience, and bring low the pride of those who'd been beaten in the war. Yet, what about the pride of men like Will? If he was so set on deposing the tyranny of the blue-bellies for his people, shouldn't he feel it only right to do the same for anybody who'd share his cause?

"Why're you ridin' with us?" Jesse asked Will at last.

Will was quiet a moment, considering how exactly he would answer that question. "You know, Jesse, I asked myself that too. I reckon in the end, I just decided we had the same enemy. Fightin' back on my own just wasn't good enough. Fightin' back with Jesse James, maybe I could make the Yankees hurt some afore I was done." A wistful look came upon the Exoduster's face. "All them years as a slave, I clung to the idea of freedom. Then the war come along and the Yankees made me free. Then there was peace and they show'd me how much my freedom was worth. I wasn't allowed in the front door of a saloon, had to sit in the back of white folk's churches, couldn't even sell my crops for the same as white sodbusters could. The same folks that went to war because I was a slave didn't care two-bits now that I wasn't." He turned and spat into the dust of the trail. "I was obliged to watch my son starve, had to bury my misses after her grief got too bad and she hung herself. All that 'cause the fort wouldn't buy supplies off'n an Exoduster – not for anythin' reasonable."

"They done a lot of bad to a lot of folk," Jesse said. "But I give you my word, Will, they're gonna answer for it. Maybe we can't get Lee to see things our way, maybe we can, but however it goes, I want you to know that I'm proud to share my revenge with you."

Will nodded and smiled. "Ain't nothin' more personal a man can offer to share than his revenge."

***

Some weeks later, the James-Younger Gang had put the prairies and forests of Texas Territory behind them. Slipping past the cordon of Union outposts, they entered the region claimed by the Confederate Rebellion. A grizzled ferryman smuggled them across the Mississippi for one of their blasters and the surveying equipment. Jesse'd been more than willing to hand over the surveyor's instruments, but he regretted the loss of even one blaster. If their plan to liberate the inmates of Camp Lincoln panned out, there'd be a lot of men in need of guns after the raid.

On the other side of the Mississippi, the gang found themselves following a narrow road winding its way through a vast stretch of bottomland. The half-sunken cypress trees rose grotesquely from winding creeks, the brown water carrying a stagnant smell as it flowed sluggishly through the swamp. Veils of Spanish moss swayed in the humid breeze, the droning buzz of cicadas filled the air and drowned out even the hum of the outlaws' RJ-powered vehicles.

Though they'd crossed beyond the Union frontier, the gang still kept a wary eye for blue-coat patrols. Infiltrators and raiders of both sides were constantly making forays across the demarcation, stealing supplies or gathering intelligence from the other side. The full weight of the Union Army might have been drawn away from the lingering Rebel presence by the double threats of the Warrior Nation and the Enlightened, but Washington had by no means forgotten about the Secessionists, and had no intention of allowing the rebellion to spread. Now that the outlaws were over the border, there'd be no discussion with any Yankee troops they stumbled upon. The blue-bellies would shoot without question and the outlaws had to be ready to oblige them in kind.

When Jesse's men were finally challenged, it wasn't by Union troops. For several miles, Jesse had felt a menace growing around them. Henderson whispered a quiet warning to him as they passed a stand of willows that the gang was no longer alone. Though they couldn't see them, they had acquired a shadow as they passed through the swamps. Henderson couldn't offer any clue as to who was following them or how many they might be, only that they were there.

Jesse passed the warning along to his men. He advised them to keep a ready hand near their blasters, but not to shoot until they were dead certain who or what it was they were shooting at. There was just a chance that the unseen lurkers might prove to be friend rather than foe.

The swamp unexpectedly flattened out, the ground becoming much more solid and substantial. Jesse could see the great sprawl of what must once have been a cotton field, but which had now been given over to more essential crops like corn and potatoes. The remnants of the Confederacy needed food more than cotton.

"Jus' y'all turn off them motors and ease away fra' yourn shootin' irons," a gruff voice challenged the outlaws as they emerged from the swamp. "Y'all got ten rifles on yeh an' don't take but the tick o' a hound's ear ter turn the lot o' yeh inta fert'lizer."

The whine of energy rifles cycling somewhere behind the cornstalks and among the willows convinced even Hardin that the unseen speaker wasn't making an empty threat. As the outlaws powered down their vehicles and raised their hands, Jesse glanced over at Cole.

"Gettin' a bit tired of folks getting' the drop on us," he remarked to his friend.

Cole scowled at the cornfield. "Well, Jesse, you wanted to be the leader." He winked at his chief and smiled. The twang in their ambusher's voice made it clear he wasn't anybody from up north. It was possible, of course, that they'd run into some Cajuns hired out as scouts to the Union or maybe a band of opportunistic bounty hunters, but both Cole and Jesse felt it was more likely they were being challenged by Confederate pickets.

Jesse flexed his arms, ripping open the seams on the sleeves of his coat. As the torn linen flopped against his side, his metal arms glistened in the sunlight. A few startled gasps sounded from behind the willows. "Lord above!" a shocked voice cried from the cornfield. "That thar's Jesse James!"

In the Union, Jesse was a feared gunfighter and robber, but to the folks of the Confederate Rebellion, he was something far different. He was a hero, a freedom fighter, a Rebel version of Robin Hood.

From out of the cornfield stepped a grizzled-looking man wearing a battered felt hat and the grubby remains of a gray shell jacket. Double bandoliers of ammunition crossed his chest and about his waist hung a massive hatchet with an ugly alligator-hide handle. The rebel's face was grimy with mud and dirt, strands of grass and weed poking out from his bristly black beard. One of his eyes was lazy, vacantly staring away to the left. The other squinted at Jesse, looking him over from head to toe.

"Thet gospel, mista?" the swampy asked, displaying a mouth of blackened teeth. "You'n heem, true an' true?"

Jesse returned the scout's stare. "I'm him," he told the sentry. Before the rebel could react, the outlaw's metal arms whipped to his holster and had both blasters drawn and pointed at his face.

Far from being terrified, the scout grinned and shouted in delight. "Tarnashun! We's got us the Jesse James!" The scout's excited cry was taken up by the other hidden rebels. In a mass they emerged from their hiding places, streaming toward Jesse, reaching trembling hands to shake his metal fingers. Cole watched the display of worshipful adoration with an expression that suggested he'd swallowed something foul. He made an effort to impress on the pickets that he was Cole Younger, but no one seemed interested.

It was Henderson who interrupted Jesse's moment with the rebels. "We've ridden a fair piece to get this far. Jesse wants to see President Lee. Wants to offer his services to the rebellion."

The grizzled swamp-rat seemed to be the man in charge. He squinted his good eye at Henderson, studying him with an almost open hostility. Jesse noticed the scout had a weird fetish hanging about his neck when the man reached up to it and crossed two fingers over it. Pressing the charm into his breast, the man turned his head and spat three times on the ground.

"Can't take ya'll nowheres," the swamp-rat said, stepping back a pace.

Even with his eyes covered by his tinted glasses, the severity of Henderson's gaze could be felt by the scout as the guerrilla leaned forward in his saddle. "Then you can take us to a higher authority who can conduct us where Jesse needs to go."

For a moment, it seemed the scout might offer up some protest. Many of the other rebels were looking at their commander with a puzzled expression, unable to account for his sudden fright. Jesse thought of Will Shaft and the gris-gris bag he sometimes held when he was around Henderson. As he glanced over at the Exoduster, he found that this was another of those times. The uneasiness in Will's face might be less, but it was certainly kindred to what gripped the swamp-rat.

When the tension in the air was almost tangible, the swamp-rat finally nodded. "Can take ya'll ter see the general," he decided. "He's the one in charge o' these here parts. It's rightly General Mosby's decision ter let ya'll pass through."

A flicker of amusement played on Henderson's gaunt visage. "So they made the 'Gray Ghost' a general, did they?" His words had just a trace of bitterness in them.

Jesse could appreciate Henderson's sentiment. During the war, his raiders had been regarded as nothing more than marauders by both sides. They were criminals that were useful to the Confederacy, but criminals just the same. Mosby had commanded a similar unit in Virginia, but his men had been esteemed as partisans and irregular cavalry by the Confederate generals. Colonel John S. Mosby had commanded rangers. Colonel William Quantrill was chief of a gang of raiders. It was a scornful distinction that still stung the Missourians who had ridden beneath the black flag.

"Take us to Mosby," Jesse told the scout. "When he hears what I aim to do, he'll make sure I see Lee."

***

"Frank's much better thanks to you, Miss Lucy." There was a boyish, almost shy smile on John Younger's face as he spoke, his eyes not quite able to maintain contact with those of the nurse.

Lucinda Loveless felt embarrassed by the boy's display of gratitude and emotion. She'd taken on the mantle of a 'rebel angel,' and infiltrated the organization of Camp Lincoln with the intention of gaining a lead on Jesse James. It was in many ways a scheme hatched from her own ingenuity, something outside the provenance of the Pinkerton Agency. Her intention had been to pump Frank for any information that might give her an insight into his brother's future plans, hints as to his hideouts, details into how he operated; anything that might give her an edge in tracking down the outlaw. Helping Frank to recover from his illness had simply been a part of that plan.

As Loveless looked over at John, however, she knew that things had changed. By slow and insidious degrees, all the things she had seen in stark black and white, right and wrong, had become distorted and muddied into a great morass of gray. The quagmire of gray that rotted away within the palisades of Camp Lincoln had dissolved many of the beliefs and ideals she had held. If a place like this could be allowed to exist on the behest of the Union, if such suffering could be inflicted solely to prosecute vengeance upon the Secessionists, then what moral justification did her government truly possess? She was reminded of the philosophical warning that maintained revenge was a disease that destroyed the perpetrator as much as the victim.

Loveless glanced across the rows of tattered tents and the muddy ground between them, at the bedraggled men who trudged through the muck to toil away in their miserable little fields. This was the fate that Pinkerton would have Jesse condemned to. She knew if they ever got their hands on Jesse alive, Pinkerton wouldn't be content for mere hanging. Jesse's numerous escapes, the brazen bravado of his escapades; these had become deeply personal to the chief of the Secret Service.

The hate that had been building up inside him wouldn't be content merely to visit justice on Jesse. He'd need his revenge, just as the men who permitted Andersonville's prison to exist needed to slake their own thirst for blood.

It could only be a matter of time before Pinkerton or some other lawman decided to announce Frank's incarceration to the country. When they did that, they'd bait a trap Jesse was certain to ride into. Loveless didn't think the outlaw would risk trying to break into Camp Lincoln for John, but she knew nothing on earth could stop him if he knew his brother was here.

Motioning to John, Loveless made a quick withdrawal from the miserable file of sickly rebels she'd been ministering to. John followed her down a muddy track running between two rows of tents in a winding, circuitous route. Only when she felt certain nobody had followed them did she stop and address the boy.

"We have to get Frank out of here," Loveless told him. "He's not out of danger unless he's someplace more healthful than this place."

John almost laughed. "That'd sure be a nice trick, if'n you could pull it. Somehow I think them blue-bellies might take poorly to such a suggestion. In any case, the 'bots on them walls certainly wouldn't listen."

"I'll figure out a way," Loveless promised. Since deciding that Frank needed to be removed from Camp Lincoln, she'd been making a careful study of the camp's routine. Sooner or later, she'd figure out the most practicable way of getting him out. In the meantime, it was essential that Frank and John had the strength to make good any escape when it came. Reaching into her white blouse, she removed a small wooden box and handed it to John.

The boy outlaw flipped the box open, staring in bewilderment at the little pellets inside. They looked like little sausages made from sawdust. Loveless noted his confusion.

"Marchtack," she said, providing the pellets with their name. "The latest in industrial convenience. Each of those pellets has enough nutrition to provide a grown man with all the rations he needs for an entire day. It's the same as what the sentries posted here are issued."

John continued to stare at the unappetizing pellets. "Look like horse-pills," he declared.

"Just take them," Loveless said. "One for yourself and one for Frank. I'll steal more from the commissary as soon as I get a chance."

"You'd better steal some extra," a scratchy voice suddenly rose from between the tents. Loveless and John both spun around, startled by the interruption. They found themselves staring into the ugly face of a scraggly prisoner. Clenched in the man's fist was a jagged piece of wood, the end filed down into a crude point.

John glowered as he recognized the rogue. "Shouldn't you be somewheres tryin' to steal boots?"

The scavenger sneered. "Can't get much nourishment off'n boots. These here pellets though, they sound like they'd turn the trick." As the rogue moved to reach for Loveless, John stepped into his path. The scavenger scrambled back, glaring hatefully at the outlaw.

"Nobody harms an angel," John reminded the vulture.

A ratty gleam crept into the scraggly rebel's eyes. He glanced from Loveless to John. "Maybe I'll just have to forget the rules," he said. He made a feint for Loveless, then whipped around and brought his stick stabbing up at John's gut. "Or maybe I'll just take 'em from you."

John caught the scavenger's hand before he could stab him. A vicious twist snapped the rogue's wrist. The vulture flailed about, howling in agony. The scream rang out over the maze of tents. The satisfied expression on John's face collapsed as he looked out across the tents and saw the immense bulk of a Warder looming above them. The 'bot was turning about, doubtlessly ordered by whoever was commanding it to investigate the scream. He could see the machine's claw reaching out and pulling down tents as it forced a path through the camp.

"Get out of here!" John yelled at Loveless, thrusting the box of marchtack back into her hands.

Loveless hesitated. It offended her to leave John to the dubious mercy of the Union guards, but at the same time she knew there was nothing she could do. Revealing herself as a

Pinkerton agent might defuse the immediate situation, but it would scuttle any plans for helping Frank and John escape.

The boy's next words decided her. "Go," he said. "Help Frank."

Resisting the urge to rush to John's aid, Loveless turned and retreated down the narrow track between the tents. Behind her, she could hear the harsh voice of a soldier demanding the submission of John and his foe. She could hear the angry growl of the Warder as its mechanized brawn forced the two combatants apart. A stab of pain shot through her heart as she heard screams and recognized one of them belonging to John.

When she gained the main path between the tents, Loveless crouched down and waited. After a few minutes, she saw a pair of Union soldiers step out onto the track, the gigantic Warder lumbering behind them. In their wake came a group of prisoners, the rebels laboring under the weight of two bloodied bodies: John and the scavenger he'd been fighting. At first glance, she thought the men must be dead, but then she heard a soft groan rise from the scavenger and saw John move one of his arms.

"What'll we do with 'em?" one of the guards asked his comrade.

"The dispensary is already full," the other said. "Besides, the way the 'bot handled them, they won't be fit to work for quite a spell."

"So what do we do with 'em?" the first soldier persisted.

Even from a distance, Loveless couldn't mistake the grim humor underlying the response from the other soldier. "They're still breathin'," he said. "So why don't we take 'em to the surgery. Tumblety is always need'n fresh materials."

Loveless suppressed a shudder as she watched the soldiers march off toward the compound, the entourage of prisoners they'd impressed to carry the wounded men following after them. Tumblety? Since coming to Andersonville she'd heard too many ugly rumors about what went on behind the locked doors and closed windows of his surgery. John Younger was little more than a boy. To think of him being subjected to the mad doctor's experiments was too awful to contemplate.

She waited until the soldiers were out of sight before making her way back through the tents. Loveless knew she'd have to tell Frank what had happened. Someone had to know where John had gone. After that, she'd have to turn her energies to two important tasks: finding a way out of Camp Lincoln and finding a way into Tumblety's lab.

Chapter 16

General Mosby's headquarters was situated in the partially burnt-out ruin of a plantation house. The old antebellum finery had been defiled by the filth of war. Gabled roofs had been torn by artillery shells, marble floors cracked and irreparably scarred by tromping boots and heavy machinery, Greek columns scorched and blackened by the heat of blaster beams, and the white facade smirched and made dingy by the dust of marching men and the smoke of battle.

The Gray Ghost remained a dashingly handsome figure, his looks as fine and remarkable as they had been during the War through the strange, preservative power of the RJ. His gray uniform was immaculate, tailored to accommodate a lean frame just beginning to trade the musculature of youth for the fat of middle-age. Several medals gleamed on his chest, and about his neck dangled the diamond Dixie Sun, the highest honor the Confederate Rebellion could bestow upon one of its soldiers. The bright feathers of a peacock protruded from the side of Mosby's hat as he entered the old ballroom that now served him as a command center, and a wide-bladed sword with a curious mechanical hilt was scabbarded at his side. When he saw his visitors, Mosby smiled and doffed his hat in a sweeping bow.

"The renowned Jesse James," Mosby said. "If something isn't done, your legend is going to eclipse my own." The general laughed and unbuckled his sword belt. A gray-uniformed aide scrambled forward to relieve his commander of both the weapon and the hat. Mosby glanced over the other men with Jesse. Most of the gang had remained outside, but both Cole Younger and Allen Henderson had insisted on accompanying their leader to this meeting. Mosby's gaze didn't linger on Cole, but when he stared at Henderson, his smile faltered. "I heard you died in the war, Henderson."

Henderson's voice was as cheery as a breeze blowing across an open grave. "Did you hear that, or hope it?" He shook his head. "Doesn't matter. What does is that I'm back."

Mosby nodded. "There's some that would celebrate your return. And there's a damn sight more who'd like to hear that I hanged you."

"That'd inconvenience me considerable, General," Jesse said. "Mr. Henderson used to represent an old friend and what's more, he has crucial information. Information that could be of great benefit to the Confederacy."

"The man has no recognized military rank," Mosby continued to scowl at Henderson's pallid face and darkened glasses. "He didn't earn any rank in the war and he damn sure hasn't earned any since."

The shadowy figure's face spread in a menacing grin. "I've earned more than anyone you know, General."

"He's spent the years since the war in Camp Lincoln," Cole explained, trying to cut the mounting tension emanating from the two officers. "Henderson's the only man to ever break out of that place."

The news seemed to shock Mosby even more than the ghastly resurrection of Henderson had. "Impossible. We've been trying for years to slip spies into Camp Lincoln, trying every trick in the book to sabotage that place and free our men. The place is an impregnable fortress.

Mosby turned and gestured to the sprawl of his command center. The old ballroom had been transformed by the demands of military intelligence into a tangle of desks and tables, each lorded over by a clerical-looking officer and littered with a chaotic profusion of reports. The walls were papered over in immense maps depicting not only the contested banks of the Mississippi, but also the rest of the Confederate Rebellion's frontier. A few harried-looking soldiers repositioned markers indicating both friendly and enemy units on the maps as reports came in, employing curious mechanized claws fitted to steel poles to move those markers too high to reach by hand.

The most arresting feature, at least to Jesse and Cole, was the corner of the command center given over to a vast array of machinery. Carpets of wire dripped away from the machines, snaking along the floor before vanishing into a trapdoor. More wire crawled up to the ceiling and then arched its way through a hole gouged into the wall to affix themselves into the base of what looked like a copper flagpole bolted to the side of the mansion. Each of the machines was fronted by a crazed array of glass tubes and crystal spheres. A soldier was seated before each machine, connected to it by a strange helmet that fitted down over his ears and which had wires slithering back into the face of the machine. A secondary apparatus, like a curved length of bull's horn, was clenched in each soldier's hand. Jesse could see them frequently raise the devices to their mouths and shout into them. A small mob of pages waited behind the banks of machines, hurrying to relay written messages from the helmeted soldiers to the officers behind the desks.

"An invention of a man named Bell," Mosby explained to Jesse when he noted the outlaw's fascination. "With these machines we can instantly communicate with stations all across the Confederacy. Something like the vocal reiterators our enemies use, but far quicker and more efficient. It isn't muddled written messages that we receive or transmit. This is even more advanced than the vocal reiterators. We send and hear the voices of the men at each end of the line clear as a bell."

Cole smiled and shook his head. "A fancy contraption, but you'll understand if'n I'm none too keen on seein' it passed along. Invention like that'd be pure murder on our profession. Sheriff in one town tells the law around him to be 'spectin' us in their area after we pull a job…"

"Where'd you get these machines?" Jesse interrupted. His metal hands clenched into fists at his sides. Before he even heard it, he felt he knew what the general was going to say.

"Carpathian," Mosby said. "The Enlightened have been most sympathetic with the aims of the Confederacy. They've supplied us with a lot of weapons and material, much of it on credit to be paid after cessation of hostilities. It's the same exact thing that Washington is using to keep tabs on the rest of the Union. This system is so rare, that we believe to have the only other one like this in existence. What more, from what Carpathian told us, it was very time consuming and expensive to create."

Jesse turned away from the machines, fixing Mosby with a reproachful look. "You should be careful about taking things on credit," he said as he again flexed his steel hands. "There's always a price to pay and sometimes it's more than you reckoned."

"The South doesn't have the luxury of picking her friends," Mosby answered, a hint of annoyance in his voice. "Carpathian, the Indians, the Europeans, we'll take whatever help we can get from wherever we can get it! The Yankee factories turn out more guns and vehicles in three days than ours can in a month. If they weren't too busy worrying about the Warrior Nation and the Enlightened, they could come down here and squash us like a bug! We're fighting for our survival, Jesse, and we'll do anything – anything – for that right to live and be let alone."

Henderson's dry chuckle hissed through the command center. "As you said, General, the South needs help and can't afford to be choosy about picking her friends. We've come here to offer you help." He pointed a gloved finger at Jesse. "He's got a plan to bust into Camp Lincoln and free all the prisoners. It's a good plan. It's a plan that will work. But he needs the resources to pull it off. He needs men, weapons, and transport."

"I've seen that place," Mosby said, shaking his head.

"I've been *in* that place," Henderson countered. "I say Jesse's plan can work. Certainly it's a gamble, but the stakes are ten thousand rebel soldiers." Again, the black-clad guerrilla laughed. "A couple of thousand rebs and the chance to jab a finger in the Yankee eagle's eye."

Jesse stepped toward one of the big maps on the wall. He waved one of his hands toward the region depicting Andersonville and Camp Lincoln. The Yankees had chosen the camp not only for its notoriety during the war but also for its proximity to fresh supplies of unrepentant Secessionists. That meant, however, that they were also close to the ever-shifting Confederate frontier. "A quick, bold strike, General," he jabbed a steel finger at the map. "A raid just like the old days. We strike, do what we need to do, and then fade back across the border."

Mosby pointed at the marks on the map indicating Union forts and outposts. "The Yankees have an entire army scattered about that area. Any effort against Andersonville and they'll turn out every one of their soldiers. They'll lock down that border so tight a coon couldn't sneak across it."

"If the Yankees had something else to occupy them, a distraction to tie them down while we were liberating the prison, it could be done," Jesse said.

"You mean a general advance? Make a feint toward their lines and hope it keeps them pinned down." Mosby frowned. "Not sure if that would turn the trick. What I do know is that it'll need authorization bigger than anything I've got to make an attack happen."

"We came here to speak with President Lee in any event," Henderson said. "Having this palaver with you has just been whistling in the wind."

"What our associate means is we're anxious to lay this plan out before President Lee," Cole said, again trying to break the tension Henderson's lack of civility threatened to cultivate.

"I know what Henderson's meaning is," Mosby said. "It doesn't change things. In good conscience I can't send notorious outlaws – even if they have been attacking our enemy – deeper into Confederate territory with a pass to see our president."

Jesse slammed one of his hands against a desk, splintering the wood. "General, them men in Camp Lincoln need help! They can't just be abandoned!"

Mosby sighed and started toward the communication machines. "I can't send you along to President Lee, but I can fix it so you can talk to him," he said, his expression became grim. "I can't promise what he'll say. All I can do is arrange so you can ask him yourselves."

"That's fine, General," Henderson said. "Once Lee has heard Jesse's plan, there's no question that he'll know it's the right thing to do."

***

General Mosby turned away from the advanced reiterator, as he called it, removing the wired helmet from his head and replacing the horn-like vocalizer into its cradle at the top of the machine. He faced the waiting Jesse, nodding to the outlaw. "I've been placed into contact with President Lee. I'll allow you to make your case to him personally."

With some hesitation, Jesse approached the bulky machine. He could see the crimson glow of the RJ disks behind the grill-work vents at the front of the machine. It was a stark reminder that this 'telephone', like the mechanical arms fixed to his body, was an invention of Dr. Carpathian's enclave of scientists. He was anxious about speaking into the device. After the experience with his arms, he wondered what other treachery Carpathian might have installed in his other inventions. Would the machine somehow recognize the voice of an enemy and explode? Would it transmit some electrical shock into his body?

Jesse shook his head. With John rotting away in that Union hell-hole, his own fears and anxieties weren't something he could afford. He had to get him out, had to get all of the imprisoned rebels out. If he had to die in doing it, well, that was just a risk he had to accept.

Removing his hat, Jesse took the helmet from Mosby and lowered it over his head. A Confederate technician helped him adjust the leather straps that would secure the helmet. He could feel the cold metal funnels fitted on the inside of the helmet slip over his ears.

The next instant, Jesse's eyes went wide with surprise. He wasn't sure what he'd expected from the telephone. Some acoustic clicking and buzzing that vaguely sounded like words, maybe a buzzing drone like the whine of an Iron Horse, perhaps even the mechanistic growl of a recharging blaster. The last thing he expected was to hear a distinct voice, much less the precise inflections of a deep and cultured speaker.

"Hello, Mr. James," the voice said. "Are you receiving me? This is President Robert E. Lee of the Confederate Rebellion."

Jesse's hand closed around the speaking horn when Mosby passed it over to him. It took the outlaw a moment to overcome his surprise and lift the tube to his mouth. "It is an honor to speak with you, Mr. President," he said.

"I fear that honor is of less consequence than necessity," Lee replied. "General Mosby has told me something about your intention to strike the Union prison camp at Andersonville."

"We intend to raid it in the same manner as we did Lawrence during the war," Jesse said. "I've Cole and Jim Younger along with a few other raiders to ensure the attack goes like it should. More, I've got Mr. Henderson to smooth out the plan and work out the logistics. All we need is some men, weapons, and transport. If you can give us that, then I can free every man-jack the Yankees have got locked up in there."

Even over the electrical apparatus, the gravity of Lee's voice was conveyed to Jesse. "I sympathize with your ambition and your enthusiasm, son, but we just can't afford such a scheme right now. It's too reckless and too antagonistic. The Confederate Rebellion is a fragile thing, still reeling from losing the War. The Warrior Nation uprisings out west and the territorial expansion of Carpathian's Enlightened have forced the Yankees to deal with other enemies, but don't make the mistake of thinking they've forgotten about us. Don't think that Washington is prepared to 'live and let live.' No, what they want is complete restoration of the Union and the Devil take what anybody else says about it. We've been given a reprieve, a stay of execution, but they haven't torn down the gallows. If we give them enough reason, the Union will turn its troops loose on us."

Jesse's hand tightened about the speaking tube, his metal fingers denting the device. "Mr. President, there's upwards of ten thousand of our people starvin' and dyin' in that place. You can't tell me you'd sit aside and let 'em suffer."

"What I am saying, Mr. James, is that the Confederacy can't afford to start a fight just now." A ragged sigh came across the wire as the rebel president weighed his conscience against the reality of his movement's situation. "We're just now starting to pick ourselves up. Carpathian's men have helped us build great factories to turn out the armaments and machines we'll need to fight the Yankees. The Europeans are sending us supplies through hidden harbors along the old Florida coast. We've formed compacts with the natives, and there are bands of Warrior Nation members that stand with us." Lee's voice became strained. "We're gathering our strength. Five more years and we might be able to match the Yankees, but we can't do it now."

"Then you won't help us?" Jesse demanded.

"What I'm saying is that I *can't* help you," Lee answered. "My political responsibilities won't allow me to condone such an attack, however much I sympathize with its aims."

Jesse's hand clenched tighter, cracking the casing of the speaking horn. "I'm glad I don't have any responsibilities to make me a coward," he growled in disgust. He didn't wait to hear whatever response Lee might make. Reaching up, he snapped the straps holding the helmet to his head. Frustrated, he threw both the speaking tube and the helmet to the floor.

"I warned you what to expect," Mosby said as Jesse stormed away from the telephone banks.

Jesse paused, turning around slowly. His eyes fairly blazed with outraged fury. "Yes, you did," he said. "I just didn't believe the South was so yellow as you made it out to be." Without another word, Jesse marched from Mosby's headquarters, brushing past the startled sentries who moved to intercept him. A gesture from Mosby sent the guards back.

"There goes a most unhappy man," Henderson said as he turned to Cole. "You might want to rein him in a bit. We're already fighting the Yankees, we don't need to be fighting the rebels too." Cole didn't need to be told twice. Pausing only to recover Jesse's hat from the telephone technician, the bushwhacker hurried after his departed leader.

"Jesse has no reason to worry," Mosby told Henderson. "I might not be able to help him, but I'm not going to stop him."

Henderson's raspy chuckle wheezed across his bloodless lips. "Stop him? After this, nothing will stop him! You and Lee have lit a fire in Jesse James today. You told him that something he knows is right can't be done. That's a challenge he won't let alone. He's going to bust up that prison without your help."

Mosby shook his head. "That's insane," he declared. "He'll just get himself killed and everyone who follows him."

Henderson adjusted his glasses as he turned away from his old rival. "He might at that," the guerrilla conceded. "But at least he'll die on his feet, not crawling around a swamp on his belly. Good day, General."

***

Jesse marched away from the mansion, making straight for the orchard where his gang had parked their 'Horses and were now lounging in the shade waiting for their leader's return. He didn't know how he was going to break the news to them. After building up their hopes so high, after encouraging them with grand plans of getting the support of the Confederate Rebellion, Jesse didn't know how he was going to tell them it wasn't going to happen. He didn't know how he could tell them that the rebels were too timid to strike back at the Yankees in a meaningful way. He didn't know how he could tell them that the Confederacy was willing to sit aside and let all those men rot away in Andersonville's prison.

Cole hurried down the broad stairway at the front of the mansion, trying to catch up with his leader. "Jesse," he hissed in a low tone as he reached out to catch the outlaw's shoulder. Jesse spun around at the first touch of Cole's fingers, his eyes just as intense and enraged as when he'd thrown down the telephone equipment. "Don't do anything crazy, Jesse. Even if'n they got a yellow streak, these're still our people."

"They ain't our people," Jesse admonished Cole, his eyes staring past the bushwhacker and up at the red and blue battle flag flying above the mansion. "Anybody'd let good soldiers rot in a place like Camp Lincoln ain't folk I'm keen to claim kinship with."

"Damnation, Jesse!" Cole cursed. "Don't you think this has me riled too? It's my brother the blue-bellies got in there. Don't you think I'm even hotter'n you are to bust him out?"

The pain in Cole's tone touched Jesse and defused some of the rage he was feeling. The responsibility and obligation that drove Jesse so hard could be distilled into his guilt over John Younger's capture. For all the lofty ideas Henderson had stirred up in his mind, at the very core it was still the plight of John that made the raid so vital and imperative to Jesse. How much worse it must be for Cole and the other Youngers, he couldn't even begin to imagine. If it was Frank in there, Jesse knew the worry and fear for his brother would drive him crazy.

"We'll get him out," Jesse vowed. He shook his metal fist at the Confederate battle flag hanging over the mansion. "We'll get them all out and to the Devil with what Lee wants."

Cole shook his head. "Fine words, Jesse, but how're we gonna turn it?"

"I'll think of somethin'," Jesse said as he turned and stalked off toward the orchard and his men. He was eager to be quit of Mosby's encampment. He wasn't afraid the rebels would try to hold the gang; it was more the feelings of despair and betrayal that he felt growing in his heart. Once he was away from the rebel headquarters, Jesse would be able to think more clearly. He'd be able to plan out his next move better.

As they approached the orchard, Jesse was met by John Wesley Hardin. The Texan gunfight caressed the grips of his smokers as he stepped out from the trees, an oily smile shaping on his face as he saw Jesse's metal hands drop to his own holsters.

"I didn't mean to scare you, chief," Hardin apologized, though the smirk on his face said otherwise. He nodded his head back toward the orchard. "No need to tell the boys that the rebs ain't gonna help us none. They've already heard."

Jesse glowered at Hardin. "Who told 'em?"

Hardin bristled at the demanding tone, but a glance at Jesse's mechanical arms convinced him not to press the issue. "One of them darkies of yourn went pokin' his nose around. Tryin' to steal supplies most like. Anyway, he was caught and frog-marched back to us. The soldiers who brought him back laughed when they heard about yer plans." The gunfighter nodded his head back at the trees. "They sent back their officer to talk some sense to you when you got back from yer palaver with the president."

Jesse stalked past Hardin, marching quickly through the orchard to where his gang was gathered. He felt a sudden rush of fury when he saw Will Shaft tending one of the other Exodusters. The black outlaw had been badly beaten, his face swollen until it looked like one big bruise. It took him a moment to understand why the sight upset him so. After all, he'd seen slaves beaten far worse when he was a child. The difference, he realized, was that he knew better now. The Exoduster wasn't some slave, some piece of property to be pampered or abused as the owner saw fit. He was a free man and he'd followed Jesse by his own choice, not because somebody had ordered him to do so.

The outlaw chief rounded on a gray-uniformed man leaning against an orange tree and talking with Jim Younger. By the shoulder boards and the braiding, Jesse knew the officer was a Confederate captain.

"Your men do that?" Jesse growled at the officer, pointing a steel finger at the injured Exoduster.

Jim turned toward his leader. "This is Captain Rufus Henry Ingram of the California Rangers," he said, introducing the officer.

"I don't care a damn who he is," Jesse snapped. "What I want to know is have his men been beatin' one of mine?"

Ingram was a stocky, heavyset man, a thick beard covering much of his face. He bore the burn-mark of a blaster across his forehead, leaving a deep furrow between brow and scalp. He had a bulky saber, the same design as Mosby's, dangling from his belt, and keeping it company were a brace of blasters with alligator-hide grips. Each of the pistols had ugly tally-marks etched across the scaly hide. The captain's face had a villainous, thuggish quality about it, reminding Jesse of Mexican bandits he'd seen in Robbers Roost. As he stepped forward, Ingram removed the wide-brimmed cavalry hat he wore, sketching the briefest bow to the outlaw.

"Weren't my boys. We plucked your man out from a tangle of swamp-rats all set to string 'im up." The ranger smiled, an expression that only served to make his face even more cruel and murderous. "Some of these Southerners ain't got so good a sense of perspective. Think it's still like the old days of Mason-Dixon and all that." He shrugged his broad shoulders. "Me an' most of mine are Californians. We ain't got so many notions about where a man's color puts him on the totem pole."

"What *do* you care about?" Cole wondered.

Ingram laughed. "Gold and glory," he said. "That's what moved us to take up the cause during the war. That's what keeps us fightin' now." He shifted his gaze back to Jesse, his voice dropping into a whisper. "Only there ain't been much of neither. Not with the way Lee wants everybody to pussy-foot around the blue-bellies. I reckon we've about hit the point where we need to be movin' on."

"You're offerin' to ride with us?" Jesse asked. "You'd join the raid on Andersonville?"

"Help free ten thousand rebels?" Ingram laughed again. "Tarnation, can you even dream o' greater glory than that?! Hellfire, we'll be laid out in the history books after that, like old King Henry strikin' it to the froggies!"

"How many are you?" Jesse asked.

"Twenty seven," Ingram said. "Born bastards, each of them. We fought our way across a continent to help the cause. You won't find harder fighters than my rangers. What's more, every man in my command has his own arms and his own 'Horse."

Cole scowled. "We'd still be too few to make it work," he cautioned Jesse.

"We'll make it work," Jesse said. He took a step toward Ingram. "Shakin' hands with me ain't so pleasant since I got these," he said, waving his mechanical arms, "but I'd be obliged if'n you'd give me your word that you'll abide by my decisions an' take orders from Cole and Mr. Henderson."

Ingram nodded, replacing his hat on his head. "I'm lookin' to make my name and my fortune, not saddle myself with the obligations of command. You can keep that if you want it and be welcome to it. My rangers are all the men I can handle."

Jesse smiled at the Californian. "Let's just hope they're more than the Yankees can handle."

***

Lucinda Loveless shook her head as she listened to the muffled groans coming from the gagged woman lying on the floor of the nurses' barracks. Rummaging about in the bottom of the wardrobe, she produced another stocking and started winding it around the bound nurse's face. The fashion in which she'd been hogtied allowed the woman only the feeblest movement as she tried to struggle against the Pinkerton operative.

"Trust me, this is for your own good," Loveless told her. She cocked her head, listening for any noise. To ensure her captive wasn't playing it smart, she reached down and tweaked her ear. While the nurse's body quivered in pain, no undue noise escaped her gag. Satisfied, Loveless dragged her prisoner across the room and stuffed her into one of the closets. Almost as soon as the captive was hidden away, the sound of tromping boots reached her. Hurriedly, she moved back across the room, sitting herself at the edge of her prisoner's bed and adopting the anxious expression befitting the role she had chosen to appropriate for herself.

The nurse she'd ambushed had been selected by the camp commandant to attend Dr. Tumblety in his surgery. It was common knowledge in the camp that the assignment was a demanding one and that any nurse who failed to measure up was quickly dismissed and summarily removed from Andersonville, removed with such dispatch that their belongings were bundled up and shipped out days after the women had been sent away.

Loveless felt a cold determination course through her. The enigmatic and reclusive Tumblety would have a different experience when it came to her. She was determined on that point.

Once the guards came into the barracks, the sergeant sent to escort her to the surgery began to address her. Loveless, playing the role of an agitated nurse fearful for her position, shook her head and slowly rose from the bed. She smoothed the front of her white uniform, and then followed the sergeant out.

Tumblety's surgery was on the far side of the fenced compound at the center of Camp Lincoln. Loveless had been impressed by the amount of security that had been afforded to the building. It was guarded better than the armory and the supply shed, better even than the commandant's house. As the sergeant led her toward the entrance, the metallic bulk of a UR-25 Warder lumbered out from the doorway, its optics glowing in the thickening darkness. The robot started to raise the blaster built into its arm. Only the magnetized identity disk the sergeant carried stemmed the automaton's aggression. The Warder shuffled aside, making way for the sergeant and his charge.

"The doctor's waiting for you," the soldier said as he thrust a pair of keys into the mechanical locks barring the door. Loveless noticed with both surprise and alarm that the steel beams that held the door fast were bolted on the *outside* of the door. For the first time she wondered if all the security around Tumblety's surgery was in place to keep people out or to keep *something* in.

The guard didn't follow her inside. Once Loveless was across the threshold, he hurriedly closed the door. She could hear the bolts locking fast behind her as the sergeant turned his keys. Getting John out of the surgery, it seemed, wasn't going to be as easy as she'd imagined.

Loveless took in the white, sterile dimensions of the ward at a glance. She could see the marks of recent damage, the ugly stains marring the specimen shelves across the room and the vacancies among those same shelves. Plaster patches had been slapped across several of the walls and there was a strange steel disc embedded in the ceiling.

At the sound of her shoes clattering across the tile floor, a tall man dressed in evening clothes rose from behind a desk. He squinted at her from behind a pair of spectacles, then smiled and brushed his fingers across the enormous moustache he wore. Setting down the anatomy book he had been perusing, Dr. Tumblety approached Loveless.

"Colonel Custer said that you required an assistant to help you in your work," Loveless told the experimenter.

Tumblety hesitated, stroking his moustache for a moment as he considered Loveless's words. Finally, he nodded. "Yes," he said. "You will be able to help me in my work. I've been under terrible stress. You will be able to relieve that affliction."

Loveless felt her skin crawl as Tumblety's eyes roved up and down her body. She must have betrayed some sign of her revulsion because the scientist was quick to make a placating gesture with his left hand.

"Oh, no. No, you mustn't misunderstand me," Tumblety said. "I have no lascivious designs upon your body. Such base vileness is beneath a man of my genius. Science is my passion! Knowledge is my lust! Invention is my purpose!"

With each exclamation, Tumblety drew closer to Loveless. She found herself backing away from him, something instinctive deep inside her recoiling before this ridiculous-looking man. When the doctor's right hand came whipping out from behind his back, the gleam of steel shone in the electric glow of the ward's lights. Like a striking cobra, Tumblety drove his blade at Loveless's throat.

Fast as the murderer was, Loveless was faster. She caught Tumblety's hand by the wrist, giving it such a savage wrench that the knife was sent flying from his numbed fingers. The twist forced the scientist's entire body into a downward sprawl, spilling him onto the floor. All the civility and pretense of a moment before was gone now. The prostrate experimenter cursed and howled, a continuous stream of profanity spilling across his lips. Keeping his arm in a firm hold, Loveless planted her foot between Tumblety's shoulders and pressed him firmly against the floor.

"You're strong enough to slip my hold," Loveless told Tumblety, "but you must know anatomy well enough to realize you'll break your own arm doing it. Now, quiet down and be a good boy."

The reprimand only incensed Tumblety further. Despite the threat, he started to force his body up from the floor. Grabbing hold of his finger, Loveless gave it a vicious twist, breaking it like an old chicken bone. The scientist wailed in pain, his effort to break free collapsing into a fit of sobbing moans.

Feeling she was safe from immediate attack, Loveless released Tumblety's arm and quickly lifted the hem of her skirt. Sight of her exposed legs drove the pain from the experimenter's mind. Snarling like an animal, Tumblety lunged at her, tackling her to the floor. All humanity was gone from the scientist's face as he glared down at her.

"Jack'll do for you, whore," Tumblety hissed, spittle flying from his gnashing teeth.

"Whore's charge for it," Loveless snarled back. "This one's free." She brought her hand swinging up, the hand that had drawn the derringer from the holster fastened to her garter belt.

The gun cracked against the side of Tumblety's head, gashing his scalp and sending the madman sprawling. Loveless kicked the stunned experimenter's body away, freeing herself of his noxious weight. Scrambling back to her feet, she aimed her derringer at the lunatic.

"Two choices, Doctor," she told him. "You can take me to John Younger or I can blast your brains out." She put the toe of her shoe into his ribs, knocking him onto his back. Tumblety's face turned pale when he saw the large-bore derringer in her fist. It was a compact model designed expressly for the Pinkerton agency, capable of the same destructive power as a full-sized blaster, though limited to a two shot capacity and severely reduced range. Either consideration wouldn't be a problem for Loveless to make good her threat. If she opened fire, all that would be left of Tumblety's head would be a plume of smoke.

"Don't shoot," Tumblety begged, raising his hands and holding them out to his sides. "I'll take you to him. He's only been here a few days."

"Where is he?" Loveless demanded, aiming the derringer at Tumblety's face.

The experimenter craned his head, glancing toward the vivisection theaters. Each station was separated by a white curtain, concealing whatever lay behind them.

Loveless kicked Tumblety again. "Get up," she ordered. "And no tricks."

Awkwardly, Tumblety picked himself off the floor. He dabbed a handkerchief at his bleeding scalp, grimacing at the sight of his own blood. "You've cut me, you filthy strumpet!"

"I'll do worse," Loveless promised. 'Take me to John."

Grumbling, Tumblety led his captor across the ward to the furthest of the vivisection theaters. With a showman-like flourish, he drew back the curtain.

Loveless blanched at what she saw lying on the operating table. It took her a moment to recognize the features of the rebel scavenger who'd attacked them. What had been done to his body was beyond description, flesh peeled away to expose the raw musculature and organs, limbs amputated and weird copper plugs stapled into the stumps. An array of bottles was suspended above the carcass on a spider-web framework, little tubes conveying a constant drip of chemicals into the body.

"I fear I was unable to help that one," Tumblety said. "But I was much more successful with your friend." He gestured toward a curtained alcove at the back of the theater.

Keeping her gun trained on Tumblety, Loveless walked over to the alcove. She ripped down the curtain in a single tug. Instantly she wished she hadn't.

True to Tumblety's words, John was there. What had been done to him was more obscene than the dead scavenger the experimenter had termed one of his failures. John's body was swollen with muscle, patches of skin and flesh stitched to his body to accommodate the extra mass. A third arm protruded from the middle of his chest, sutures and staples surrounding the place where the shoulder merged with breastbone. New legs were sewn to his pelvis, again without any concession to symmetry or conformity, one leg appreciably longer than its opposite. Hoses and pipes ran from bottles of chemicals into the monstrosity and about the whole there was a foul stink not unlike that of an embalmer's studio.

While she gawked in horror at this thing, this obscenity that had been John Younger, Loveless momentarily forgot Tumblety. The scientist scurried behind a cart of surgical tools and then shouted at the creature his madness had made. "Disarm her!"

Distracted by the madman's cry, Loveless didn't react quickly enough when John's misshapen bulk lurched into life. The ghastly arm protruding from his chest smashed down with tremendous force, nearly breaking her hand as the derringer was knocked from her grip. The monster's other arms caught her at waist and shoulder, holding her fast as Tumblety emerged from his refuge.

"What do you think of my lovely Reconstructed?" Tumblety asked, grinning as he stalked toward the captive woman. "A marvelous discovery that will advance medicine by an order of magnitude not seen since… well… since forever."

"It's monstrous!" Loveless snarled at him, struggling to pull free from John's iron-like grip. "It's insane!"

Tumblety shook his head. "All genius is called 'insane' by those too stupid to understand. But I am too magnanimous to hold a grudge. I shall help the world, even if they don't want my help." He leaned down and recovered Loveless's gun from the floor.

"I'm a Pinkerton agent," Loveless warned him as she watched him study the weapon.

Tumblety stuffed the derringer into his pocket. "That might be true," he said. "But who knows you are? Just you and me and John. And none of us are going to say anything." He shook his head. "Things would have been so much simpler if you had cooperated. Now, I fear, it will go harder on you. So very much harder. I'll have to take my time with you now. Nothing quick. Nothing simple."

Tumblety pointed to the specimen racks across the ward. "As you may have noticed, I had an accident and part of my collection was ruined. We'll have to see how much of what I'm missing you will be able to replace."

Chapter 17

The Richmond Terminal Company had gained control over the old railways in what had been Georgia, an aspect of the Union's reconstruction efforts to consolidate the infrastructure of the vanquished South into the hands of a few Northern companies and 'right-minded' Southern establishments. At great expense, the Richmond Terminal Company, imported hundreds of miles of new rail to repair pathways that had been willfully heated and twisted by the invading army as part of Sherman's scorched earth policy. In many places, the malformed knots of iron, grimly termed 'Sherman's neckties,' still lay beside the fresh track, slowly rusting in the humid Georgian climate.

Sherman's intention had been to wreck the track and make it completely unusable to the Confederacy. The neckties of iron were an almost total loss to a mineral-poor nation. It was bitterly ironic that these mementos of the Confederate defeat should now repose beside the newly-constructed symbol of Yankee occupation.

It was still more ironic that these mangled knots should now be put to good purpose by a new breed of rebel. Jesse James admired the scheme Cole Younger and Captain Ingram had hatched between them. Chaining Sherman's neckties to the backs of their Iron Horses, the outlaws could speedily drag the things onto the fresh track. One or two of the knots might be easily brushed aside by a train, but with each 'Horse able to drag a pair of the twisted rails up onto the track, the combined mass would stop the RJ-powered locomotive cold.

It was like the first big heist all over again. Jesse felt a wave of nostalgia wash over him as he thought about the effect that the neckties would have. Well over fifteen years ago, he had sat with an agitated Cole and his brother Frank, as they blew-up the Union train carrying Yankee technology. That heist gave the outlaw parties the technology that they all desperately needed to keep up with the Yankee bastards. Now, here they were again, without Frank, and a lot less of their gang, but it still sent shivers down Jesse's back as he remembered the feel of success from all those years ago.

From the shadows of a stand of willows, Jesse and Allen Henderson looked over the site they had chosen for their ambush. The old guerrilla was particularly happy with the way the track turned at a sharp angle to avoid a rocky slope. The railway company had been lax in allowing the trees to grow so close to the tracks; Jesse thought they would have learned to be more careful with their trains after what he had done. When the train came to the turn, the engineers would have no warning of what lay around the bend until they were right on top of it. The location seemed purposely made for an ambush.

"You'll have to move fast," Henderson reminded Jesse. "I'm sure you remember that the Yankees make it a habit to send a stalking horse ahead of the main engine. You have to let the bait slip through before making any move to catch the real prize."

Jesse frowned, shaking his head. "Yeah, I remember. Still disgusts me that they let the boys in the front stick their head in the noose while the train is left free to skedaddle." He turned and posed a question to Captain Ingram. The Californian's rangers had scouted this area many times on behalf of General Mosby and had more than a passing familiarity with how the Yankees moved supplies through the region. "You're certain about the disposition of guards?"

Captain Ingram ran a finger along the scar across his forehead. "I've been close enough to hear 'em holler," he said. "You can expect ten troopers and a half-dozen 'bots in the Malediction they have running out front. That engine'll have ten inch armor plate all about and enough repeatin' blasters to cut down a forest. If the blue-bellies get that thing rollin' back on us, we're through."

"They won't," Jesse promised with a smile. "You can say that I'm familiar with how to get this part of the job done." He looked over at Will Shaft. Of all the men with him, the Exoduster was the man most familiar with deploying explosives. It was only natural for a man who'd once been a slave in a rock quarry and 'entrusted' with the hazardous job of setting demolition charges to become an expert at handling the stuff.

"I won't let you down, Jesse," Will promised. "That stalking horse won't be comin' back after it passes by."

The Exoduster's vow brought a sneer onto John Wesley Hardin's face. The gunfighter slapped his hand against one of his smokers. "See to it, boy, or I'll tell you right now you'll burn like a pig if'n you betray us."

It took Jesse only six steps to be standing in front of Hardin. His mechanical arm whipped out, cracking across Hardin's face and knocking him from the saddle of his 'Horse. The gunfighter landed in a sprawl. He spit out a broken tooth and then drew his smoker from its holster. Before he could take aim, Cole kicked the weapon out of his hand.

"Damn Free-Soiler!" Hardin cursed at Jesse. "Takin' up for that no good horse thief!"

"Hardin, right now you should be thankful I showed some restraint," Jesse growled down at the Texan. "Otherwise we'd be kicking the bushes lookin' for your head. Will's here to fight the Union, same as any of us. You can't appreciate that, it's all the same to me. But you damn sure are gonna keep them notions to yerself." He turned his eyes across the rest of his gang and the rangers. "Same applies to everyone else. Don't make no nevermind what a man was afore, you're all ridin' with the James Gang now. Pull your weight, and I don't give a hoot in hell what color yer skin is. All that matters is you do yer job."

Wiping the blood from his lip, a sullen Hardin recovered his smoker and stuffed it back into its holster. He glared at Jesse, but his temper had cooled enough to appreciate that there was no way he'd be able to outdraw those quick-devil arms. Chastened, he climbed back into the saddle of his 'Horse.

The distant toot of a steam whistle roused the gang back to the present. One of the Exodusters had staged himself further down the line with a few head of cattle that the rangers had rustled. Positioning the animals on the tracks, he'd wait for the Malediction to come right up to him and blast its whistle to scare the animals out of its way. That would be the signal to the waiting outlaws that their prey was drawing near.

Jesse hurried back to his own steed. He glanced to his left, watching as Ingram's rangers formed up with a precision and discipline that belied their commander's claims about them being merely marauding brigands. Jesse's gang mustered with commendable speed but with a deal less polish. It was something that nagged at his pride and he resolved that once the Andersonville raid was over, he'd be making some changes about what it took to become a member of the James Gang and what was expected of a man once he was in. Meeting Henderson again had impressed on Jesse the difference between acting like a military unit, even a company of irregulars, and behaving like robbers and road agents. If he was going to aspire toward something greater than simple outlawry, then he'd have to change a lot of things.

"Keep to the willows," Henderson hissed to the men, rangers and outlaws alike. Ingram, commanding the rangers, set about ensuring his men were well within the cover of the trees, as Cole did the same with the outlaws. The screen of the willows would hide them from the men on the train, but the drooping branches would provide no obstacle at all once the time came to gun their Iron Horses and speed down across the tracks.

Jesse smiled at the appropriateness of the old term 'going among the willows,' which meant a man had turned outlaw. They were certainly among the willows now, and quite soon they'd impress on the Yankees the veracity of the old slang.

The Malediction came rumbling past, playing its role as scout for the train behind it. The armored engine looked like some prehistoric behemoth, its dull steel plates layered atop one another like the interlocking scales of a snake's belly. Cupolas jutted from the sides of the single car following behind the engine, a murderous scatter-blaster array fixed into each of the basket-like projections, and a blue-uniformed gunner was poised behind each weapon. A much larger turret rose above the car. A massive blast-cannon scented the air, with two more scatter-blasters situated above it on the sloping armor; an array of weaponry designed to deal with large targets at a distance and smaller ones at closer range. The car was armored like the engine, and along its sides was a covered walkway upon which the steel frames of robots could be seen, rifles clenched in their metal claws. Magnetic clamps built into their feet kept each 'bot in place, defying the momentum of the Malediction as it roared through the countryside.

The outlaws watched the armored train pass, each of them feeling a sensation of dread well up inside him. More than a few turned a worried glance at Will Shaft, praying that the Exoduster's explosives would knock out the Malediction before its vicious armaments could be brought into play against them.

Jesse was one of the few who didn't doubt Will's capability. He kept his eyes on the Malediction, not on the man he was trusting to eliminate it. When the armored train rumbled around the bend, he lifted his mechanical arm and brought it chopping down. At his signal, the outlaws spurred their Iron Horses into motion. Like a horde of wolves, they howled out from the willows and across the tracks. Behind each vehicle, the ambushers dragged a pair of Sherman's neckties. The twisted rails smashed their way through bushes, tore chunks of bark from the willows, gouged furrows in the ground, but the impetus of the Iron Horses pulled them onto the tracks just the same. As each outlaw brought his burden onto the tracks, he leaned back and released the chains holding it. In short order, what had been a section of clear railway was now cluttered with over a hundred heavy lumps of twisted metal.

The Ford brothers were the last of the outlaws to clear the tracks when the Union train came into view. The engine's whistle blared as the crew saw the obstruction on the tracks ahead. Frantically, the engineer tried to brake the locomotive, but the momentum of the speeding train and the over laden cars behind it was too great to be arrested.

The locomotive slammed into the mass of twisted iron with a thunderous screech. The debris was thrust forward by the force of the hurtling train, pushed along the track in a rolling, grinding mass of tortured metal. The track was ripped apart by the knots of iron, ties reduced to splinters and rails ripped clean from their fastenings. As the train neared the turn, its wheels left the track. The entire engine was propelled onward into the rocks, slamming into it with such violence that the front of the locomotive crumpled and was pushed back into the control cabin.

The crew vanished, crushed into bloody pulp by the fury of the wreck.

The cars behind the engine slammed into one another, some of them flung dozens of yards into the trees, others leaping upward and hurling themselves atop the cars ahead of them. One flat-car, its length taken up by a dozen Iron Horses, was sent whipping around crosswise across the rails only to be cut in half by the plowing momentum of the car behind it.

The outlaws waited until every car had come to a stop, then with a mighty Rebel yell, they shot out from where they lurked in the trees. Like a flock of buzzards, the ambushers swarmed about the train. Blasters barked out as the attackers fired on blue-coated soldiers crawling out from the wreckage.

Jesse held back, waiting and listening for the explosion that would alert him that the Malediction had been eliminated. The ruination of the train had been achieved, but if its escort returned, then the outlaws' success would be eradicated in a frenzy of vengeance.

From his place among the rocks, Jesse watched his gang and Ingram's rangers rove across the smashed train. He saw Jim Younger shoot a Yankee sergeant as the man stumbled out from the shattered window of a passenger car. He watched as Bob Younger cut down an enraged rail man who came at him with an axe, the seasoned knife-fighter ducking beneath the cleaving blade to open his enemy's belly. He shook his head as he observed John Wesley Hardin immolate a pair of blue-bellies who came crawling out from an upturned supply wagon, the incendiary ammunition of his smokers turning the two soldiers into shrieking pillars of flame.

Most sickening to Jesse, however, was the sight of the man that used to represent his old commander, and supposedly everything he stood for, Allen Henderson. The black-garbed guerrilla had dismounted and was stalking among the cars, dragging injured men from the wreckage. However mangled by the crash the wretch might be, Henderson showed them no mercy. Pressing his blaster against each forehead, he murdered the wounded with icy callousness. Jesse felt a shiver crawl down his spine as he wondered at the cruelty he witnessed, the inhuman monstrousness exhibited by the guerrilla. There seemed no emotion, no rage in the man as he killed his victims. They might have been ants for all the feeling Henderson expressed. That feeling of deja-vu overcame him in a sickening way, as it reminded him of Jake 'Smiley' Williamson and the way he brutalized the victims from the first train robbery.

The deafening bellow of Will Shaft's explosives boomed across the landscape. Jesse could see the fingers of flame and smoke that shot hundreds of feet into the sky as the Malediction was obliterated. The armored gun-car's turret went spinning through the air, smashing down among the trees. Human forms, like tiny motes, went sailing through the heavens. Speeding back to help the train, the escort had tripped the Exoduster's trap perfectly.

Jesse didn't wait, now that he knew the Malediction wasn't coming back. He gunned his Iron Horse and sped down from his lookout post. The outlaw zipped around the smashed and burning coaches and cars. Everywhere, he could see outlaws and rangers plundering supplies from the wreck. Professional railroad wrecking crews couldn't have pillaged the cars more thoroughly. Jesse could see Cole guiding a pair of outlaws as they tried to drive a hulking transport wagon off one of the flat-cars. The bushwhacker waved his arms excitedly when he saw Jesse.

"There's five of 'em!" Cole shouted. "Big ore-cars for some mine outfit down the pike! Each of these lummoxes could haul a hundred men in their beds, maybe even more!"

"We'll make salvagin' those a priority," Jesse said. "We'll need 'em to get our boys away from Andersonville."

Cole's expression grew grave. "Henderson says they're in a bad way. Sick and starvin' and all." He studied the big ore wagon as it rumbled down from the smashed flat-car, the glow of RJ shining from a gash in its engine casing. "If'n we rigged up some sort of tiers inside, like bunks, we'd maybe carry off three times as many men."

"Fix it up, then," Jesse ordered. "Just do it quick." The outlaw chief was already speeding away. He passed Captain Ingram, noticing the way the Californian and his rangers were dragging crates of blasters from a burning supply car. Again, Jesse was struck by the military discipline and efficiency Ingram had drilled into his followers. Not without a twinge of envy, Jesse left the Californians to their work.

He had a different sort of confrontation to address. Speeding around the mangled wreck of a passenger car that had been transfixed by a box car, Jesse found Henderson still pulling men from the wreck and shooting them in the coldest blood. Jesse glared at the guerrilla, and then revved his 'Horse so that the noise of the engine would draw Allen Henderson's attention away from his vicious labor.

"Allen!" Jesse shouted. "What in Hell are you doin'?"

Henderson didn't look up until he'd turned the face of the man he'd pulled from the wreck into a steaming hole. When he did turn to face Jesse, the shadowy man's eyes were inscrutable behind his glasses. "I'm doing what needs to be done," Henderson said. He waved his hand at the smashed train. "You've taken the whole pot with a full house. Now you have to be careful that you don't give away the bigger game. It'll take the Yankees days to figure out what happened here. Their first guess will be Mosby's men, and then they might start wondering about Warrior Nation war parties sneaking around the countryside. They won't think somebody has designs on Andersonville. Not unless you leave somebody around to tell what happened." Henderson pointed at Jesse's mechanical arms. "There aren't too many men with arms like that. The Yankees realize that you're here, it won't take them too long to reckon why you're here."

Jesse felt sick at the bottom of his stomach. What Henderson said made sense. Brutal, horrific, even obscene, but sense just the same. Any witness they left behind, anyone who could even hint that they'd seen Jesse or one of the Younger brothers and they could alert the Yankees, cause them to bolster the guards at Camp Lincoln. Their chances were long already, any significant enlargement of the defenses at Camp Lincoln could spoil them entirely.

"We can take 'em with us," Jesse said, pointing toward the wagons Cole was salvaging. "We can ride into Andersonville with a load of Yankees and leave with a load of rebs."

Henderson stood up, loading a fresh cartridge into his blaster. "And what if something happened? What if one of the Yankees got loose? This is safer, Jesse, and you know it. We didn't put the fear of God into the Jayhawkers during the war by being squeamish."

"Maybe we didn't fight the war the right way," Jesse said. He thrust a steel finger at the armed man. "No more killin'. I want prisoners. Things can go wrong at the other end, too. If'n they do, it might be convenient to have hostages for bargainin'. Don't you go forgettin' who's the one in charge here. You mighta been second to Quantrill once, but he ain't here."

The shadowy figure kept his eyes trained on Jesse for a few moments before he shrugged. "My apologies, Jesse. I'll pass the word along," he said. There was no resentment or hostility in his expression, only a suggestion of disappointment, and an almost fatherly sense of disapproval at the outlaw's compassion. Jesse wasn't sure what made him more uneasy, the thought that this man represented his old commander's ideas, or that Camp Lincoln had changed him so much to act like a savage on the warpath.

The return of Will Shaft turned Jesse's attention away from Henderson. The Exoduster's Iron Horse was coated in soot, as was the outlaw himself. It was obvious that he'd been close when the Malediction had struck the explosives. Jesse'd given him the job of making certain the escort engine was knocked out, but he hadn't expected the man to linger so close to his work.

Beneath his mantle of soot, Will's face was grim. It wasn't the demolition of the armored train that upset him however. "If I'd knowed this was the sort of thing you was goin' to do Mr. James, I'd stayed put in Robbers Roost."

Jesse shook his head. "Henderson was tryin' to make sure the Yankees weren't warned. I've already told him I want prisoners, not a massacre."

Will glowered at the bodies left by Henderson. "I didn't know nothin' about Henderson murderin' nobody. Seein' you've put a stop to him, maybe you'd put a stop to Hardin too."

The Exoduster didn't wait to explain further, he just turned his 'Horse around and sped away. Jesse bit back an outburst and hurried to follow Will. Together, the outlaws rode around the periphery of the wreck to where a flat-car had lodged itself among the trees. Still strapped down to the car's bed were two immense steel juggernauts, mammoth machines that made the Judgement Wyatt Earp had brought against the gang look feeble by comparison. They were the mechanized artillery designated 'Rolling Thunder' by the Union Army and they looked to be perfectly intact.

Less intact were the men cowering on the ground around the flat-car. Crouched down on their knees, their hands folded behind their necks, the men wore the soiled tatters of their Union uniforms. They'd been badly bruised and battered by the wreck, but the ordeal of the crash was the least of the horrors the night held in store for them. Standing before them, smokers gripped in each hand, was John Wesley Hardin. An ugly, sick expression was on the gunslinger's face as he glared at the cowering soldiers. Picking one at random, he lashed out with his boot and knocked the man sprawling.

"Get up, blue-belly. Run fer it! Maybe you'll get further than yer friends!" Hardin laughed as the soldier started to run. Keeping one smoker trained on the other prisoners, he aimed the other at the fleeing man. Before he'd gone a dozen paces, the soldier was struck down by a shot from Hardin's gun. The incendiary struck him square in the back, the chemical splashing over the man's body and turning him into a blazing bonfire. The screaming figure raced on for several yards, then collapsed to the ground in a smoldering heap. The scorched bodies of three other soldiers gave mute testament to how long Hardin had been indulging in his sadistic sport.

Jesse had been appalled by Henderson's cold, calculated murder of the Yankees; he had expected something like that by Smiley back in the day, but not from Henderson. Seeing Hardin's vicious enjoyment of slaughtering helpless men brought raw fury flowing through his veins. Opening the throttle of his Iron Horse, Jesse swooped down toward the Texan. "Hardin!" he shouted. "Stop it, you murderin' cur!"

Hardin swung around at Jesse's yell. For an instant there was a twinge of panic when he saw the outlaw chief, but then he spotted Will riding alongside Jesse. The black gunman's presence enflamed the hate already boiling inside him.

"I'm fixin' these Yankees so's they won't be bringin' their high-falutin' ideas no place 'cept Hell!" Hardin said. He kicked out with his boot, knocking another soldier to the ground.

"Please!" the man howled, reaching his hands imploringly toward Jesse. "I ain't no Yankee! I'm from Virginia! I'm jus' tryin' to make some money for my family back home!"

Hardin kicked the man again. "Then yer a damn galvanized Yankee! Get on yer feet an' start runnin'!"

"Leave him alone," Jesse told the gunfighter. "Leave all of 'em alone. You've murdered enough men tonight."

"Murder hell!" Hardin cursed. "I'm avengin' the indignities heaped up on the South by these blue-belly tyrants!" He glared at Will, then back to Jesse. "Maybe if'n yer head weren't so took up with miscegenation, you'd appreciate that."

"I appreciate I jus' told you to do somethin' and you ain't doin' it," Jesse warned.

Hardin turned away, back toward the prisoners. Suddenly, the Texan swung back around. Will shouted in alarm, but Jesse's reaction was still quicker. His mechanical hands flew to his holsters, ripped the Hyper-velocity blasters free and fired at the Texan before Hardin could pull the triggers of his already drawn smokers. Jesse's blasters picked off the guns in Hardin's hands. The left smoker went spinning off into the coming night, but the one in the Texan's right hand exploded under the impact of Jesse's shot. The incendiary charge contained inside the gun's chamber splashed across Hardin's body.

The gunfighter screamed as the chemical burned his flesh. Hardin threw himself to the ground, rolling in the dirt in a desperate attempt to smother the fires engulfing him. Will raised one of his pistols, pointing it at the Texan to administer a coup de grace and end his suffering.

"Leave him be," Jesse said, waving his hand at Will. "Leave him burn." He glared down at the writhing shape of the Texan. "He should get used to it. He'll find it a might hotter when he gets to Hell."

Will shuddered at the cruelty of Jesse's decision. Hardin was a monster and Jesse'd paid him back in his own coin. Will didn't want to think about what that made the outlaw chief. Instead he nodded to the still cowering Union soldiers. The duel had happened so quickly none of the men had been given the chance to even think about running. "What'll we do with them?"

Jesse turned in his saddle and stared down at the soldiers. He noticed the cannon patch of artillerymen on the jackets a few of them wore. "You're responsible for those?" he asked, gesturing to the Rolling Thunder wagons strapped to the flat-car.

The galvanized Yankee from Virginia was the first to answer Jesse. "Yes sir, we're engineers, 21st Ohio Mobile Artillery Brigade."

Jesse smiled at the statement. He pointed at Hardin's agonized figure rolling in the dust. "You've been given a reprieve, so now yer gonna earn it. Yer gonna show my boys how to operate them juggernauts." A hard edge crept into the outlaw's tone. "If'n you don't, then you'll be prayin' I'd left you to Hardin."

***

Frank James tried to maintain just the right mix of timidity and uneasiness that the Yankees would expect from one of their turnkeys. Walking down the halls of the Union barracks, he was careful to keep his eyes averted any time a soldier in blue marched past him. When an officer approached, he was quick to snap to attention and salute, a performance that always brought a sneering smile to the face of the Union commanders. He remembered all the little details he'd been told that would help him blend in and allay any hint of suspicion on the part of Camp Lincoln's administrators.

It had been an entire day since he'd seen Lucy the nurse escorted into Tumblety's surgery. Frank had expected he might see her ejected from the place, but since she'd gone in, no one had either visited or left the old hospital building. That simple fact had done more to exacerbate his worry than anything else. If she'd been successful, he would have seen her and John leaving. If she'd failed, then Colonel Custer's troops should have collected her and dragged her off to their guardhouse. Neither had occurred, and that had set his mind to pondering other, darker possibilities.

Even more, Frank wondered why the girl that he had seen all that time ago in the saloon, at the start of the big to-do with Billy the Kid, had suddenly appeared here and now?

Eventually, Frank's worry grew to the point where he couldn't just sit idle and maintain his vigil. Using the marchtack Lucy had given him, he was able to bribe one of the turnkeys. The Union administrators employed trusted prisoners to clean up the buildings inside their compound and handle all the drudgery of day-to-day life. Prisoners represented the cheapest labor, working for only a meager increase in their food ration. For the budget-conscious Custer, they were a boon to his economy.

The turnkey had given Frank the special armbands that would mark him out for admittance into the compound and the magnetized disk that would keep the Warders from firing on him if he was inside the fence – though he warned that the 'bots on the walls and around Tumblety's surgery would still shoot if he got too close. Frank remembered both warnings. The story he'd given the turnkey was one that elicited the man's cooperation to the fullest – a promise that he knew where more marchtack was hidden and that he would share with the turnkey if he recovered it – so Frank was certain the man had left out no detail that would ensure the outlaw's safe return.

If the prisoner had known Frank's objective was the surgery, he'd probably have been a good deal less cooperative. Frank, however, had a good idea about how he'd get inside the old hospital without the man's help. All he needed was the identity disk of the sergeant who'd taken Lucy to Tumblety. For two hours he prowled the halls of the barracks sweeping up and cleaning, his eyes ever on the lookout for the man he wanted. At last he found him.

The sergeant was sitting at a poker game in one of the guardrooms off the main gallery. Frank leaned into the room, watching as the off-duty soldiers made wagers and drew cards. He waited until the sergeant looked up, and then waved his hand in a subtle, beckoning gesture. The sergeant didn't pay attention the first time, but when he looked up and saw Frank repeat the motion, it aroused the soldier's interest. When he lost the next hand, he excused himself and walked out into the corridor. He didn't look at Frank, but he made certain to brush against him as he walked past, his arm nudging the supposed turnkey. Frank waited a few seconds, and then followed after the sergeant.

The sergeant was waiting for him in the darkened doorway of a linen closet. "Well, Johnny Reb, what's so all-fired important?" the soldier growled.

Frank glanced down the hallway, an apprehensive look on his face. "There's a Texas boy who had himself a fine-looking gold ring. It's been took."

The sergeant's eyes gleamed with the glint of greed. It wasn't the ring that excited the soldier's avarice, but rather the prospect of catching the thief. "Who took it? One of us?" Custer had an unbending mania for discipline in his command. It wasn't the crime itself that upset the commandant but rather the breech of discipline the theft represented. He'd deal out harsh punishment to any soldier caught stealing. At the same time, he'd reward any soldier who uncovered such an indiscretion.

"Yeah," Frank said, lowering his voice to a whisper. He glanced around again, smiling at the dearth of potential witnesses. The sergeant had found an admirably isolated spot for their conversation. One that suited Frank's purposes exceedingly well. When the outlaw continued to whisper, the sergeant leaned forward to hear him. Frank brought both hands smashing down into the back of the soldier's neck, flattening him against the floor. Before anyone could come along, he picked up the stunned sergeant and shuffled him back into the linen closet.

It was only a matter of minutes before Frank was wearing the sergeant's uniform and carrying his identity disk. He discarded the turnkey's disk as he walked from the barracks. Two disks had the potential to confuse the mechanical brain of a 'bot. A confused Warder tended to shoot at whatever was confusing it. As he approached the surgery, the hulking Warder on guard outside the door watched him with its glowing optics, the omnipresent threat of its rifle-arm all too prominent. Frank felt as though his legs were jelly. The sergeant had been unarmed when he'd waylaid the man. If the Warder decided to start shooting, there was nothing he could use to defend himself.

The 'bot, however, paid no notice to Frank's anxiety. The only thing that mattered to it was the disk he carried. Holding the stolen disk, Frank was able to walk past the Warder and to the door. It took him a moment to work the keys and slide back the bolts, but the 'bot didn't pay attention to his fumbling uncertainty with the locks.

Slipping inside the door, Frank at once was struck by the size of the surgery and the sterile white walls. For a man engaged in so furtive an enterprise as a rescue, the surgery offered an appalling lack of shadows and clutter to conceal his movements. At the same time, the well-lit conditions made it easy to spy at a glance the whole of the ward room. Almost at once, Frank saw one of his objectives. The sight made him rush across the surgery, outraged by the implications of what he'd seen.

Lucy was lying strapped to a steel table in one of the vivisection stations. Arms and legs bound at her sides, her uniform had been slashed and cut to expose the trunk of her body. Frank noticed that her bare flesh had been marked up with paint, different spots circled or X-marked, often with a number written beside them. Stretched upon a stand beside her was an anatomical chart with the organs designated in similar fashion. A gurney was lying at the opposite end of the table, a motley collection of jars filled with chemical preservatives strewn across it. Beside the jars was a gruesome array of knives and hooks.

The nurse was alive, her captor had gathered the instruments for her butchery, but he hadn't started the operation yet. Lucy stared at Frank, a desperate appeal in her gaze. She struggled to push words through the gag that had been tied across her face. Frank hurried to remove it.

"Hold up," the outlaw told her. "I can't understand you."

"I believe the whore's trying to warn you about me," a mocking voice chuckled from behind Frank.

The outlaw spun around, his hands clenched into fists. With what he'd seen, Frank would happily beat Lucy's captor to death with his bare hands.

Unfortunately, Dr. Tumblety wasn't unarmed. Wearing an ostentatious military uniform, a Prussian-style spiked helmet on his head, the experimenter strode out from behind the shelves holding his anatomical collection. Each of the madman's hands was closed inside a strange metal gauntlet. Upon each forearm there was a little hopper into which tiny steel disks were fed. At the front of each gauntlet was the menacing darkness of a slit-edged barrel.

"I don't know who you are, or how you got here," Tumblety said. "But you've come at an opportune time. One of my subjects is rejecting the last enhancements I endowed him with. I'm afraid I'll need to borrow some of your organs to fix him up again."

Frank took a pace back. He turned his head and started to reach for one of the knives on the gurney.

Tumblety laughed and pointed one of his gauntlets at Frank. "I'll give you a choice," he said. "You can help me with one experiment or you can help me with another." The gauntlet on his arm screeched as one of the saw-edged disks left the hopper and dropped into the magazine below. "I've just been *dying* to try out my Rippers on a free and unfettered target."

Chapter 18

The lieutenant commanding the gates of Camp Lincoln scowled down at the group of men gathered before the wrought-iron portals. He didn't appreciate being called away from his poker game in the middle of the night. The sergeant on duty should have handled these men on his own. Simply because they clamored for an officer didn't mean the guards had to acknowledge such demands. He almost wished they could get away with posting Warders throughout the prison and do away with soldiers entirely. A 'bot simply obeyed orders; it didn't suffer any failures of initiative. With a little more versatility, 'bots would replace human troops entirely. The lieutenant was convinced of that fact and he was certain that Tesla was already working on the improvements to the robot brain that would make such implementation practical. It would be a happy day when every soldier under his command simply did as they were told.

There were seven men below standing just beyond the stakes that demarked the dead line, the point beyond which any trespass would provoke the Warders patrolling the walls to open fire. The group was gathered around one of the electric lamps lining the approach to Camp Lincoln. By the lamp's light, the lieutenant could see that four of the men were dressed in Union uniforms and that three of them had the dusky color of Africans. A third man was, standing nearby. His pale features standing out stark against the somber color of his clothes and the shadow cast by his wide-brimmed hat. There was a glint of brass armor under his duster. The other two men were wearing gray linen dusters and stood between the others. Their stance was stiff and tense, but they had their faces averted from the prison so the officer wasn't able to form a more distinct impression of their attitude. He could tell that the soldiers were in a state of heightened agitation, their eyes never leaving the two men in the dusters.

"What's all this ballyhoo about?" the lieutenant called down.

The only white soldier among the group muttered a command to the black troopers and then stepped forward. "I'm Sergeant Iverson, 23rd Pennsylvania, detached from Fort Stimson to render aid to Mr. Thomas Tate Tobin." The sergeant nodded toward the man in black.

The lieutenant tapped his chin thoughtfully as he tried to recall where he had heard that name before. He'd read it somewhere, he was certain of that. After a moment, the connection came to him. "Tobin? The bounty hunter?"

"The same, sir," Iverson said. The man in black simply brushed the brim of his hat in a mocking semblance of a salute when the lieutenant looked at him. "We've been helping him track down the James-Younger Gang."

The lieutenant was taken aback by that news. If the James-Younger Gang was in the area, then it was likely the outlaws had learned that Frank James had been confined in Camp Lincoln. The officer blanched at the idea of facing the vengeful outlaws. Jesse James was infamous for the murderous speed of his mechanical arms. What a garrison of some second-string infantry and second rank 'bots of Camp Lincoln could do against the rage of the James-Younger Gang was a question that brought him to the edge of panic. He was just turning to order a message relayed back to Colonel Custer when Sergeant Iverson called up to him again.

"It's been a hard day and we'd like to get our prisoners put away."

"Prisoners?" the lieutenant looked again at the two men in the linen dusters. While he stared at them, one of the black soldiers stepped over to them and pulled back the dusters. The officer could see now that the older of the two men had his hands tied in front of him with rope. He didn't study the captive long, however, for when the duster was pulled off the other prisoner, that man commanded the lieutenant's full attention. He wasn't bound with rope but with chain; chains that were wrapped around his body and pinned his arms at his sides. They weren't natural arms, but powerful steel mechanisms.

"Cole Younger and Jesse James," Sergeant Iverson said, gesturing from one to the other. "We managed to take them alive. The other Younger brothers weren't so fortunate." He gestured to a burlap sack which the black-clad bounty hunter had tied to his belt.

The mere suggestion of what was inside Tobin's bag made the lieutenant shudder. The idea of a white man behaving in such savage, bestial fashion was offensive to him. Just because he was a paid killer didn't mean he had to comport himself like a jungle heathen. "We'll take your prisoners, but that killer and his trophies can stay right where he is."

"Then so do my prisoners," the man in black declared. "Jesse's worth $10,000 to me. I'm not letting him out of my sight." His gloved hand tapped the bag hanging from his belt. "These are worth a thousand each, so they're coming along too."

The lieutenant bristled at the imperious tone and frowned at the faint trace of Southern twang in Tobin's voice. He was tempted to tell the psychopath and his escort to leave, but the idea of Jesse and Cole somehow escaping custody made him hold his tongue. "Turn your weapons over to Sergeant Iverson. I'll be hanged if I let you come in armed."

The bounty hunter shrugged and began turning over his blasters and rifle to the sergeant. He hesitated when he drew the knife from his boot, staring at it a moment before handing it over. "That's the whole caboodle."

"Open up," the lieutenant told the troopers manning the gate. While his men set the machinery in motion, the officer snapped orders to Iverson. "Make sure your darkies keep their guns trained on them outlaws. I don't want any slip ups."

Iverson turned around and snapped a string of orders to the black soldiers. The men kept their rifles at the ready, prodding their prisoners forward with the muzzles when the gates swung open.

The lieutenant met them in the assembly area just past the gate. Like the perimeter outside, there was a series of stakes set into the ground to mark off the forbidden region where the Warders would open fire on trespassers. Beyond the open ground meant for assembly, the squalid sprawl of the prisoner tents stretched across the enclosure. Beyond the tents, rising above them like a distant range of mountains, were the buildings of the command compound.

"Come along," the lieutenant said. "I'll take you to see Colonel Custer. He's commandant here. He'll know what to do with your prisoners." He glanced over at Tobin. "He'll make the arrangements to see that you get paid," he added with disgust.

***

As they were escorted through the prison camp, Jesse heard his name shouted many times. Prisoners rushed toward the small procession, lining the sides of the pathway the lieutenant was leading them down. In addition to Iverson and his black soldiers, the lieutenant had brought three men from the gate and one of the Warders from the wall. The menace of so many blasters combined with the mechanical strength of the 'bot kept the rebels back.

The prisoners weren't so cowed, however, that they kept silent. Few were the voices not raised in some call of encouragement to Jesse or lowered to spit some derisive curse against the Yankees. The tumult made the lieutenant more uneasy with each step. It wasn't long before he had his pistol drawn. He barked at the prisoners, ordering them back to their tents. The rebels just jeered at his demands.

A motion to his right brought the lieutenant's head turning around. He scowled when he saw Iverson returning one of Tobin's blasters to the bounty hunter. "I don't want that civilian armed!"

Sergeant Iverson nodded at the crowd of angry rebels. "My apologies, sir, but I thought we might need him armed afore long."

The lieutenant shouted at the crowd of prisoners, again enjoining them to disperse. On his command, the Warder swung around and raised its weapon-arm, aiming the built-in blaster at the ragged mob. Snarling, the officer gave the 'bot the command to fire. A bolt of energy slammed into one of the rebels, hurling his charred body back into the crowd. The prisoners fell silent, stunned by the sudden barbarity.

They found their voices again a moment later, screeching a defiant cheer. The Union officer moaned in horror when he looked at Jesse James. The outlaw was straining against the chains binding him. His mechanical arms snapped the steel links before the lieutenant knew what was going on. Terrified, the lieutenant snapped an order to the Warder. Before the 'bot could spin around, a shot rang out and its head was torn from its shoulders. Smoke rose from the barrel of the bounty hunter's gun.

Other shots quickly followed as each of the black troopers gunned down one of the camp guards. The lieutenant didn't have time to process this act of treachery before he felt something sharp punching into his back.

"The name ain't Iverson," the blue-coated sergeant said as he dug the big Bowie-knife deeper into the officer's flesh. "When yer get ta Hell, tell 'em it were Bob Younger sent you there, yer murderin' Yankee bastard!" Bob let the dying lieutenant sink to the ground, freeing his knife with a savage twist of the blade.

Will Shaft threw away his blue-coat and kepi, and then hurried to Jesse James. He handed the freed outlaw the blasters he'd been holding for him. The Exoduster wore a broad grin. "I believe these are yourn," he said.

Cole snatched his own weapons from one of the other Exodusters, the loosened ropes still hanging from his left wrist. The bushwhacker cursed lividly. "We should have been inside the compound afore startin' the shootin'."

As if to confirm Cole's statement, a loud roar boomed through the air. One of the watchtowers vanished in a ball of flame as the artillery from one of the Rolling Thunders slammed into it. The destruction was so swift that the Yankee guards inside didn't even have time to scream. A moment later, the second Rolling Thunder obliterated another of the towers. Soon after, the bark of small arms and the rumble of Iron Horses echoed from outside the palisade walls.

Captain Ingram, Jim Younger, and the Ford brothers had been waiting outside with the rest of the men, waiting for the sound of gunfire inside the prison. That was their signal to attack, to assault the sections of wall Henderson had declared were the most vulnerable.

Jesse shook his head. "Ain't nothin' can be done about it now. That Yankee forced the hand."

Henderson had already tossed aside the black hat he had worn in his bounty hunter disguise and retrieved his rebel-gray cavalry hat from beneath his coat. Straightening it back into some semblance of shape, he set it on his head and began bellowing orders to the stunned, confused throng of prisoners around them. "This here's Jesse James and he's come to fetch you luckless ruffians out of this Yankee hellhole. I need twenty men who haven't gone yellow to step forward and get themselves armed! You want to go free again; you'll have to earn it!"

The former prisoner's raspy snarl electrified the captives surrounding the outlaws. Almost to a man, they forgot their alarm at the carnage they had witnessed and the turmoil unfolding around the palisade. Surging forward with an animalistic bellow of rage, the rebels snatched up the guns of the dead guards. Will and the other Exodusters handed out spare pistols they had smuggled in beneath their coats. True to Henderson's request, there were soon another twenty armed men waiting for Jesse to tell them what to do. Hundreds more crowded close, watching with the keenness of hungry dogs as the notorious outlaw stepped up onto the wreck of the Warder.

"I'm intendin' to get every man in Andersonville out of here!" Jesse told the prisoners. He swung his steel arm down, pointing his hand at the fenced compound. "To do that, we've gotta take the headquarters. Stop the Yankees from tracking us from Hell to Christmas. I need them that've been given guns to help take the compound. The rest of yer go an' spread the word. Get everybody set to charge them gates the moment the men outside have busted through!"

Jesse felt strangely empty when the raucous cheer of affirmation rose from the prisoners. His eyes were roving over every face, seeking out any trace of John Younger. He knew that Cole and Bob were likewise hoping for some glimpse of their brother, listening desperately for the sound of his voice. Jesse's anxiety was the more onerous, however, rooted not in filial devotion and the love of family, but from the pangs of guilt and responsibility. As the crowd began to disperse, as the prisoners started to rush back into the maze of tents to carry Jesse's orders to every corner of the camp, the outlaw kept praying for some trace of John.

Finally, Jesse grabbed one of the armed rebels. "The Yankees brought a new prisoner a few weeks back. A boy named John Younger. Do you know where he is?" The prisoner shook his head regretfully. When Jesse turned his attention on a second man, he also could only shake his head.

"I ain't see any John Younger," a third rebel told Jesse, "but I have seen yourn brother, Frank. He borrowed my badge ter get inter the compound." The prisoner pointed his hand at the fenced area, thrusting a finger at one building in particular. "Saw Frank gussied up liken a Yankee sergeant waltz'n straight inter the doctor's surgery. Never did see him come out."

Jesse couldn't believe his ears. Frank? Frank James, alive and in Andersonville! It was too miraculous to believe, but when they saw the incredulity on his face, several of the other armed prisoners told Jesse that his brother had been imprisoned in Camp Lincoln, though only the turnkey had seen him go into the old hospital building.

Alive! His brother, alive! A warmth Jesse hadn't felt in months rushed through him. He turned toward the compound. It took all the restraint he possessed to keep from running straight to the fence and tearing it down with his bare hands. Frank was in there, somewhere, and he was alive.

Or at least he had been. Jesse's eyes narrowed to pinpoints as he glared at the menacing hospital building.

"Jesse, we've still got to capture their headquarters. That vocal reiterator has to be knocked out afore we start movin' men out of here," Cole shouted at the outlaw. He laid his hand on Jesse's shoulder when his friend failed to respond. "I know what yer thinkin', I'm thinkin' it too, about John, but we can't set aside the plan."

"And they got some o' them heavy wagons in there, too, boys!" A scarred and battered prisoner pushed himself to the front of the crowd. "You gotta get in there fast afore those crews can get all buttoned up!"

Jesse watched the Union troopers scrambling around inside the compound, hurrying to defensive points they'd dug into the ground or quickly created from upturned carts and sledges. Several were running for a darkened corner where heavy, menacing shapes hulked in the shadows: Rolling Thunder Assault Wagons. Will's grenades would make short work of the Yankee positions. The real trouble would come from the soldiers taking shelter inside the big stone buildings, and the heavy wagons, if their crews could get them up and running in time.

Even recognizing that fact, Jesse couldn't set aside the image of his brother languishing inside the old hospital. "You and Henderson will have to see the plan through," he growled through clenched teeth. "Ain't nothin' comin' between me an' what I need to do."

***

Jesse rushed toward the old hospital, dodging around the smoldering craters left behind by Will's explosives, sometimes forced to leap over the smoking husk of a Yankee guard who had been caught in one of the blasts. He ignored the grisly remains with the same cold determination that kept him from worrying about how the fight for the administration building was faring. That was a conflict that Cole, Henderson, and the men under their command would have to settle on their own; all Jesse needed them to do was keep the guards pinned down while he charged the old hospital.

Only one man was crazy enough to follow Jesse. Bob hurried behind Jesse, supporting his advance with his blaster. Fixated upon the hospital, Jesse directed his fire against the Warders on the building's roof. Trading shots with the hulking robots had been an uneven contest. The mechanical brains in the 'bots weren't capable of the kind of accuracy an Enforcer could muster. There was a reason the Warders weren't considered suitable for front-line deployment. Perfect for guarding unarmed prisoners, they simply weren't equal to the challenge posed by a determined man with a gun. Steel plate designed to withstand early model weapons wasn't equal to the searing heat of a blaster. Each time Jesse fired, he saw the spot he struck turn red hot, the armor of the 'bot become a molten wound that dripped down its body. Arms and legs would seize and lock in place when the molten metal flowed across joints, blasts to the head would cripple the optics and blind the machines. It took several shots to bring down a Warder, for the automatons fought on without regard to their injuries, but Jesse's attack was too remorseless to be denied.

Every time a Warder showed itself, they were brought down by Jesse but he only needed one to end his life. Bob threw himself into the battle trying to protect his chief as they assaulted the hospital. He watched the scarred ground within the compound and picked off lurking Union troops who thought to attack the outlaws by ambush. By the time they neared the steel door of the hospital, Bob had accounted for four lurking soldiers. He was thankful for Jesse's visibility and notoriety; the Yankees had been so intent on the infamous robber that they'd completely ignored Bob, which left them easy targets for his blaster.

A final Warder stood guard before the door. The robot leveled its rifle-arm at Jesse as the outlaw came charging toward it. From each of his blasters, a bolt of energy blazed into the automaton. The first shot slammed into the muzzle of its rifle, reducing it to a blob of smoldering slag. The second blast scored against the Warder's chest, opening a fist-sized gap in its armor. Before Jesse could fire again, the Warder tried to gun him down. Oblivious to the damage inflicted to its arm, the 'bot sent a pulse of energy hurtling down the chamber. Unable to leave the melted barrel of the weapon, the energy blast redoubled against itself. The resultant detonation exploded through the Warder's arm and turned it into a cloud of metal splinters, in turn, throwing the 'bot to the ground by the force of the explosion. It crashed to earth like an overturned turtle, flailing at the dirt as it tried to right itself.

Jesse didn't give it the chance. Aiming at the wound in its chest, he sent a shot searing through the 'bot's internal machinery. With a final shudder, the Warder froze, all animation burned from its frame by Jesse's shot.

The outlaw chief stepped over the inert Warder. He scowled for an instant at the steel door and then brought both pistols to bear against it. In a shriek of tortured metal, the locks and bolts securing the door were blasted apart. A kick from Jesse's boot sent the massive portal crashing inwards.

Smoke from the savaged door billowed about Jesse as he stepped into the old hospital, into the great ward that had become the surgery and laboratory of Dr. Tumblety. It took several steps before he was clear of the smoke, before he could see with his own eyes the place where the Yankees were holding his brother.

What Jesse saw sent a rage of emotions flowing through him. Lucinda Loveless, the beautiful young woman he'd encountered months before, lay shackled and prone on the operating table in the tattered remains of her clothes, her flesh stained with marks that reminded him of a butcher's chart. Looming over her, a knife gleaming in his hand, was a tall man dressed in an ostentatious military uniform. He had a crazed look in his eyes when he spun around and glared at Jesse. Briefly, the surgeon's gaze darted to a nearby table where a pair of strange-looking gauntlets lay.

"Jesse! Don't let that maniac get near them fancy gloves!"

Jesse felt his heart quicken when he heard that cry. He spun around, staring in amazement at the man shackled to the wall of the surgery. It was Frank! It was his brother! Alive! Despite everything he'd been told by the prisoners of Andersonville, Jesse was still stunned to find Frank alive after the long months he'd thought his brother dead.

Tumblety seized upon Jesse's moment of distraction. Like the outlaw, he'd heard Frank's cry of warning. The experimenter made no move to regain the Rippers he'd removed to conduct his vivisection of Loveless. Instead, he dashed across the surgery and threw back one of the curtains. The madman grinned triumphantly at Jesse as the outlaw realized his mistake and swung back around to cover him with his blasters.

"Jesse James!" Dr Tumblety crowed. "You've seen your brother, now let me reunite you with another old friend!"

Before Jesse could fire, a hulking shape emerged from behind the curtain. Recognition of the brute's twisted face froze Jesse as utterly as the Warder he'd disabled outside. The creature that came lumbering out from the darkness was almost twice the size of a normal man, its flesh a patchwork of stitches and scars, its body swollen with immense knots of muscle. The limbs were mismatched, one leg longer and bulkier than the other, and one arm bifurcated near the elbow to allow a second forearm to protrude from its side. An arm dangled from the center of the thing's breastbone, its fingers clenching and unclenching with each step. Yet above this travesty, this abomination of surgery and madness, there sat the recognizable countenance of John Younger – the boy Jesse had traveled across the country to save.

"My God! It's John!" Bob cried out as he entered the surgery and saw the monster lumbering out from the shadows.

The monster's face twisted into a pained grimace as he heard his brother's shout. For a moment, the Reconstructed hesitated in his menacing advance.

Tumblety held his hand toward John, displaying for the creature the vial of cloudy liquid gripped in his fingers. "You're mine! That menagerie of organs and tissues I sewed up inside your carcass is screaming in pain right now! You want the hurt to go away? You obey me! I'm in control; I have the drugs that can hold your pain in check. Only I can make the pain go away."

His face assuming an almost regretful expression, John turned back toward Jesse and resumed his lumbering march.

"Don't damage them too badly," Tumblety warned his creature. "I'll need unharmed parts if I'm to build you some new friends."

***

Colonel Custer leaned over the terminal, using the vocal reiterators as he tapped the alert signal on the key. It grated on his sensibilities to be down here in the communications center instead of out with his men leading them in battle. Only the vital importance of ensuring the message was relayed as far and wide as possible made him linger in the room. The fact that rebels had somehow broken into Camp Lincoln and smuggled weapons to the prisoners was disastrous enough, but if Custer allowed any of them to escape through negligence, he was apt to see his military career come to an abrupt and ignominious end.

"Ain't you sent that alert yet?" Custer growled at the operator.

The anxious soldier looked up at his commander and shook his head. "Fort Stimson wants to know numbers and their armaments before dispatching any cavalry our way."

"Just tell them to head for the frontier," Custer snapped. The offer of sending a troop of cavalry to relieve the prison was something that stung his pride. The situation might be slipping beyond his control, but he had no intention of letting anybody else see it for themselves. "If they can stop the rebs from linking up with the rest of the Secesh, we can stop 'em cold." The strategy was a sound one; there were enough troops and forts between Camp Lincoln and the Confederate Rebellion to intercept the prisoners as soon as they started south. By suggesting such a course to the other commands, Custer would be able to salvage something from this disaster. His plan was to claim responsibility for the recapture of the prisoners. If he got enough newspapers to print that line, the War Department wouldn't be able to dismiss him out of hand for allowing the escape in the first place.

"I've told them, Colonel," the soldier at the console said. "They still feel…"

Before the man could finish, sounds of violence erupted in the corridor outside the room. Custer drew his pistols and started to step around the terminal. As he began to draw a bead on the door, the portal was kicked inward by a powerful blow. The Union officer fired at the rebel prisoners who started to surge through the doorway. Two men pitched and fell, their chests ripped to shreds by his shots. Custer fired again, driving the rest of the prisoners back.

"Surrender, Colonel," a voice snarled from the corridor outside. "You don't have a chance."

"Then I'll die with my boots on," Custer growled back. He lunged toward the doorway, intending to make good his vow. Just as he started to move, however, a burst of eerily precise marksmanship stabbed at him, and his pistols were ripped from his hands. He could only gape in astonishment as his guns went clattering across the room.

A second mob of prisoners appeared at the doorway. Leading them was a pale man dressed in black, his eyes hidden behind a set of tinted goggles. The man's lean face curled into a sneer as he studied Custer.

"Did you already send out the alarm?" the man asked, pointing one of the blasters gripped in his hand at the vocal reiterator.

Custer nodded, a triumphant smile on his face. "Every fort from here to the border knows about the breakout."

"Much obliged," Henderson said. He wagged his pistol from side to side. The men behind him opened fire on the operator and his equipment. The fusillade blasted both man and machine into a heap of twisted wreckage.

"Now we settle with the commandant," one of the prisoners said, rushing into the room. Before he could close upon Custer, the rebel was struck from behind by the butt of Henderson's pistol. The man staggered, clutching at his bloodied scalp.

"I tell you who dies and when," Henderson warned the prisoners.

The rebels glared daggers at him. "What we've been through, this cur needs to hang!"

Henderson reached up to his face, pulling away the tinted glasses. The rebels cringed in fright when they saw his unveiled eyes. In the darkness of the signal room, Henderson's eyes burned like two crimson fires.

The prisoners didn't get the chance to recover from their fright. Mercilessly, Henderson blasted the four men in the hall with his pistols. The betrayed rebels were splashed across the corridor, dismembered by the murderous salvo. The mysterious man turned back toward Custer, a mocking smile on his face as he regarded the Union officer's bewilderment.

"There's some that feel you're worth more alive than dead," Henderson said. Without hesitation, he put an energy bolt into the head of the prisoner he'd struck with the butt of his pistol. The shot all but decapitated the reeling rebel and dropped his twitching body to the floor. "My friends expect big things from you, General," the gaunt man continued, his red eyes still blazing with an inhuman vibrancy.

"Who… who are you?" Custer stammered.

Henderson shook his head. "A question for another time." He backed through the doorway, keeping the threat of his guns on Custer as he retreated from the room. He pulled the door shut behind him. Custer could hear the bark of Henderson's pistol as the rebel melted the lock and sealed him inside the room.

Looking at the carnage around him, Custer was unable to fathom the stranger's ruthless betrayal of his own men. Destroying the reiterator relays was something he could understand, but killing his followers to spare the life of an enemy was madness!

As he reflected on that insanity, and thought about Henderson's crimson eyes, Custer realized that who the villain was wasn't the important question. It was *what* he was – that was the bigger question.

A question that Custer knew he might never find an answer for.

***

Jesse aimed his blasters at John as the hideous beast came lumbering across the ward. He closed his eyes, tried to tell himself that the Reconstructed wasn't really John Younger, that it had no connection to the boy who'd followed him with such worshipful adoration. This wasn't the boy he'd led into ambush and capture.

"Don't shoot!" Bob cried out. "It's still John!"

Jesse shook his head. He wanted to shout down Bob's cry, to tell the outlaw that the Reconstructed wasn't his brother anymore. When he opened his eyes and saw John's face staring at him from atop the gigantic brute, he found the effort impossible.

"Get Frank out of here!" Jesse snarled at Bob. He turned and grabbed the outlaw by the shoulder, shoving him toward the wall where Frank was shackled.

"That thing's not John!" Frank shouted, thrashing against his chains in impotent fury. "Tumblety's destroyed his brain with torture and chemicals! There ain't nothin' left of him!"

"Get Frank out of here!" Jesse repeated. He again tried to train his guns on John, but his determination faltered when he saw the Reconstructed's face twist into the familiar, exuberant smile he'd seen so often. Holstering one of his pistols, Jesse made a soothing gesture to the advancing monster. "John, it's me. Jesse James."

The beast hesitated, blinking in confusion at the metal-armed outlaw. Despite Frank's claims, to the contrary there was still something of John Younger buried inside the grotesque giant. Jesse had to appeal to that, draw it out from whatever foulness Tumblety had inflicted on the boy with his insidious experiments.

Tumblety noticed his monster's hesitation. Some of the crazed light faded from his eyes, replaced with a hunted, rat-like cunning. He could see his triumph collapsing before his eyes. Failure was something the experimenter couldn't allow, not when he was so close to the success that would set his name above Tesla and all the others who'd scoffed at his theories.

Tumblety dashed back across the vivisection theater, dodging around the table upon which Loveless had been strapped down, intent upon seizing the Rippers lying on the wheeled instrument tray. He froze as Jesse noticed him, as the outlaw swung around and trained the blaster he still held on the madman. A nervous twitch flickered across Tumblety's face as he felt the gun aimed at him. Only his proximity to Loveless and Jesse's fear of striking her made the gunman hold his fire. Tumblety noticed the restraint and ducked down behind the edge of the surgery table.

Before Jesse could move, before he could find some fresh angle from which to draw a bead on Tumblety without threatening Loveless, an inarticulate bellow rose from John's mutilated body. Bob and Frank, close to the door of the surgery, shouted a warning to Jesse. Jesse did not react quickly enough when he swung around to meet the Reconstructed. Like a crazed bull, John charged into Jesse, slamming into him headfirst and throwing him back. The outlaw's free hand closed on John's arm, clinging to the monster as it drove him across the room.

"Get away!" Jesse shouted to Bob and Frank. "Find Cole! Find help!" Frank looked as though he would argue, but

Bob shoved him through the door and spurred him on in a desperate rush to find the manpower they'd need to subdue the monstrous John.

John's charge ended in a clamorous crash as he drove Jesse against one of the wooden walls acting as a partition between the vivisection theaters. The wall splintered beneath the impact, Jesse felt his bones shiver with the violence of the blow. Still, he retained his grip on the Reconstructed's arm. Pivoting his body, the mechanical strength in his arm pulled John around and slammed the brute into the partition. Beneath John's muscled bulk, the wall more than splintered; it disintegrated, reduced to splinters by the beast's weight.

Jesse loosed his hold on John as the monster crashed to the floor. The pistol he'd still been holding had been knocked from his hand by the impact, but its companion was still holstered at his side. In a flash, Jesse drew the blaster and took aim. From the ground, the creature stared up at him with a bloodied, battered face. Jesse hesitated, once again frozen by the thought that somewhere inside this thing there endured the mind of John Younger.

Even as he hesitated, a whirring noise sliced through the air. The partition a few inches from Jesse's face was suddenly gouged by a razor-sharp disk of steel. The outlaw threw himself into a dive, sprawling across the floor as another saw-blade came streaking across the surgery toward him. This blade struck the floor, skipping as it went whirling through the ward. He took aim at his attacker, and then felt raw horror pulse through his body.

Tumblety had regained his Rippers, but the crafty fiend hadn't depended entirely on his skill with the experimental weapons to finish Jesse quickly. He'd taken the precaution of upending the table Loveless was strapped to, employing it as a bulwark against Jesse's marksmanship. As the experimenter ducked down, all Jesse could see was Loveless tied to the front of his refuge. Gagged by her captor, all she could do was stare at him with hard determined eyes, struggling to escape even though she knew it was useless. He knew the message she was trying to convey. Whatever it took, she wanted him to finish Tumblety.

Jesse's reluctance to fire on John was nothing compared to how repugnant the idea of jeopardizing Loveless was. "Come out of there, yeh yellow dog!" he shouted at Tumblety.

The madman kept himself low behind the table. "Come now, Jesse," he called. "I expect fools to think me insane, but I find it insulting when they think I am stupid. Throw down your blaster and perhaps we can talk things over."

"In a pig's eye!" Jesse spat. He started to make a dash toward the racks of specimen jars, thinking to use Tumblety's morbid collection as cover while he crept up on the lunatic's flank. Just as he began his run, he was struck from behind. Jesse was spun around as John's brawny arms closed about him, the limb stitched to his chest reaching out and locking its fingers around his throat. Jesse pounded at the brute with his steel hands, trying to force the Reconstructed to let him go.

"It seems the situation has changed," Tumblety smirked, stepping out from behind Loveless. He pointed one of his Rippers at Jesse. "Know that your death will advance the cause of science, Mr. James."

Exerting the full power of his mechanical arms, Jesse swung John's immense bulk around just as Tumblety fired. The saw-edged blade from the Ripper went scything through the arm holding Jesse by the neck, slicing clean through flesh and bone, severing the limb just behind the elbow. John bellowed in pain, releasing Jesse and staggering back as black chemicals spurted from the stump sewn to his chest. Frantic, Tumblety aimed the other Ripper and tried to drop Jesse in his tracks. The blade went whirring through the air, but instead of striking vulnerable flesh, it hit the unyielding steel of Jesse's arm. The blade was deflected by the metal and sent ricocheting off through the surgery. Tumblety wailed in dismay as the blade smashed through specimen jars before burying itself in the RJ generator that powered the laboratory equipment and supplemented Tesla's electric lights.

The madman rushed across the operation room, kneeling amid the rancid organs that had spilled from the shattered bottles. Mewing like a panicked child, he tried to salvage the mangled specimens, oblivious both to the enemy at his back and the flames spurting from the side of the damaged generator.

Only one thing granted Tumblety a reprieve. In his struggle with the Reconstructed, Jesse's remaining blaster had been knocked from his hand. The outlaw might have spared a moment to look for it, but sight of the flames billowing from the generator and the vision of the fire spreading along the spilled alcohol from the doctor's shattered jars, decided him upon a different course. Removing the knife tucked into his boot, the outlaw rushed over to the vivisection theater. "Sorry about all the distractions," Jesse apologized as he crouched beside the overturned table and began sawing away at the straps holding Loveless down.

A loud explosion rocked the surgery before Jesse had Loveless free. He glanced up from his work to see the generator engulfed in flames. The fire was rapidly spreading through the spilled alcohol, sending fiery streamers running up the curtains and along the shelves. Several of the intact bottles began to burst as the heat set their contents to a boil. Amid the havoc, the deranged Tumblety still scrambled to preserve the scraps of his collection.

"We've gotta get," Jesse swore as he slashed through the final binding. Loveless slumped to the floor and pulled the gag free from her mouth. Gratefully, she accepted the duster Jesse handed her to cover herself.

Any words of gratitude that might have found purchase on her tongue evaporated when Loveless saw the hulking figure of John come rushing at the outlaw. The Reconstructed held one hand against the set the whole in his chest, but the other reached toward Jesse with all the malignance of the Devil's own claw. Jesse pushed Loveless aside, and in the same motion he caught the edge of the table and flipped it toward the monster. John caught it in his outstretched hand, crumpling it beneath his fingers as though it were an old tin can.

"You have to kill him!" Loveless shouted to Jesse. "Any sympathy you have for John should find solace in the knowledge that death is a mercy after what Tumblety has done to the boy".

Jesse recoiled as the Reconstructed reached for him again. "Good idea. How do I do it without a blaster?" Even as he asked the question, John lunged at him and caught him by the wrist. The brute lifted Jesse from the floor and shook him like a rag doll. The knife in Jesse's hand raked across John's flesh, but the monster didn't seem to notice. What flowed from the slashes and cuts wasn't blood, but more of the black ichor.

Loveless glanced about, searching for any weapon that might stop the Reconstructed and save Jesse. The outlaw had risked his life to save her, it was only fitting she should do the same for him. Tumblety's surgical instruments, for all their horror, wouldn't be much use against John. If she was going to help Jesse, she needed something far more effective.

The spreading flames gave Loveless an idea. Running across the theater, she snatched up a strip Tumblety had cut from her uniform. Passing the cloth through the flame, she soon set it alight. Loveless turned about and ran back to the embattled outlaw and the monster that held him. Holding the burning cloth high, she thrust it full into John's face, scorching the creature's enraged eyes.

A demonic screech echoed through the surgery. John flung Jesse away and clamped both hands about his burnt eyes. Screaming in pain, the monster lurched across the surgery.

From where the beast had thrown him, Jesse cried out a warning to John. If the Reconstructed heard him, the creature didn't show any sign of understanding. He continued to shamble blindly across the theater until he crashed full into one of the specimen racks. Shelves, jars, and monster came toppling to the floor in a calamitous collapse. The alcohol from the jars splashed through the surgery, forming a great morass that quickly took light.

Jesse lurched to his feet, even now intent on trying to help John. Loveless caught him before he could make such a suicidal gesture. "You can't help him," she scolded the outlaw. "It's too late!" Sternly she turned Jesse around, hurrying him along as they dashed for the doorway.

They paused only once, glancing back at the conflagration that was consuming the laboratory. Tumblety was still dashing about among the burning racks, trying to salvage his grisly collection. John's misshapen body lay sprawled among the shelves, thrashing and flailing as the fire began to consume it.

With a groaning rumble, one of the roof beams came crashing down, spilling the upper floor into the surgery and obliterating any trace of Tumblety and his creation.

Grimly, Jesse James and Lucinda Loveless retreated out into the comparatively wholesome bedlam of the compound.

***

Cole Younger and a dozen other men were rushing toward Tumblety's laboratory when Jesse and Lucinda came stumbling out of the burning building. The outlaws and rebels were taken aback when they saw the people they had come to rescue advancing toward them. Frank James ran to his brother, catching Jesse in a fierce embrace. Bob Younger looked past the two bank robbers, staring hopefully at the dark doorway leading into the burning hospital.

Jesse noted Bob's agitation. Pulling away from Frank, he turned to face the two Younger brothers. "I... I couldn't save John. It was too late. Whatever that Yankee devil did to him, there weren't enough left of John to help." He locked eyes with Cole, wincing when he saw the deep hurt in the elder Younger's gaze. Jesse'd recovered his brother, but Cole had lost his. "I'm sorry," Jesse said, appreciating how hollow those words were. "But it's better this way. Better John's dead than walkin' around as some Yankee monster."

Bob dropped to his knees, pounding his fists against the ground. "They're all gonna pay! Every damn blue-belly!"

Cole closed a hand on Bob's shoulder and lifted him to his feet. "They'll pay," he assured his brother. "But not today. Today we've gotta get all these prisoners somewheres safe. After that, then we can talk about revenge."

"The guards been taken care of?" Jesse asked.

It was Robert Ford who answered the outlaw chief. "There's a few blue-bellies in the barracks, but they've barricaded themselves into a few isolated rooms. Trapped themselves in their own cages. Jim and Captain Ingram took care of the guard towers and the 'bots on the walls. Some of the boys got learned on the Rolling Thunders've got the new wagons runnin', and they're guardin' the main gate". Robert's expression turned grim.

"With you gone, Mr. Henderson took it on himself to gather all the prisoners and start leadin' them out the main gate."

Jesse was struck by Will's tone. There was something about Henderson's assumption of command that had disturbed the gunman and which, in turn, now aroused Jesse's own suspicions. "Let's head for the gate," Jesse told the outlaws around him. "It might be that Allen needs to be reminded that he ain't in command of this outfit."

Despite the beating he had endured at the hands of John, Jesse hurried through the now abandoned prison camp. Even with the magnitude of their victory over the Yankees and the liberation of not only his brother Frank, but the thousands of captives, he felt a sense of panic welling up inside him: a feeling that this great triumph was going to be snatched away from him in the final instant.

When he neared the gates of Camp Lincoln, Jesse knew his unease was well founded. Allen Henderson stood at the top of the gate, barking out orders to the liberated prisoners, whipping them up into a vengeful fury. Around him, the bodies of lynched guards twitched and squirmed. The revenge Henderson called for, however, wasn't against the guards or other Union soldiers. He was calling upon the rebels to sack the camp itself, to put the nearby town of Andersonville to the torch and slaughter the inhabitants. Jesse felt himself go sick inside when he heard the vitriol spewed by the bespectacled warmonger, remembering another time he had whipped up his troops to a murderous frenzy. Lawrence had been the town to suffer that time under Quantrill. Now, Henderson wanted to unleash the same rage against Andersonville.

Loveless clutched at Jesse's arm. "You can't let him do this," she said, entreaty in her voice.

"I don't intend to," Jesse told her. Leaving Loveless with Frank and Cole, Jesse marched straight toward the gate. Without his duster, the outlaw chief's mechanical arms were fully exposed and visible. The rebels parted in awe and respect before the man who had won them their freedom. He stepped through the ranks of prisoners until he was standing before the gate and looking straight up at Henderson. "What're yeh doin', Allen?" Jesse demanded.

Henderson adjusted his goggles and looked down at the outraged outlaw. "We're going to teach the Yankees a lesson. Pay them back in kind."

Jesse shook his head. He turned and faced the rest of the rebels. "Not like this we ain't. Fightin' soldiers, lawmen, carpet baggers, and robber barons is one thing. This, this ain't any of that! This ain't fightin' at all. It's killin', killin' for the sake of plum meanness." He pointed his hand in the direction of Andersonville. "That ain't even a Yankee town. Them people there are Southerners. They're the same folk as you fought a war to defend. Now you want to kill 'em because they've been conquered? Them are the ones we should be fightin' for, not agin!"

"We need supplies, Jesse," impatience was etched into Henderson's face. "Wagons to transport all these men. Food to feed them. Clothes to replace the rags they're wearing. Guns..."

"Did the guards get off their alarm on the Reiterator?" Jesse asked him.

Henderson nodded. "They sent the alarm. The blue-bellies will be waiting for us if we move toward the Confederate Rebellion."

Jesse grimiced. "Then we gotta put a wiggle on," he said, raising his voice so the prisoners could hear him. "Because we ain't goin' south. We're headin' west, out to where there's open land we can make our own. Land where we can lick our wounds and make our plans without havin' a Yankee boot on our necks. We ain't got enough time to bundle ya'll up. So, those that can, make for the big wagons just this side of town. Spread the word in the camp: the rest of ya'll, scatter. Union'll be down on us shortly, but they won't be able to get you all. We'll take as many north with us as we can."

"We still need supplies," Henderson reminded him.

"We'll get 'em," Jesse answered. "We'll take 'em from Andersonville as we ride through. We'll steal if we have to, but there ain't to be any killin'." He glared up at Henderson. "This ain't gonna be Lawrence all over agin." The shadowy man sketched a slight nod and climbed down from the gate.

Jesse rejoined Loveless and the members of his gang. Will Shaft clapped him on the back as he came close.

"You got more sand'n I have," the Exoduster said. "I don't think I'd ever have the gumption to talk down that man."

Frank's expression was even graver. "I never expected to see you again, Jesse. I damn sure never expected to see *him* again."

Loveless suppressed a shudder. The murderous intensity she'd felt exuding from the black-clad warmonger during his harangue had been, in its way, even more terrifying than the madness of Tumblety. "Who is he?" she asked Jesse. She was proud that Jesse had stood up to the strange man and could even find it in her to be sympathetic to Jesse's ambition to lead these men away from the reach of the Union. But both pride and sympathy were suborned to the feeling of alarm hammering inside her. This man calling for violence, she felt, was a menace to the safety of not just the government and military of the Union, but to every man, woman, and child who lived in it.

Jesse watched Henderson stalk out through the gates and into the growing night. It was some time before he answered Loveless's question. Who was Allen Henderson?

"I'm not sure I know who he is anymore," Jesse said. "I'm not sure it's somethin' I want to know."

Epilogue

"I ain't goin' for it, Virg. Yer a plum fool to even be thinkin' that way!" Wyatt Earp's voice was livid in its tone; the imperious, unyielding bellow that had tamed towns across the west.

"Take a good damn look at me," Virgil snarled back, weakness and pain underlying the emotion in his words. "Them sawbones mightn't have cut it off, but this arm's useless as a lump of lead! How in Hell am I supposed to help you when I've only got one arm?"

"Who said anythin' about needin' yer help, Virg?" Wyatt retorted. "Me, Warren, and Doc can handle things ourselves."

Virgil laughed, a hollow and cheerless sound. "Yer fergettin' Morg," he said. "Or don't you count him as yer brother anymore?"

"I do, but damnit, Virg, look at him!" Wyatt swung his arm out pointing to his brother. "He's just standing there like a 'bot, starin' down at his crippled brother with all the emotion of a brick wall. I loved Morg, and I don't want you to end up like that!"

Morgan Earp's cold eyes shifted from their wounded brother to the livid Over-marshal without a hint of emotion. When they slid back to Virgil's broken form, something akin to sympathy may have resided in their dark depths, but the face remained impassive and immobile.

"It's only my arm," Virgil retorted. "It's not like I need him to do what he did for Morg. And you'll need my help if'n yer goin' after Ike Clanton and the rest of the Cowboys."

"I've already settled with the Old Man and Phin," Wyatt snapped back. "I'll get the others too. And I'll get 'em without any more help from Carpathian."

Back in his lab, the scientist smiled as he heard the remark transmitted across the audiophonic transposer. The voices of the marshal and his elder brother had a distorted, tinny quality as they left the elaborately funneled transmission horn fitted to the side of the bulky, boxy machine, but the words were distinct enough for Carpathian's purposes. He rose from the claw-footed chair he'd been sitting in for the last hour as he listened to Wyatt and Virgil Earp arguing about the medical miracles only Dr. Carpathian could bestow.

"My invention is remarkable, is it not?" The question came from a bespectacled young man wearing a long white coat and sporting a many-pocketed work belt around his waist. He stepped around from behind the machine, a proud smile on his face.

Carpathian always felt that Thomas Edison's smile belonged to something from the fox family rather than any product of human evolution. The inventor was brilliant, naturally, that was why he'd been recruited into the Enlightened. That brilliance, however, was married to a personality utterly devoid of ethics or conscience. Edison was proud of his inventions – both those of his own creation and those which could more justly be credited to engineers and scientists working under him. Carpathian happened to know that the credit for the audiophonic transposer could be equally divided between the Scotsman, Alexander Graham Bell, and the Italian, Guglielmo Marconi. Edison's contribution had come in the area of miniaturization, a crucial development for the purpose to which Carpathian wanted to put the invention.

Nestled inside the cyborg body of Morgan Earp was a cylindrical audiophone that, when actuated by Hertzian waves emanating from an electromagnetic key, would transmit the sounds of whatever was unfolding around it to a receiver hundreds of miles away. By such means, Carpathian could gain access to the most intimate secrets, the most candid of conversations. There would be no confusion about what was overheard, for wax cylinders fitted to the receiver would record every word and preserve them for later consultation.

"It is a remarkable achievement, Thomas," Carpathian conceded as he set his hand atop the receiver. "Be certain to make a record of the rest of their talk in case one of them should divulge anything useful."

Edison stared in puzzlement as his mentor turned and started from the room. "Where are you going?"

Carpathian turned and pointed at the audiophonic transposer. "You heard the lawmen, Thomas. Virgil Earp is in the market for a new arm, so I think I might make some modifications to existing devices. It would be a shame to disappoint him, after all. I do so have such plans for the west and I'd rather have the Earps beholden to us than working against us." The old scientist shook his head. "Violence is so terribly distressing when it isn't necessary."

***

The blackened heap of timbers that had once been the old hospital continued to send up streamers of greasy smoke into the overcast sky. Buzzards and crows circled the ruin, squawking hungrily at each other as though complaining about the lingering heat which prevented them from scavenging among the rubble.

Heat didn't keep a very different sort of scavenger from sniffing around the ruin. From where he stood at the edge of the rubble, Colonel George Armstrong Custer could see the hunched figure scurrying about the wreckage like some gigantic spider black from soot. Sometimes the shape would pounce on some bit of twisted metal with a happy yelp, at other times the ghoul would pull an unrecognizable lump of charred refuse out from under a timber and utter a despairing wail.

Custer shook his head. Any sane man would count it a miracle that he'd escaped such a conflagration with his life. Dr. Tumblety, however, was very far from sane. He capered about the smoldering rubble bewailing the loss of his equipment and the destruction of his test subjects. Most of all, he cursed the obliteration of his prize collection, that menagerie of pickled organs he had exhibited with such pride to anyone with stomach enough to gaze upon them and listen to the experimenter's grisly lecturing.

The vivisectionist was insane and so was the ghastly chain of experimentation he had sought to perfect. Custer wasn't sure who it was in the War Department that was crazed or desperate enough to put any stock in Tumblety, but he knew they must have been both powerful and ruthless. Only power could protect a murderous fiend like Tumblety – especially after what he had done in London. Only absolute ruthlessness would try to harness the demonic madness of Jack the Ripper.

"He's here! He's here!" Tumblety suddenly cried out, waving his arms and gesticulating wildly at something lying partially buried under the rubble.

Custer looked worriedly at the soldiers arrayed about the compound. Most of them were reinforcements from Fort Stimson, busy forcing the crowd of prisoners that had been left behind - those too sick or injured to make the trek out to the massive ore-haulers the rebels had brought to the edge of town.. Few of them had any idea what sort of grisly work Tumblety had been engaged in. The commandant hoped that whatever Tumblety had turned up, it wouldn't draw too much attention from the men. He was almost thankful that the experimenter was carrying on in so audacious a fashion. Such was the contempt the troops held Tumblety in, that the louder he carried on, the more the soldiers tried to ignore him.

Keeping a ready grip on the sword sheathed at his side, Custer walked across the jumbled debris and joined Tumblety amid the rubble. He looked down at the thing that had so excited the madman. It looked like the charred body of a twisted giant, a boyish face still visible amid the burnt flesh. He removed a scented handkerchief from his pocket and held it across his face as the stench wafting from the corpse struck his nose.

"Whatever it is, it's dead now."

Tumblety scowled at the commandant. "Do not speak to me of death. That is a technical definition that has no place in my experiments!" He pointed back at the charred body of John Younger. "Perhaps he is without the spark of life, but I was the one who put it there to begin with. It will be a comparatively easy thing to revive him again."

Custer blanched at the very thought. "To what purpose? Look around you! The prisoners are all gone, the camp is a shambles, most of my men are dead. Your experiment is over!"

The madman clucked his tongue in disapproval. "You fail to understand the importance of my work. They appreciate my genius in Washington. This… unpleasantness… is only a setback. A rut in the road to discovery. Discovery that will revolutionize science!" Tumblety tugged at his thick mustache and looked across the destruction. "You are right, however. The camp was a desolate ruin. All but the least-hearty prisoners had fled, heading north with the outlaws or scattering far and wide across the surrounding countryside. Only those barely clinging to death had remained, and they had been moved to other camps or put down, whichever had seemed easiest to the troopers who found them. We will need to move the facilities to someplace more conducive to research. I mentioned to Stimson once that it would be interesting to see how efficient my procedures might be when adopted upon aboriginal subjects. There's a certain recalcitrance when it comes to experimenting with civilized men, even when they are rebels. But to use savages! No one would gainsay my experiments then."

The image of Tumblety working his insane science upon entire Indian villages was so vile that Custer nearly drew his saber from its scabbard. He was too pragmatic, however, to let his loathing of the experimenter carry him toward an act that would see the end of his career. "I imagine you've already formed an idea about where you want to set up shop?"

Tumblety smiled. "I think the Black Hills would prove ideal. The Nations have some quaint notions about that place being sacred. There have always been savages guarding the hills, and the Warrior Nation can be counted on to maintain a presence there." A cunning twinkle shone in his eye. "I'll need a full facility there. Troops to collect subjects for me and a fort to garrison them in. Naturally, a fort will need a commander."

"You mean me?" Custer said, both shocked and disgusted by the suggestion that he continue his relationship with Tumblety.

"Of course," the madman said. "Who better to help me in my work than an officer who already appreciates what I am trying to accomplish." Tumblety pointed again at the gigantic carcass of John Younger. "That is but the beginning. They will make you a general when I show them what my Reconstructed are capable of!"

Custer listened to the madman rant and plot, but his ears only half heard what Tumblety said. He was thinking about the possibility that the experimenter was right, that by sticking with him he'd be able to aggrandize his own career and reclaim the rank of general once more. It was a temptation too great to resist.

In the back of his mind, however, Custer recalled a red-eyed rebel dressed in black, a sinister enigma who had unaccountably spared his life. The rebel had called him 'general,' almost a prophetic declaration. It was a coincidence that Custer found uncanny. Almost as though some dark force was guiding him and propelling him to some terrible doom.

About the Author

C. L. Werner was a diseased servant of the Horned Rat long before his first story in *Inferno! magazine*. His Black Library credits include the Warhammer Hero books Wulfrik and The Red Duke, Mathias Thulmann: Witch Hunter, the ongoing saga of Grey Seer Thanquol and the Brunner the Bounty Hunter trilogy. His first full-fledged foray into the gothic sci-fi universe of Warhammer 40k occurred in 2012 with The Siege of Castellax. He is the author of Moving Targets, a novella set in Privateer Press' Iron Kingdoms featuring the iconic heroes Taryn and Rutger. He has also written several fantasy stories about the wandering samurai Shintaro Oba for Rogue Blades Enterprises. Currently he is labouring upon further instalments of the Black Plague series for Warhammer's Time of Legends line, as well as more adventures of mercenaries Taryn and Rutger in the Iron Kingdoms. An inveterate bibliophile, he squanders the proceeds from his writing on hoary old volumes – or at least reasonably affordable reprints of same – to further his library of fantasy fiction, horror stories and occult tomes.

WILD WEST EXODUS™

Experience These Tales
On the Table Top
With the Official
35mm Miniature
Skirmish Game!

OUTLAW™

Purchase Models, Rule Books, Templates, Dice and More At:

WWW.WILDWESTEXODUS.COM

Zmok Books – Action, Adventure and Imagination

Zmok Books offers science fiction and fantasy books in the classic tradition as well as the new and different takes on the genre.

Winged Hussar Publishing, LLC is the parent company of Zmok Publishing, focused on military history from ancient times to the modern day.

Follow all the latest news on Winged Hussar and Zmok Books at

www.wingedhussarpublishing.com

Look for the other books in this series

WILD WEST EXODUS

™

THE JESSE JAMES ARCHIVES

HONOR AMONG OUTLAWS

CRAIG GALLANT

OUTLAW

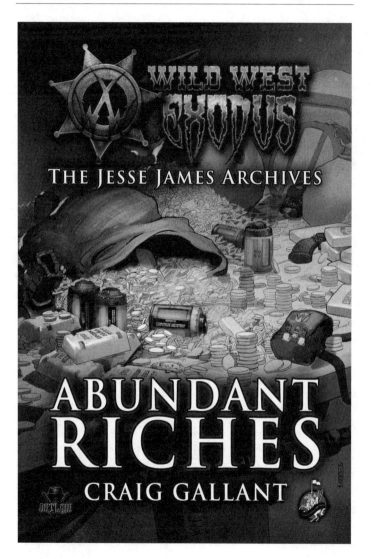

Prologue from "Abundant Riches"

Shadows stretched over the northern plains as the sun sank into the west. Gently rolling hills swept away to the south, fading to a dull brown in the distance. Lush grass and full trees dominated this border region; a last bastion of quiet, serene greenery. As far as the eye could see, all was at peace.

As darkness settled in, a spray of sparkling lights sprang up across the plains, echoing the stars appearing overhead. Guttering campfires stretched for nearly a mile in every direction. Iron Hawk settled into the grass and eased one hand, palm flat, behind him. Unseen in the growing shadows, a band of Warrior Nation scouts lowered themselves to the ground.

The large force of easterners had moved into Warrior Nation territory several days ago. Armed, they rode a mismatched variety of loud, loathsome vehicles that defiled the land with their foul vapors. Dispatched by the united chiefs of the Warrior Nation, Iron Hawk had stalked into the prairie with his most experience fighters, shadowing these outsiders as a larger war party followed along behind. The invaders would spread across the plains in disorderly camps each night, easy to spot and track. When Iron Hawk's scouts caught up to them, they were settled around a shallow dale, many camping in a series of limestone caves beneath the hills.

There was no real pattern to the mongrel exodus. They had violated the territory of the People, fleeing from the south east. Moving at a slow crawl, they had advanced across the plains in an arch that brought them gradually back around towards the south. Behind them they left a foul trail of discarded equipment, empty containers, and shallow graves.

Iron Hawk touched the medallion at his neck. The stylized bird of prey had been painstakingly carved from a plate of Union armor, its chain had once held a plain gold band and had been snapped from the neck of the armor's previous owner. The rough feel of the iron on his fingers always served to remind the war leader of the new world that had risen up to overtake his people. The men spread across the plains ahead had violated an immutable law of that new world. He had been sent to see that they were punished.

Iron Hawk looked back into the lengthening shadows. He could just make out the shapes of his scouting party crouching in the darkness. He nodded to himself and then made a quick series of gestures. Each warrior raised two fingers in silent acknowledgment and settled deeper into the grass. The sun was nearly gone now, the western sky washed with warm, muted colors that did little to illuminate the dell below.

The war leader lowered his head and began a low, sonorous chant. He felt the power of the Great Spirit rising from the earth, answering his call. Although he had not yet mastered the ability to surrender his body to the shapes of his spirit guides, he had inherited vast reserves of power from his father, the imminent medicine man, White Tree. When his father and the band he had been sent west with had disappeared, Iron Hawk knew in his soul that the worst had occurred, and had been searching, ever since, for every opportunity for vengeance.

The shaman stood as the colors and shadows around him began to swirl together, answering his call. Like a massive, impenetrable cloak, the powers of the Earth rose up to conceal him from the eyes of his enemies. He looked back to his warriors, each seeing with clear eyes through the illusion, and nodded once. With calm, measured steps he strodetowards the haphazard encampment of his enemies.

The sentries posted by the invaders were nothing to fear. The scent of their unwashed bodies carried for hundreds of paces downwind, further tainted with the acrid trace of tobacco and the sour smell of alcohol. The inescapable stench of their unnatural energy hung over everything. Iron Hawk was certain that, even without the power of the Great Spirit, he could have walked through the camp unnoticed.

The shaman walked among the enemy, his dark gaze passing unseen over the invaders. These poor apparitions radiated wary, brutalized exhaustion. They clung to their ragged belongings as if the horrible conditions of the encampment were a paradise they feared could be stripped away at any moment. The warrior snorted softly in contempt.

Even shadowing the enormous mob for days had not fully prepared him for the number of dispossessed. There were thousands, most dressed in tattered rags, their feet bare; their bodies shrunken by starvation. As darkness descended, most of the men were lying down upon the grass without any sense of order, merely falling asleep where they had come to rest. Here or there were the massive shadows of vehicles, most unarmed and unarmored; rusting wrecks, their twinkling crimson lights dim and dying. Men stood atop some, watching everyone who passed with a suspicious glare, ill-kept weapons clutched in shaking hands.

Moving through the camp, he caught bits and pieces of conversation in their harsh, alien tongue. They crouched in fear; pathetic, flickering fires all the comfort they could claim. Most were silent. Those that spoke did so in dull, stunned tones. Iron Hawk was passingly familiar with the language of his foes and the conversations all seemed to revolve around a deep sense of betrayal and disappointment.

A sense of disbelief made them numb to their current state, and of the world at large. It was as if the changes that had wracked the world for a generation had finally, in their darkest moment, been made manifest. Their reality consisted of their immediate, pathetic surroundings; huddled around ramshackle vehicles in the middle of hostile territory, watching each man that passed as if the whole, shifting world were there enemy.

Iron Hawk shook his head as he passed among them. The trucks likely contained what food and supplies these outcasts had left, and yet he was not surprised to see that no unified organization had been made for their defense. Each mob acted on its own, huddled around its own vehicle, or glaring jealously at the vehicles of others. It became more and more apparent that this was not a single army, or even a single united mob. It was, rather, countless smaller bodies of tired, frightened wretches determined to hold their own against the wider world. There was no unity or trust here among his enemies.

Rather than take heart from their obvious weakness, he found it sad.

Iron Hawk moved through the camp, making his way towards the sunken valley at its center. As he came up on the lip of the depression, he wrapped the concealing shadows more closely around himself, peering down into the dell. A series of caves were visible around the edges of the depression. Some were no larger than a rabbit warren, but others could hold entire parties of the enemy. More of the defiling vehicles were parked all along the floor of the valley. These seemed to be in better repair and included several heavily armored monsters bristling with weaponry. Scattered among the larger machines were over a hundred of the smaller, horse-sized contraptions capable of carrying men gliding over the ground like low-flying birds.

There was far more organization here than with the rest of the rabble above: the leaders of this ragtag band, must be camped within. He wanted to get as close as he could, to learn more about these men, before unleashing the full might of the Warrior Nations with the rising sun. His chest reverberated with a low hum, and the shadows grew even darker around him. A ring of more alert sentries watched the valley, but hidden by the power of the Great Spirit, he stalked right through them.

As Iron Hawk moved further into the hollow, he saw that tattered sheets of rough fabric had been hung across the mouths of the largest caves. Dancing firelight or the muted, crimson-edged illumination of their foul lanterns flickered weakly around the edges. One of the curtains sheltering a cave nearby was suddenly pulled back. Light washed out into the clearing as a man emerged, a rifle held in one hand. With his free hand he pulled the cloth shut behind him, killing the wash of light.

The shaman stopped, trusting to his spectral cloak, and the man walked past, oblivious. He found himself wondering at the man's story. Iron Hawk shrugged. It mattered little. Soon enough, they would all be dead. He eased his way closer to the cave mouth and settled in the shadows of a rocky fracture, craning his head towards the opening.

"—left the place standin' at all!" An angry voice muttered from the cave.

"Well, I blame that fast trick he's been ridin' with since the breakout; you want to know what I think. Ain't no way she was a normal nurse, no how." Another voice, bitter but resigned. Both spoke in soft, conspiratorial tones.

"Loveless? She's a bitch Union spy an' you can take that to the bank." The first voice, speaking again, quavered with barely-suppressed emotion. "How else would she have gotten out of there alive? That burg was a nest of whores' sons, and deserved to be burned out after everythin' they done! Weren't gonna be nothin' but pure justice, plain an' simple!"

"Henderson had it right, an' that's true enough." A third voice now, stoking the fires of resentment in the other two. There was an edge to this one that set Iron Hawk's skin crawling. "Burn a place like that to the ground, you send a message that the damned blue-bellies'll get loud an' clear!"

"Shut yer, mouth!" The second voice spoke. "You want 'im to gut us an' leave us behind fer the savages to pick over? Jesse done made uphis mind, and it's done. That woman might o' got in his head, might o' turned him soft, but that don't matter none now. We been duckin' and runnin' through Injun territory like we was the ones that lost, an' that's Gospel." Someone spat. "But Jesse hears you bad mouthin' that Rebel angel or second guessin' his call? We're gonna be staked out fer the scorpions faster'n you can say Billy Yank."

"Ain'tno scorpions out there, Galen." The first voice again. "Not in all that grass."

Iron Hawk heard the sharp rip of another spit, then a grunt. "Then snakes, 'r gophers, 'r whatever in the name o' hades it is up here eats folks staked out – It don't' matter none, Colton, fer the sake 'o the Lord! Just hobble yerlip afore he ends us, will you?"

"I was just sayin'," that angry voice, Colton, again. "We should'a burnt down that town when we had the chance. Hell. We'd a been better off staying in Robbers Roosts for all the boodle we're comin' out'a this little adventure with."

Iron Hawk eased away from the cave and scanned the bottom of the dell. There were other caves, and he could hear the low mutterings of other conversations. Most of the caverns were connected, farther back beneath the hills, he knew. He doubted that the men hiding within them had taken the time investigate, however. They probably thought they were safe, talking about each other as long as they were huddled within different mouths. The warrior smirked. If this Jesse was the bad medicine these cowards were making him out to be, he hoped he was listening. Watching easterners kill each other was always good sport.

He spotted a larger cavern nearby, several strips of cloth obscuring the light within. Iron Hawk slid down next to the opening and settled in to listen.

"—would have wanted someone to come after me, that's for sure." This voice carried no anger or resentment. It was calm and relaxed; louder than the other voices. There was no fear of being overheardhere. Iron Hawk was sure that would change before long.

"Nah, I get it. And if my brother was being held by those rat bastards, I would have gone in all guns a-blazin' too." There was a crunch and hiss as someone stirred a large fire. When this voice continued, it was pitched lower than before. "Just not sure I would have wanted to be dragged in myself, is all. We could have stayed back with General Mosby and been none the worse for wear. Lost a lot of good men going in there."

The first voice muttered grudging agreement. "We did. And there's still some more might not make it. But Frank James seems like a good man. Captain Ingram says Jesse needs him, if we're gonna be able to turn any of this around."

"He seems like a good man, right enough." Another voice spoke. "But is he better than any of the men who fell fetching him out? Better than Shady Joe, or Johnny Fu, or any of the other guys we lost?"

"You best keep words like that to yourself, Cord." All of the voices around the fire quieted down. "Don't you be in any doubt: Frank's more important to him than any of us he picked up along the way. You know he's been on the shoot since long before Captain Ingram offered up our services. Only safe place to be when he's like that, seems to me, is behind him or beside him, and that's a fact."

"I'm just saying," continued Cord, in a softer voice. "Something to keep in mind, as touching on the man's loyalties, is all."

"And your loyalties wouldn't lie with your own brother?" This voice was edged with contempt.

"I ain't got a brother." There was a sullen tone to the second voice now. "And I'm not sure I would have traded a bunch of good men for him if I did."

"Well, if he was YOUR brother, he wouldn't have been worth trading good men for in the first place." The contemptuous voice deepened. "If you're so concerned, go back to Cali. It's just about three thousand miles that way, is all. Now shut your trap. I'm trying to enjoy the fire."

Iron Hawk ignored the muttered response as he pivoted on his heel to survey the bowl around him. The man with the rifle had not yet returned. Whether he was heading out to water the grass or to relieve a sentry, someone would be coming back towards the caves soon. He passed several of the larger vehicles as he moved towards another cave. He summoned the Great Spirit's energy, his hands warm as the familiar sensation of ghostly knife handles filled them. But he held the burning fire in check, the radiance of the spirit power the merest aquamarine lightning skittering around his fists and deep within his eyes.

A man surged out of the cave he was approaching, and Iron Hawk lurched back into the deepest shadows, hiding behind an armored brute on metal wheels. The man was careless with the hanging fabric and left it askew as he stomped into the central clearing.

"I don't wanna talk about it no more!" The man gestured behind him, one hand filled with a vicious-looking fighting knife. It was a comment that made no sense to Iron Hawk until another man rushed out into the night after him.

The second man's voice was hushed but urgent as he grabbed the first's arm. "Well, you gotta talk about it some more. He was our brother!"

Iron Hawk looked more closely. He could just make out the family resemblance between the two men in the light from the cavern. The first man spun around to confront his older brother, knife glittering as he spread his hands wide in a dismissive gesture that the older man ignored.

"He weren't our brother when Jesse did for him. They changed 'im in that Union camp, an' that thing in that building?

That weren't Johnny." There was pleading in the man's eyes, and Iron Hawk could tell that it did not sit easily there. "C'mon, Bobbie. I heard what both you and Jesse said. It weren't John. John was gone."

The younger man shook his head, the knife vibrating. "An' Jesse couldn't o' saved 'im? He saved Frank, though, din't he. An' that woman from KC." It was a statement, not a question, and the older man shrank from it.

"Bobbie, there weren't none of John left to rescue, you told me yourself. He was like one o' Carpathian's monsters, only worse! Ya'lldin't have no choice!"

The younger man, Bobbie, grabbed the other by the shoulder. "Cole, he was our brother, an' we left 'im to die in a hole like an animal, put down by Jesse DAMNED James!"

Iron Hawk did not hear the response, whatever it might have been. As soon as he heard that name his heart surged in his chest and he lurched backwards, fetching up against the iron tire.

Jesse James? The man was known by all the Warrior Nation as an avatar of the darkest powers that had come to grip the land. Those unnatural arms of his, monstrous creations of the vile outsider, marked him as a demon of the first order.

If this band was running at the command of Jesse James, then a tribute truly worth of White Tree was near at hand. In the morning, the Warrior Nation would claim a major victory against the darkness and remove the blight of this infamous monster from the sun's sight.

Iron Hawk rose and moved back towards the gently-sloping wall of the vale. When he turned, however, the man with the rifle was there.

"Hey, who—"The sentry tried to bring the weapon up across his body to defend himself. He took in a lungful of cool night air, preparing to sound the alarm and bring James' entire posse flooding out to destroy the intruder.

The shaman did not hesitate. His eyes flared with a burning hatred. His empty hand floated up and past the startled sentry's face, sliding around his jaw and head, grabbing a filthy hank of hair at the base of the man's neck. The white man's eyes went wide.

Iron Hawk pulled with all his might as he brought the other hand, a sliver of burning azure shadow appearing in a reversed, knife-fighter's hold, up and across. The phantom blade dripped with blue flame as the warrior's eyes ignited in an answering surge of power.

The outlaw twisted around, his head yanked in a disorienting spin. He clutched the rifle more tightly to his chest, helpless. As the man's face came back around, pulled by the native warrior's off hand, the burning blade slid across his throat, opening his veins and spraying a fan of burgundy into the grass at their feet. The blue flames flickered into darkness, reflecting once in the depths of the dying man's eyes as he stared, disbelieving, into the face of his killer.

Iron Hawk lowered the body to the grass and glanced around to be sure the scuffle had not been heard. There were no shouts of alarm, only the muffled voices of the two men still arguing over their brother's fate.

With a grim smile, Iron Hawk sneered down at the quivering body. The first blow in retribution for his father's death had been dealt, and with the rising sun, countless more would follow. His father's spirit would rise upon their cries of pain and despair. He made his way casually back up the slope. The other war leaders needed to know who led this tattered army of derelicts.

It was a new world, with new laws and new punishments. And Jesse James, the man whose very body defied the Great Spirit, the wretch who symbolized everything the Warrior N

For all your fantasy, science fiction or history needs look at the latest from Winged Hussar Publishing